BURDEN OF TRUTH

A British Murder Mystery

THE WILD FENS MURDER MYSTERY SERIES

JACK CARTWRIGHT

CHESTNUT PRESS

ALSO BY JACK CARTWRIGHT

The DCI Cook Murder Mysteries

A Winter of Blood

A Secret to Die For

The Wild Fens Murder Mysteries

Secrets In Blood

One For Sorrow

In Cold Blood

Suffer In Silence

Dying To Tell

Never To Return

Lie Beside Me

Dance With Death

In Dead Water

One Deadly Night

Her Dying Mind

Into Death's Arms

No More Blood

Burden of Truth

Run From Evil

DEDICATION

It's 7:09 p.m. on August 1ˢᵗ, 2024 as I write this. I have just finished writing chapter fifty-five, with the last three chapters already mapped out and ready to be written.

The weather has been hot this week, hot enough that our dog, Blue, came back from his walk and could barely breathe. He has laryngeal paralysis, so can only take in half the air a normal dog can. It took us over an hour to calm him down, and we were praying he would pull through. His tongue had turned blue, and his eyes were wide with fright. He's a poorly dog. But we love him.

Our three-year-old daughter, Olivia, has been at preschool and is now in bed. We spent the last two hours just admiring her.

My wife, Erica, is snoozing on the sofa with her finger on the contraction timer app on her phone. That's right. Contractions. It's happening. Or at least, we think it is...

You aren't born yet. You're either minutes, hours, or days away. That's okay. Take your time.

We don't even know if you're a boy or a girl. But we can't wait to find out.

You don't even have a name yet, although we're pretty sure

you'll be a Poppy or a George, or maybe a Teddy. We don't mind which.

The important thing is that we're here to take care of you. Everything is going to be fine. In fact, it's going to be wonderful. You have been on my mind for the entire time it has taken me to write this book. The past few days have been hard work, as I want to send the finished manuscript to Ceri, my editor, so I can forget about work and spend some time with you. I want to know you. I want to be there for you. We all do.

One day, when you're old enough to reach the snack drawer, old enough to drive, and old enough to stay out late, I'll let you read my books. And if that moment has been and gone; if you've already met Freya, Ben, and the team, and you've worked your way through the series and finally discovered this page in book fourteen, then you should know...this one is for you.

Dad. xxx

BURDEN OF TRUTH

JACK
CARTWRIGHT

PROLOGUE

The world passed by in a blur. The horizon was in the dying throes of azure, clinging on as darkness claimed its space. Through the honey stems, crunching underfoot and tripping him, cutting into his bare skin, he ran across the field.

And the air he breathed was lacking as if his body needed more.

He stumbled and fell, and lay in the crops, listening for footsteps above his thumping heart as the darkening sky above him swirled like vultures.

Something scurried nearby, a mouse or a vole.

Or maybe it was *him* growing close. His captor. Maybe he had found his path through the broken stems and was on the hunt.

Lee Constantine sat up. But still the world spun. His eyes, unable to focus on a single stem, found only shadow, and that distant strip of light to the west.

Again, he ran.

Even the ground was a blur, and each mistimed step was like miscalculating the final stair. Sometimes his feet hit the ground earlier than he had anticipated, while other times, the soil seemed to have disappeared altogether.

Ahead of him, a line of trees marked the edge of the field. In the light of day, when the world did not turn and his eyes could focus, he might have named his position.

But in the meagre, mid-evening light, he could have been anywhere – Scotland, Yorkshire, Cornwall. Any number of places. A part of him, that part that he recalled from an hour or so ago, knew the field was a Lincolnshire field. But the mind has a way of giving in to the doubt that delusion propagates.

"Lee?"

A whisper. A hiss in his right ear.

He stopped and turned, but found nobody.

"Lee?"

The same whisper. The same voice, but this time to his left.

And still, nobody was there.

"Leave me alone," he screamed, first to his left and then to his right. "Just let me be."

He edged backwards.

"There's nowhere to run," the whispered voice taunted. "I know what you saw."

"I didn't see anything," Lee replied. Even his repeated blinking would not clear the blur, and the tears that rolled from his eyes only served to make focusing harder.

He reached behind him, feeling the bushes of sharp thorns digging into his skin. But he pushed through. It was his only escape. With one hand reaching through the thicket and the other covering his genitals, he forced himself into the bush to the tune of his captor's laughter.

"Where are you going, Lee? You can't get away. I'm in your head."

"Just leave me alone. I won't say owt."

He stayed still, with sharp thorns pressing into his sides and backside. He couldn't get him here.

Could he?

But then he appeared. A face. A sneer.

Anger.

"No," Lee said and forced himself through the hedge as a hand groped for him. He fell through the second half and landed in a heap on the ground. He scrambled clear, backing away on his hands and feet.

But nobody came after him.

No voices called out.

No laughter taunted him.

He was alone.

Slowly, he climbed to his feet, blinking to regain some clarity but finding only the inescapable blur.

He took a step back, searching for movement where detail lacked. Listening for footsteps, for a breath, for anything.

"I know you're there," the whisper came, and Lee froze as the face emerged from the hedge and grinned at him. "Found you."

Lee backed away – one step, two steps.

But the third step was different. There was no hard ground to take his weight. It was that gut-wrenching sensation of descending dark stairs, imagining that his foot would find the step.

But no such step existed and he felt his weight shift. He groped the air for a hold of something. Anything.

But nothing was in reach, and as he fell backwards, his captor grinned at him.

The image of that grin filled Lee's mind until his broken body hit the rocks below, where the sneering face faded into the swirling sky above.

And the darkness gave way to a light so bright that Lee had to squint.

But there was clarity. The world around him was as vivid and detailed as he could ever remember. So clear was the dying world, so detailed, that he saw his captor peer down at him from above. And that grin was gone from his face.

He let his head rest on the rocks. He let a smile form on his cracked lips. And he let peace take him, along with a deadly secret.

CHAPTER ONE

"Morning, Inspector," the nurse said from behind her desk. She was young, lithe, and wore a cheeky smirk in response to his wink. "You'll have to be quick, I'm afraid. You're later than usual."

"Oh, you know how it goes," he told her. "I honestly believe that whenever I manage to have a weekend to myself, fairies let themselves into my office and double the pile of paperwork I have to do."

"We have those," she replied. "Although, I don't call them fairies." She checked nobody was within earshot, leaned forward, and whispered, "I call them doctors. Lazy gits."

The entire interaction had taken place without Ben breaking step; the nurse must have understood why, as she watched him along the corridor and peer through the window in the door. He turned back to her briefly and nodded his appreciation before pushing into the room.

Outside, in the reception with the nurse, and even at the station with the team, he wore his bravado like a suit of armour. Inside this room was the one place he could hang that suit up. It was the one place where he could air his vulnerabilities.

"Evening," he said, though he expected no response from the woman on the bed.

Her entire left side was bandaged, including her ear, which had melted before his eyes. Spaces remained, providing access to her mouth and nose for the tubes that aided her breathing. But one eye, her right eye, the unbandaged one he had stared at for what seemed like hours now, remained closed. He sat to her right, where the nurse had uncovered her hand, and he resumed the position he had adopted during every visit – perched on the edge of a chair, leaning forward, and holding her hand in both of his.

"You've had some more cards," he told her, eyeing the bedside table on which the nurses had displayed a plethora of cards. Most of the well-wishers were on the force, from constables who admired and held her in great esteem as an ambassador of female leadership, and even one from the Chief Constable of Lincolnshire. Although Ben presumed he had never even seen the card, but his secretary had seen fit to send one on his behalf. No doubt when Freya was able to, she too would draw the same conclusion.

"You'll be pleased to know the team is doing well. Gillespie has stepped up, and so has Nillson. Anderson and Cruz are both edging towards the sergeant's exam. And Gold, well, you know her. She's like everyone's mother. If I'm honest, I don't know what I'd do without her. I don't know what I'd do without any of them, come to think of it. Chapman has become my unofficial diary. She's always telling me when I need to be somewhere. And what with Gold always trying to gauge my mental well-being, I feel like I have a pair of nurses pulling me this way and that." He realised his choice of words and grimaced. "Not that that's a bad thing."

He cleared his throat, trying desperately to find a new topic, however mundane. The doctor had said it might help her to hear his voice, and to be kept abreast of life outside those four walls. A sense of normality, he had called it. Initially, Ben had scoffed at the idea and told him exactly what he thought.

"She's had half her face burned off. She might have lost an eye, most of her left ear has gone, and as for her hair...I don't think she's going to be interested in the weather, Doctor," he had said.

"You're right," the small Indian man had agreed. "It'll be months before the plastic surgeons can get to work. And as for her mind, Mr Savage, most people with injuries of this magnitude would benefit from some element of counselling. Some never fully recover, you know."

"Right," Ben had said, sensing the agreement was one of those roundabout ways of delivering a message.

"When she's awake, she seems quite short-tempered," the doctor said, then added some justification. "It's probably the pain. Most of which we can address, of course. But not all of it. You might find that she sleeps a lot. That's the medication. Her body is healing." Ben recalled how the doctor had stared down at Freya with sorrow in his eyes. "I don't envy her, you know? I wouldn't want to lie here day after day, in pain, wondering what was happening. Wondering who would come to see me today, if anybody. Wondering if my circle of friends would have moved on, or if I'd ever fit in again. If I'll ever be up to date—"

"Okay, okay," Ben had said. "I get the message."

The doctor grinned. "Be her eyes and ears, Mr Savage. Say it as you see it and let her interpret it as she sees fit. Give her a sense of normality. We'll be discharging her soon. We've done all we can here. Any rehabilitation and aesthetic procedure will be done by the specialists at Nottingham."

"Nottingham?"

The doctor had smiled warmly.

"Just talk to her."

"What about?"

"Anything," he replied. "Anything but her injuries and this place."

It was an odd sensation, Ben thought. To gossip. He'd always rolled his eyes whenever he heard somebody gossiping. But now he saw why they did. Because without gossip, life, for them at least, would be empty. Nothing would happen.

"I was at your house yesterday," he told her. "The neighbours, that young couple, they've put some shrubs in. Nicely done, too. There's a red robin, a few hebes, and I noticed some hostas behind the front wall, where the sun doesn't get to. Not a bad idea, really. I was thinking I might do something like that in yours. It's all easy maintenance. I could put some ground cover beneath them. Some saxifrage and campanula. They should flower for months and they'll stop the weeds coming through."

Freya was still. He wondered if his words were penetrating. If the vibrations from his voice were somehow resonating.

"I also noticed the old house on the other side has been sold. Going to take some work to get that place livable. I spoke to the woman on the other side of the green. You know, the one with the spaniel. She reckons the new couple are going to live there. Half the village was worried it would be modernised and flipped or rented out or something. But she reckons they'll retain the original features as much as they can. It might be an interesting project, that one. I wouldn't mind doing that, you know? Buying an old place and doing it up before it gets torn down. Maybe that'll be my retirement project. I can take my time then. Do it all myself, you know?"

A knock at the door disturbed his train of thought, and he looked up to find a man peering into the room. Ben rose and approached the door, opening it with caution.

"Can I help?"

The man was around Ben's height and build. He wore smart jeans, a button-down shirt, and tan leather brogues, the suede type that, not so long ago, Freya had been pushing him into buying. From the look of the man's watch, his clothing, and his tan, Ben assumed the man was financially comfortable.

"I'm looking for Freya," the man said.

"And you are?"

"Greg," he said, extending a hand for Ben to shake. "Greg Bloom."

CHAPTER TWO

The two men shared a silence, which grew in discomfort as the seconds passed.

"Sorry, and you are?" Greg asked.

"Me?" Ben said. "Oh, I'm Ben." He realised how immature or flustered he appeared and corrected himself with a formal introduction. "Sorry, I'm miles away. DI Savage. I um...I work with Freya." He stepped to one side to allow Greg a view of Freya and her injuries.

His face paled and his gullet rose and fell.

"It's bad then?" Greg asked.

"Oh, you know. The bandages make it look worse than it actually is," Ben told him, eyeing the clock on the wall. He peered along the corridor at the nurse, who held up her wrist and tapped at her watch to signify they were nearing the end of visiting time.

"Do you want to get a drink or something?"

"A copper that drinks?" Greg scoffed.

"Well, no. I meant a coffee. There's a place near the entrance. It's not exactly fine dining, but the coffee's okay, and the tables are clean."

"I was hoping to see her," Greg replied.

"I'm afraid times up, gentlemen," the nurse called out. "I'm going to have to ask you to leave, if you don't mind."

Greg smiled politely.

"Well, that's put me in my place, hasn't it?" he said. "Coffee it is, then."

Dutybound, Ben led him away from Freya's room, pausing to shut the door and blow a kiss her way without Greg seeing.

The nurse closed the ward doors and Ben fell into step with Greg.

"How did you find out?" he asked.

"About Freya? It was on the news," Greg told him.

"On the news? I thought you were down south. South London, isn't it?"

"You are well informed, aren't you?" he replied, then eyed Ben. "It wasn't the local news, and it's not the first time she's made the national headlines. Although I have to say, she's doing a proper job this time around. She has the scars to prove it."

"The national headlines? Blimey! I didn't realise."

Greg seemed to hesitate before continuing.

"So, are you and Freya..."

"Me? Oh, no. No, we're just..."

He didn't know why he didn't just come out and tell the truth. It was, after all, none of Greg's business. It just came out that way. He chose the easy option.

"Friends?"

"Right," Ben said. "We're in the same team. I just...I look out for her. That's all."

"And how's that going?" Greg asked, a loaded question with more than one undertone.

"It's going very well if you must know," Ben said, stopping to stare into the man's eye. "Freya's accident is not my doing."

"Sorry," Greg said, and he nodded down at Ben's hand. "I just saw the burn and figured–"

"Jumped to conclusions, you mean?"

"I thought you might be the officer they mentioned on the six o'clock news," Greg said flatly. "The officer who Freya saved." He met Ben's stare with defiance as if daring him to push for more information. None of which would be to Ben's credit. "Perhaps I was mistaken."

"Perhaps you were," Ben told him.

"Listen, I'm not here to cause trouble. I just thought—"

"Thought what? That you would come to her rescue?"

"I just wondered how she is, that's all," Greg said, softening. "I didn't mean any upset."

He looked up apologetically and Ben inhaled a deep breath.

"I was standing in front of a van filled with petrol," Ben said, simplifying the events that had led them all to this place. "I told Freya to stay back, but she didn't listen—"

"That sounds like her alright."

"She shoved me out of the way just as the fumes ignited," Ben continued, then left a pause for Greg to appreciate the image. "The doctor said the only thing that saved her was the fact that she fell to the ground and let the fire blaze above her. But even so, she's still badly hurt."

"But she's conscious?"

"She is. Well, she *was* anyway," Ben said. "The work they do to her during the day means that she's either exhausted by the evening or still sedated. I haven't spoken to her for two weeks now. Not properly anyway. She tires easily."

"Two weeks? How often do you—"

"Every day," Ben said. "Without fail." He watched as Greg processed the information. Ben added commentary to embellish the images and answer any further questions Greg might have. "There's a chance she could lose her left eye. Her left ear is functional but unrecognisable. The skin on the left side of her face will need a full skin graft, as will her left arm and hand. The hair she lost may grow back. If not, she'll need a hair transplant." Greg stood in awe of the list of injuries. "And that's before we even begin on her internal injuries."

"Internal injuries?"

"Her body went into shock, Greg. The doctor on the air ambulance pulled her back."

"Pulled her back? From where?"

Ben was silent.

"No," Greg said. "No, she can't have—"

"She was gone, Greg. I was sure of it. The doctor said it was shock or something. Her heart just gave up under the pain. I don't know. To be honest, when they explained it, I wasn't in a good place."

"Oh, Jesus. I knew I should have come sooner."

"Oh, I don't think that's necessary," Ben told him. "I'll tell her you came."

"You'll tell her I came, will you?"

"Well, what do you want me to do?" Ben said, as his phone rumbled to life. "Hide it from her? If so, what was the point in coming if you're just going to leave?"

"Oh, I think you've misunderstood me," he replied, and he glanced back along the corridor. "I'm not going anywhere."

He stared at Ben, perhaps vying for a reaction. But Ben simply turned his back and answered the call.

"Ben Savage," he said.

"Ben, it's Chapman," came the soft-spoken voice. "I'm sorry to bother you. But we've had a call. We need you out near Nocton."

"I'm on my way," he replied, then ended the call. He smiled an apology at Greg. "That was the office."

"Nothing changes, does it?" he replied. "I can't tell you how many times I witnessed Freya having the same conversation, and then giving me the same pathetic look." He stared quizzically at Ben. "What's wrong?"

"I'm sorry, it's just... I'm just not sure how she'll react if she sees you," Ben said, testing a theory which was proved almost immediately.

"She doesn't have to react," he replied. "I'm her husband. I have a right to see her."

"Can I ask you something?" Ben said. "You're a Bloom. You said you were Greg Bloom."

"I can see why they pay you the big bucks," he replied, which Ben chose to ignore.

"Her dad was a Bloom, wasn't he? How does that work? Are you cousins or something?"

"Freya refused to take my name," Greg replied, as if the topic were a tender wound he would rather leave to heal of its own accord.

"That sounds like her."

"Which left me with two choices," Greg explained. "Keep my own name and have to explain to everyone we met that my wife is both a snob and a feminist, or..." He paused there, wondering if he had said too much.

"And you didn't change it after the divorce?" Ben asked. "I thought you would have gone back to your own name?"

"I might have," Greg said, plunging his hands into his jeans pockets. "Had she signed the divorce papers, that is." He studied Ben's reaction with more than a hint of amusement. "Sorry, I thought you would have known. We're still married."

CHAPTER THREE

"You Mr Willis?" Gillespie asked, as he climbed from his car and spotted the larger-than-average man. He wore a high-visibility vest, hard hat, and jeans, which were surprisingly clean, considering his profession. The man nodded briefly, then stepped away from the portacabins, holding his hand out for Gillespie to shake. "Sergeant Gillespie. I came as fast as I could."

"Some of your lot are already here," Willis replied, and he gestured at the two liveried police cars parked at the end of the little car park. "This take long, will it?"

"It'll take as long as it takes, Mr. Willis," Gillespie replied. "Where are my officers?"

"Sent them over," Willis said, and again he gestured with a nod of his head into the distance. "S'where he is."

In the distance, Gillespie caught sight of three uniformed officers at the edge of a pond in the corner of the quarry and one more a little further afield. He positioned his first and third fingers beneath his tongue and blew, issuing a shrill whistle that echoed around the rocky void. One of the uniforms looked up and Gillespie waved an arm, beckoning them back.

"Haven't touched him, have you?" Gillespie asked.

"Touch him?" Willis said. "It's a dead body, mate. Why the bloody hell would I touch it? Besides, bloody deep, that pond is. Wouldn't catch me in there if you paid me."

"I'm just getting a lay of the land," Gillespie replied. "Did anybody else see him? Any of your colleagues, maybe?"

"They've all gone home," Willis replied. "As I should be, I might add. I'm the quarry manager, see? I was up there." He pointed to one of the portacabins which sat atop another like a giant version of a child's building blocks. "I stayed late. I had to finish some paperwork and the like. Anyway, I did what I had to do, cleaned my cup and was just setting it down by the kettle when I saw him out of the window. Didn't know what it was, course, but I knew it weren't nothing that ought to be there."

"So, you took a wander over there, did you?"

"Aye, I did. But I never touched him. And as far as I know, none of the others even knows he's there. They would have said something."

"You alright, Sarge?" one of the uniforms said as the foursome approached. He wore sergeant's stripes on his shoulders, setting him apart from his constable colleagues. "MacAllister. Sergeant MacAllister."

"You new?"

"Transferred in from Mablethorpe," MacAllister replied.

"Right. Well, if this isn't a baptism of fire, I don't know what is," Gillespie replied. "Let's have one of your team at the entrance and the other two walking the quarry perimeter. It's seven p.m. now, so we've got about two hours of daylight left. Not nearly enough. We'll need lights, generators, and more uniforms. Think you can manage that?"

"I think I can stretch that far," MacAllister replied, as a little, red hatchback trundled into the car park, and MacAllister clicked his fingers for one of his constables to attend.

"It's alright, Sergeant," Gillespie said, spying the little man in the driver's seat. "He's one of ours."

Detective Constable Cruz climbed from his car, eyed the quarry and the men huddled together, and deeming Willis to be a member of the public, adopted a professional disposition. He pulled his shoulders back and wore a frown that did little to his appearance except give him the look of a constipated monkey.

"Sarge," he called out, as he pulled on his wellies. "Where do you want me?"

Gillespie eyed Willis, and then the portacabin from which the manager had seen the body in the water.

"With me," he replied and led both him and Willis to a steel staircase. He shoved open the door and found a table and chairs large enough to accommodate twelve people. At the far end of the room was another table, on which was the kettle and tea-making facilities Willis had spoken of.

"Cruz," he said. "Make mine strong, will you?"

"Coffee?" Cruz said, unable to hide his disappointment. "You're kidding me, aren't you?"

"Mr. Willis? Tea or coffee?"

Willis shook his head.

"I'll have a hard enough job sleeping as it is," he said.

Cruz's attempts at coming across as a serious player dissipated with every step he took towards the kettle, shaking his head as he went.

"So, this is it, is it?" Gillespie asked Willis. He stepped over to the window by the kettle. "This is where you saw him?"

"It is," Willis replied, coming to stand beside him. "Though, you can't see him now. He must be behind those rushes."

"So, he's floating, is he?"

"He is," Willis replied.

"And what are the odds of him coming through your main gate? I noticed you have CCTV up."

"Slim to none," Willis replied. "To get over there, he'd have had to walk past the weighbridge, plus half a dozen or so machines. There's only a handful of us here full time, so any guests are fairly easy to spot, and nobody has the run of the place, trust me."

"What makes you so confident?"

"Well, my men are driving diggers, lorries, and earth movers. Last thing they want is to knock someone down," Willis told him. "Mark my words, if someone was to walk through here, they'd have been stopped and dragged up to the office."

Cruz raised an eyebrow at the comment.

"Probably shouldn't rule it out, though," he said.

"Agreed," Gillespie replied. "But if they didn't come through the gate, then how did they get here?"

"Over the top, I'm afraid," Willis replied, and he gestured at the pond in the distance, and the rocky wall on the far side reached up to the original ground level. "There's no other way."

"You think he fell in? That's a good forty feet."

"It's not impossible," Willis said. "There's nowt up there but fields."

"Can I ask something?" Cruz said, then continued before anybody agreed. "What is a pond like that doing in a quarry?"

"Excuse me?" Willis said.

"I mean, look at it," Cruz said, staring out of the window. "There's rushes and reeds and whatnot. There're birds and wildlife." Cruz swept a hand across the view. "And then look at the rest of it. I feel like we've landed on Mars."

"It's a restoration pond," Willis said.

"A what?" Gillespie said.

"A restoration pond," Willis repeated. "It's land we've finished with. We're obliged to restore the areas when we've dug as much as we can. Ponds are good for wildlife, so there you have it. A pond."

"So, this whole area will be restored?"

"Every inch of it," Willis said, and he stared out of the window with pride in his eyes. "We take looking after the area quite seriously, you know? If it weren't for the local community, then we wouldn't be here at all. We don't want to create any ill-feeling. That's not good for us and it's not good for them."

"Do they complain, then?" Cruz asked.

"They've no reason to," Willis said as if he had expected the question. "We don't dig down to the water table, so they can't complain about contamination. We don't dig until eight a.m. every day, and we stop in time for tea, so they can't say we're a nuisance. We even draw any water we need for the filtering process during off-peak hours, so we don't leave the locals with dribbling showers in the mornings."

"That's quite the commitment," Gillespie replied.

"Trust me, when you've been in this game as long as I have, you know only too well how easily locals are upset by a quarry on their doorstep."

"If I understand you correctly, Mr. Willis, you're saying this is unlikely to be a local do-gooder falling foul of his own intentions."

"What I'm saying, Sergeant, is that whoever that is in that pond, has nowt to do with this place. If you ask me, he came out of the fields and fell."

"It sounds to me like you're trying to steer our investigation," Gillespie told him.

Willis stiffened. "Maybe I am. But ask yourself this," he said. "If he came through that gate, then where are his clothes?"

"Eh?" Cruz said.

"He's naked?" Gillespie said.

"As the day he were born," Willis replied, his tone serious and sombre. He turned to look Gillespie in the eye. "You want to find out where he came from, then you look in them fields, Sergeant."

"Oh, we'll be looking everywhere," Gillespie replied, and he held Willis' stare, searching for a sign of deceit, or guilt even. He turned to face him, sizing the quarry manager up in a single glance. "In fact, we won't leave a single stone unturned."

Willis stiffened, perhaps sensing that Gillespie's stare was more scrutinizing than it was casual.

"Well, then I should leave you to it," he said.

Gillespie nodded slowly, still unsure of the man.

"Cruz, have Chapman search the missing persons list, will you? When you're done, you can have MacAllister put a search team together, and then you can process Mr Willis here," he said, still holding Willis' stare.

"Process me?" Willis said. "I bloody reported it. I'm hardly likely to have—"

"As I said, Mr. Willis," Gillespie replied. "No stone unturned."

CHAPTER FOUR

A uniformed officer holding a clipboard held her hand up as Ben pulled into the quarry. He lowered his window and held his warrant card up for her to see.

"Oh sorry, Inspector," she said, scribbling his name onto the board. "Didn't recognise you there."

"No problem at all," he told her. "It's nice to see processes being followed. Nothing wrong with a tight ship, is there?"

"Nothing at all," she replied and then stepped out of the way to let him pass. He entered through the gates and followed the makeshift road around to the left, where he found a small car park and two large portacabins, one stacked atop the other. Among the various liveried cars, Ben recognised Gillespie and Cruz's cars, plus the trademark small white vans belonging to CSI, a large white van with the Lincolnshire Underwater Search Team livery, and a sleek Jaguar that looked utterly out of place in a quarry car park.

He pulled his old Ford into the space beside Cruz's car and took a few moments to gather his thoughts, to set Freya to one side and focus on the job at hand.

Although, as if she were sitting beside him, her alluring yet loathsome tentacles were far-reaching.

"Ben, you made it," Gillespie called out as Ben opened his car door. Before Ben could climb out, the big Glaswegian barked an order to a female uniform across the car park. "You, what are you doing? You should be up top with Sergeant MacAllister."

"Just getting my boots on, Sarge," came the reply.

"Never mind your boots, lassie. We've got an hour of daylight left. Unless you want to be out here in the dark, of course?"

"No, Sarge," she said, as Ben climbed out and caught the embittered expression on her face.

"I wondered if you'd be at the helm of the ship," Ben said, and he gestured at the line of vehicles. "Looks like you have things in hand. What are we looking at, anyway?"

He began a slow walk towards the corner of the property, where a group of white-suited individuals were crouched on the ground before a few other people, some in uniform, some in plain clothes.

"Young lad found floating in the pond," Gillespie began. "Early to mid-twenties."

"Drowned swimmer?"

"I'm not sure if he was swimming," Gillespie replied. "In fact, I'm not sure of much right now. Jacob Willis, the quarry manager, was just closing the office for the night when he saw something in the pond. He claims that nobody could have gotten through the gates without being seen."

"Hence them lot?" Ben asked, nodding at the line of uniformed officers at the top of the rock face.

"We're running out of daylight, Ben," Gillespie explained. "I've got lights coming for the crime scene, but we can't light an entire field."

"Good call," Ben replied. "I'd have done the same. How long has he been there?"

"No idea, mate. Kate is down there now, but you know how it is."

"You didn't want your relationship to get in the way of your job? Your idea or hers?"

"Aye, well. You know how she can be. She's a pro. She knows what she's doing. Doesn't need me sticking my nose in, does she?"

"I saw Doctor Saint's Jag in the car park."

"Aye, he's here, too. He's waiting his turn like the rest of us."

They stopped midway through the quarry to take in the surroundings. The quarry was a good sixty or seventy feet deep, and the sides were sheer limestone faces. A large piece of machinery took pride of place somewhere near the centre, comprising eight conveyor belt legs with a central network of small structures, steel stairs and gangways, all connected by a complex series of pipes. In the distance, two large diggers stood idle, each armed with a hardened point not unlike a pick, with which the operator could hammer into the rock face.

The side of the pond closest to them was at ground level, while the rock face that encircled the property served as the pond's far reaches. Wild grasses and rushes filled the spaces around, and trees, which Ben presumed had been planted, dotted the surrounding ground.

"It's a wildlife pond," Ben said. "I've heard about quarries doing this to restore the land."

"Aye, he's quite proud of it too," Gillespie told him.

"Yeah, my dad has some," Ben replied, then caught Gillespie's confused expression. "The government pays him a grant to install ponds on unfarmable land. They started off as a few holes in the ground a few years ago. Now they're his pride and joy. You'd be amazed at how fast life finds them."

"Well, our little pond seems to have attracted death," Gillespie said, and he coaxed them forward. "I've got Chapman on the local police stations and mispers, Cruz is heading up the search, and I've got a local unit out looking for any parked cars on the lanes."

"That's a good shout," Ben replied.

"Aye, I thought so," Gillespie said, never one for modesty. "The entire site is framed by Sleaford Road to the east, Grange Lane to the north, Dunston Heath Lane to the south, and a farm track to the west, connecting Grange Lane and Dunston Heath Lane. Aside from a few fields, there's bugger all else there, and if our lad did come over the top and fall in, then my guess is that he came from one of those roads."

"Any local properties?"

"Farms," Gillespie said. "Cruz is going to create a door-to-door strategy when he's done. You never know. Someone might have seen something."

"Does he know that yet?"

Gillespie grinned.

"You don't give your bairns every present on Christmas morning, do you? No, you give them wee surprises throughout the day. Keeps them excited, eh?"

"Well, I can't wait to see the excitement on Cruz's face when you tell him he has to traipse across the fields, Jim," Ben told him. "But there's a chance somebody saw something. This time of year, farmers are out all hours. Especially since we haven't had rain for God knows how long. My old man is struggling with the weather and you can bet others are too. Too much rain in the winter and not enough in the summer. They're being attacked on both sides." He caught Gillespie smiling politely. "Sorry, it's in my blood. Talk to me about the body before we get there," Ben said, leading them on again.

"Head wound," Gillespie replied. "And naked."

"Naked?"

"We've checked the immediate area. No sign of any clothes."

"You don't think he could have been diving off the top, do

you?" Ben asked. "You know? He could have been here with some mates. It happens, doesn't it? They might have panicked and legged it. We were always in the farmer's reservoirs when I was young."

"Naked?"

"Well, no, not with my mates, anyway. Okay, so maybe he was out here with a girl? Maybe he was trying to impress her and he misjudged his dive?"

"It crossed my mind," Gillespie replied. "I've asked Kate to have a wee look around. If he was here with somebody, then they might have left a sign somewhere beside the pond."

"I doubt he was here alone," Ben said.

"You're ruling out suicide?"

"Not ruling it out, exactly. But let's face it, it's hardly certain death, is it? What is that, forty feet? He had a good chance of ending up in a wheelchair for the rest of his life."

"I'm not sure which I'd prefer," Gillespie reflected.

"Life," Ben said immediately. "Always life."

They neared the pond and Gillespie caught hold of Ben's sleeve.

"Listen, Ben. Before we get into this, I just…"

"What?" Ben said, and he eyed Gillespie's hand until he let go. "You just what?"

"Mate, are you okay? Are you up for this? I mean, I could take care of it if you needed some time—"

"I'm fine," Ben said. "In fact, the distraction will do me good."

"And Freya?" Gillespie said. "The boss, I mean. Is she…"

"Awake?" Ben asked, shaking his head. "She's undergoing surgery during the day, so by the time I get there, she's out for the count."

"But the doctors? They're happy, are they?"

"Hard to say if they're happy, Jim. But she's in good hands, and all we can do is trust the process."

Gillespie nodded slowly and held Ben's gaze.

"You'll tell me," he said, "if there's something I can do? I can cover for you if you want me to. Anything, alright?"

Ben smiled gratefully.

"Cheers, Jim," he said. "Now then, let's see about this dead body, eh?"

CHAPTER FIVE

"Evening, Katy," Ben said, his eyes dancing from one crouched white-suit to the next, until Southwell rose from her duties. She peeled off a glove, dragged her hood back, and then lifted her goggles onto her forehead.

"Evening, Inspector Savage," she replied, a little too enthused considering her role. She nodded a brief hello to Jim but cut the interaction short before he could say anything. "I suppose you want an update, do you?"

Ben glanced up at the sky, and then at the little group of people around the pond – Doctor Saint, the dive team, and a few of Katy's team working on various tasks. Finally, his eyes rested on the cadaver behind her.

"Jim, can you gather everyone?" he asked. "Let's have the FME, and whoever is heading up the dive team. I don't want to go over everything three times."

"Aye," Gillespie replied, before walking away to carry out the request. At the car park, he had yelled to the young uniformed officer without constraint, yet at the crime scene, mannerisms were far more reserved.

"How are you keeping, Ben?" Southwell replied. "Is she progressing?"

"She is," Ben said, hoping to push past the awkward yet inevitable conversation about Freya.

"I suppose we won't know for sure until she's out of hospital," Southwell said.

"She's in good hands," Ben found himself saying for the second time in only a few minutes. "We can't ask for more than that, can we?"

She opened her mouth to speak but held her tongue when Gillespie returned with Doctor Saint by his side.

"Peter, how are you?" Ben said, pleased at the interruption. He held out a hand for him to shake, and marvelled, not for the first time, at how the forensic medical examiner's hand seemed to engulf Ben's. He was one of life's giants, a tall, lean man, whose extremities seemed to have outgrown the rest of his body. His ears were larger than average, as was his nose. No jacket or shirt Ben had ever seen him wearing had ever fully covered his arms, and if he were to have committed a crime, the size of his shoes would have placed him in a very small niche of suspects. They had to be a size thirteen or fourteen, at least.

"Hello, Ben," he replied, his tone soft and warm. "I heard about the news. I'm so sorry."

"Now then," a new voice said from behind Saint, and a perfectly dry sergeant appeared in uniform. "Geoff Fletcher."

"You're heading up the underwater search, are you?"

"Aye, we are," he replied, a hint of Yorkshire in his accent. "Fished the fella out for Doctor Saint here and we've been over the bottom of the pond twice." He shook his head. "Not a scrap of anything down there, so far."

"Nothing buried in the silt?" Ben asked.

"No. Pond is too new for that. Can't be more than a year old. Didn't even find a Coke can. That's got to be some kind of record."

"So, you're wrapping up then, are you?"

"Aye, we are. We'll be out of here in the next hour or so. We're doing another sweep to make sure. I'll send the report over to you, Sergeant Gillespie." He realised he might have mistaken the chain of command and then added, "Unless you want it directly, Inspector...?"

"Savage," Ben said. "And no. Send it to Sergeant Gillespie if you would. He's more than capable."

Fletcher nodded then retreated, leaving Ben with Gillespie, Saint, and Southwell.

"And then there were four," Saint said, clearly hoping to elevate the mood. It was a trait Ben had noticed in the individuals he worked alongside. A young man's dead body lay only feet away, yet jokes were often cracked and smiles often raised.

"What do we have, Pete?" Ben asked the big man, to which he sucked in a lungful of air.

"Not much, I'm afraid. The fall killed him. That much I'm sure of."

"Head wound?"

"That and a broken neck," Saint replied.

"At least he didn't suffer, then," Ben said.

"Not before he died, at any rate," Saint added.

"You're suggesting he suffered beforehand?" Ben said, and Saint nodded.

"He has cuts all over the lower half of his body," he replied. "And when I say all over, I mean all over."

The additional description wasn't necessary, but Ben was grateful not to be the one making the discovery.

"Time of death?" Ben asked. "Approximately?"

"Can't give you a time, Ben," Saint said. "But I can give you a day."

"Sorry?"

"Saturday," Saint said.

"Saturday? It's Monday now. Are you saying he's been in there all this time?"

"I could be stretched to Sunday morning," Saint explained. "But my money is on Saturday night sometime. He's been through rigor mortis, he's taken on a fair amount of water, and there's enough decomposition to suggest it didn't happen while you were eating your breakfast, Ben."

"I suppose the heat hasn't helped," Southwell said, to which Saint nodded his agreement.

"If you ask me, he came from the fields up top," Saint added, turning briefly to indicate the rock face above them. "I had a quick look. I know I shouldn't have, but you can't do this job and not be a little curious."

"And you have a theory, do you?" Ben asked, mildly amused at the man who, in all the years Ben had known him, had never put a foot out of place.

"Winter barley," Saint said, then put his hand up to his waist palm down. "About so high."

"Which correlates with the cuts on the body?"

"If you ask me, he came from the fields sometime on Saturday night and stumbled into the pond. He wouldn't have known what happened."

"Is death immediate?" Ben asked. "Under the circumstances, that is."

"There are theories," Saint said. "Some say the brain remains active for up to a minute. Others state that death occurs the moment the spinal cord is broken."

"And you?" Ben asked, and Saint grinned softly.

"Somewhere in between. A few seconds. Worst case scenario is that his broken neck resulted in paralysis."

"In which case he would have drowned anyway."

"Yet there are no signs of drowning," Saint replied. "Which is why I think that death was almost immediate."

"Well, it's a theory," Ben said, inhaling long and hard. "Better than a blank sheet of paper."

"I'll send my report through when I'm back in the office," Saint said.

"Thank you, Peter," Ben said, and shook his hand again.

"You take care of yourself now, Ben. Mind you eat well. Keep your strength up, won't you?"

Ben smiled. It was hard not to be warmed by the man's sentiment.

"We're keeping him on track," Gillespie said, which pleased Ben as he was struggling to maintain a hold on his emotions.

"I'll be seeing you," Saint said, then made his way back across the quarry.

"And then there were three?" Southwell said, and Ben laughed.

"Why am I always last?"

"Because you have the biggest task of them all," Ben told her. "And I don't envy you in the slightest."

They turned as a threesome to face the rock wall and the pond before it. To their right, the body bag lay unmoving. The pond was approximately eighty or ninety feet across, in Ben's estimation, and the light was fading fast.

"How are those lights coming on, Jim?" Ben asked.

"They're coming," Gillespie replied. "Give it thirty minutes and this place will be lit up like Christmas."

"If Doctor Saint is right," Ben started before Southwell began her report, "then our victim has been in there for close to forty-eight hours. It hasn't rained, and there's barely been a breath of wind."

"In other words, I have no excuses?" Southwell said.

"Something like that."

"Well, let's rule a few things out, shall we?" she began. "We've been over the perimeter of the pond and can find only one set of bootprints."

"Clearly not belonging to the victim," Gillespie said.

"What about Willis? The man who found him?" Ben suggested.

"It's unlikely but worth double checking," Southwell replied. "Aside from that, there's not a single print to be found, and as you rightly said, Ben, there's been no rain for a week or more."

"All roads lead to Doctor Saint's theory then, do they?"

"We've taken a few samples from the rocks on the far side. If our victim did fall from the top, then we should be able to pinpoint where exactly."

"And the body?" Ben asked.

"Not much to go on until we get him out of here," she explained. "We can't exactly strip him of his birthday suit, can we?"

"Right," Ben said. "So, how long do you need?"

"I'll be here all night," she replied, eyeing Gillespie as if taking the opportunity to tell him he would be eating alone that evening. "If you could arrange for a couple of officers to stay, I'd be grateful."

"Jim?" Ben said.

"Aye, I can arrange that."

"Good," Ben replied. "If you're done with the body, let's get him to the morgue, shall we?"

"Don't tell me, another job for me?" Gillespie said.

"You could always go door to door," Ben replied with a smile.

"Boss?" a little voice called out from atop the rock face. Ben glanced up and found Cruz up there, waving to catch their attention.

"Cruz? What are you doing up there?"

"I'm leading the search, and erm..." Cruz called out, then glanced over his shoulder.

"What is it, Cruz? Come on, I don't want to be out here all night."

"Some of us don't have that option," Southwell muttered.

"Well, it's just..." Cruz continued. "You might want to see this."

CHAPTER SIX

It took Gillespie and Ben a few minutes to walk around the pond to the far reaches of the quarry, where they could make their way up to surface level. The sun was low in the sky, casting long shadows across the near-flat landscape, and the temperature had dropped a few degrees. From the top of the rock face, the view over the quarry was vastly different to that of being inside it.

"The diggers look like wee toys from up here," Gillespie said, more to make conversation than for any other reason. "Like every schoolboy's dream, eh? Diggers and dumpers, and whatever the hell that spider-looking thing is."

"I don't know the official name for it," Ben said rather unenthusiastically. "But it sorts the stones into sizes."

"Eh?"

Ben took an irritated breath but continued to explain.

"You see those conveyor belts?"

"The legs, you mean?"

He nodded.

"You stick a whole load of rocks in the machinery at one end, then they're split into different sizes and sent along the various belts, giving you a pile of aggregate of different sizes."

"Right," Gillespie said, surprised at Ben's knowledge and slightly disappointed not to have induced some humour. Ben glanced across at him as they walked.

"Are you regretting asking me?" Ben said.

"No, not at all," Gillespie lied, as they rounded a corner, and for the first time in a long time, he was actually glad to see Cruz waiting for them fifty yards ahead. "I should have known you'd have some kind of explanation. But if you don't mind, I'm going to keep referring to it as the spider thing."

"Just as long as I don't see that description in any of your reports," Ben said, before addressing Cruz from afar. "Now then, Cruz. What have you got, mate?"

Cruz waited for them to get closer, and then, with a sweep of his arm, presented the hedge that segregated the quarry and the neighbouring farmland.

"What is it?" Ben said to which Cruz seemed slightly dumb-founded.

"It's a hole," he said. "I think this is where he came through. I've checked all along the hedge, and this is probably the weakest spot."

"I wouldn't call that a hole," Gillespie said. "I mean, a man couldn't get through it, could he?"

"I reckon I could," Cruz said.

"Aye, well. There's your benchmark," Gillespie said. "A wee hobbit like you could get through it. But a man? The question is, is our victim a man or a hobbit?"

"Why do you have to be so bloody rude—"

"You're right," Ben said, with enough venom in his tone to shut the pair of them up. "Cruz, well done. What's on the far side of this?"

"Ah," Cruz replied. "That's where it gets interesting. We'll have to walk to the end of the hedge though."

He turned on his heels and led them back the way they had come, like a small boy eager to show his parents his latest painting masterpiece.

"I'm guessing this won't be as interesting as he makes out," Gillespie muttered quietly to Ben. "If you want to slope off, I'll cover it. I don't mind. Kate's going to be working all night, anyway."

"I'll stay," Ben replied, then must have sensed Gillespie's inquisitive stare. "What else am I going to do, go home and think? Open a bottle of wine?" He shook his head. "I want to keep busy, Jim. I'll let you know if I need help."

"Aye," Gillespie grumbled. "Aye, as long as you know..." He stopped and, in the process of doing so, forced Ben to stop, leaving Cruz to amble on ahead of them. "I'm not going to wait for you to tell me you need help, Ben. In fact, I'm going to be by your side as often as possible. So often, you're going to be sick of me, and even then, I'll not leave you alone. You've been through hell, mate. Your bird nearly died—"

"My what?"

"Your...missus. Freya, for God's sake. Not to mention seeing a lass being flattened by a bus." He tapped his temple with an index finger. "It's going to have some kind of effect, Ben. You're not bloody Superman, you know? You might feel like it, but you're not." He let that last sentence sink in before continuing. "I'm your mate, Ben. I can't sit back and watch you pretend nothing has happened. I can't let you try to convince me and the others that working all day and then visiting Freya in hospital in the evening, every night, every week, is healthy. Because it's not. It's not healthy, Ben. You're going to break one day, and if you don't have people like me looking out for you, then that 'one day' will come sooner than you think."

Ben stared at him, and Gillespie read in his eyes that he was refraining from speaking his mind.

"Something wrong?" Cruz called out from the far end of the hedge.

Ben glanced his way briefly, raised his hand to acknowledge the constable, and then spoke quietly to Gillespie.

"I know you have my best interests at heart," he said. "But let me deal with this in my own way. There's a lot going on right now. More than you know—"

"Then tell me," Gillespie hissed at him.

"It's getting dark," Cruz called.

"Tell me what's going on, Ben," Gillespie continued. "For God's sake, man. You're like a closed book, and one I know the ending of, I might add. And it isn't a happy one. Not happy at all. It ends in tears, heartache, or..."

"Or what, Jim?" Ben said. "How does my story end?"

He stared at Gillespie as if daring him to voice his opinion.

"Misery, Ben," Gillespie whispered. "You'll bury yourself in work, you'll bottle your emotions, and every day you do that, the load will get heavier. But you're a stubborn bastard. You'll push on. Tenacious to a fault. That's what you are. Then one day, when you think it's just another miserable day at work, another day of hauling your...baggage around with you, something will happen. Something small and insignificant. Something that, had you not been carrying the weight of the world on your shoulders, you could have dealt with. But you will be carrying it. And you'll break. In fact, no. Break is the wrong word. You'll crumble, Ben. And do you know what? You'll need mates like me to pick you up and dust you off. So you'll do well not to push me away."

"You're right about one thing," Ben said.

"Come on, guys," Cruz called again. "Is there a problem?"

Gillespie glanced up at him, held up his hand signalling him to wait, then refixed on Ben. "What's that? What am I right about?"

"It isn't a happy ending," Ben said. "Not happy at all."

"Are you two talking about me?" Cruz yelled.

"Just hold on, Gabby, will you?" Gillespie shouted back, then took a step closer to Ben. "Go home, Ben. Get some sleep," he said. "Let me deal with this."

"I *need* to be here," Ben said, his tone sharpening with irritation. "I can't go home and do nothing."

"Well, then you leave me no choice," Gillespie said. "If you won't open up and you won't get some rest..."

"What?" Ben said. "Go on. What is it you're going to do? I might remind you that I'm an inspector, I'm the SIO on this investigation, and you're a sergeant who, I might add, is sailing very close to the wind right now."

"Don't push me away, Ben," Gillespie replied. "Not if you expect me to pick you up and dust you off when you crumble."

"I don't expect anything of the sort," Ben replied, and Gillespie released a sad smile.

"Well then, respectfully, Ben," he said, with a quick check of his watch, "I'm going to call it a night."

"You're going home? I haven't dismissed you. What do I write in my report, that you abandoned your duties? How do I phrase that?"

"Abandoned my..." Gillespie tugged at his hair in frustration. "I've arranged CSI, the FME, lights, and the search team. I've got Chapman working on the mispers list, calling round to all the stations in case they've dealt with somebody who matches the victim's description. I've got Gold lined up for family liaison when we find the next of kin. I've had units patrolling the surrounding lanes. Don't you see? While you've been pining over Freya, I've done everything we need to do, Ben. I've covered for you, just like I'm supposed to," Gillespie said, as he walked away back towards the portacabins. "The least I expect in return is a little respect, as a mate, if not a colleague. And if you won't listen to reason, Ben, then I can't stand by and watch. Tomorrow morning, we'll have the pathologist to see, we'll have CSI reports, and we'll have suspects to talk to. One of us will need to be switched on." He held Ben's stare for as long as he could before turning away.

"I haven't dismissed you, Jim," Ben said.

"I'm dismissing myself," Gillespie growled back at him. "I'll see you in the morning, Inspector Savage."

CHAPTER SEVEN

By the time Ben had walked back along the far side of the hedge to the other side of the hole in the hedge that Cruz had found, the sun's dying embers were the only light they had to work with.

"Where did the rest of the search team go?" Ben asked to which Cruz shrugged. "I can't see any torchlights."

"They've reconvened at the quarry entrance, ready to start again tomorrow."

"Any finds?"

"Nothing tangible," Cruz replied, which was cryptic enough to catch Ben's attention.

"Anything intangible?" he said, and Cruz's white teeth gleamed.

"Look," he said, turning his back on the hole in the hedge. He dropped into a crouch, and pointed out into the field, then waited for Ben to follow suit. "You see that?"

He could. From standing height, the crops in the field were as uniform as any farmer could hope for. But crouched down, with the remnants of sun illuminating the distant sky, a faint trail was visible – erratic, but visible.

"Bloody hell, Cruz," he said, and he turned to find the young constable beaming up at him. "Have you sent anyone up there? Do we know where it leads?"

"I've only just found it," Cruz replied. "Bent down to tie my shoe and there it was."

"You could have investigated," Ben said.

"Well, I wanted to be sure, boss. Besides, I didn't want half a dozen fifteen-stone men trampling all over it."

"Please don't call me boss," Ben said. "The boss is lying in hospital having her face rebuilt." He straightened and peered along the trail into the distance, then turned to face Cruz. "Do you have plans for the evening?"

"Plans? Me? No..." He stopped himself from using an incorrect salutation. "Inspector."

"Guv will do," Ben told him. "And if that seems weird, then why don't you use my name? Gillespie doesn't seem to have much trouble with it."

"Guv it is then," Cruz said.

"Come on," Ben said. "I reckon we can make it to the far side of the field before the light goes completely."

"What? Now?"

"Well, yeah. Unless you want to wait until morning? I mean, you're running the search."

"Well, I suppose..."

"We could just go home and come back in the morning? Obviously, any evidence might have gone by then but..."

"Alright," Cruz said, suddenly enthused. "Alright, let's see where it leads us."

"That's more like it," Ben told him, and he checked the sky, gauging the dying light. "We've got about two hours until it's pitch black. Not scared of the dark, are you, Cruz?"

"Me, guv? Sorry, boss...erm, Inspector." Ben raised his eyebrows at Cruz's sudden awkward disposition. "No. Not scared of the dark. Not at all."

"Good," Ben said, presenting the beginning of the trail with a sweep of his arm. "You can lead, then."

Cruz set off slowly and Ben watched as he scoured the ground before him. The soil was rich and dark, and dry from the incessant heat so each step Cruz took left a fine print on the earth for Ben to step into. The victim's prints were evident; his bare toes had left clear indentations.

"He definitely came this way," Cruz called out, taking care to avoid the victim's obvious trail. But he hadn't taken a dozen more steps before he stopped and trampled the crops to the side of the trail. "Here we go."

"What is it?"

Cruz dropped to a crouch, studied the ground, and then looked up.

"Another print."

Ben moved beside Cruz, then dropped down alongside him.

"It's a trainer," he said. "Look, there's the Reebok logo."

"So, either our victim took his shoes off here and flung them somewhere," Ben began, and then looked into the fields for a sign of them. "Or..."

"Or someone was with him."

"Not *with* him," Ben said, eyeing a spot further along the trail where the bare footprints were clear. "Following him, more like. Look, there's our victim's prints. He couldn't have taken them off here."

Cruz followed the trail of Reebok prints further from the crime scene. "They didn't make much of an effort to hide their prints."

Ben trampled the surrounding crops, wincing at what the farmer might have to say about the negligence.

"What does that tell you?" he asked.

"He's not forensically aware?" Cruz suggested.

"Maybe, but think harder. Why might somebody make no effort not to cover their prints?"

Cruz gazed up at the trail into the distance.

"The victim was running along here, naked," he said aloud, "and somebody was behind him. Somebody fully dressed."

"What do you notice about the trail?" Ben asked.

"Eh?"

"Look at it."

Cruz crouched again to see the faint variation in the uniform crops.

"It's all over the place," he said. "He didn't run straight."

"It also looks like he fell a few times," Ben added. "Now look at the footprints, the victim's prints, not the third party's."

"What about them?" Cruz asked, looking slightly bemused.

Ben strode over to him and together they studied a line of prints before them.

"He was either two foot tall with size ten feet, or..."

"Oh Jesus," Cruz said. "He wasn't running. His stride is too short."

"A fast walk, maybe," Ben replied. "Now, if you were naked and someone was after you, for one reason or another, why wouldn't your strides be long? Why wouldn't you be sprinting your backside off to get away?"

"And why wouldn't you run in a straight line?" Cruz said. Ben grinned. He always enjoyed watching the cogs fall into place, especially when the cogs in question belonged to somebody as keen as Cruz. "It was dark," Cruz continued. "It was pitch black. He didn't know where he was running."

"Which suggests?"

"He wasn't from around here. He's not local," Cruz said. "A local lad would know these fields. They'd at least know which direction to run to reach the road."

"Which leads me to my next questions," Ben said. "Where was he running from? Why was he running? And why was he naked?"

"The trainer is definitely a man's," Cruz said, then peered up at Ben with his face screwed up. "You don't think..."

"I don't think what?" Ben asked.

"You know. Maybe he and the other bloke were...you know?"

Tempted to feign ignorance to prolong Cruz's discomfort, Ben studied him and relented. "We can't rule it out," he said. "If I'm honest, I had my fair share of outdoor pursuits when I was young."

"Eh? You mean...you're...no, surely not? I had you down as a ladies' man through and through."

"No, not with men. With girls, Cruz. There's something about being outside with someone. Maybe it's the risk of being caught? Maybe it's the feeling of fresh air on bare skin? There's no reason homosexual couples don't feel the same, you know?"

Cruz nodded.

"It's a decent theory," he said. "A young gay couple seeking adventure. It goes wrong, somehow. Maybe the victim was upset by something the other bloke did?"

"Maybe they weren't a couple," Cruz added. "The killer could have just picked him up. It happens to girls all the time. Why shouldn't it happen to men?"

"Why not indeed," Ben said, checking his watch. "I want to see where this trail leads. But not tonight. If we're right, we could stomp all over important evidence." He pulled his phone from his pocket and took a deep breath, slightly annoyed at having to call their little adventure off prematurely. "In the meantime, I'll get Southwell and her mob up here to take some casts of these prints." No sooner as he uttered the words than the phone lit up and Katy Southwell's name flashed across the screen. "Speak of the devil," he said, as he answered the call. "Katy, your ears must have been burning."

"I could say the same thing," she said.

"Oh really? I'm a topic of discussion for you and your team, am I? I feel quite privileged."

"I wouldn't get carried away," she said. "I was referring to a chat I've just been having with Geoff Fletcher."

"Geoff Fletcher?" Ben said, trying to place the name.

"From the dive team," she said.

"Oh, that Geoff Fletcher. Go on. What did he have to say?"

"It's not what he had to say, Ben," she replied. "It's what one of his team found during the last sweep of the pond."

CHAPTER EIGHT

"Well, that's our theory out the window," Ben said, and he held up the clear plastic bag for Cruz to see. In the fields, the dying light had been plentiful enough for them to make out the footprints in the soil. But in the confines of the quarry's high walls, they relied on the bright lights and generators that Gillespie had organised.

"Well, it was just a theory," Cruz said, leaning in to study the name on the exposed driver's license. "Lee Constantine." He squinted and leaned in closer. "Metheringham."

"A mile away," Ben said.

"So, he was local. Surely any of the local lads could find their way home from a mile away."

"We'll need to do some digging," Ben replied. "How long had he lived here? He might be new to the area."

"That driving licence is old," Cruz said. "It's not a new issue."

"We're heading up to the field," Southwell announced from a few metres away. "Care to join us?"

"I'll go," Cruz said, then smiled meekly at Ben. "If you wanted to get off, that is...Inspector."

Ben wanted to tell him to go home. He wanted to stay and see the night through with his team.

"You look done in," Southwell added. "Go on. Get some rest. You're no good to her like that, are you?"

Her. Freya. The memories of his chat with Greg came flooding back.

"You're sure?" Ben said to Cruz, who nodded emphatically.

"I'll update you in the morning."

"Good. Good, we'll have a briefing and make a plan," Ben said, as he turned to walk back to his car. He stopped and called back. "Oh, and Cruz?"

"Boss? Sorry, Inspector?"

Ben dismissed his flustering with an appreciative smile.

"In case you're wondering if you'll be handed the joys of going door to door, you won't be. You've done well today, mate. Keep it up, eh?"

"Oh, that doesn't bother me," he replied. "I'm happy to knock on a few doors if it helps. Besides, I want to know what's at the end of that trail."

"Don't we all," Ben said, then nodded a goodnight, and left them to it.

He hadn't taken four steps when somebody grabbed onto his shirt sleeve, tugging him back. He turned to find Katy Southwell staring up at him. Aside from her obvious intelligence and personable nature, she was an attractive woman. Her wide-set eyes gave her a unique look, which was far from unattractive. Gillespie was a lucky man.

"Ben," she began. "I hope you don't mind me saying but..."

"But what?" Ben said, sensing the victim, the evidence, and the results were not going to be the topic of conversation.

"You're going to see her, aren't you?"

"Sorry?"

"Freya," she said. "You're going to see her."

"I don't see what business that is of yours, Katy."

"Have a night off," she said. "Honestly, you look awful. You're burning the candle at both ends."

A part of him wanted to tell her to mind her own business. But the fact was that every piece of advice she had given him about Freya had been right. She had told him not to have a relationship with a colleague. She had told him to question his priorities. It was he who had been the fool not to have listened to her.

"I admire you," he told her. "I really do."

"I don't want your admiration, Ben."

"Well, you have it," he said. "And you're right. I look like death warmed up."

"Oh, Ben—"

"I'm not sleeping, Katy. I spend most of my life at work, and when I'm not there, I'm with her. If I go home, I feel guilty that it wasn't me who was hurt. That it isn't me lying in hospital. So I go to her house, where I'm constantly reminded of her. There's no escape," he said.

"You don't need to escape from her, Ben," she said. "You just need rest. There's nothing wrong with being loyal. There's nothing wrong with loving somebody. God knows she's all you have, and you're all she's got."

"That's just it," he said. "I'm not, am I? I'm not all she's got. I've been an idiot, Katy. I've been a bloody idiot."

"Oh, Ben, you're tired—"

"I am tired," he told her. "And I've been a fool." He stared into those glistening eyes of hers, marvelling at how Gillespie had landed on his feet by working his way into her heart. "If you talk to Jim, tell him something, will you?"

"Of course, but what?"

"Just tell him I'm sorry," Ben said. "He's another one I should have listened to." Southwell's expression softened and Ben felt his shoulder sag. "He's a good mate. He should know that."

"Then tell him," she replied, and she closed the gap between them. "You once told me to give him a chance. You said he was a good man, and he is. He really is."

"You listened to me, you mean?" Ben said. "And I didn't listen to you? You told me to keep my relationship and my career separate, and I didn't listen. She's married, you know?"

"Eh?"

"She's married. Freya."

"I don't understand, I thought—"

"That we were engaged?" Ben said. "Oh, that too. Well, I thought we were engaged. I proposed, and she as good as said yes, albeit with a few caveats. But the fact remains that her husband showed up at the hospital today. I thought she was divorced. All this time, I thought she was divorced and she wasn't. How do you think that made me feel?"

"Oh, Ben," she said, and she reached out to squeeze his arm. "I'm sure there's a good reason—"

"I'm sure there is," he told her. "But I can't get past the fact that she lied to me."

"Did you ask if she was divorced?"

"Well, no," he said.

"And did she tell you, specifically that she was divorced?"

"Not in so many words, no."

"And did she commit to marrying you?"

"Again, not in so many words," he said. "But she didn't say no. She didn't exactly say, '*Sorry, Ben, I can't marry you because I'm still married*'. She just kept me hanging on. She kept dangling the carrot."

"And you would have preferred more stick, would you?" Southwell said. "Would you have preferred her to tell you no?"

He stared at her but said nothing.

"Look, go home. Get some rest," she said. "You can't go on like this, and without speaking to her, all you're going to do is jump to conclusions."

"You're right," he said. "Of course, you're right. You're always right."

"I just have one request, Ben," she said softly, to which he raised his eyebrows in anticipation. "Bloody well listen to me this time, will you?"

CHAPTER NINE

The tenacious summer light had finally succumbed to the clutches of darkness by the time Ben pulled out of the quarry, which sat in the parish of Dunston where Freya's house was but some way from the village. He considered the drive to his own house, which was a mere fifteen minutes further, but no matter how much he thought of his own bed, his own kitchen, and all those housework chores he had neglected of late, he still found himself pulling up outside Freya's cottage less than two minutes later.

He pondered driving on but was easily convinced otherwise, and a few moments later, he was unlocking the front door.

Less than five minutes after that, he was pouring himself a glass of wine in Freya's kitchen, much as he would have done had she been there. Except, she would be flitting from room to room or poring over the evidence at the dining table.

But he had no appetite for death or investigations. Nor did his appetite extend to Freya. For now, he was content just to be in her house, where maybe he could find a way into her mind.

"Find a way," he said to himself, as a thought struck him. "Find a way."

Carrying his glass, he locked the front door and then took the stairs two at a time. He burst into Freya's spare room, which served as both a dressing room and an office, the former taking precedence over the latter. Careful not to leave a ring, he placed his glass down on the little table and then reached for the handle on her wooden filing cabinet, where his hand seemed to hang in the air.

He felt betrayal's bony finger trace its way around his heart. This was her private space. This was her life. The life she had led before they had even met. That part of her that he had no claim to. It was a line in the sand that he had no right to cross. He dropped down into the wooden chair and then folded one leg over the other.

The answer to his questions would likely be inside that filing cabinet. It wasn't locked. All he had to do was open it, rummage through what he imagined would be a chaotic filing system, if there was a filing system at all, and he would find it.

But that was a level he couldn't sink to. That would make him no better than her.

He drank the last of his wine and pictured Freya giving him a filthy look for drinking fine wine in such a manner. In the end, he was who he was. He had fallen for Freya because, aside from her looks and her charm, she had a brilliant mind. He knew how abrasive she could be and had learned to see past it. He knew that she could start, maintain, and finish an argument all without him uttering a single word, only to be left bewildered and wondering what on earth had just happened.

But he did love her. There was something about her. The way she took pride in her appearance, the way she took care of herself, and the way she could enter a room and raise every head through presence alone.

He snatched up his empty glass and wandered downstairs. Had she been there, no doubt she would have commented on him not removing his shoes. But she wasn't there. She was lying in a hospital bed having her face rebuilt. And in those brief moments of consciousness between doses of God knows what drugs she was being given, she would be considering her future and rebuilding her mind.

The thought of her rehabilitation stopped him on the stairs. He wondered if it was him she would be thinking of, or... The front door closed, dragging him from his thoughts like a blazing fire seeking oxygen through an open van door.

Quietly, he took the last three stairs and then stared at the newcomer.

"Greg?" he said.

"Ah, I wondered whose car that is," he replied. "Do all Freya's colleagues have keys to her house, or are you the exception?"

"I'm the exception," Ben heard himself saying, while his mind was elsewhere in a rage.

"I thought so."

"I might ask what you're doing here," Ben said. "She won't like it, you know? She won't like you being here."

"Oh?" he said, taking a few steps inside as if to cement his position. "I would have thought I had more right to be in my wife's house than you, Inspector Savage, was it?"

Ben glanced down at the object in Greg's hands.

"Where did you get a key?" he said, to which Greg held up a bunch.

"Oh these? Well, she won't be needing them, will she? Not for the time being anyway."

"You stole them from her bag?"

"Stole is a bit strong, given she's my wife," Greg said, and in turn, he glanced down at the object in Ben's hand.

"Helping yourself to her wine?" he said. "Now, if there's one thing Freya is possessive about, it's her wine."

"She won't mind," Ben said. "But I suggest you leave. Give me her keys and leave. I won't tell her you were here. I don't want to upset her."

Greg placed the keys on the cabinet near the front door, then put his hands in his pockets. He had an air of authority about him that rivalled even Freya's. Perhaps that's why they split, he thought. They were too similar.

But even Freya's arrogance paled in the shadow of Greg's. He took a few more steps, coming to one of the armchairs, where he turned and dropped into it, sighing like the chair was an old friend.

"Don't make me be rude, Greg," Ben said. "Let's keep this amicable."

"Amicable?" Greg replied. "You're sleeping with my wife. What do you suggest, we cook dinner together and talk about her?"

"I'd rather go hungry," Ben said.

"Do you honestly think I'm going to let a man like you worm your way into Freya's heart? Do you expect me to stand aside and watch?"

Since Freya's accident, Ben's emotions had run high, which, coupled with his fatigue, only served to fuel the fire inside him. He wanted to walk over to Freya's husband and teach him a lesson in manners.

But that was not how Freya would have had it. That was not what she would have called proper behaviour. Instead, he walked into the kitchen, collected another glass from the cupboard, and filled them both.

"Here," he said, handing Greg the fresh glass, and then he dropped into the armchair opposite. Greg sniffed once, closed his eyes, and then grinned.

"Chianti," he said eventually. "Her favourite."

"What are you doing here, Greg?" Ben said, letting his tone dictate the mood.

"I've come to see my wife, Mr Savage. She had a little accident. I wanted to make sure she's okay."

"What are you doing in her house? How do you know where she lives?"

"Oh, come on. If I give you a name, I'll bet you can get their address in under ten minutes."

"I'm a copper, Greg."

"And I am married to one," he replied without hesitation. "Which means I know other coppers."

"Bent coppers, you mean?"

"Bent ones, straight ones, fat ones, thin ones, rich ones, skint ones." He sneered at Ben. "You're all the same. You might act like you've got a ticket to the pearly gates, but deep down, you're all the same. Most of you are so scared of being called a racist, sexist, or whatever else you can think, that you can barely do your job. One little word in your earhole, Mr Savage, and I can have whatever I want."

"Not from my earhole," Ben told him.

"You all start off like that," he said, sitting back in his seat. "But it doesn't matter anyway. I found myself a copper who can help and I exploited it. I call that good business."

"You still haven't told me what you want," Ben said. "You don't care about her. If you cared about her, you would have been to see her. Before the accident, I mean. You would have helped her when she needed someone to help her."

"Oh, I see," Greg said, grinning from ear to ear. "She needed an arm around her and along comes Mr Savage with his big size twelves. Is that it?"

"I'm not her only friend."

"Right, but you're the only one with a key to her house." He glanced around the room, nodding to himself. "You don't live here, though, do you?"

Ben said nothing.

"No, you don't live here. This is all Freya. The fancy furniture, the nice paintings. I'll bet the frames are worth more than the prints."

"I wouldn't know."

"No. No, I don't suppose you would, being a farm boy and all that."

"You what?"

"Oh, come on. Let's not be coy, Ben. You're a farmer's son. You're her bit of rough, that's all. You didn't think she was actually going to marry you, did you?"

"Get out."

"It's nothing to be ashamed of."

"I said get out."

"You should feel privileged. She has very high standards, you know?"

Ben placed his glass down on the coffee table – to hell with the ring marks. He shoved himself from his seat.

"You've got ten seconds to get out of this house," he said.

"Get out?" Greg said. "You must be joking. I'm not going anywhere." He sank the remains of his wine and placed his glass on a coaster close to Ben's. Slowly, he pushed himself out of the seat and stood, matching Ben's six-foot-something height. "Freya is still my wife, which means I own half this house." He took two confident strides towards Ben, leaving just twelve inches between them. "If anyone's leaving, farm boy, it's you."

CHAPTER TEN

The incident room whiteboard was usually Freya's domain. It was her comfort blanket, her notebook, and her planner, and yet to Ben's surprise, he experienced very little in the way of guilt when he scrubbed her scrawled notes from its surface and began a new investigation.

In the centre of the board, he wrote a single name. *Lee Constantine*. Beside the name, he listed the scraps of information that cluttered his mind. *Naked*, *trail*, and *chased*, followed by three question marks.

And there, his momentum faded.

It was early morning, too early for the team to be in, and the silence was as comforting as the surroundings. Like every other incident room Ben had seen, the space was far from welcoming. The walls were dotted with faces of wanted or missing individuals, maps, and posters to remind them all what good police work entails.

But it wasn't his house, and it wasn't Freya's house, and those facts alone pleased him. It was a neutral surrounding. A place with more professional memories than personal.

The sun was up but still hung low in the sky, illuminating the

Wolds on the horizon and the Fens before them. It was a view he had admired for most of his career, and one he could lose himself in if he let his mind wander, which he nearly did. Had he not caught his thoughts from drifting towards Freya, he might have stared at that landscape until the team came in. But he pulled himself free, cast Freya aside, and returned to the board.

The beginning of any investigation was always light on fact, thick with loose theories, and dizzied by the various opinions of the team.

He drew a rough circle in the lower half of the board and placed an X inside it. The circle represented the quarry, and the X represented where the pond was located, and by default, where the body had been discovered. He enclosed his rough map in a large square, with each side representing the roads Gillespie had stated. Finally, using a red marker, he added a rough dotted line to represent the trail that Cruz had found. Using the maps app on his phone, he added the various properties on each of the roads, adding in the property names, where possible. He took a step back to admire his handiwork, before moving on and adding in the rough location of Metheringham, and the road on which Constantine had lived. According to the app, Alfred Avenue was one point four miles from the quarry, so he added in the fact.

"You would have been better printing a map off," a voice said from behind him. The tone was gruff and the accent familiar.

"Morning, Jim," Ben said, turning to look him in the eye. "Bit early for you, isn't it?"

Gillespie placed a takeaway coffee on Ben's desk, took a sip of his own, and then perched on his own desk.

"Kate told me," he said. "About the whole Freya thing."

"I'd rather not talk about it," Ben replied. "We've got a job to do, right?"

"Aye, we've got a job to do," Gillespie said. "But can we do it when our minds are elsewhere?"

"We have to," Ben told him, each of them skirting around the topic like it was contagious. "Or try, at least." He clicked the lid back on the pen. "And for the record, my laptop is still playing up."

"Eh?"

"The map," he said, gesturing at the whiteboard. "I'd have had to come in an hour earlier if I wanted a map printed."

"Fair enough," Gillespie said, and he held Ben's stare long enough to convey that he didn't buy Ben's diversion tactics and would get him to open up sooner or later.

"Listen, Jim. About last night," Ben began.

"It's okay, Ben," Gillespie said. "The least said, the better, eh?"

"No, I'm sorry. I was out of order. You were being a mate and I was being stubborn."

"It's no bother—"

"It is to me," Ben said, cutting him off. "I don't have many mates. I should listen to the ones I do have."

"Ben—"

"I mean it, Jim," he said. "Listen, meeting Freya's husband in the hospital really threw me. You know? I've put everything into her."

"I don't need to know about your sex life, Ben—"

"You know what I mean. I committed to her. I've given up a lot to be with her. To the detriment of my career, I might add. And even though she hadn't said yes, deep down, I suppose I thought she would eventually. I figured she was just playing a game. Seeing how long I'd wait. And so, I hung around. I've been with her every night since the accident. I've taken care of her house, her bills, everything. You name it, I've done it for her. I've been the one to pick up the pieces so that when she finally gets out, her life will have some kind of normality. She'd be able to get back on her feet with no distractions, you know?"

"I do," Gillespie said, his usual brash tone giving way to something more akin to empathetic.

"Then he came along. Greg," Ben said. "And now I realise I've just been a complete idiot. At the quarry last night, I just wanted something to take my mind off it all. I was pleased with the distraction. I even let Cruz lead me through a field when I should have listened to you, mate."

"Ah, I wouldn't have listened to me if I were you," Gillespie said. "I'm not exactly a role model, am I?"

"You're doing yourself an injustice if you think that," Ben told him. "Anyway, your missus told me once that I should keep my professional and personal lives separate, and I didn't listen. I mean, look at you two. You were both there in the quarry and nobody would have even guessed you were a couple."

"Yeah, she's pretty tight on that. She barely even looks my way."

"And that's a good thing," Ben said. "It's the right thing to do. She's right. And she was right when she told me last night that I should go home, to my own house, and get some sleep. But did I? Did I hell."

"You went to Freya's?" Gillespie said. "Why?"

"Why? I don't know why. It's around the corner from the quarry. It has Freya's stuff in there. It reminds me of her. It smells of her."

"The girls' toilet smells of her, mate. If you needed reminding."

"And then he turned up," Ben said and left the statement hanging there.

Gillespie took a sip of his coffee, licked his teeth, and then waited for Ben to stop fidgeting.

"I take it you're referring to her husband?" he said, and Ben nodded. "How did he know where she lives?"

"I don't know. Somebody Freya used to work with. It doesn't matter how. The fact is that he took her keys from her bag and let himself in."

"He did what? He took her keys? That's theft."

"He's entitled to," Ben said. "Legally, I mean."

"Because they're still married?" Gillespie said, shaking his head. "Jesus, Ben. What did you do? Don't tell me you hit him. God, please—"

"I didn't hit him," Ben said. "Although the thought crossed my mind, I have to admit. Besides, what was I going to do? He's her husband. He has a right to be there."

"Oh, come on—"

"And I have no claim to anything," Ben finished. "What am I really? To Freya, I mean. What am I? A bit of rough? A plaything?"

"You're more than that, mate. Any idiot can see that."

"This idiot can't," Ben said. "But they say the first step in rehabilitation is to recognise you have a problem. So that's what I'm doing."

"What do you mean?"

"I'm going to listen to your missus. Kate," Ben said. "It's time I took a step back from it all."

"You're giving up on her? Oh, come on, Ben. How many times have you been here before? You two are off and on more than a McDonald's microwave. You're going to give all that up for this Greg bloke?"

"She lied to me, Jim," he said, holding his hands up in surrender. "All this time I thought she was just playing a game and I was wrong. She's still married."

"And you think she still wants her husband, do you?"

"What am I supposed to think?"

"Not that, you daft sod. If she wanted to be with her husband, she'd have damn well been with him. You know her. She wouldn't move halfway across the country to get away from him if she still wanted to be with him, would she? No, is the answer."

"Well, it doesn't matter now, does it? I've given all I can give."

"You can't give up on her, mate. She's got nobody else, except us lot, and let's face it, who would she rather have visit her? A bunch of misfits or a nice wee bit of rough."

Ben gave a little laugh at how Gillespie always seemed to add an insult to any pep talk he gave and somehow got away with it.

"I'm not giving up on her," Ben said. "She's a good friend, and I'll be there when I can. When she needs me." He shook his head sadly. "But that's where it ends. It's the line in the sand that we both knew was coming sooner or later. I'm only glad it's me who gets to draw it. From now on, I'll listen to your missus."

"Kate? What's she told you now?"

"To put myself and my career first," Ben said. "So, when it comes to all things police work, the gloves are officially off."

The incident room door squealed, and both Ben and Gillespie turned to find DCs Cruz, Gold, and Chapman entering the room, each of them grinning from something that had been said.

"Morning," Gold said. "What are you two conspiring about?"

Ben heard the words but said nothing. He stared at the door, which for years had squealed open and banged closed, until Freya's predecessor, Steve Standing, had had it repaired. Since then, for some unexplained reason, the place hadn't quite been the same.

"What is it?" Gold said, her faint Edinburgh accent sweetening those three simple words. She glanced at the door and back at him. "Ben? What's wrong? Has something happened? Is it the boss? Is she okay?"

"It's nothing," he said, finally, just as DS Nillson pushed through into the room, and the door hinge gave another quiet squeal. "It's just..."

"Go on," Gold said.

He smiled at her and chose his words carefully.

"You might think I'm going mad," he said. "But I think things are getting back to normal."

CHAPTER ELEVEN

A bemused look visited each of their faces in turn, finally resting on DC Anderson, the last of the team to arrive. She took her place beside Nillson, opened her laptop, and stared up at Ben.

"What? Have I missed something?"

He grinned at her.

"Nothing. You're just in time," he said and then clapped his hands three times, just as Freya used to do. "Briefing in five minutes. If you need the washroom or a coffee, then now is the time."

Nobody moved an inch. Those who wanted a drink already had tea or coffee. Nillson sipped from a water bottle, glanced at her teammates, and then back at Ben.

"Looks like we're ready when you are, boss," she said.

"Please," he said. "I'm only standing in for Freya. I'm not the boss. Just use my rank, if you must."

Never one to miss an opportunity to prove a point, Nillson glanced around at her colleagues once more.

"You're the boss to us, boss," she said. "Besides, Detective Inspector is so stuffy, don't you think?"

"Far too many syllables," Gillespie added.

"Alright, alright," he said. "I'm not going to spend the morning debating what to call me. If my rank is too much to deal with, then call me by my name. You've all known me long enough."

"Thank God for that," Gillespie said.

"Except..." Ben added before a noisy agreement took place. "Except when Granger is around."

"You mean Detective Chief Superintendent Granger?" Nilson said, grinning again.

"Don't stir it up, Anna," he said, then tapped the whiteboard. "Now a few of us have already had the pleasure of spending an evening on this one, but for the benefit of those who enjoyed a night off, a man's naked body was found in Dunston quarry last night at around six p.m."

"I had my own naked man's body to deal with," Nillson remarked, which for the sake of progress, Ben let slide. "The dive team discovered a wallet in the pond belonging to a Lee Constantine from Metheringham." He turned to Chapman briefly. "How did you get on with the mispers?"

Chapman was what Ben's father would have called prim and proper. She was an old woman in a young woman's body, preferring knitting and crosswords to dancing and drinking. But there was little doubt that the team would not operate as well as it did without her.

"Nothing that matches his description," she said. "I called around to the local stations too, just to see if they had any dealings with anyone matching the description. Nothing."

"Okay, at least we've ticked the box," Ben said. "The good news is that we have an address that will need checking out. In the meantime, Chapman, do some digging on Lee Constantine of Alfred Avenue. See what you can find on him." He turned to face the rest of the team and then tapped the board again. "The body was discovered by a Jacob Willis. Quarry manager. He was locking up when he saw something floating in one of the restoration ponds in the northern corner of the plot. As far as he knows, nobody else saw anything, but that doesn't mean we can rule anybody out just yet."

"So, he drowned, did he?" Nillson asked.

"The FME is leaning towards a broken neck," Ben said. "One side of the pond is a sheer rock face leading up to the fields above. The theory is that he fell from the top and broke his neck on the rocks below."

"Naked?" Nillson said.

"That's right."

"He was in a field naked?"

"As far as we can tell," Ben said.

"So, he was shagging then."

"Sorry?"

"Why else would he be out there naked? He's had a sexy rendezvous with somebody and somehow fallen off the top. That's death by misadventure, which is a job for CID, isn't it?"

"Not a bad start, Anna," he said. "But perhaps wait until I've given you all the facts before we palm this one off to our friends upstairs, eh?"

She held her hands up defensively. "Sorry, sorry. Just brainstorming."

He winked at her to let her know there was no harm done and then continued. "DS Gillespie was first on scene and arranged for CSI, the FME, and the underwater search team to attend."

"Eh?" Nillson said, interrupting again.

Ben bit his tongue and raised his eyebrows. "What is it, Anna?"

"Jim was first on scene? How come I wasn't called? I was the on-call sergeant."

It was a conversation Ben had foreseen and was ready for.

"DS Gillespie was nearer," Ben said. "It wasn't a matter of preference. It was a case of who could respond the fastest while I was with Freya."

"Right," Nillson said, unconvinced.

"How is she?" Gold asked, and Ben felt the irritation rising in his chest.

"Let's keep to the topic, shall we?" he said politely. "DC Cruz was tasked with managing a search of the local area and discovered a faint trail through the fields," Ben continued, pointing to the dotted, red line he added to his map.

"Is that a map?" Anderson asked. "You should have printed one off, Ben. It would have been clearer."

"I know," he said and debated if he should explain that his laptop had not worked properly for more than a year, despite receiving several new ones from IT. "Can we just…"

"I'll print one off for you," she said, and immediately set about working on her laptop. For a moment, Ben considered pulling her back into the briefing but thought better of it. Nillson could explain anything she missed.

"So Cruz and I took a walk along the trail to see where it led," Ben said, hoping the remaining members of the team were following. "Where we found two sets of prints. The first was made by bare feet and the other was a male, approximately a size nine or a ten. CSI have taken casts and will confirm the details later. All we know is that it was a Reebok trainer."

"So, he was with a bloke then?" Nillson said.

"With or being chased by," Ben said, then perched on his desk, much as Freya used to. "You see, this trail Cruz found wasn't a straight line. We won't know for sure until we talk to the pathologist, but he wasn't running straight."

"So?" Nillson said.

"So, a local lad could have found his way home in a heartbeat," Ben said. "The trail looks like he was changing his mind or changing direction to avoid being captured."

"So, not a sexy rendezvous, then?"

"I don't know," Ben said. "It's certainly a possibility. The other thing was that the footsteps were fairly close together. If he was running full pelt, they would have been further apart."

"What are you getting at?" Gold asked.

"I don't know," he said. "There's something there, but I can't quite place it. He was naked in a field walking in a zig-zag with no real purpose. Why was he naked? Where was he going? Was he heading to the pond?"

"Did the FME give a time?"

"He gave an approximation," Ben replied. "Anytime between Saturday night and Sunday morning."

"So, it was dark?" Nillson said. "Out in a field in the middle of the night, he wouldn't have had a clue where he was going."

"He would have seen Metheringham. He would have at least seen the glow of the village," Ben said.

"Right, but he wouldn't have been able to see his hand in front of his face. No wonder the trail was all over the place."

"Again, I agree, but we need to put some meat on that bone, and the only way we're going to do that is by talking to the pathologist. Chapman, anything on Constantine yet?"

"Not much," she replied. "The address is correct, although it's rented by a Vicky Fraser. I'm looking at his social media now, and if I'm right, then she's his girlfriend."

"Right," Ben said. "Here's what's going to happen. Gillespie and Gold, the three of us are going to pay a visit to Vicky Fraser. If need be, we'll deliver the bad news, and then it's over to you, Gold, to act as family liaison while we go on to see the pathologist. Once she's calmed down, I want you to propose a viewing to give us a formal ID."

"Will do," she said.

"Cruz, if your offer of going door to door still stands, can you hit the properties on my map? Take a uniformed officer if you need to. I want to know if anyone saw or heard anything at all. Any strange cars at night, any voices. Anything at all."

"Not a problem, boss, sorry, Inspector," he said, kicking himself for his mistake.

"Nillson and Anderson, work with Chapman, will you? Find

out where he worked and have a snoop around. Just remember, we cannot bring anyone in until we have a positive ID. All being well, he's known to us already and CSI can confirm his DNA. Until then, all we can do is the groundwork. Understood?"

They chorused a confirmation, and some of them even offered a smile, which caught him off guard. Nillson stood, scraping her chair back, and the printer whirred into life, presumably being Anderson's printed map.

"Just one more thing," he said, before pandemonium ensued. They stopped in their tracks and looked at him with anticipation. He nodded his appreciation. "I just wanted to say that things are going to be a little different from here on in. We don't know how long Freya will be out for. We don't even know if she'll be coming back. So, we need to pull together. There's still a murder to solve, and it falls to us to do so."

"Goes without saying, Ben," Gillespie said.

"I know. I just wanted to say it. I wanted to make sure," he said. "Before Freya arrived in Lincolnshire, it was us. We've lost a few people along the way, but for the most part, we're all still here. And now it's only us again. We know we're capable. So, let's show her what we can do, eh?"

CHAPTER TWELVE

"Sounds to me like you're ready to draw a line under her," Gillespie said, as they made their way across the car park to Ben's car.

"Not quite," he replied. "But what else can I do apart from getting on with life? Would you rather I mope about like a lovesick puppy?

He pulled his car door open and tossed his jacket onto the rear seat.

"Well, no–"

"Shall I follow you?" Gold called out. She descended the few steps that led up to the custody suite, and Ben couldn't help but notice she had done something with her hair. He wasn't sure what it was, but she looked different somehow. More confident.

"If you don't mind, Jackie," he replied. "Jim and I will go in and deliver the bad news, then we'll get you inside. We don't want to go in heavy-handed."

"Fine by me," she said, and just as Ben was about to climb into his car, another voice called out.

"Ben? Got a minute?"

It was Nillson, and she stood at the door to the custody suite waiting for a response.

"If you're quick," he said. There were perhaps twenty metres between them, and the fact that she didn't budge an inch suggested the word she wanted to have, was for his ears only, and he had a good idea of the topic.

"Give me a minute, Jim, will you?" he said, leaning into the car, to find Gillespie busying himself with his phone.

"Aye, no bother," he replied in his typical carefree tone.

Ben made the journey back across the car park, questioning himself as to whether Freya would have made the effort, or if she would have called out for Nillson to come to her, or more likely, for Nillson to arrange a meeting later that day. But Ben knew Nillson. He knew that private words were few and far between and that they were often of a serious nature.

"You alright?" he asked, as he drew near to her.

Slowly, she descended the steps, glancing about the yard to ensure neither Gold nor Gillespie could hear.

"I need to say something," she said. "And I realise that you're going through a difficult time, what with the boss and all that."

"We're all going through a difficult time, Anna," he told her.

"We're not all in a relationship with her," she replied, to which he nodded his agreement, but kept quiet about any recent developments. No doubt once Gillespie had a chance, he would spread that little scrap of gossip on Ben's behalf. "The thing is, Ben. What you said in the incident room, about there being a chance of Freya not coming back-."

"I said it was a possibility. It's not set in stone, Anna–"

"I know, but still, I need you to know something," she said, and her expression altered. It was perhaps the first time in all the years he had known her that she displayed any kind of weakness.

"What is it? Your job's safe. You know that, right?"

"I know. Well, I think I know anyway. But if she doesn't come back, and I know it's a big if, but if she doesn't come back, then there's a strong chance that you'd take her place."

"I've been a DI for five minutes, Anna. I doubt very much Granger or his superiors would be in a position to promote me so soon even if they wanted to."

"Oh, come off it. If it wasn't for Freya, you'd have made DI over a year ago. When David died—"

"When David died, Granger considered me for the role," he told her. "At no point did he make an offer and he certainly didn't guarantee me the position."

"Even so," she said. "Whatever happens, if she doesn't come back there'll be a hole to fill. Either above you, or below you."

"And you want to be considered for it?" he said. "You don't want me to overlook you. Is that it?"

She folded her arms, which was a typical defensive posture for Anna. Growing up with several older brothers had instilled a strength in her far beyond any other women he had known, not just mentally, but physically.

"Jim got the investigation last night, despite my name being down as the on-call sergeant."

"I explained that," he said. He was closer, and I was...otherwise engaged."

"And now it looks like you've buddied up with him. What am I supposed to think, Ben?"

"I haven't buddied up with him," he said. "He's with me because he was buddied up with Cruz, but that relationship clearly wasn't working. Cruz works better without him. He actually works well with Gold. And you and Anderson are a solid team. I wouldn't dream of breaking the pair of you up." He watched her expression shift from disappointment to frustration, and then regret, perhaps for speaking out in the first place and exposing a weakness. "If you really want the truth, Anna, then listen to this. You are a fine sergeant, and I have absolutely no doubt at all that you're ready for the DI role."

"But?"

"No buts,' he said. "Jim is in the same position, but you both need some work."

"Eh?"

"He has a tendency to find the easy way out, whereas you have a tendency to go in guns blazing," he told her. "Now, if you were me, which of those two individuals would you want to keep a close eye on, and which of them would you trust to work alone?" She eyed him, perhaps seeking some kind of sincerity in his gaze. "Carry on as you are, Anna," he said. "But remember this. We have our parts to play in this team, and if Freya doesn't come back, then I'm going to need every one of you. Especially you and Jim."

"Right," she said, sounding more convinced than before, but still not entirely. "I get that. But can I ask something? A request, as it were?"

"Anything," he said. "Anything at all."

"Give me something. Give me something to work on."

"Like what?"

"I don't know. More responsibility. Give me someone else to manage."

"I hear you, but I need to be careful. We don't want to appear top-heavy or Granger and his cronies will soon find a way to over-load us."

She smiled a smile that wasn't a smile, more of a reluctant acceptance. Ben sensed the conversation coming to an end. If she were a burst pipe, then he had stemmed the flow with his finger but had yet to fix the leak.

"Give me time to think about that," he said, as an idea sprung to mind. "In the meantime, carry on as you are, Anna, and picture the team without you. Imagine Anderson working with somebody else. Imagine somebody else in your seat. But more importantly, ask yourself this. Who else could I trust to do the things I ask of you?"

"I don't know," she said, with a feeble shrug.

He grinned.

"Neither do I," he told her, as he walked back to his car and called out over his shoulder. "And what does that tell you?"

CHAPTER THIRTEEN

The houses on Alfred Avenue had the look of old council houses with their red-brick finish. They reminded Ben of a place where an old girlfriend of his used to live. A two-up-two-down, his father would have called it. As modest as the houses were, they were well-kept and, being so close to the road into Lincoln and the village high street, would be sought after.

"This one here," Gillespie said, shifting in his seat in preparation to get out. It was these small differences that Ben noticed. Freya would have sat calmly, composed and collected. Gillespie made such an effort to sit upright that the entire car rocked under his weight. He leaned forward to tuck his shirt tails in just as Ben was reversing into a spot and blocking the mirror in the process.

"Jim?"

"Aye?" he groaned, as he carelessly stuffed the excess material into his pants. Ben squeezed his eyes shut, regretting having witnessed such an atrocity.

"Can't see the mirror, mate."

"Eh?" Gillespie said, then realised what Ben had said. "Oh, sorry. My bad. I'm used to Cruz driving."

"Doesn't he use his mirrors?" Ben asked.

"Aye, he uses his mirrors, alright. He drives like he's on his driving test every bloody day. But he's only wee. He sits so far forward, a bloody rhino could be in the passenger seat and he'd still see the mirror." He mimicked Cruz's driving, adopting a ten-to-two posture as the Driving Standards Agency recommends, and Ben gave a light laugh, climbing out of the car quickly before Gillespie had a chance to enquire into the subject of Nillson's little chat, a topic he'd successfully avoided during the journey. A few cars along, Gold was reversing into another spot, and she gave a polite wave as Ben waited for Gillespie, and then together they walked up the footpath, where he gave three firm but discreet knocks.

"You, erm, you want me to leave this one to you?" Gillespie asked, fingering his collar.

"Aren't you up to it?"

"Aye, course. But you know. It's been a while. You and the boss usually take care of it."

There was little room for argument on the matter. Delivering bad news was something that Freya preferred to attend to herself. Even if Ben was left to do the talking, she liked to be present. If ever there was an opportunity for a member of the public to cause a fuss, it was these sensitive and regrettable moments.

"Why don't I do this one to give you a refresher?" Ben suggested, as the door opened and a young lady gazed out at them. "The next one's yours, though."

"Aye," Gillespie said.

"Yes?" the woman said, her eyes dancing from Ben to Gillespie and back again.

"Miss Fraser?" Ben said, and he flashed his warrant card, which usually removed the need for an explanation.

"That's me. What's wrong?"

Her accent suggested she was a local girl, and her faded jeans and creased T-shirt, along with the fact that she had opened the door at ten-thirty in the morning told Ben she was either on a day off, unemployed, or sick. He peered past her into the house, eyeing a messy kitchen, and a threadbare hallway carpet. She didn't look sick and there was no sign that she was getting ready for work.

"I wonder if we might come in," he said.

"Come in? What for?"

"It's probably better if we do this inside," he said, giving her a look that he hoped she would pay heed to. Slowly, she stepped to one side and opened the door fully. "Is there somewhere we can sit?"

"In there," she replied, pointing to one of two doors, the second being to the messy kitchen. But when Ben walked into the living room, a part of him wished she had suggested the kitchen. The only place to sit was a small two-seater setter which was unusable as a week's worth of laundry was spread out in various stages of being folded. As predicted, a few items of clothing were quite clearly a man's.

A long glass coffee table occupied most of the standing room, and even that was covered in a range of used crockery, tissues, and what appeared to be a nappy. He caught Gillespie's eye, and glanced down at it discreetly, receiving a confused expression in reply. "Sorry, it's a bit of a mess."

"It's quite alright," Ben said, moving around the coffee table to make room for Gillespie. "We're here regarding a Lee Constantine. We have this as his address."

"S'right," she said, a look of panic washing over her face, draining any remaining colour along with it. "What's he done? What's happened?"

"Well, before we go into specifics, can I ask what your relationship with him is?"

"Me? I'm his girlfriend. Why? You're scaring me."

"I think it might be best if you sit down, Miss Fraser."

"Oh God, no," she said, covering her mouth with her hands, showing a range of fingernails of various lengths and conditions.

Her eyes widened and she seemed to freeze. "He's not in trouble, is he?"

"Miss Fraser, there's no easy way to tell you this—"

"No," she screamed, dropping onto the pile of washing. "No, not Lee." She shook her head and began to hyperventilate. But such conversations were rarely best left to linger and Ben pressed on in an effort to limit the pain she was enduring.

"Can you tell me when you last saw Lee?" he asked, and he dropped to a crouch before her. "Miss Fraser, I know this is hard, and we'll help you where we can."

"Saturday," she said, between breaths, and Ben glanced up at Gillespie, gestured to the kitchen, and hoped he would take the hint to fetch some water. The big Scot nodded and slipped from the room. "It was Saturday evening. He went out."

"Do you know where, Vicky? Do you mind if I call you Vicky?"

She shook her head, and Ben handed the box of tissues from the coffee table. She took a handful and dabbed her nose.

"A party, I think."

"And has he been home since then?"

"Eh?" she said, as if his questions were little more than an irritation. "No. No, he hasn't."

"Well, the last thing I want to do is prolong this for you," Ben said, as Gillespie handed him a glass of water, which he held out for Fraser to take. "But a man's body was discovered not far from here, yesterday evening."

"Where?" she asked, her voice light like a child's. "Where was he?"

"The body was found in the quarry on Sleaford Road."

"In the quarry?"

"But before we jump to conclusions, we really need to make a formal identification," Ben said, and slowly, she let her hands slide from her face.

"See him, you mean?"

"Unless there's anybody else who you can suggest. Parents or a friend, maybe?"

She gazed into space, and Ben gave her mind some room to stretch its legs for a moment.

"You don't have to make a decision now," he told her. "I have a family liaison officer outside, ready to come and sit with you. She's been trained to help people in your situation, and she's very experienced. Anything you need, you ask her, alright? And when you feel ready to see him, then she'll make the arrangements. And don't worry. She'll be with you every step of the way."

"Can she breastfeed?" Fraser said, and Gillespie's wide-eyed expression mirrored what Ben was thinking.

"Sorry?"

"Can she breastfeed?" Fraser asked again, and she peered down at Ben. "I can't seem to."

"Vicky, is there a child in the house?"

She nodded and gestured at the room above them.

"He's sleeping," she said, and Ben gave some thought on how to handle the situation.

"Like I said, she'll help you in any way she can. You just let her know when you're ready."

"How?" she asked, as Ben rose to his feet. "How did it happen?"

"We don't know for sure, right now. In fact, our next port of call is the pathologist," he told her. "But don't worry. We'll find out and we'll keep you informed via DC Gold."

"The family liaison officer?"

"That's right," Ben said. It was at times like this that he wished he could sit beside her and put his arm around her. But rules were rules. Instead, he watched as she processed the information in a state of numb denial. He gave Gillespie the nod for him to fetch Jackie from the car, then dropped to a crouch before her again.

"Nothing can prepare you for this, Vicky. DC Gold will take

care of you, and we'll keep you abreast of our investigation every step of the way. You're not alone, okay?"

"Investigation?" she said. "What do you mean?"

"Well, we need to look into his death," Ben said, pleased to have intrigued her enough to take his bait.

"You mean it wasn't an accident?"

"I didn't say that," Ben said, offering a reassuring smile. "However, if there's something you think might help us, then now is the time to say."

She turned away, wiped her nose, and then cleared her throat.

"Vicky?" Ben said. "Vicky, why didn't you report him as missing?"

She said nothing at first until they heard Gold's heels on the concrete footpath outside.

"There is something you should know," she said, quietly, and she held his gaze for an awful moment. "But if I tell you, you can't let anyone know it was me."

"Go on," Ben said.

"No," she said, and she grabbed onto his wrists. "I need you to promise it'll go no further than these four walls."

He turned her hands in his own and held them tight, as he heard Gillespie and Gold at the front door in the hallway.

"If there's something you need to tell me, Vicky. If he was in trouble, somehow..." he hissed. "Give me something to work with. Anything at all."

CHAPTER FOURTEEN

"Lee Constantine was troubled," Ben said, and he heard the hushed whispers from the incident room coming over the call. Gillespie made himself comfortable in the passenger seat, and Ben waited for the car to settle. "Vicky Fraser nearly told me something."

"What do you mean nearly?" Nillson said.

"She was about to tell me something. I'm sure of it. But Jim and Jackie came in."

"Aye, right. Blame me, why don't you?"

"But that goes no further," Ben said. "Not in any reports. Nothing. Not yet anyway."

"What do you mean?" Chapman said. "We're not allowed to use a piece of information we don't even know?"

"We don't necessarily need to know what it was, although it would be useful, just as we don't need to use it," Ben said.

"Bloody hell. You're talking in riddles, Ben," Nillson said. "She hasn't told us something we don't need to know, and even if we did know what it was, we can't use it anyway. Am I missing something here?"

"She's scared of something or somebody," Ben said. "We find

out what she's scared of and we're on our way."

"How the bloody hell are we supposed to do that?" Gillespie asked. "The girl's a mess."

"Chapman, draft Jackie an email, will you?"

"I can call her if you like?"

"No," Ben said, a little too abruptly, as a mother walked past the car pushing a pram. She eyed them with obvious suspicion, then turned her head when Ben stared at her. "No, don't call her. Send an email. Vicky will hear a phone call and know what you're talking about. We want her to open up to Jackie, not close up for good. What we need to do is understand where she's been recently, who she's been with. Let's start building a picture, shall we? Gold can help where she can."

"Understood," Chapman replied.

"Nillson, Anderson. Get yourself to Constantine's workplace. Where is it, anyway?"

"In Lincoln," Nillson replied. "Looks like some kind of electrical appliance shop. He was a delivery driver."

The woman with the pram moved to one side to allow a young man to pass. He wore work boots, dirty jeans, and he walked with purpose. But when he slowed and turned into Vicky Fraser's front garden, Gillespie gave Ben a tap on his leg. He nodded that he'd seen the man, but continued with the call.

"See what you can find out. See what his demeanour was like. If Vicky Fraser is scared of something or somebody, then maybe he was too. See if that correlates with his colleagues' description."

"Will do," she replied. "Are we meeting this afternoon?"

"With any luck," Ben said. "Jim and I are heading to the pathologist now. Cruz, how's that door-to-door going?"

"I was just about to leave," he replied. "I've spoken to Sergeant MacAllister. He's given me one of his support officers."

The young man knocked on Vicky's door, then waited on the doorstep expectantly.

"Better than nothing, I suppose. While you're out there, have a quick look at that trail. I want to know where he entered the field. It's only a handful of properties, so you should be back by half past two. Let's do a debrief at three and make a plan for tomorrow. Chapman, can you get hold of Katy Southwell? Let's see what else she's come up with."

"Already done," she replied, and Ben imagined her in her knitted cardigan, her face as neutral as the paint on the walls. "The casts of the footprints are a size ten Reebok, most likely belonging to a male or a large female."

Jackie opened the door, and after a brief interaction, the man nodded, walked backwards a few steps, then walked back the way he had come. A well-wisher, maybe?

"Christ," Gillespie said. "Wouldn't want to meet her in a dark alley. Never date a lass with bigger feet than you or who is taller than you. That's my rule."

"What makes you think she'd want to meet *you* in a dark alley?" Nillson added. "Or a well-lit one, for that matter."

"Alright, alright," Ben said, calming them down before the argument escalated. "Let's just do what we need to do, and if it turns out our Reebok owner resembles a female shotput champion, then we know who can question her, don't we?"

"She also had some news about the area surrounding the pond," Chapman explained. "She found no evidence that anybody had walked on the area, but there were traces of blood on the rocks beneath the rock face, if that makes any sense to you?"

"She's suggesting that Constantine fell from the top and landed on the rocks below. Doctor Saint was under the impression he died from a broken neck, which fits. I suppose he just rolled into the water."

"Bloody awful business," Gillespie said. "Any other time of the year and he'd have walked away with a headache. But we've not had rain for weeks. The pond was a good two feet lower than normal."

"Yeah, I saw the water marks on the rocks," Ben agreed.

"Makes you wonder if he knew the pond was there and dove in to get away from his pursuer."

"The shotput champion, you mean?"

"Whoever it was," Ben said, rolling his eyes. "Anything else, Chapman?"

"Not yet. She's testing the blood to make sure it's his and she's seeing what she can find on the wallet to link it to him."

"I think we've made the link already," Ben told her. "But let's leave her to it. She knows what she's doing. Right, I'll see you all at three."

He ended the call and started the engine, dragging his seatbelt across his chest and fitting it into the receiver. Then he paused.

"Are we off to see the mad Welshwoman?" Gillespie asked, wondering why Ben had stalled.

"Jim, have you considered what would happen if Freya didn't come back?"

"What do you mean?"

"Exactly what I said. What if she doesn't come back?"

"Ben, we both know she's coming back. It's just..."

"Just what?" Ben asked.

"It's just a matter of time," he said. "I mean, this is Freya Bloom we're talking about. You know her better than any of us. Yes, she's experienced life-changing injuries, but they're superficial."

"Yeah, they're superficial," Ben agreed. "But do you honestly know how much effort she puts into her appearance?"

"Well, aye—"

"No, you don't. Honestly, it's a wonder she has time to actually go to work most of the time, what with all her routines, her creams, and... God knows what else. But I honestly think there's a chance she won't even want to leave the house when she's allowed out of the hospital, let alone come back to work."

"Ah, the cursed vanity, you mean?"

"Something like that."

"Ben, did you ever hear of those acid attacks down south?"

"Of course. They're bloody vicious."

"Aye, they are. But have you seen what the doctors have done with some of the victims? Bloody miracle workers, I tell you. Honestly, there's this one girl who had her entire face doused in the stuff and aye, she may not look as she did, but what the doctors or the surgeons, whoever it was, what they did to her was nothing short of a miracle. I swear, she can walk down the road with her head held high that girl."

"I'm sure she can—"

"What were the boss' injuries, again? Her ear, wasn't it?"

"Her ear took the brunt of the fire, but the left side of her face will be badly scarred. Not to the extent of her ear, but still pretty bad. The doctor said she was lucky the fire was inside the van and that she fell to the ground. That twelve or eighteen inches between the ground and the van made all the difference, apparently."

"Ben, if they can rebuild a lass's entire face from an acid attack, I'm sure they can do something with Freya with a few minor burns."

"They're hardly minor, Jim—"

"Aye, you know what I mean. She hasn't lost her entire face, has she?"

"It's bad enough that they're talking about sending her to Nottingham Hospital for treatment."

"Nottingham?"

"It's a specialist burns unit. Lincoln has done a good job of saving her life, and her lungs and whatnot. But they're not really equipped to deal with severe burns."

"Bit of trek to visit her after work, eh?" Gillespie said.

"Bit of trek, indeed," Ben replied thoughtfully. "But what I was saying was—"

"That should she not come back to work, there will be some changes," Gillespie cut in, finishing the sentence for him. He cleared his throat and shifted in his seat again, rocking the car from side to side. "I might be a lowly sergeant, Ben, but I'm not a complete dummy."

"Clearly," Ben said.

"And neither is Anna, eh?"

Ben smiled away at his embarrassment.

"And that's what she wanted to talk to you about, eh?" Gillespie said. "If Freya doesn't come back, then she thinks you'll be moved up, leaving a gaping hole in the team."

"She just wants to be considered, Jim," Ben said. "Nothing more. She wasn't bad-mouthing you."

"Oh, I know. Even Anna wouldn't stoop that low."

Ben stared at the big Glaswegian, who despite his flaws, had somehow become the closest thing he had to a best friend.

"Aren't you going to try to convince me that you're the best man for the job?"

"Me?" Gillespie replied with a laugh. "Christ, Ben. Don't you know me better than that?"

"I know you pretty well, but–"

"You *know* I'm not the best man for the job," he said. "Nillson has the edge on me, and you know it. She's sharper, she dresses better–"

"You have more experience."

"And she's hungry for it," Gillespie finished.

"Don't tell me your appetite for promotion has waned, Jim," Ben said.

"It'll come when the time's right," Gillespie replied. "Besides, if you move up and Anna moves up, you're going to need someone like me to keep the rabble under control, Benny boy." He winked at Ben and gave the type of smile that belied his confidence and offered an insight into Gillespie's true thoughts.

"Don't put yourself down," Ben said. "The truth is that I'd be proud to have either one of you under me as DI."

"But?" Gillespie said, letting his unrivalled intuition shine for a moment, purposefully or not.

"But the truth is," Ben replied heavily. "I'm not ready to take Freya's place. I've been DI for a matter of months. They won't promote me just because there's a gap to fill. Which means that we'll have somebody new." He put the car into drive and took a breath. "And in my experience, when somebody new comes in, lives change."

CHAPTER FIFTEEN

"Thank you for your time," Cruz said to the old man who seemed far more interested in his pickup engine than anything Cruz had asked him. "Miserable old scrote," he muttered as he and PSCO Jewson walked away. "Barely even looked up, did he?"

"Poor old bloke's busy," Jewson replied. Her voice was light and sharp and reminded Cruz of a Monty Python sketch he had seen. Except that the Pythons had been fully-grown men wearing dresses and Jewson was a young girl who might have been more suited to a passive role. She was one of the few people on the force who was shorter than Cruz, and even he had experienced his fair share of struggles with unruly ne'er-do-wells. "Besides, how can you expect him to have heard anything late on Saturday night when he could barely hear you from three feet away?"

"Ah, I suppose," Cruz replied. "This is the last one, isn't it?" He gestured up at the next house, which although it was a good few hundred metres away, was far closer than any of the previous six houses had been. "Shall we walk? Seems silly to get in the car for such a short distance." She shrugged, adjusted her hat, and fell into step beside him. "I'm not sure I'd enjoy living out here."

"What do you mean?" she asked.

"You know? With no real neighbours."

"It's very private," she countered.

"Yeah, I know, but...there's a certain reassurance you get from having someone next door, isn't there? I mean, even if you don't speak to them most of the year, they're still there, aren't they? You can still call on them if you need to."

"And do you need to?" she asked.

"Well, no. But I might, mightn't I? I mean, if somebody broke in one night."

"You're a copper. Why on earth would you need to call on help from your neighbours?"

"Well, I mean, I could handle them. Course, I could. But you know? Witnesses and whatnot..." He felt his voice trail off and his collar seemed far tighter than it had been. He dug his finger into his neck and released his top button, loosening his tie.

"I'm teasing," she told him, and he looked across to find her highly amused. "You can't fool me, you know?"

"Eh?"

"I mean if somebody broke into my house, I'd scream the bloody street down, copper or no copper, let me tell you."

"Yeah, well. It's to be expected, isn't it?"

Her smile faded.

"What's that supposed to mean?"

"Well, only that you're..." He gestured wildly with his hands, realising they might have well been holding a spade for him to dig himself a hole.

"I'm what?" she said. "A girl? Is that what you were going to say?"

"No, course not—"

"You were," she said. "You just made a sexist remark."

"Oh, leave off."

"My God. They told me you were alright. They said you were nice and friendly and wouldn't hurt a fly."

"I am. Honest, I am. I didn't mean that. I'm not sexist. Ask anyone."

"Well, you do a marvellous impression of one," she said. "You just said that it was to be expected that, should my house be broken into, I'd scream the bloody street down. How am I supposed to take that, if not as a sexist remark?"

"I was talking about your size, that's all."

"My what? My size?"

"Yeah, honest. I wasn't being sexist. I'd never–"

"My *size*?" she said, and Cruz recognised the tone that she shared with both his mother and Hermione, his ex-girlfriend.

"Well, you're only little, aren't you?"

"That's bloody rich, coming from an Oompa Loompa. What are you, five-foot-five? I'm surprised you've even got a driving licence. There's barely a hair on your chin. Honestly, my nephew could grow more of a beard than you, and he's only ten."

"I'm five-foot-five and a half, if you must know. I'm nearly thirty years old, and as it happens, I shave every day. Some of us have standards to maintain."

"Standards? Yeah, right. Your shirt's too small and your trousers look like they belong to your older brother. What is this standard exactly?"

"I don't have an older brother."

"No, of course not," she told him. "No, you're a prime example of an only child."

"What?"

"I'll bet you've never had to fight for anything in your life. In fact, I'll go as far as to say that mummy and daddy gave you every-thing you wanted."

"Where is this coming from?" he said, unable to comprehend how, in a matter of moments, she had turned on him like a rabid dog.

"No, actually, your parents are divorced."

"What are you talking about?"

"No older siblings to look up to, no father figure." She looked him up and down with clear repugnance. "I suppose you didn't stand a chance, did you? No benchmark to aim for, except good old British mediocracy."

"You have lost the plot, Jewson," he said, raising his voice and surprising himself in the process. He checked behind him to make sure nobody was in earshot. "I suggest you get a grip."

"And I suggest you learn to think before you speak, DC Cruz. One word from me into MacAllister's ear, and you'll be up in front of the deputy chief constable."

"What for?"

"Another word in a particular reporter's ear and you'll be in the papers. You might even make the front page."

"Hold on, hold on," he said, suddenly realising how serious this little mishap could turn out. "What do you want me to do?"

"Sorry?"

"To make it better. What do you want me to do? Honestly, I didn't mean to cause offence, but if I have, then I'll make it better. You just tell me what I need to do."

She raised her chin thoughtfully and looked down at him along the length of her button nose.

"I'll think about it," she said.

"You'll think about it?"

"That's right," she replied, as she moved past him and headed towards the final house.

"And in the meantime?" he said. "What am I supposed to do?"

"Behave yourself," she called back over her shoulder.

He stared after her for a moment then ran a few steps to catch up, which only coaxed her into walking faster.

"I didn't mean it," he said. "I can put a good word in for you if you like. You know? To MacAllister. He'll listen to me. He's alright, he is."

The last house on their list was a small farmhouse. Perhaps a few decades ago it might have been the beating heart of sprawling, active farmland. But one look at the surroundings suggested that, like many others, the land had been sold off to the most prosperous of farmers, save for half a dozen acres which was surrounded by a tall hedge, unkempt on the inside but neatly shaved on the other.

"I said I'd think about it," she said, as she made her way towards the front door, where she stopped and waited, her hands folded neatly before her. The front door was in need of a good sanding down and a lick of paint. When Cruz banged on it, three times, just as Ben often did, he thought it might shed some of the flaky, green paint, like Gillespie when he scratched his head. He prepared his warrant card and waited in silence, not daring to provoke another earful from the pitbull he'd been assigned. No wonder MacAllister had been keen to offload her, he thought. He'd heard about officers like her from Gillespie but had always dismissed the notion that career-enders even existed in this day and age.

He grimaced at the idea of Gillespie being right and that he'd fallen foul of the very type of person he'd been warned of.

He knocked again, but still nobody answered.

"Do you want to check around the back?" he asked Jewson.

"Not really," she said, with an exaggerated smile. "I'm quite happy here. Why don't you pop round the back and I'll make sure nobody comes out the front?"

She even offered a little wink to punctuate her position, and Cruz, shaking his head, made his way to the side of the old house.

Like many old farmhouses, it had been rendered and painted white. But this particular example was in dire need of some love and attention. Huge sections of render had fallen off, exposing the brickwork beneath.

There was no real path to follow that would lead him to the rear, only a muddy line between patches of unkempt grass. But it was when he reached the rear of the house that his opinion of the owners shifted almost entirely.

He inhaled long and hard, following a particular sweet scent to a row of greenhouses.

"Jewson?" he called out, as he slid one of the doors open. "Jewson?"

Despite her flagrant disregard for authority and penchant for blackmail, she appeared at the side of the house looking less than cheerful to be summoned and in no particular hurry.

"What?" she said, leaning against the house.

"Call it in," he replied, which seemed to drag her from her confidence enough to at least alter her expression. "We're going to need support." He looked back into the greenhouse. "And we're going to need a lot of it."

CHAPTER SIXTEEN

Compared to the newer shops along the high street, Dick's Appliances was archaic. The shopfront windows were wood framed and single pane, the sign above the top could have come straight from the set of a period drama, and when Nillson opened the door, she half expected to see an old-fashioned bell to sing out, announcing their arrival to a shopkeeper in a brown coat who might peer from the back room. But when a man looked up from the counter at her arrival, all thoughts of Albert Arkwright were banished from her mind. He was broad in the shoulders, narrow in the waist, and his facial hair was so well-groomed that it appeared to be painted on. He removed his glasses and waited for either Anna or Anderson to speak.

"Barry Coleman?" Nillson said, reluctant to display her warrant card just yet.

"Who's asking?" he replied, sliding his glasses back onto his nose and returning his attention to his open laptop.

Nillson felt rather than saw Anderson's amused grin, and she slowly stepped up to the counter, letting the knocks of her boot heels illuminate the carefree pace.

She opened her warrant card, held it up with one hand, and pushed the laptop closed with the other.

"Detective Sergeant Nillson," she said, then gestured at Anderson. "This is DC Anderson."

He made no attempt to hide his irritation, and moved his glasses once more, perhaps to get a better look at them.

"Might have known," he grumbled and attempted to reopen his laptop.

"Are you Barry Coleman?" Nillson asked, forcing the computer closed. "Please don't make me ask again."

Keeping her hand on the laptop, she waited for him to raise his head and look her in the eye.

"And what if I am?"

"I wonder if we might have a word," she said.

"Well, the world is a wondrous place."

"About Lee Constantine," Nillson said, ensuring that humour would have no part in the conversation.

He sighed heavily and leaned on the counter, folding his arms defensively.

"What's he done? Whatever it is, I had no part in it. He comes in here to load up and comes back to unload. What he does out there is his own business."

"Surely you have some responsibility for him? You're his boss, aren't you?"

"Boss, yes. Mother, no." He shook his head as if to accentuate his point. "If he's jumped a red light, or been involved in road rage, it's not my doing." He stared back at them both as if daring one of them to make an accusation. "So? What's he done then?"

"That's a strange question," Nillson said. "Tell me, Mr Coleman. When was the last time you saw him?"

As far as high street shops go, Dick's Appliances was small, verging on tiny, yet there had to have been at least fifty machines of various purposes on display – used dishwashers, washing machines, tumble dryers, upright fridge freezers, chest freezers, countertop fridges, and even smaller appliances such as kettles, toasters, and an air fryer.

"Last Tuesday," he said, and his demeanour shifted as if he sensed that they were not there to question him about a crime that Constantine had committed. "Called in on Wednesday morning. Said he wasn't feeling up to it."

"Up to working?"

"S'pose so," Coleman said.

"And you haven't seen or heard from him since?"

"What do you want, a signed bleeding confession?"

"To what?"

"To not seeing him," he said. "Look, are you going to tell me what this is about?"

"Eventually," Nillson said, and she watched as Anderson took a slow mooch around the shop. "I have a few questions I'd like to ask before then."

"Right, well if you're not going to tell me what he's done, lady, I'm afraid my time is needed elsewhere—"

"He died, Mr. Coleman. That's what he did."

Coleman paused, then laughed as if she might suddenly announce that it had been a joke. But Nillson's neutral expression was well-practised, and she performed it to a tee.

"You're kidding, right?" he said, to which she shook her head slowly. "Lee Constantine? Slim fellow, 'bout so high?" He held his hand up at approximately six feet.

"We've had his DNA checked. It's him," Nillson said, which seemed to come as a blow to Coleman, who took a step back and dropped onto a nearby stool.

"Well, I'll be."

"So?" Nillson said.

"So what?"

"So, have you seen or heard from him since he called in on Wednesday?"

"No. I told you," he said, his tone rising in defence.

"If you say you haven't seen or heard from him, Mr Coleman, then that's good enough for me." She offered a broad smile to remind him she would hold him to that statement if necessary. "But he did work on Monday and Tuesday?"

Coleman shrugged. "Of course. Yeah, he was in just like normal. He came in, took his job sheets, loaded up, and went."

"And then he came back in the evening, I suppose? Once he'd completed his round?"

"Well..." Coleman gave the question some thought. "Actually no. Not on Monday. He went straight home when he was done."

"Is this usual?"

"It's not unusual," Coleman said. "If he finishes late or near his house, then he just goes straight home and brings the van back in the morning."

"And you're okay with that?"

"Yeah, why not? The van's probably safer at his house than out the back." He gestured behind him into the backroom and beyond.

"And that's where he would have loaded up, is it?"

"Well, he can't exactly park outside, can he? You ever seen the parking wardens around here?"

"Actually, no," Anderson said from the far side of the shop.

"Well, let me tell you something. You can go a month without seeing a single one. But park outside and they'll be on it in seconds. Bastards."

The addition of an insult added very little weight to the statement but told Nillson a great deal about Coleman's personality. He might have been a handsome man, but bitterness was ugly whoever the bearer.

"And did you notice any unusual behaviour from him?"

"On Monday or Tuesday, you mean?"

"Just recently," Nillson said. "Doesn't matter when."

He looked up at the ceiling in thought, puffed his cheeks, and then shrugged.

"Not really."

"Thank you," Nillson said, then gave the signal to Anderson that they were leaving. "One more thing," she said to Coleman, who was about to reopen his laptop.

"Yes?"

Nillson waited a moment for his irritation to settle and for his intrigue to grow.

"Can we see out back?"

"Eh?"

"The back," she said. "You know? Where the deliveries come in and out?"

"What do you want to see out there for?"

"Just curious, that's all."

"I'd have to lock the shop up," he said.

"No need," Anderson said. "I'll wait here. I'll make sure nobody steals anything."

Coleman looked between them both and then relented.

"I don't know what you expect to find."

"Well, I'll give you a clue," Nillson said. "It has four wheels and an engine."

"The van?"

"Presumably, it's out the back. Heaven forbid you should park it out the front."

"Well, yeah. It's out there, but–"

"I just thought I'd have a quick look inside if you don't mind. You never know."

"I'm sorry, but this conversation has gone from vague to downright bloody barmy," Coleman said. "Look, he was a good bloke. I didn't know him that well. I think he joined us around Christmas time, but what little I did know about him is that he keeps himself to himself. He's got a girlfriend and a newborn baby. I suppose it'll be them who suffer."

"It usually is," Nillson said.

"Yet all you've told me is that he died. You haven't said how."

"Ah," Nillson said, "we can't really go into details at the minute."

"Well, let me paint you a little picture," Coleman said. "If he say, had a heart attack, you wouldn't be here, and you certainly wouldn't want to look in my van." He leaned on the counter, his arms ramrod straight, and his eyes bore into Nillson. "So, tell me, missy. What exactly happened to Lee, and what is it you want from me?"

CHAPTER SEVENTEEN

For more than a year now, during visits to the pathology department at Lincoln Hospital, Freya, who had proved a worthy adversary to the formidable and renowned Welsh pathologist, Doctor Pippa Bell, had accompanied Ben. In fact, the two women were so contrasting that they often worked together against Ben, coming at him from two different angles. Freya, the educated snob, and Pip, the brutish, fiery Welsh dragon.

"God, I hate this place," Gillespie muttered as they neared the doors to pathology.

"The hospital?"

"No," he said and nodded along the corridor at the two doors ahead of them. "This place"

Like many of the wards and departments at the hospital, people gained access along a long, glass-lined corridor, overlooking patches of tall grass and little else. It had always amazed Ben that the original design had factored in such a colossal waste of land. Granted, the buildings were not all part of the original design, and there had been add-ons over the years, but the volume of the wasted real estate likely added up to a whole new ward.

"The place or the host?" Ben asked, and Gillespie gave him a knowing sideways look.

"I'm not a fan, Ben," he grumbled. "As good as she is at what she does, I'm yet to walk out of here with a resting heart rate."

Ben laughed as they came to the doors and he reached up to push the bell.

"You get used to it," Ben told him, to which Gillespie simply shook his head. "I'd rather not, if I'm honest. Anyway, we'll have some time after if you wanted to..." He gave a sideways nod.

"If I wanted to what, Jim?"

"You know? Go and see her. Freya."

Ben turned away and rang the bell again, wishing for once that Pippa would hurry up and answer the door.

"Not during work hours, mate."

"Be a nice surprise for her."

"I'm sure it would," Ben replied, aiming for politeness but fearing that his response was abrupt and dismissive.

A squat shape appeared in the frosted glass window, and the door opened to reveal Doctor Pippa Bell in all her glory. She wore a light blue smock over a black t-shirt. Her short sleeves revealed a melee of tattoos along both arms and, as usual, she wasted no time in claiming her dominance.

"Christ, give me strength," she muttered by way of a greeting.

"Good morning to you, too, Pip," Ben said, and with a wave of his hands, presented Gillespie. "You're already acquainted with Sergeant Gillespie, I believe."

"I am," she said, turning to the big Scot. "Where's the other one, then? The little one with the muck in his hair?"

"Cruz, you mean?" Gillespie said. "Ah, he's walking the streets."

"You fired him?"

"No, he's knocking on doors."

"Ah, gotcha. Well, nice day for it, isn't it?" she said, clearly aware that they were itching to get inside. But she lingered in the doorway a moment longer, turning her devilish stare to Ben. "What about you, then? Heard about your boss, I did. She alright, is she?"

Ben had been expecting some kind of comment and was surprised to hear a touch of sympathy in her tone.

"She'll be fine," he replied. "Her left ear took the worst of it. The side of her face will be scarred, but a plastic surgeon should be able to do something with it."

"What about up here?" Pip said, tapping her temple with a short, fat index finger. "Thing like that has to mess with you, if you know what I mean?"

"Pip, I know you mean well, but do you think we can get on with the job at hand? We've a busy day, and I'm sure you don't want us hanging around."

She eyed him curiously, pursing her lips in thought, and then stepped to one side.

"I expect you'll be seeing her while you're here, will you?" she asked, as Ben entered the little reception room and immediately made for the cupboards holding the PPE. He tossed Gillespie a gown and a mask.

"I expect I'll be leaving here and getting on with the investigation," he replied. "That is, assuming you have anything for us to go on."

Gillespie tore the plastic wrapper from the gown and gave her a warning look.

"Best not to press it," he said quietly to her. "He's a little sensitive right now."

"Well, it's to be expected, isn't it?" Pip replied as she made her way towards the two insulated doors that led into the mortuary. "Been pining after her like a lost puppy for more than a year now, he has. Fending for himself now. Leaderless—"

"Can we just drop the subject?" Ben said, raising his voice to a level that left little doubt as to his mood. "We've come here to do a job, not to visit hospital patients. If the roles were reversed and

it was me in here, then she'd say the same and you know it." He
snatched the gown closed and tied an old knot to keep it that way.
"And as for being lost and leaderless," he continued. "If you
remember, I managed perfectly well before Freya came to
Lincolnshire."

"Ah yes," Pip said, as she pushed open the heavy door,
releasing a blast of cold air into the room. "You mean those few
weeks you had to cope when DI Foster died? What was it, three
weeks before Freya came riding in on her white horse to save the
day?"

"I can manage," he told her.

"I hope so, for your sake," she replied, as she walked away and
called over her shoulder. "Come and find me when you're ready."

Gillespie snapped his mask into place, which by concealing his
expression, somehow accentuated his wide eyes so they appeared
animated.

"Don't encourage her, Jim," Ben said.

"Eh?"

"Just..." Ben said, then stopped himself from saying too much.
"Let's just get this over with, shall we?"

He barged into the mortuary and strode over to the stainless-
steel bench where Pip was standing. A thin, blue sheet covered
the large mound on the bench, and Pip watched them grow near
as a lion might wait in the foliage for a wayward frolicking foal.

"Now then," Ben said, hearing his voice crack with fatigue.
"What do we have?"

Usually, Pip demonstrated some decency and revealed only
those parts of the anatomy in question. But perhaps for the
purpose of shock, she whipped the sheet back to expose Lee
Constantine from his head to his toes. The standard forensic
pathology procedure dictated that the subject be opened up via
cuts. The first cuts were from beneath the ears to the sternum,
where a single cut then ran down to the navel. It was via this Y-
shaped cut that access to the internal organs was granted.

She rested the sheet on the empty table behind her and watched them both for some sort of reaction. Gillespie turned away and cleared his throat, while Ben's eyes never left Pip's.

"Doctor Saint suggested a broken neck," Ben said. "How does that sit with you?"

"Well, from my initial examinations, I can't see any other cause of death. The blow to the head is quite severe, but unlikely to have been the cause of death. The skull is fractured, but not so bad as to have caused any kind of haemorrhage."

"That's pretty much what he said," Ben replied glumly.

"Bad fall, was it?"

"Bad enough to break his neck," Ben replied. "Our working hypothesis is that he fell onto the rocks, hit his head, broke his neck, and then slumped into the water."

"Ah, yes. The water. Plenty of it too, there was."

"I thought bodies floated," Gillespie said. "Unless they're drowned, of course."

"Typically, if death occurs out of water, there's enough air left in the body for it to float. But give it long enough and water will find a way in. Muscles contract, air is released. You don't need a physics lesson, do you, Sergeant?"

"No," he said. "No, I was just thinking aloud."

"Oh," Pip said. "I thought you were going to come out with something intelligent."

"Me?" Gillespie said. "No. Not today."

The sight before them was grotesque enough to distract even Gillespie from the joke, and Ben was in no mood for humour.

"I expect you'll want to know when it happened," she said. "That's what you normally ask, isn't it?"

"The time of death is quite crucial to developing a case for prosecution, Pip. We don't ask out of curiosity."

"No. No, I don't suppose you do," she replied. "What did Doctor Saint tell you?"

"You know what he told us. You received the report just as we did."

"True," she said. "Sometime between Saturday night and Sunday morning. That's right, isn't it?"

"If you say so," Ben said, not wishing to enter into her little mind games. "I presume given that he made that estimation on the side of the pond the body was pulled from, and you have the luxury of a mortuary to work in, that you'll be able to narrow that down somewhat?"

"Somewhat," she replied quietly. "But not much."

"What's not much?" Gillespie asked.

"Between ten p.m. on Sunday night and three a.m. on Sunday morning. Give or take, anyway."

"How do you know?"

"I don't," Pip said. "It's an educated guess." She grinned up at them, and Ben took a breath to stop himself from asking to hurry up. Visits from police officers and distraught family members were the only real contact with the outside world, so she was bound to make them count. "Psychodidae."

"What?" Ben said.

"Psychodidae," she repeated. "Or drain flies. Similar to fruit flies, really."

"What about them?"

"Nocturnal, they are."

"Nocturnal flies?"

"Breed around stagnant water, they do. Bats love them." She made a pucking sound with her lips as if to suggest the little flies were delicious.

"You're going to have to be more specific, Pip," Ben said. "I'm afraid my imagination is somewhat lacking."

"Larvae. It's that time of year, I'm afraid." She stared down at Lee Constantine. "And then he comes along, hits his head, breaks his neck and floats around, his mouth wide open."

"You found larvae of a fly in his mouth?"

"Not much. But unless he had dinner in a sewer, then I can't see any other way for them to get there."

"Surely he could have died earlier," Gillespie said. "The larvae could have just floated into his mouth hours later."

"Oh, these larvae didn't float into his mouth," Pip replied. "I found it in his teeth. The fly laid it there."

CHAPTER EIGHTEEN

The touch felt nice against her skin. Unlike her face, her hands had escaped the flames, and for that, she was grateful. She could still raise a bottle to her lips, even if she had to drink through a straw. But even that minute moment of normality was a godsend compared to two weeks spent connected to the drip.

She squeezed his hand, wondering how many more days she would have to wear the bandage over her eyes, and when she could see herself in the mirror.

Ben had played her injuries down like she was a child with a broken leg. But she knew. She felt it. She felt the intensity of the heat as if the flame still burned above her. She felt the tautness of the skin on the left side of her face, and her ear...well, that just felt wrong.

"It's early," she said. "I might not be able to see, but I do know the difference between night and day." She smiled, one-sided, then winced as a blister opened up. "It's all in the noise, you see," she continued. "This place is dead at night. But during the day, it's like Piccadilly Circus."

"I'm surprised you remember what Piccadilly Circus is like," he replied, and she snatched her hand away.

"Ben?"

"Wrong," the voice said, and she fumbled for the emergency cord. "I wouldn't bother with that, sweetheart."

Sweetheart?

"Greg?"

"Hello, Freya."

She pulled the sheet up to her chin and went to raise the lip of the bandage, but he stopped her with a strong hand and made a shushing sound, just like he used to do when Billy was crying.

"It's okay," he said. "I'm here. Everything's going to be okay."

"Everything is not okay," she told him. "What the bloody hell are you doing here?"

"I came to see my wife," he said.

Again, she tried to raise the bandage from her right eye to peer at him, but he held her wrists.

"I don't need to call the nurse, do I?" he hissed. "She's nice, you know? Especially when I told her who I was. I'm sure if I explained you were trying to pull your bandages off, she'd give you something. A sedative, maybe?"

"Get off me," she said and snatched her hands away, and she heard him settle into the chair Ben normally sits in. "How on earth did you find me?"

"I thought you'd be pleased," he said, and it had been so long since she had spoken to him that she could no longer gauge his sincerity. "I thought you were pleased. I mean, the way you held my hand just then."

"Get out, Greg. You have no right to—"

"I have every right," he said. "You're my wife. Besides, you're not exactly inundated with visitors, are you?"

"I have visitors," she said. "It's just that they usually come at a reasonable hour, and they usually give me warning."

"Oh, yeah. That's right. The farm boy. I met him."

"You what?"

"I met him," he said. "And to be honest, Freya, I was quite surprised. Not your usual type."

"What did you say to him?"

"But then I thought, ah, she's probably just having a good time. A bit of rough. One of Freya's playthings."

"You bastard," she hissed.

"I bet you opened his eyes, didn't you? Farm boy like him, probably never been with someone like you."

"Get out."

"Does he tie you up, Freya?" he whispered. "With those big strong farm hands?"

"I said, get out."

"Or are you saving that? Or maybe you left kinky Freya behind when you walked out on Billy and me." The mention of that name took her breath away. "What's wrong? Oh, you're wondering about Billy, are you? You're wondering where he is."

She paused for a moment. If she was to play his game, then it would to her timeline.

"You weren't there when I needed you, Greg," she said quietly. "When I needed you the most, you weren't there. You were shagging that tart from across the street."

"Here we go. The same old Freya," he said. "It's all about you, isn't it? It's all about Freya. When you needed me the most? What about if I needed you? Where were you, eh? Lying in bed."

"With PT-bloody-SD, Greg."

"Oh, come off it. You were skiving. You were after a claim. Hoping the police force would give you a payout. You didn't fool me then and you don't fool me now."

"Can you just leave?" she said, clutching her sheets to her throat. "I've had a serious accident, and I need rest."

"I can take you home, if you like."

"What?"

"Oh, not home to London. No, I could take you to your little cottage. Round-the-clock care, Freya. What do you think about that?" She hesitated. So many thoughts swirled against the blackness in front of her eyes. "I've been quite comfortable there, if I'm honest. I mean, don't get me wrong, it's not a patch on our house, is it? But it's got that country vibe you were always after. The beams are a nice touch, too.

"You've been to my house?"

"Of course, I have. I mean, I was going to stay in a hotel, but then I thought, why should I when I've got a house?"

"You don't have a house. That's my house. I've worked for that."

"Ben was a bit put out," he said, and she could almost hear the smile on his lips. He waited for her reaction, and she pictured him.

"Ben?"

"Your bit of rough, Freya. The farm boy," he said. "I think he's been staying there, you know? I hope you hide your secret toys. You never know who might be prying."

"Greg, I'm going to ask you one more time. Can you please just leave? I can't deal with this right now."

"I know," he said with sympathy in his tone. "You're going through a lot, right now. The doctor said he wanted to transfer you to Nottingham—"

"Greg, I mean it."

"But don't worry. I've made some arrangements. Pulled some strings, as it were," he said. "I'm taking you private. There's a place out in Kent that specialises in severe burns."

"Greg, we're over," she said. "I want you out of my house, and out of my life."

"Of course, it'll be harder for any of your new friends to visit you, but they can't give you the sort of care that I can, can they?"

"I have all the care I need," she said, feeling her blood pressure begin to rise, which had an effect on the machine she was hooked up to. The beeps that became the metronome of her life, increased in tempo. She licked her lips and took a deep breath trying to bring the tempo down again.

"The doctor said he'll release you later this week," he continued. "You should see this place, Freya. They have in-house plastic surgeons. And therapists. You'll need therapy, of course."

"Greg—"

"They even have a team of people that specialise in cosmetics. You know, tattoos and make-up and whatnot, to make you feel normal again."

"I can't do this—"

"Billy will be pleased to see you, of course. He's with Mum at the minute. Didn't want to take him out of school."

"You've overstepped the mark, Greg."

"And then we can bring you home, where you belong," he said. "I mean, you don't belong here, do you? What do you know about the countryside, anyway? You're a city girl, through and through. Although, I'll have money on it you've kit yourself out in a nice Barbour jacket and those tall boots."

"Greg, there's something you should know," she said, which seemed to stop him in his tracks. "It's about Ben."

"Farm boy, you mean?"

"He proposed," she said. "He wants to marry me."

Greg was silent for a moment, and she pictured him straightening his collar as he always did when he'd been caught off guard.

"I don't think that's going to happen," he said eventually. "Especially when I explained that we were still married."

"What?"

"Well, how was I to know?" he said. "I come to see my wife and bump into one of her colleagues. How was I to know he was your bit of rough?"

"You told him we were married?"

"You never signed the papers, Freya," Greg said. "And as far as I can see, there's only one reason why you wouldn't sign them."

"Greg, no—"

"You still love me. After all this time, you still want me."

"You're insane if you think that's remotely true," she hissed at him, to the ever-increasing tempo of the machine. "I didn't sign because I didn't agree with the terms."

"The terms? What did you want me to do, give you everything? Did you expect me to give you half my money so you could sleep with some farm boy from the sticks?"

"You were shagging our neighbour, Greg. At least I had the decency to wait until we were separated."

The door burst open, allowing the hustle and bustle from the corridor into the room, which was a welcome break from the incessant beeping.

"Are you okay, Miss Bloom?" a nurse asked, and Freya recognised the voice. She was Asian of some description. Sri Lankan, maybe. She had kind eyes. One day, when the bandages were removed, she might find out.

But before Freya could respond, Greg interfered.

"Actually, my wife is suffering," he said to the nurse. "She's too stubborn to admit it, but I'm afraid she's been pulling on her bandages and crying. I think she needs something for the pain. Maybe something to help her sleep?"

There was a pause, during which presumably the nurse was checking her watch, and then she heard the clatter of the clipboard at the foot of the bed.

"I can help you there. She's due some painkillers," she said, which at any other time would have been reassuring. The nurse came to Freya's side and fiddled with the canula in her hand.

Then Freya felt it. The cool sensation of foreign liquid entering her bloodstream.

"Bye, baby," Greg whispered, much closer than he had been before. He kissed her right cheek and squeezed her hand. "You sleep tight now."

CHAPTER NINETEEN

"The fly laid larvae in his mouth?"

"I'd have to consult a specialist to be sure, but yes. I'm as sure as I can be."

"But surely that doesn't rule out him dying earlier than ten p.m.?" Gillespie said. "He could have been floating around for hours. It could have been the middle of the day for all we know. The fly could have...done his business in his mouth hours later."

"Saturday, yeah?" Pip said to him, then turned to Ben. "Ben, do you remember Saturday?"

"I do," he replied, wondering where she was going with the line of questioning.

"Recall the weather, do you?"

Ben shook his head. "It was hot."

"Hottest day of the year," she added, then glanced down at the corpse. "See a sunburn, do you?"

"Ah," Gillespie said. "Dead bodies don't get sunburned. Everyone knows that."

"You're right," Pip said, smiling up at Gillespie. "Kind of, anyway."

"Eh?"

"You see, sunburn is a natural defence mechanism against the sun's UV rays. It's essentially a chemical reaction, resulting in what we perceive as sunburn. Skin cells produce a pigment called melanin. But the skin must be living." Even with his mask on, Gillespie appeared confused. "Or recently dead," she added.

"*Recently* dead?" Ben said.

"Enough melanin is retained in the flesh for the reaction to take place even shortly after death. Not long, but enough."

"How on earth does that happen?" Ben asked.

"It's a chemical reaction. It neither knows nor cares if the heart's beating." She nodded, as if the explanation had done nothing but solidify her professional opinion.

"So, had he entered the water during the day–"

"Not entered the water," she said. "He was naked. Had his naked flesh been exposed to the sun during the day, we would see some signs of the chemical reaction, even after death."

"Okay," Ben said. "I'm not wholly convinced, but I trust you."

"Oh, you will be convinced by the time I'm done," she replied cryptically.

"I'm also curious about the lacerations on his legs," Ben said, and Pip looked down at the two great slabs of white flesh.

"Have a theory, do you?"

"I do, but I'd like your opinion," he replied.

"My opinion is that these were made prior to death, but not long. Not much more than an hour and the healing process would have begun. Apart from that, as far as I can see, they aren't man-made. That what you wanted to know, is it?"

"Kind of," he said, and she offered a warm smile in contrast to her earlier behaviour. But not being one to linger on emotions, she moved on hastily.

"I will say this," she continued. "The cuts on his legs are shallower than those on his arms and chest, and his genitals."

"Nice observation," Ben said.

"Same goes for his feet. Red raw, they are."

Ben and Gillespie took a few steps to the end of the bench, where Pip was holding up one of the specimens.

"Must have hurt like buggery," she mused aloud. "Made by rocks and stones, mostly. No sign of human interference."

"Is there any way we can work out where he ran from the debris in the wounds?" Ben asked.

"Already done," she said. "Well, I've sent the samples to the lab, anyway. Expect they'll be in touch when they've worked it out." She pulled the sheet from the bench behind her and like a maid laying a table, she whipped the sheet up and let it fill with air, then let it settle gently on Constantine's body. A few tugs of the corners to get it into place and she seemed content. But instead of walking away to her desk to show them some kind of report, she leaned on the bench and stared at Ben. "So? What's this working hypothesis, then?"

"I thought you only dealt in facts?" Ben said, and she smiled back at him. "He ran through a field as naked as he is now," he began. "The smaller lacerations on his legs were made from the crops."

"Ah," Pip said, nodding.

"At the edge of the field is a hawthorn hedge. He forced himself through a small gap."

"Hence the cuts to his chest and genitals," she said, shaking her head. "Running away from something, was he?"

"That's the idea," Ben continued. "Blindly, too, if your time of death is anything to go by."

"Oh, it's something to go by," she replied, and she gestured over at her computer. "I've something to show you."

She wandered off towards her desk, leaving Ben to share a bemused look with Gillespie.

"You coming?" she asked, and they joined her. She wiggled the mouse to wake the laptop from its slumber, and then opened an image, which at first glance looked like the screen had been damaged, but only when he looked closer did he see that it was something far more complex.

"What the hell is that?"

"That is a blood cell," she said proudly, sitting back to savour the expression on their faces.

"So?" Ben said. "Honestly, this means nothing to us. You're going to have to explain it."

"Alright, then, this middle part here is normal. But do you see all this colour?" she said, and Ben nodded.

"It's like a child's kaleidoscope."

"Kind of," she said. "But in medical terms, we call it something else." She grinned again. "I mean, technically speaking, I should have left this for the lab to pick up."

"But?" Ben said.

"But I did my thesis on the effects of lysergic acid on the respiratory system." She shrugged. "So, I couldn't resist."

"Lysergic acid?" Gillespie said. "What is that, battery acid?"

"Battery acid doesn't look like that," she replied, pointing at the screen and tapping the wild colours at the edges of the blood cell. "No, there's only one thing that creates those colours."

"And that is?" Ben asked.

"LSD," she said flatly. "Let me tell you something. That man was as high as a kite when he died."

"Bloody hell. I didn't even know kids still did that stuff. I thought it was all ecstasy and weed."

"Lysergic acid is metabolised after two to three hours. The body deals with drugs like any other toxin. But the effects of the drug can last anything up to twelve hours." She tapped the screen again. "However, unlike sunburn, the body's metabolism shuts down almost immediately upon death." She peered across at them both in turn. "There're no muscles screaming for energy."

"Right," Ben said.

"Yeah, right," Gillespie agreed.

"Now, the levels of lysergic acid in this particular blood cell indicate that Lee Constantine hadn't long taken the drug. A normal acid tab you could buy from some bloke in a hoody on a park bench would contain around two hundred micrograms—"

"Pip," Ben said, cutting her off. "We're not scientists."

"Right. You want the short story," she said, and Ben nodded. "I took the blood and urine samples and worked backwards to work out how degenerated the levels of lysergic acid were." Neither Ben nor Gillespie said a word. "And that's how I came to ten p.m.," she said. "Give or take."

"Give or take?" Ben repeated, to which she nodded.

"Give or take," she said again and then sucked in a lungful of air. "In short, our victim was out of his head when he was running across that field."

"That explains the zig-zagging," Ben said.

"Have you ever taken acid, Ben?" Pip said.

He looked up at her and shrugged.

"Of course not."

"Well, I did. Back in my uni days, and believe me," she said, "if he was that out of his head, there's no guarantee he was running from anything but his mind."

"How sure are you?" Ben asked, not wanting to delve into Pip's past.

"Sure enough that I re-examined the contents of his stomach," she replied, then held up a clear plastic bag containing a tiny dab of mush in one corner.

"What is that?"

"This," she replied, proudly, "is the culprit. An acid tab." She set the bag back down and pointed back to the cadaver on the bench. "That man was out of his brains when he died."

"The question is," Ben said, glancing up at Gillespie. "Why are there two sets of footprints?"

CHAPTER TWENTY

"He was off his head on drugs?" Cruz said.

"Aye. Can you believe it?" Gillespie replied into the phone. He settled into the passenger seat, keeping a watchful eye out for Ben. "I didn't even know kids still did acid these days."

"Where's Ben?" Nillson asked.

"Oh, he's..." He paused, unsure if he should say. "He's using the little boy's room. Anyway, at least we know why the trail Lee Constantine made through the field was all over the show. The bloke was so wasted he probably couldn't even stand up."

"It doesn't explain why he was out there and why he was naked," Nillson added. "It also doesn't explain the Reebok prints that Cruz found. What did she say about the cause of death?"

"Ah, she agreed with Doctor Saint. Broken neck. Died sometime between ten p.m. Saturday night and three a.m. the next morning."

"Bloody hell," Cruz said. "So, he was out of his head on acid, stumbling around in the dark with no clothes on."

"Aye, could have been a good night had it not ended so badly."

"Jim, you can't say that." Chapman cut in, not usually one to voice her opinion so freely. "He died, for God's sake." A woman with a pushchair was making her way through the hospital car park and the breeze bellowed her long flowing dress, revealing just enough leg to catch Gillespie's attention. "Jim?"

"Eh?"

"Are you listening?"

"Aye, course I am," he replied, as the woman passed by the car, caught Gillespie watching her, and smiled wryly. He grinned back, unabashed. "What about you lot? Have we learned anything?"

"We paid a visit to Constantine's workplace," Nillson said. "Hard to say if there's anything there or not. The owner wasn't exactly forthcoming with information."

"Aye," Gillespie said, admiring those swaying hips before him.

"I think we should press him more," Nillson continued. "It was hard to get anything out of him without giving away any details, but I think if we leaned on him, he might know a thing or two."

"Anything you say, Anna," Gillespie muttered, still transfixed. "Anything at all."

"We also found something," Cruz said.

"What about Jackie?" Gillespie said. "Has she called in yet?"

"Not yet," Chapman replied. "I've left her a message as Ben asked."

"Righto," he said, lost in all kinds of inappropriate thoughts at the sight before him. But somewhere, beyond his thoughts, Cruz's whiny voice rattled on.

"I think it could be something," he said.

"Listen," Gillespie said, as the woman disappeared from view. "Why don't we all collate everything we've got for the briefing? Get the facts straight, prepare the next actions, and double-check everything? Ben's got a lot on his plate at the minute, so let's smooth the way, eh? Let's make this as easy as we can for him."

"Jim, did you hear me?" Cruz said.

"Just pull it all together and we'll hear about it this afternoon,

Gabby," Gillespie told him. "And can somebody give Gold a call? He's going to want to know how she's getting on."

"I'll do that," Chapman said.

"This one isn't going to be straightforward," Gillespie said. "Vicky Fraser mentioned something about a party on Saturday night. Somebody find out where it was, and who was there. That's going to give us a list of people to talk to. I suggest when Ben asks for volunteers to speak to them that each of us take our share. He's fragile. Let's not give him a reason to break."

———

The glass fogged at the touch of his warm breath. But he'd seen enough to know that Freya was sound asleep. Someone had pulled the blind down, casting the room into near darkness, save for the glow from dozens of tiny leads on various machines – green, orange, and red, none of which Ben knew the meaning of.

He pushed open the door, slid inside, and then closed it quietly behind him. A machine beeped every couple of seconds, and in the silent spaces, Freya's breath hissed. She looked at peace, and her sleep must have been deep, as Ben recognised the way her lips were parted. It wasn't a look she would relish anybody witnessing, but it warmed him to know she was resting. He dropped into the chair beside the bed and took her hand, noting how warm the seat was. Gently, he caressed her finger, the way she often did to him.

It was the small things. The details.

"So, here's a conundrum," he said quietly. "Naked man found in a pond in the quarry just outside Dunston. Both the FME and Pip agree the cause of death was a broken neck, which leads me to a powerful hypothesis that he fell from the field above the pond, hit his head on the rocks, and rolled into the water. Nothing suspicious there, but we found a winding trail through the crops in the field, along with his footprints, and those belonging to a man wearing Reebok trainers."

Verbalising his thoughts proved to be quite therapeutic, and although Freya was virtually unconscious, just getting his ideas out there gave his mind some room to work on the facts.

"If the accident had happened during the day, I could put it down to misadventure. You know what people are like on hot days. They'd swim in a puddle if it was deep enough. But Pip is adamant this happened sometime between ten p.m. and three a.m. She's also convinced he was under the influence of LSD. I'm not sure how she did it, but she reverse-engineered the amount of the drug in his blood and urine samples. She also found some fly larvae in his mouth, which I think convinced her." He sighed, then laughed at how pathetic he sounded. "God, I wish you were with me on this one. Even if we find out who was wearing the Reeboks, it's going to be hard to get a conviction for murder. The best we're looking at is manslaughter, and even then, they'll probably walk. It's not like we even have any eyewitnesses."

Her chest rose suddenly then fell slowly with a long exhale, and he wondered if, in some faraway dream world, she had heard him. Perhaps his words had influenced her dreams, and she was there now, in the dark, playing the role of Lee Constantine. Empathising. Imagining.

"His girlfriend said he left the house on Saturday evening around five p.m., and she hasn't seen him since. She thought he'd gone to a party and just hadn't come home. Poor girl. There's a baby, too. Another kid growing up without a father." He stopped. The last of his thoughts assembled among the haze. "She was worried about something. She was going to tell me something. Something about him. There's more to this, Freya. There's more to this than a bloody manslaughter charge."

He let go of her hand and sat back in his seat.

"Ah, what do you care? I don't even know if you're coming back."

He stared at the gentle rise and fall of her chest beneath the sheet. He looked around at the scant possessions on the bedside table – her handbag, a glass of water, get-well-soon cards from the team and the few locals. The flowers in the vase were beginning to wilt and somebody had brought a fresh bouquet.

But something was missing. The photograph. He leaned forward to see if someone had moved it. Then he stood and searched between the get-well-soon cards, snatching them up in haste.

And then he saw it, the card affixed to the fresh flowers. And the name inside.

With all my love...Greg xxx.

––––––––

The remit of a family liaison officer did not extend to folding ironing, yet Jackie felt compelled to keep busy while Vicky Fraser tended to her baby. It was one of the monotonous jobs that required little thought, and just as if she was at home folding her son's washing, she found herself gazing around the room, staring into space, and wondering. She wondered what was in store for the baby. She wondered if Vicky had family nearby to help out. And she wondered what life was truly like with Lee Constantine.

Already, she had established certain clues about their relationship. The fact that he had left her with a newborn baby to attend a party, for one. And that, despite him being missing for more than twenty-four hours, Vicky had decided against bringing it to anybody's attention.

She placed a baby grow on the pile, marvelling at how small it was. There had been a time when Charlie had been that small, and it should be a time for Vicky that she could look back on with pleasure. But grief leaves scant room for fond memories to bloom.

Jackie had had her mother to lean on when she had found herself alone. She wondered if Vicky had a mother close by.

The baby cried out as she folded the last of the baby grows, but just as she was about to scoop the pile up, she felt a small vibration in her pocket. She unlocked her phone and found an email from Chapman, who, despite their close bond, never failed to present even the most informal of messages as properly as could be.

Hi Jackie,

Message from DI Savage. I am keen to discover more about the following:

- *The party Lee Constantine attended on Saturday night.*
- *The reason for Vicky Fraser's anxiety. She was trying to tell me something but was obviously scared to.*

Please use your time with Vicky Fraser to develop answers to these questions. Needless to say, discretion is paramount.

Kind regards,

DC Chapman.

Jackie grinned at the tone. Sitting beside Chapman in the office, Chapman could have passed the same information across in a far less informal manner. But, she supposed, should anyone use the internal emails as evidence in a trial, as they often were used, there would be little cause for the prosecution lawyer to accuse her of negligence or low standards.

She pocketed her phone, scooped the washing into her hands, and then ventured upstairs, calling out as she went. "Vicky?" she said, halfway up. "Vicky, it's me. Do you need anything?"

During her first few engagements as FLO, Jackie had fallen into a trap that caught many people off guard. Tentatively, she would ask if the family of the victim was okay. It had taken a few cold stares from bloodshot eyes to realise that rarely is anybody experiencing grief even almost okay.

But even with Jackie's cautious approach, Vicky didn't respond. Only one of the doors was closed, which she presumed was the bathroom. An open door revealed a wall covered in rainbow stencils, which she surmised to be the nursery, so she leaned inside.

"You in here, Vicky?" she said quietly.

Vicky wasn't inside. But lying in a Moses basket, staring at the ceiling, was a small baby. Perhaps it was the motherly instinct inside her that yearned to collect the child in her arms for a cuddle. But touching another mother's baby, especially one who was beginning her journey through grief, was a huge no-no. She set the washing down on the nursing chair and, tearing herself from the desire to hold the baby, she left the room and bumped straight into Vicky.

"Oh, my apologies," she said.

But Vicky just glared at her with bloodshot eyes that flicked to the baby and back to her. "What were you doing?"

"I was just bringing your washing up."

"You were with my baby. Did you touch him?"

"No, I just thought I'd help out—"

"You had no right," Vicky said, rushing into the room and raising the baby to her bosom. "Get out."

"Wait, no. Vicky, I wouldn't—"

"I said, get out."

Jackie could have argued. She could have fought her corner or perhaps reassured the distraught mother that she hadn't touched her child, despite wanting to. But there was something in her eyes. Something that was beyond reason.

So instead, she found herself nodding sadly. From her pocket, she pulled out a contact card, which she offered. But Vicky didn't even look down at it. She refused even to make eye contact. So, Jackie set the card down on the chair beside the washing.

"Very well," she said, as softly as she could. "Listen, Vicky. I know what you're going through, and I understand how it might have looked." Vicky did not attempt to demonstrate that she had even heard Jackie. "Call me. If you need to, just call me. Anytime, okay?"

She made her way to the stairs, wondering how on earth she was going to explain the situation to Ben. She was near the bottom when Vicky called out to her, so she stopped and peered up. Vicky was at the top of the stairs, clutching the baby to her chest.

"He didn't deserve it, you know?" she said. "None of us deserve this."

Jackie climbed up a step to be closer. "I can help you, Vicky. It's okay."

"It's not okay," she said, shaking her head with her bottom lip protruding as if she might break down any second. "I want to be alone." She glanced down at her child. "We want to be alone."

CHAPTER TWENTY-ONE

Pity was the last thing Ben needed. Yet, it was the one thing the team seemed hell-bent on giving. The moment he had walked into the incident room, the hum of activity had ceased, and ever since, while he had been adding notes to the whiteboard, he'd heard only whispers and seen only brief movement from the corner of his eye as Anderson leaned into Nillson to pass some judgement or other, or when Cruz had mimed a question to Chapman, no doubt asking if he, Ben, was okay.

"Right," Ben said, adding a dot to Barry Coleman's name with a little too much vigour. He clicked the pen lid on, tossed it onto the desk behind him, and then turned on his heels with his hands on his hips. "I need to say something."

Nobody said a word, and even Chapman's fingers, which never seemed to stop typing, froze. He gestured for her to close her laptop, then glanced at every one of them in turn.

"Come on then," he said. "Say what you have to say." He looked into each of their eyes and found only sorrow. "Anyone?"

"There's nothing to say," Nillson said, never one to back down from a challenge. "Maybe if you tell us what's going on, we can help?"

"What's going on? In what regard?" he said. "We have the dead body of a man lying in the morgue and it's our job to understand how he died, and if our investigation deems an individual guilty, and if we can demonstrate to the CPS that we have sufficient evidence to prove an MMO, then we can consider our jobs done. What's not to understand?"

"I, erm... I think they want to know about Freya, Ben," Gillespie said.

"Freya? What does she have to do with the investigation?"

"Nothing but—"

"So, why are we discussing her? Why are our attentions distracted from the job at hand and focused on Freya?"

"We're just worried about you, Ben. That's all."

"Well, let's have less of the chat and more focus on the job at hand. We're less than a day into the investigation and we have a long way to go. If you want to go and visit her in hospital, that's fine. But please don't...no, please *stop* treating me like a child with a grazed knee. Whatever went on between Freya and me is over. I'll continue to support her. She's still a good friend. But she's in hospital being taken care of. We don't have the luxury of people looking after us. If you want to know the truth, we don't even know if she'll be coming back to work. All right? So, let's do what we do best."

"You do want her back, don't you?" Anderson asked, just as Gold pushed into the room.

"Sorry I'm late," she said in a fluster of bags which she slung onto the floor before taking her seat beside Chapman.

Ben waved the apology off and returned his attention to Anderson.

"What I want doesn't matter. All we can do is deal with certainty. Freya coming back is uncertain, so we need to plan for it. Lee Constantine's death is a certainty, so let's focus on that, shall we?"

She smiled sadly at him, and he glanced around the room. "Anything else?"

Gillespie shook his head, glaring at the team to follow suit. Ben collected the pen from the desk, snatched off the lid and, after a deep breath, returned his attention to the investigation. "Jackie, you're back early. What did you find out?"

She opened her mouth to speak, but nothing came out, until at last she composed herself, rid her mind of the stories she had concocted, and spewed the truth.

"She kicked me out, Ben," she said, and the strength from Ben's arms conceded. They fell to his side in dismay.

"How did that happen?"

"I don't really know," she said. "I was helping her out. You know? Folding washing and stuff. I took it upstairs, and she caught me staring at the baby."

"What?"

"I didn't touch him. I was just looking. Charlie was that age once, you know? And if you recall, I also had to go through it alone."

"Jackie," Ben began, and he was about to remind her of what did and did not fall within the remit of her duties. But that was a conversation to be had in private. Nobody enjoyed those chats in front of an audience.

"Did she say anything at all?"

"Only that Lee didn't deserve what happened. That, none of them deserved it."

"Nothing about the party or what she was scared of?"

She shook her head.

"I didn't get a chance," she said. "I spent all morning rubbing her back while she cried her eyes out. She went upstairs for a sleep and to clean herself up, and that was the last I saw of her until..."

"Until?"

"Until I went upstairs with the washing. You know how the rest of it went."

"Tell me you at least managed to arrange a viewing of the body?"

She winced, then shook her head slowly.

"Sorry."

"Okay, it is what it is. We are where we are," he replied, taking another breath. "Anna, give me some good news."

Nillson sat back in her seat. It was as if somebody had once told her that a casual posture signified confidence. Yet something Freya had once told Ben was that obvious demonstrations of confidence usually meant the exact opposite. It was one of dozens of nuggets of information she had inferred to him over the past year or more.

"Barry Coleman is a bit of a character," she said. "Hard to say if he's up to no good. I imagine in a business like his, he has to bend the rules a little, but nothing serious. According to him, Constantine called in sick last Wednesday and was off all week."

"And he was the delivery driver?" Ben asked.

"Yep," Nillson replied. "He came in, loaded up, did his deliveries, then either went back to the yard or went straight home, depending on the time and location of his last drop."

"And what did he do on Tuesday night?"

"Dropped the van off, then went home," Nillson replied.

"Did you manage to look inside the van?"

She shook her head.

"Coleman was having none of it. He was fishing for information, so we are kind of at a stalemate."

"How did you leave it?"

"I told him that if we needed to come back to search the premises, we would."

"And what did he say to that?"

"He was fine with it, providing we can show him a warrant."

"So, it was a dead end, was it?"

"An open end," she said, after a pause for thought. "I think he's worth looking into." She glanced across at Chapman, who in turn waited for Ben's feedback.

"Go ahead, Chapman," he said, taking a final deep breath and turning to the last source of information in the room. "Cruz," he said. "Come on then. How did you get on?"

"Me?"

"You did manage to get out today, didn't you?"

"Oh, yeah," he said. "It wasn't much of a morning really. Quite warm."

"I was referring to the houses I asked you to knock at, Cruz," Ben said, recalling the number of times Freya had spoken to him in the same exasperated tone.

"Oh, right. Well, the first five houses weren't much cop. One bloke was as deaf as a post, another couple were unloading their car from a caravan trip–"

"Tell me about the sixth house," Ben said, cutting to the point.

Cruz gave a wry smile.

"Well, this is what I found interesting," he said. "See, when Gillespie called us earlier, he mentioned that Lee Constantine was under the influence of drugs when he died."

"That's right," Ben said, turning to the notes he'd made on the board. "LSD. And he died of a broken neck sometime between ten p.m. and three a.m." He tapped the board to reiterate the point.

"Well, see. We found something quite interesting," Cruz continued. "Well, it was Jewson who found it. She deserves the credit more than me, if I'm being honest."

"Jewson?"

"The PCSO Sergeant Macmillan assigned me," Cruz said. "She'll go far that one. Said I'd put a good word in for her–"

"Oh, here we go," Nillson cut in. "One sniff of a female in uniform and Constable Cruz has gone all soft."

"Soft?" Gillespie added. "I doubt he's gone soft. He'll be walking with a limp for a week. Jingling his change, as they say."

"Just get to the point, Cruz, please," Ben said, finding that deep breaths were having little effect on his patience.

"Oh, yeah," Cruz replied. "Well, if it's good news you're after, I might have found the golden ticket."

"Just tell us, damn it," Gillespie said. "For Christ's sake. It's like listening to an old woman tell me about her shopping trip."

"Talk to many old women, do you, Jim?" Nillson asked.

"Cruz?" Ben said, before an argument broke out, and both Gillespie and Nillson backed down.

"You said he died under the influence," Cruz said. "Well, what if I were to tell you that there's a weed farm less than five hundred metres from where Lee Constantine entered the field?"

CHAPTER TWENTY-TWO

"A weed farm?" Gillespie said. "Why the bloody hell didn't you tell me that earlier when I called?"

"I tried," Cruz protested.

"Did you hell," Gillespie said. "For Christ's sake, Gabby."

"Cruz, talk me through it, will you?" Ben said. "How was it left?"

"Sergeant MacAllister got CID involved," Cruz replied. "We waited there for support to arrive, then I came back here."

"And Jewson?"

"She stayed," he said. "There was nothing really for me to do. A weed farm isn't really of interest to us, and the owners weren't home."

"And who are the owners?"

"Oh," Cruz said, and he referred to his notebook. "It's two brothers. Andrew and Colin Major."

"Were there any vehicles parked up?"

"None," Cruz replied. "We knocked on the front door, but nobody answered, so I just popped around the back to see if they were in the garden."

"In the garden?" Gillespie said.

"Yeah. It's a nice day. People like to sit in the garden on days like this."

"Oh, aye. I can see it now," Gillespie said. "Two drug barons sitting in a forest of cannabis plants on stripy deckchairs eating ice cream. I suppose they had handkerchiefs on their heads as well, did they?"

"They weren't home," Cruz said. "And anyway, there was no forest of cannabis plants. It was a pro set-up. Five massive poly-tunnels with sprayers and heaters. Biggest one I've ever seen."

"And I suppose because Andrew and Colin Major didn't come to the door, you immediately assume they're not in? What did you expect them to do, invite you in for tea and a special cookie?"

"They weren't home," Cruz protested. "Besides, when CID arrived, they broke the door down."

It was this statement that caught Ben's attention.

"Did they search the place?" he asked to which Cruz nodded.

"They had a warrant issued in minutes. Apparently, there's a big crackdown across the county on places like that."

"Damn," Ben muttered, and he sat back on the desk, tapping the end of the pen against his teeth in thought. "Did they find anything?"

"I suppose so," Cruz said. "They took enough stuff away."

Ben shook his head in dismay.

"What's up?" Nillson asked. "It might not be one for us, but it's a win, isn't it?"

"Not really. If either Andrew or Colin Major had anything to do with our investigation and there was evidence inside that house, how do you think it'll stand up in court when the defence lawyer tells the jury that a dozen officers entered the house while the defendants were out and seized property? If there was evidence in there and it was usable, it won't be now. Even if it is still intact, there's enough reasonable doubt to sway a jury. The CPS will never go for it."

"Nice one, Gabby," Gillespie muttered.

"What? I found a bloody weed farm. What was I supposed to do, walk away?"

"I thought you said it was Jewson who found it?"

"Well, yeah. I mean, she did. But you know what I mean? I was there."

"Right," Gillespie said, nodding disbelievingly. "And this Jewson, this lass who you're going to put a good word in for, pretty, is she?"

"Oh, for God's sake, Jim," Nillson said. "Does everything have to have a misogynist slant on it?"

"Alright, alright," Ben said, thinking on his feet. He turned to his right. "Chapman, do some research on the Major brothers, will you? Who are they? What do they do? Where are they from? Do they have previous? What vehicles do they drive? You know the routine."

"Will do," she replied.

"Jackie, we need to know more about the party Lee Constantine attended. Have a look at his social media. See who he's friends with, who he engages with, and more importantly, who he engaged with last."

"Right," she replied.

"Nillson, Anderson, in light of Vicky Fraser's reluctance to work with us, we're going to have to contact Lee's next of kin. I usually prefer to have the spouse or partner break the bad news, but in this instance, I don't think that's an option."

"I don't know," Nillson replied. "Just because she's mad at Jackie, doesn't mean she won't give them a call."

"I have no doubt she will," Ben replied. "But it'll be a good excuse to get them talking. Perhaps Lee mentioned something to them. Maybe they knew who he was friends with. They might even have a number for us to call."

"Gotcha," Nillson replied. "You want us to break the news of their son's death as an excuse to get close to them."

"We're exploring avenues," Ben said. "We're establishing Lee's last movements and crossing people off our list. That's all we're doing." He pointed at the board. "So far, we have Barry Coleman who needs a bit more work, the weed farmers, and Vicky Fraser. None of whom lead us to the party."

"Vicky Fraser isn't a suspect?" Gold said. "She's got a newborn baby, Ben."

"As far as I'm aware, having a baby is not a golden ticket," Ben replied. "It does not clear her name. If she wants to play games with us, we'll play games with her."

"For Christ's sake, Ben. She's grieving."

"Right, which means you'll need to adopt a delicate approach with her, won't you?" Ben replied. "Give her a day or so to come to terms with her loss. Then go at her again.

"Ruthless," Nillson said. "Sounds like something the boss would do."

The statement caught Ben off guard. He stared at her but refrained from reacting until he had his emotions in check.

"Have you ever known her to fail in an investigation, Anna?" he replied calmly.

She gave it some thought, then shrugged. "I suppose not."

"Somebody was with Lee Constantine when he walked across that field. We need to find out who. It's our job to find out who it was," he said. "Gillespie and I will talk to CID to see what they seized. I suggest we meet again tomorrow morning and see where we are."

"What about me?" Cruz said, and he glanced at the rest of the team in turn. "What do you want me to do?"

"Well, you clearly work well with PCSO Jewson," Ben said. "I'll talk to MacAllister and see if she can be released. Why don't you continue your search of the field, seeing as you get along so well?" He slid from the desk and tossed the pen onto the table, letting it roll onto the floor. "And if any of you are still interested in Freya and if she's coming back, why don't you visit her for yourself? Ask her." He snatched his jacket, nodded for Gillespie to follow, and headed for the door. "Because quite frankly, I can't be bothered to explain it anymore."

CHAPTER TWENTY-THREE

Rarely was there cause for Ben to venture to the second floor, where CID operated. Dealing with crimes that ranged from burglaries to assault and drug-related offences, their incident room was far busier than that of the Major Crimes Team that Ben now found himself running. It was a sad state of affairs that Ben could recall a time when CID dealt with crimes of a sexual nature, but the volume of that particular category had increased to record-breaking levels, and any police force that did not invest in specialist teams was seen to be behind the times, incompetent, or merely uncaring.

A few heads turned when Ben and Gillespie entered the room, but as with any police station, people were too busy to stop what they were doing. But it wasn't difficult to identify the officer Ben needed to talk to. DI Wiltshire was a lifer. He had entered the force around the same time as Ben and had progressed through the ranks. They had been in uniform together, been on the same dawn raids, and on a few occasions, had even been on patrol together. But when the opportunity came, as it does for many career police officers, to branch off on a particular career path, both Ben and Wiltshire had entered the world of CID, sidestepping from uniformed tasks to become detective constables. It wasn't a promotion, as so many had thought. It was a decision. Transferring from a constable in uniform to a detective constable was, in Ben's mind at least, an affirmation. It said, 'Yes, I enjoy working for the force. I enjoy making a difference. But now I want more. I want to get deeper into the world of crime'.

At the time, the move had been huge for Ben. It had been life-changing. Yet it had barely registered on the force's radar. Both he and Wiltshire had entered that very incident room all those years ago, expecting to dive straight into a heavy investigation. They had expected huge busts and high-fives when they nailed a particular crime to a particular offender. They expected great success. And that is what they got in some respects, if you counted wading through stacks of historical investigations in search of some mundane fact to connect said crime to said offender. It just lacked glamour. All of a sudden, the days of riding around in a patrol car and dealing with the public felt like a joy.

But opportunities come when we least expect them, and when they do, only a fool lets them breeze past. A reshuffle of CID had created forks in career paths. Ben had gone one way, following his then sergeant down the path of major crimes, whilst Wiltshire had stayed on track with CID in a much larger team that offered greater opportunity. And as a result, Wiltshire was now four years into his term as detective inspector, while Ben could only claim a matter of months in the rank.

"Chris," he said, spotting a break in the chat Wiltshire was having with his team. He extended his hand to his old friend. "Looking good, mate."

"DI Savage," Wiltshire said, always a stickler for rank before his team. "What brings you up to these lofty heights?" He eyed Gillespie and greeted him with a curt nod. His experience had clearly empowered him with mistrust.

"Can't I pay an old friend a visit?" Ben asked.

"I can't remember the last time you were up here, and aside

from passing each other in the yard, I can't remember the last time we actually spoke. Therefore, a visit seems rather unlikely." He nodded at his team. "Give me a moment, will you?"

"The handful of officers took their leave and Wiltshire leaned on a nearby desk, brimming with confidence. The move allowed Ben to see the whiteboard behind him, and he gestured at the names at the top of the board. "A mutual interest."

Wiltshire followed his gaze, then grinned.

"Andrew Major and Colin Major? What would you want with them?"

"I want to ask them some questions, that's all."

"Ah, the body in the pond. Is that it?" Wiltshire said. "Do you really think a pair of inbred brothers are capable of murder?"

"Their house is one of six houses in reasonable proximity to the crime scene," Ben explained. "I merely wish to ask them a few questions. Where they were, what they saw or heard. The usual."

"You realise we're in the middle of a major drug bust here?" Wiltshire said. "I hope you don't think I'm going to let you interfere with that over what's nothing more than a suicide. Death by misadventure at best."

"You're well informed," Ben said.

"I'm not an idiot, Ben," he said, folding his arms. "Their faces and names are with every officer in the county. I expect them to be in custody by the end of the day."

"I can wait."

"You're not understanding me," Wiltshire said. "I have enough to charge them with intent to supply a class B drug. It's not enough to hold them until their court appearance, so they'll be bailed, and when they are, you can do as you want with them."

"Five polytunnels full of weed hardly constitutes a major drug bust, Chris," Ben said. "This is likely a murder investigation. Manslaughter, at worst."

"It was four, actually. The fifth had been recently harvested."

"Four then. What is that, a few hundred grand on the street? Hardly national headlines, is it?"

"Leave them alone," Wiltshire said. "I'll call you when we're done with them. If you decide you've grounds to rearrest them, then that's over to you, but I'm not having my investigation muddied by something we don't even know is connected."

He shoved off the desk and started towards where his team were sitting around a table.

"You're putting me in an awkward position, Chris," Ben said to which Wiltshire turned and raised an eyebrow.

"Oh?"

"Look, we all know the only reason you made that bust was because one of my officers discovered the weed farm. If we hadn't been there, you'd still be working on a street dealer looking for a way up the food chain."

"Oh, I know who made the discovery, Ben," Wiltshire said. "PCSO Jewson. So, if there's any gratitude owing, I'll make sure MacAllister hears it."

"For God's sake," Ben said, a little too loud, and as a result, a few heads raised, then slowly dipped again. Ben lowered his voice to a hiss. "I'm stuck here. Help me out, will you? Half a dozen of your officers charged into that house and, for all we know, destroyed evidence in the first place."

"Ah, now I see," Wiltshire muttered.

"Even if we do pay them a visit when you release them, who's to say they won't clean up? How do we know any evidence hasn't already been destroyed, and even if by some miracle there's something there that can help my investigation, who's to say it would even be admissible in court? Any defence lawyer would claim it was a plant made during your raid. I've got nothing here, Chris."

Wiltshire returned to his position by the desk, then slowly slid a cheek onto it and refolded his arms.

"You're not talking to them. Not yet."

"My officer said you seized goods," Ben told him. "Let me see it. Let me see what you took out."

"Is that all?"

"It's a start."

Wiltshire mulled it over. His lower jaw rolled from side to side.

"You realise that anything my officers seized is part of a drugs charge and therefore would run the same risk of being inadmissible in an unrelated investigation, don't you?"

"I need a start," Ben explained. "If we found something, then we'll work out if and how we can use it."

Wiltshire unfolded his arms and shoved his hands into his pockets. He clicked his fingers at his team and a young male officer looked up expectantly.

"Gibson, take DI Savage and Sergeant Gillespie to the evidence locker. Eyes only, alright? Nothing is to be taken away. Not until we've had a chance to go through it."

"Guv," Gibson replied and made a show of locking his laptop. He stood, pushed his chair under the desk, and then waited.

"Cheers, Chris," Ben said, hating that he'd had to ask for help.

"That's alright, Ben," Wiltshire said, holding his stare. "Just remember where the favour came from, eh? You never know, I might need one myself one day."

CHAPTER TWENTY-FOUR

The address Chapman had provided led Nillson and Anderson to a house on the edge of Heighington. It was a large, detached house sitting in walled grounds, with neat flower beds, established plants, and a gravel driveway.

"Jesus, how's this for life goals," she muttered as she drew the car up beside a small pond. "There're a few boxes being ticked right here, look. Gravel driveway, detached garages – plural – and more outbuildings than I have dinner plates."

"Does that tick your boxes?" Anderson replied. "You always struck me as a neat little new-build somewhere. No fuss, no mod cons, and no age-related maintenance jobs to stay on top of."

"Well, there is that," Nillson conceded. "I might choose to live like that for now, but one day..." She nodded through the windscreen. "A girl can dream, can't she?"

Nillson reached for the door handle but Anderson grabbed her arm to stop her, and she stared down at the hand.

"What is it?"

Anderson hesitated, then relaxed her grip.

"Before we go in, I just wanted to ask you something," she said, then took a breath. "It's about Freya."

"Oh, for God's sake, Jenny. Haven't we heard enough about this? Ben just told us that if we want to know how she is, then we should go and see her ourselves."

"It's not about how she is," Anderson replied. "Although, obviously, I do care. I just... I'd feel like I was intruding. She doesn't know me well enough for me to visit."

"She's been in hospital for weeks, Jenny. She's had nothing but nurses and Ben for company. Believe me, she'd appreciate a visit from Jimmy bloody Saville if it meant some decent conversation—"

"I'm thinking of leaving," Anderson said, then took a deep breath, like she'd just confessed to being an alcoholic in front of the group.

"What? You're leaving?"

"I'm thinking of it, that's all." She sighed and stared through the passenger window. "Look, you know my story, right? I'm here because of Freya. I worked with her in London, and I looked up to her. Trust me, when she was down there, she was a thorn in the sides of all the men. She was everything I wanted to be."

"A nice-smelling thorn with polished nails and impeccable taste, you mean?"

Anderson gave a soft laugh, then smiled briefly. "What if she doesn't come back?"

"Oh, come on. She'll be back."

"But what if she doesn't?" Anderson said. "I mean, it's not like I make a huge difference to the team, is it?"

"What on earth are you talking about?"

"Well, I don't, do I? I'm one of four detective constables in a team of eight, soon to be seven."

"We don't know that."

"If she doesn't come back, then Ben will move up, which means that either you or Jim will move up."

"That's not a given."

"None of it's a given, Anna. But it's the best-case scenario. And where does that leave me? One of four constables looking to move up to sergeant, that's where." She shuffled into her seat and cleared her throat. "So, let's look at what I've contributed to the team since I arrived in Lincolnshire." She made a show of counting on her fingers, then made a fist. "Oh, that's right. Nothing."

"What?"

"Then there's Chapman. The team wouldn't even function without her. Gold, everyone's mother. The voice of reason. And then there's Cruz."

Nillson laughed aloud.

"You're worried about Cruz being your competition?" she said. "Listen, Chapman is one of the best researchers in the force. Freya's words, not mine. Gold is a single mother trying to keep her head above water, and Cruz? Jesus, Jenny."

"He's doing well, Anna," she said. "Since Freya separated him and Gillespie, he's doing really well. He's more confident, he gets results–"

"He's a man-child," Nillson said. "As is Gillespie, FYI."

"But the fact remains that if you or Gillespie or Ben were to look at us all, I wouldn't be your first choice."

"You'd be mine."

"Plus, I'm not ready for the sergeant's exam."

"Oh, behave. It's easy. There's nothing you don't know already." Anderson smiled appreciatively, then looked away. "Jenny, you have nothing to worry about. You certainly don't need to worry about reporting into Sergeant bloody Cruz. Christ, the thought of it makes my skin crawl."

"There's a spot come up," Anderson said quietly. "It's back in London."

"What? No–"

"I wanted you to know. I wanted you to know that I've sent a request for transfer."

"Without discussing it?"

"It hasn't been approved. Not yet anyway. And even if it is, I still get the final say."

The front door of the house opened, and a man wearing tan chinos and a light blue shirt peered out. Slowly, he began walking towards the car.

"So, what you're saying is that, if Freya doesn't come back and you don't get the promotion, then you're leaving."

"That's not what I'm saying–"

"It sounds like it to me," Nillson said, and Anderson stared at her with guilt in her eyes.

"I'm a bit lost," she said, as the man's pale hand tapped on Nillson's window. "I'm trying to find my way."

Nillson shoved open the car door, climbed out, and displayed her warrant card for the man to see.

"Good morning, sir," she said. "I'm Detective Sergeant Nillson, this is Detective Constable Anderson, and we're looking for a Graham Constantine."

"That's me," he said, his inquisitive expression shifting into one of fear.

The anger and disappointment ran riot in Nillson's mind, and she hesitated as she regained control of her emotions.

"Perhaps we can speak inside," she said, smiling as warmly as she could.

"We can speak out here," he replied, and he steered her view with a sweep of his hand to a bench beneath a rose arch.

She eyed the bench and Anderson came to her side.

"Is your wife home?" Nillson asked. "I was told there was a Samantha Constantine."

"She's busy," he said, clearly deflecting any attention from her. It was a typical protective husband behaviour Nillson loathed. "Listen, if there's something I need to know–"

"May I ask when you last spoke to your son, Mr Constantine? Or his girlfriend, for that matter."

He stared down at her, his head cocked to one side as if he could read her mind in the whites of her eyes.

"Just tell me," he grumbled.

"We found the body of a young man, Mr Constantine," she said. "I'm afraid it's your son."

He silenced. The corners of his mouth raised like he expected her to announce that it was a sick joke.

"Sorry?" he said, for want of anything else to say.

"Shall we go inside?" Nillson asked. Before he could answer, she took him by the arm and led him back towards the house with Anderson trailing behind.

"I don't understand," he said. "He was here. He was here last week. He can't—"

He stopped and stared at the front door, and Nillson turned to find his wife standing there. She wore an apron and had a tea towel draped over her shoulder.

"Graham?" she said, doing her best to sound strong but failing. It was one of those scenarios that damn near every adult in the country had seen take place in a TV show but had always thought themselves immune. But when one day the scene played out, they knew instinctively what it was about. "What's happened?"

Nillson tapped Anderson to walk ahead while she led the father into the house. Gently, Anderson moved Mrs Constantine into the house to make room for her husband.

The ground floor was open plan and appeared to have been furnished almost entirely from the same tree. The side table, consoles, coffee tables, and even the picture frames were all the same shade, with the same bevelled edges and joinery techniques. Two large couches, deep enough for two people to lie side by side on, faced each other before a large open fireplace framed in the same brick as the house's exterior. The floor was a similar shade to the furniture, but very obviously older, as if it had been reclaimed from an old manor house.

"We can talk here," Graham said when they were inside, and he gestured at the couches.

"I don't understand," his wife said. "What's going on? What's all this about?"

Graham leaned into Nillson, took a breath, and muttered to her, "Leave this to me, will you?"

It was the first time she had seen strength in his eyes, and she nodded once and remained standing while he made his way over to the couches, where he dropped down beside his wife and took her hand.

From afar, Anderson looked up at Nillson sorrowfully and the two shared a moment. It was as if everything that had been said in the car had paled into insignificance; the private conversation that was taking place on the other side of the huge space was little more than a reminder that life is short and that you should grab every opportunity that comes your way.

She nodded once back at Anderson, hoping she understood what it meant.

"God, no," Mrs Constantine cried, and she fell into her husband's waiting arms.

Nillson scanned the room, noticing the freshly cut flowers most likely picked that morning and the dainty ornaments that only people of a certain age enjoyed – plus Chapman, of course. Her house was full of the stuff. Nillson noticed again the photo frames that matched the floor, tables, and sideboard.

And that was where she stopped.

She caught Anderson's eye and nodded at the sideboard, then watched as the constable who, over the past year, had become a solid friend, saw what she was referring to.

Nillson took a slow walk over to the grieving pair and dropped down onto the couch opposite them.

"There's no easy time for this," she began, "but there are a few questions I need to ask."

Mrs Constantine peered up at her, her face screwed up in disgust.

"I've just lost the last son I had," she sobbed. "Can't your bloody questions wait?"

"Sam, come on," her husband said. "She's just doing her job–"

"Well, it can wait," she said. "It can bloody well wait until I've asked my questions."

"Sam–"

"No, Graham. No," she said, turning on Nillson again. The emotions were understandable, expected, and tolerable, and Nillson had skin like rawhide to deal with it. "How? How did he die? And when? Do you even know it's him?"

"We've matched his DNA," Nillson replied. "I'm sorry, we have no intention of making this any harder, but as you can appreciate, there are procedures we need to follow."

"Procedures?" she said, rising from her seat and shrugging off her husband's grip. "Procedures? I'll tell you what my procedures are, shall I?"

"Mrs Constantine, I'm happy to share the details with you–"

"My procedure is to find out how and why this happened," she barked.

"He fell from the quarry just outside Dunston," Nillson said, then watched as the statement was processed, probably running over and over in the mother's mind. "It happened sometime on Saturday night. He'd been to a party, and early indications are that he was inebriated."

"Inebriated? My Lee, drunk?"

"We're still waiting on the toxicology results for the precise cause," Nillson continued. "But I'm afraid it wasn't alcohol."

Mrs Constantine shook her head a little, displaying the early signs of denial.

"No," she said. "No, he wouldn't–"

"Like I said, we're still waiting for toxicology."

"He doesn't take drugs. He never has. He wouldn't touch them with a barge pole."

"Look, without knowing the full details, I can only say what I know. We've been dealing with Victoria Fraser, his girlfriend."

"He wasn't a druggie," she said flatly, to which Nillson listened and remained respectful. "My Lee is a good boy."

"With all due respect, Mrs Constantine, I'm not here to judge. It's not my job to–"

"I know he didn't touch them," she spat, and she turned on her heels to march across the room to the sideboard, where she collected the framed photograph Nillson had spotted, and then returned to stand before her, a bony index finger jabbing at the image of two boys. "Do you know who this is? Eh? Do you?"

Nillson waited, hoping the silence would pacify her a little.

"Lee?" she said softly.

"And?" Mrs Constantine asked, her finger pointing at the other boy. "Do you know who this is?" Nillson shook her head and felt a pang of guilt that she should have known somehow. Mrs Constantine leaned in. Her face screwed so that every line around her eyes became a deep chasm of grief. "It's his brother. His dead brother."

"I'm so sorry, Mrs. Constantine."

"And do you know he died?" she continued, her voice rising into a tremble like a violinist's vibrato. She swallowed hard, then cleared her throat, preparing to spit the next words at Nillson. "Drugs. So don't you dare come here and tell me my last remaining son is dead from drugs because he knows damn well what they do to people. They killed his brother."

CHAPTER TWENTY-FIVE

"Why don't you get off, Jim?" Ben said, as the three of them made their way down the stairs to the evidence locker. "I'm sure you've got better things to do."

"Aye, well, I mean Katy's at work. So, I suppose I could clean the house up," Gillespie replied. "Or I could stay and help you."

"I'm sure I can go through a pile of junk on my own, mate. Go on. Get off. Go and clean, or whatever it is you need to do. Have a rest. You've earned it."

"You sure?"

"Listen, you told me to go and get some rest yesterday. The least you can do is return the favour."

"Aye, but you didn't get any rest, did you? You didn't listen to me."

"Yeah, well, the difference is that I'm SIO on this investigation, and you...well, you're not, are you?" Ben said, as he followed the young detective constable into the evidence room foyer and called back over his shoulder. "That's an order, Jim."

He held the door open long enough to witness the little lost puppy look in Gillespie's eyes, then let it close before he felt sorry for the big Scot. DC Gibson gave the investigation number to the duty officer standing behind the desk.

"That just came in. I've just finished putting it all back there," the officer said, jabbing a thumb over his shoulder at the cages of evidence behind him. "Do you know which box you want?"

"Erm..." Gibson began, suddenly unsure of himself.

"All of them," Ben said. "I need to see all of them."

Gibson opened his mouth to speak, and although he thought better of it, he allowed his dismay to form on his brow.

"Do you have plans?" Ben asked him.

"Well, no, but–"

"I might be here a while."

Gibson looked unsure of himself and peered up at the duty officer before giving a nod. The duty officer unlocked the cages and then disappeared into the back room. Florescent tubes pinged on and they heard him shuffling around among the aisles.

"You and DI Wiltshire seemed pretty pally," Gibson said.

"We started off together." Ben stared at the cages behind the desk, sensing Gibson's roving eye rather than watching him.

"Must be good mates, then," Gibson replied.

"Good enough. There's always a bond with the ones you start off with. Like a shared journey," Ben said. "Something like that, anyway. It's probably less to do with the dawn raids and big busts, and more to do with being locked in a room together wading through paperwork."

"Yeah, I know that one," Gibson replied, to which Ben gave a knowing laugh.

"Look, I don't need you to hold my hand. The duty's here to help if I need it."

"I'm not sure DI Wiltshire would agree to that."

"DI Wiltshire?" Ben said with another laugh. "Let me guess, before I came in, he was holding a late afternoon briefing, dishing out tasks for you all to go through tomorrow."

"Well, yeah."

"Right," Ben said. "He's probably getting into his car now. Go on. I won't tell him if you want to get off. I know what it's like."

A squeak from the aisles drew their attention and the duty officer wheeled a trolley containing four large plastic crates around the corner.

"Big haul," Ben said.

"This is just half of it," the officer replied. "Another four boxes back there, plus the bin bags full of weed. You don't want that, do you?"

"I think I can do without the weed," Ben said with a pleasant smile.

The officer unloaded the boxes onto the desk and disappeared around the corner to get the others. Ben opened the first box, withdrew the first clear plastic bag he came across, and studied the notebook inside. He dragged a chair across the room and made himself comfortable before donning a pair of latex gloves from the dispenser on the desk and opening the bag.

Then he stopped and looked up at Gibson.

"You might want to make yourself comfortable," he said, as the officer returned with the other four boxes. Ben opened the bag, pulled out the notebook, and flicked through the pages. "It's going to be a long night."

———

"The old ones are the best, eh?" the duty officer said from the desk, as the door closed behind Gibson and the sound of his boots trailed off along the corridor. "One day, he'll be pulling that trick himself."

"Maybe," Ben replied, and he tossed the bag containing the notepad back into the box. "I don't suppose they gave you an inventory, did they?" As if he had been expecting the request, the duty officer collected a few sheets of paper from a nearby file and handed them to Ben, who then perused the list of seized belongings. "Trainers," he said, eyeing the boxes, and the officer began helping him search them.

It took a few moments before he dragged a large bag from the furthest box. "These?"

Ben strode over to him, held the bag up, and then sighed. "We're looking for Reeboks," he said and snatched the list up again. "There's got to be something in here."

"Trouble, are they?" the officer said.

"What makes you say that?"

"Well, DI Wiltshire has every copper in the county on the lookout for them with regards to a weed farm. But you're Major Crimes, aren't you? What would you want with a weed farm, and why would two detective inspectors be looking into them? Unless, of course, it's two unrelated offences?"

"Very intuitive," Ben said.

"The joys of working in here," he said. "It's like living in a cave. I live vicariously through my visitors." He leaned on the counter casually and folded his arms. "I reckon the next time I'm let out, everyone will be wearing space suits and driving flying cars."

"I don't think we're quite there yet," Ben told him, and he studied the man. "Why don't I know you?"

"Transferred from the coast," he said. "Been out in Mablethorpe for five years."

"Mablethorpe? I thought they closed the station down."

"Hence the transfer," he said, then offered his hand. "Henry, guv."

"Henry?" Ben said, shaking his hand. "Do you have a last name?"

"Henry, guv. James Henry."

Ben nodded.

"Well, James Henry, you seem at home in the evidence locker. Are exhibits your thing? I didn't realise it was a speciality."

"Oh, it's not really a speciality," Henry replied. He heaved his right boot onto the desk and pulled up his trouser leg to reveal the lower half of a prosthetic leg. "More of a necessity. Not much good at chasing after drug dealers anymore."

Ben was slightly taken aback by the sight of the man's leg and watched with admiration as he dropped his boot to the floor and straightened his trousers.

"I wouldn't have known," he said. "You walk normally. I didn't even see a limp."

"You weren't looking for a limp, guv," he replied. "But you will now."

"How did it happen?" Ben asked. "In service?"

"Sadly not. The payout would have been nice. No, this was the result of a car accident. Deer ran across the road one night. I swerved and put the car into a dyke."

"Crikey," Ben said, unable to think of anything to say that didn't sound pitiful.

"They might have been able to save it had it been daylight. Four hours, I was trapped there. My bloody phone fell into the passenger footwell." He grinned at his own misfortunes. "By the time they cut me out, I knew it was gone. It's funny, like you and everyone else, the thought of losing a limb would have horrified me. But the longer I was trapped there, the easier it became. It's like I learned to accept the loss and planned a life without it, you know? I think if I hadn't come to terms with a new way of life, the ordeal would have beaten me. Eighteen months of physio, shrinks, and the rest of it. It's enough to put you over the edge, if you know what I mean. Losing a part of you is hard, let me tell you."

Ben let the inventory fall to his side to study the man once more, noting how normal he looked. Yet, his mental strength was clearly extraordinary.

"I think there's a few of us who could take a lesson from that," he said, reflecting on his own dilemma. "I just don't think the rest of us have the strength."

"Well, if ever you find yourself in a hospital bed for weeks on end, without the ability to run away, then maybe you will find it. Trust me, when there's bugger all else to do, you analyse everything in your life. You soon realise what's important, and what's not."

"Maybe," Ben said thoughtfully. "Maybe you're right." He took a deep breath, ran his eyes across the boxes, and then stared at the inventory once more. The items were mundane, hardly even worth taking. Until he turned to the final page. He looked up at Henry and held the page for him to see. "Mobile phone?"

"Might be worth looking at," he replied, and the two of them tore into the boxes in search of the device. Henry was on his third box when he called out, "Got it." He dragged the bag from the plastic crate and held it out for Ben. "Although, I doubt it'll do you much good."

Ben grabbed the bag from him and stared at the contents.

"It's an old Nokia. Jesus, they don't make them like this anymore," Ben said, and through the bag, he pushed the power button. To both of their surprise, the phone lit up and began the Nokia boot sequence. "Must have been charged recently."

"Could be a burner," Henry suggested. "Why else would it be charged? I mean, I know those old phones only needed charging once a week, but..."

"There's only one number in the call history," Ben said. "I think you're right." He pulled his own phone from his pocket, opened the camera, and took a photo of the number. "You didn't see that, Henry."

"See what, guv?" he replied, and then winked at Ben, just as the doors opened. Ben stuffed the bag back into the box, slipped the inventory on top and then turned, expecting to find Wiltshire looming over him.

But it wasn't Wiltshire.

"You alright, Ben?" Chapman said. "It's late, you know?"

"I could ask you the same," he replied, then turned to Henry. "I think that's enough for now, Henry. Do you need a hand?"

The officer began dragging the heavy boxes back onto the trolley and gave him a warning look not to pity him.

"I was just finishing a few things off," Chapman said. "I imagine tomorrow is going to be a busy one. I wanted to get a head start."

"I think you're right," Ben said, then waited for Henry to push his trolley around the corner. He held his phone up to Chapman. "Make a note of this phone number and look into it, will you?"

She inferred the discretion Ben was hoping to achieve and noted the number in her pad, slipping it into her bag before Henry returned.

"That's us, Henry," Ben said. "Thanks for your help."

"Thanks for your company," he replied. "Always a pleasure to learn what's going on outside."

"I'll keep you posted on those space suits, shall I?"

"Ah, I was never one for fashion," Henry replied with a smile. "But if you start seeing cars flying about, give me a shout, will you?"

He nodded a bye to Chapman, then began dragging more boxes onto his trolley. Ben held the door for her and ushered her outside.

"Don't worry about it tonight," he said. "But make that number a priority tomorrow, will you? It would be nice to have something to go on. Right now, I'm at a loss."

Chapman smiled politely.

"Can I tell you something, Ben?" she said.

"Of course," he replied and began walking her towards the door to the station yard.

She seemed hesitant to speak, then stopped before the doors, checking around to make sure they weren't being overheard.

"You don't need Freya for this. You're more than capable."

"Excuse me?" he said.

"Sorry. I don't mean to speak out of turn. But I get the impression you're wishing she was with you. Even if it's just to bounce ideas off."

"Chapman, I hope you don't think I'm being rude, or ungrate-ful, but–"

"It's okay," she said. "I overstepped the mark. I'm sorry."

He paused and studied the young woman who, in all the years he had known her, had never displayed malice in the slightest.

"I do miss her," he said honestly. "And I know I don't need her. I know we can do this without her."

"But?" she said, as if she could read his mind and was pressing for him to verbalise his thoughts.

"I suppose it's a habit," he said. "You know, we used to spend our evenings working on theories. We used to come up with all kinds of ideas, some of them utterly ludicrous. But they needed voicing. I think that's why we worked so well together. By the time we got you all in the incident room the next morning, we'd have theories coming out of our ears, and we'd have a plan." He stopped and sighed. "Right now, I haven't got a plan. I'm winging it, Denise."

"Well, how would you like something to mull over tonight?" she said. "Maybe you can come up with a plan for us all without her."

"Go on," he replied, intrigued, but not too hopeful.

"I checked Lee Constantine's phone records with the provider," she said. "Three text messages on Saturday night, all from the same number."

"Any details?"

"Where did you go? Where are you? Give me a call in the morning," she said. "All sent between nine-thirty and ten o'clock."

"I don't suppose you managed to find out–"

"That's where it gets interesting," she said with a grin. "The sender was a female. Margot Major."

"Major?" he said, and his voice carried along the corridor. "As in—"

"The weed farmers' sister," she said, then slowly peeled herself away from the conversation, tugged open the door to the yard and looked back at him with a friendly smile. "That should keep you busy tonight."

CHAPTER TWENTY-SIX

There had been times in Gillespie's life when he had known his actions were wrong. He had stolen, lied, and fought his way through the network of foster homes and carers as a child, never quite belonging and never quite feeling wanted. That had all changed when he joined the force. He had found a sense of place. A purpose in life. But that hadn't stopped him from breaking the odd rule here and there.

Yet rarely did he ever embark on breaking a rule and doubt his reasons for doing so. Staring at Freya through the window in the door, however, he felt the pang of betrayal coursing through his veins. Was it immoral? Was he overstepping the mark? Or was he being a friend?

He knocked once, then pushed the door open. The curtains were pulled and the summer sun glowed through the heavy fabric, allowing him to navigate his way to the chair with ease. She was still, save for the rise and fall of her chest. Her mouth was closed and judging by the half-empty glass on the bedside table, she had recently been awake and able to have a drink.

The other bedside table was home to a vase of flowers, and

Gillespie took a peek at the card, noting the name that gave reason for Ben's mood.

"Well, this makes a nice change," she said, startling him to the point where he felt like an intruder. He placed the card back into the bouquet and considered retreating to the door. "It's okay. You don't have to make a run for it, Gillespie."

"Eh?" he said. "How on earth–"

"You'd be surprised how efficient your other senses become when you lose your sight," she said. "I recognise your breathing and your scent."

"My scent? I don't wear any–"

"And that is precisely how I recognised you," she said. "Sit. Please."

He sniffed at his jacket discreetly and then his armpits, finding neither to be offensive, and then slowly dropped into the chair.

"I thought you were sleeping," he said.

"That is almost certainly the only perk of having my eyes bandaged over," she replied. "Nobody knows if I'm sleeping or not." She gave a loud exhale and then shifted her position, pulling herself a little more upright. Gillespie immediately rose, and she held out a hand. "It's okay, it's okay. I've had my ear burned off. My arms still work just fine."

"Aye," he said, returning to his seat. "I just came to see how you were doing. The others are asking after you."

"Lying never was your strong point, was it?" she said and then grinned at his silence. "I've been lying here for weeks, Gillespie. That's plenty of time to think about things. Too much time, if I'm honest. You came here because Ben has decided not to."

"Well, I wouldn't put it quite like that."

"He visited me every day since my arrival," she said, cutting him off. "Then one day my husband turns up out of the blue and Ben stops."

"Aye, well. I mean, that's none of my business."

"So now Ben is in a state of depression, is he?" she said. "I imagine he has thrown himself into the investigation, leaving very little time to think about his personal life." She cleared her throat, then groped for the glass, raising a hand to still him when he tried to help. "So, there we have it. Here's me with all the time in the world to consider my life, and there's Ben refusing to even consider it. Don't worry. I won't ask you to betray him."

He sat back in his chair and folded one leg over the other.

"He's...not himself," he said. "I'll give you that."

"He's sulking," she told him. "He's feeling sorry for himself. He always does it. You know that as well as I do."

"Look, it's not my place to–"

"So why did you come?" she asked.

"Well, I...like I said, I wanted to see how you were doing. See if there's anything you need."

"Something that you could provide that neither Ben nor my husband can? Is that right?" she said.

"It's not my business, boss," he said. "I just feel for him, you know? I know he loves you. If he didn't love you, he wouldn't have come, would he? But it's–"

"Greg?" she suggested. "My husband? So, I was right? He's sulking." She shook her head. "You'd think he'd have a bit of fight left in him, wouldn't you?"

"I think it's the whole marriage thing," Gillespie said. "You know, he's not really into breaking up marriages."

"Unlike you, you mean?"

"Hey, I never broke one up."

"But you have had more than one encounter with a married woman."

"Aye, well... I mean, what was I supposed to do, stop them halfway through and ask them?"

"Halfway through what?" she said. "Oh, never mind. Anyway, Ben is burying himself in the investigation, is he?"

"He is, aye."

"Two out of two," she said, with a smile.

"Aye, you should do this for a living," he said, hoping she would take the bait.

"Is that a question?" she asked. "And if so, am I meant to read more into it?" She licked her lips, then bit down in thought. "You're not here to talk about Ben, are you? No, you're too loyal to discuss Ben. Even you have morals, don't you?"

"He's a mate, boss. A good mate."

"Which means that you're here because there is uncertainty in the team. People are wondering if I'm coming back to work."

"Don't take it the wrong way, boss."

"Is there a right way?"

"Well, I mean. Ben mentioned them transferring you to Nottingham to see a specialist."

"And did he mention Kent?"

"Kent?"

"That's a no, then," she said. "My husband has booked me into a private clinic. Kind of him, isn't it? And here was me thinking he couldn't care less about me."

"You can't go, boss. Not down south, surely?"

"If I don't come back," she continued, ignoring his question, "then either Ben will be moved up or somebody will be transferred in from another team. I'm not sure if Ben is time served enough as a DI to be considered."

"He might not have been a DI for long, but he's capable," Gillespie said.

"Oh, there's no doubt he's capable. I know it. You know it. Granger knows it."

"The only one who doesn't know it is Ben," Gillespie said heavily, to which Freya cocked her head thoughtfully.

"Is he struggling?"

Gillespie nodded, then voiced his response.

"Like I said, he misses you."

"And you? If Ben were to move up, either you or Nillson would move up behind him," she said, nodding. "You're here to work out if there's a chance of promotion."

"Well, no–"

"You want to know if I'm coming back or if you should brush up on your exam technique?"

"I'm here because he's struggling, boss," Gillespie said. "Not just with his head. That's none of my business. But the investigation? That's my business. That's why I'm here."

He imagined her eyes narrowing in thought, the way she often did. He wondered if she would still do that or if those little foibles would alter.

"What is it exactly that he's struggling with?" she asked quietly.

Gillespie thought about his response, regretting his decision to come in the first place.

"Direction," he said. "There's bugger all to go on, and he needs to demonstrate progress. We're going round in circles. We've got Lee Constantine–"

"Yes, I know. He fell into a pond and broke his neck. Has Pip confirmed it?"

Gillespie was a little taken aback

"Aye, she's confirmed it, alright. Time of death was sometime between ten p.m. on Saturday night and three a.m. on Sunday morning."

"What else did she say?"

"Well, she's still waiting for the toxicology report so–"

"What did she say, Gillespie?" she asked. "I know Pip well enough to know that she wouldn't leave it there. This one would intrigue her."

"LSD," Gillespie said. "He was high as a kite."

"Acid?" she replied. "That's interesting."

"Interesting as in you have an idea, or interesting as in you have no idea?" Gillespie asked.

"LSD is perhaps the least criminal drug you can find. One of them, anyway. Everything else is highly addictive, even weed, and as we know, drug addicts often fall into crime to feed their habits."

"But LSD isn't?"

"LSD is something somebody takes when they're with friends, in a safe place, and they don't have to be anywhere for a day. It's a once-in-a-while drug, and it's certainly not the type of drug you find gangs fighting over. Not at the domestic level, anyway. What does that tell you?"

"Well, we know he went to a party."

"Did he know the host?" she asked.

"We're still looking into that part."

"Prioritise it," she said. "You've got to think like Lee Constantine. Did he have anywhere to be the next day? An LSD trip can last hours. Twelve or more, and the following come down would be horrific."

"Right," Gillespie said.

"Would he have felt safe at the party? Was he with friends? Understand all that, and you'll understand the motive for taking the drug."

"The motive?"

"Well, if he felt safe, had a free diary, and was with friends, then he might have taken it willingly."

"If not, you think he might have been spiked?"

She cleared her throat and shifted her position again.

"Have you ever seen anyone on acid, Gillespie?"

"Not recently," he said. "I mean, I nicked a few hippies in my time."

"They have no control. They'll talk to trees. They'll pull their hair out thinking it's on fire."

"How about running across a field starkers?" Gillespie asked.

"That as well," she said. "Find out about the host of the party. Maybe you can ask his girlfriend. Vicky Fraser, wasn't it?"

"Christ, have you got a copy of the file in here somewhere?"

She smiled broadly.

"Ben told me," she replied. "When he used to come to see me."

"Well, that avenue might be closed to us now," Gillespie explained. "Vicky Fraser kicked Gold out of the house. Found her looking at the baby and went nuts at her, apparently."

"Kicked her out?" Freya said. "What about the thing she was hiding?"

"What thing?"

"Ben mentioned something about her wanting to tell him something but changing her mind. Did Gold manage to get to the bottom of that?"

"She didn't have time, by all accounts," Gillespie replied, to which Freya nodded.

"And there lies your answer," she said. "If Vicky Fraser is hiding something pertinent to the investigation, it means that either Lee Constantine was in trouble or had done something. My guess is that he was in trouble somehow."

"Trouble? Like what?"

"Does he owe money? Has he upset anybody? I don't know. But you need to either separate the party from whatever trouble he was in or link him to it."

"Sorry, boss. I'm not following."

"Well, if you were in trouble or had done something stupid, would you go to a party and drop acid, knowing that for the next day or so, you would have absolutely no control over what you said or did?"

"Aye, probably not," he said, to which she nodded.

"Do that, and then come back to me."

"Eh?"

"You heard me. Work that out, and then come back to me," she said. "You can't imagine I'll rest easy until I know what happens next, can you?"

"I'm not sure if I should be telling you any of this–"

"Gillespie, you have come to my bedside under the guise of caring for me. Yet we both know that all you want to know is if I'm coming back or not. If I'm not coming back, then there's a chance, albeit slim, of a promotion for you. Hence, you speak to me, I tell you what I would do, and you go away and reap the rewards."

"Well, aye. I mean—"

"We both know you will be back, so why not go and tell me if I'm right? You never know, you might just get that promotion."

"You'll help us, you mean?"

"I'm not helping you, Gillespie. If I know Ben, he wouldn't entertain the idea of having me help him. Not in his current mindset anyway. But I do find myself in need of stimulation," she said. "So, think of it as rehab. You're helping me. That's got to ease your conscience, hasn't it?"

CHAPTER TWENTY-SEVEN

It was one of those summer mornings that followed a damp night. It was one of those mornings that Ben loved. It was one of those mornings that made long and hard winters worthwhile. But it wasn't the morning sun burning the dew from the grass so that it hung in the air as a low fog that he loved. And it wasn't the pastel sky that God could have painted himself – if there even was a God. No, it was the smell. The fragrance of a summer morning, the scent of the trees and the plants and the animals.

He leaned on his car, checked his watch, and then sipped his coffee. The old, steel thermos mug was battered and bruised, but that was okay. The coffee wasn't even made with fresh beans, as Freya would have done. It was just some old instant granules he found in his cupboard from before Freya had...changed him. Was that the right phrase? No doubt she would call his transformation an education or refinement. But that was just snobbery.

He took a sip of coffee. It wasn't bad. It served a purpose. Maybe tonight he would reach past the bottles of fine wine she had stocked his kitchen with and choose the cheap bottle he'd been saving. The one with the little sailing boat on the label.

The lane was quiet enough for him to hear Gillespie's old

Volvo trundling along before it even rolled into view, so he took another sip, fitted the plastic lid on the cup, and then reached in through his open window to stuff it into the cup holder.

And that was when he smelled it. Not the summer morning. His car had never smelled of a summer morning. It was just a normal car. No expensive handbags on the back seat, no designer shoes in the footwell, and no lingering smell of perfume.

"If you want a game of hide and seek, you'll have to do better than that," Gillespie said. "I spotted you a mile off."

Ben pulled himself from the car, feeling the urge to laugh, but not quite having the mental energy to smile.

"Plenty of places to hide around here, Jim," he said.

"Aye, one problem, though," Gillespie replied. "I can't count to ten. We'd be here all bloody day."

"Well, it's a good job we're not here for a game of hide and seek then, isn't it?" Ben told him, then nodded at the end cottage in a terrace of three. They sat alone on a stretch of lane between Metheringham and Blankney, and it wasn't hard to imagine them a hundred years before. They would have started as part of the local estate. Then, as the decades rolled by and the land was sold off, they would have been sold to locals, villagers who worked in the village or ran local businesses. But they still had their charm. The modern world couldn't rid them of that.

"I hope you're going to tell me why we're here then," Gillespie said. "All I got was a message to meet you here. I mean, am I dressed for the occasion?"

Ben eyed him and felt a grin form. It was weird to see Gillespie's transformation. He'd gone from being a man who almost never ironed his clothes, rarely washed his hair, and almost always had the sweet scent of last night's beer on his breath to being the best-dressed person in the team. There was no doubt it had been Katy Southwell's influence, though Ben doubted it could be called an education or a refinement. It was just him wanting to keep hold of something good.

"Margot Major," he said.

"Who?"

"Margot Major," Ben repeated. "The younger sister of Messrs Andrew and Colin Major."

"Right," Gillespie replied, staring up at the cottage. "And what do we want with her? She involved?"

"That's what we're going to find out," Ben told him. "You ready?"

"Would have been nice to have a coffee first," he replied. "But you can get me one on the way back to the station."

"Is that right?"

"You'll want to when I tell you my idea," Gillespie said.

"Do I need to hear it before we go in?" Ben said, hesitating on the footpath.

"No. No, it can wait. I'm still fine-tuning the details."

"Jim, if you have something to say, just say it. I'm scratching here."

Gillespie opened the garden gate, which appeared to be as old as the old stone house. "Let's just say, if it's direction you're after, then I think I might have it."

"Direction?" Ben said, as they made their way up the garden path. He reached up and knocked three times. "What the hell is that supposed to mean? Don't tell me you've done something stupid, Jim. I haven't got the mental bandwidth to deal with anything else right now."

"Just trust me," Gillespie said. "By the time we're done, we'll be on our way to a motive."

"A motive? What about a suspect?"

"One thing at a time, Ben, eh? One thing at a time."

Bare feet padded on wooden stairs inside and the door opened to reveal a confused and bleary-eyed female in her late twenties. She tugged the cord of her dressing gown tight, which may have secured the lower half of her gown, but seemed to reveal more of the area above the cord. Ben averted his eyes, but Gillespie made no attempt to hide his approval.

"Miss Major?" Ben said, holding up his warrant card.

She gave it a cursory glance, then screwed her face up in confusion.

"Yeah. Is there a problem?"

"It might be best if we speak inside," Ben said, as he pocketed his warrant card.

"I'm not letting you in. I'm a single female. I'm not letting two men into my house."

"We are police officers—"

"I don't care who you are. What will my neighbours think?"

"Well, you can either let their imaginations run wild or we can have a conversation right here about how you were the last person to message Lee Constantine before he died on Saturday night."

"What? Lee Constantine?"

"His body was found not far from here," Ben explained.

"Oh my God," she said, holding her hands to her mouth. "That's awful. How did it happen?"

"Well, that's what we're trying to find out, and seeing as you were the last person to see him alive."

"I'm sorry, I have no idea what you're talking about. I saw him at a party. There were lots of people there."

"But only you messaged him," Ben said, and a silence followed as the gravity of the situation became apparent.

"Coffee would be good," Gillespie said, taking her off guard even further. "Come on, Margot. Let's not do this the hard way, eh? Not at this time of the morning."

"It's just a few questions, Margot," Ben added. "The alternative is that we have the same conversation at the station."

"The police station?" she said. "I haven't done anything."

"Then you have nothing to worry about, do you?" Ben said. She peered out of the door along the lane, clutching her dressing gown collars. "Look, if we wanted to arrest you, we would have, and you'd be on the way to the station right now. All we want is a chat."

"Why don't you call somebody?" Gillespie said. "Tell them you're about to let two police officers into your house. Gillespie and Savage. Anything happens, and you've got somebody on the outside who knows we were here."

She considered it for a moment, then relented, stepping back and pulling the door open.

"That-a-girl," Gillespie said, as he entered the hallway. "Kitchen okay with you?"

He didn't wait for a response, choosing instead to duck beneath the low doorframe in the kitchen. Ben followed suit and Margo Major came after, although she waited at the doorway, hesitant to join them, leaving Ben little option but to proceed in the hope that his line of questioning might reassure her that they meant no harm.

"Margot, can you tell us about your relationship with Lee Constantine?"

"My relationship? I don't have a relationship with him. I don't even bloody know him."

Ben gave her a quizzical look.

"So, how do you explain the messages on his phone state-ment?" He retrieved his notepad from his pocket, flicked to the correct page, and then read aloud. "Three messages. Where did you go? Where are you? Give me a call in the morning." He waited for her expression to alter, but it remained steadfast. "You have to agree, Margot, those messages indicate that you were with him."

"I never said I wasn't, did I?" she said.

"So, can you tell me a bit more about this meeting with him?"

"It was at the party," she said. "He was there, and we...we just got chatting, that's all."

"Chatting? About what, Margot?"

Reluctantly, she stepped into the room, sliding along the

counter to the furthest reaches. Behind her large eyes, an internal battle appeared to be taking place. They flicked left, then right, never staying in one place for too long.

"Margot?" Gillespie said. "If there's something you need to say, sweetheart—"

"I'm not your sweetheart," she replied, folding her arms and finally looking across the room to Ben. "I'd already heard about Lee. It's a small village. Everyone knows everyone."

"But you didn't know Lee personally?"

"He's not from Metheringham. I think his parents are up the road in Washingborough or Heighington. Somewhere around there. But you know how it is when someone moves in. People are friendly. They gossip. Before you know it, the name Lee Constantine started cropping up."

"In what context?"

"There was no context," she replied. "It wasn't even gossip, really. He was friends with Paul, so I suppose he would have known the people Paul knocks around with."

"Paul?"

"Stoneman," she said. "He's a local lad. Works up at the quarry."

Ben watched Gillespie make a note of the name. Then he took a few steps further into the room to peer out of the rear window. The garden was small and quintessentially British. Long tendrils of lavender spilled onto the small lawn, while foxgloves in their dozens grew as tall as the brick wall.

"Was this Paul Stoneman with Lee on Saturday night? At the party, I mean."

"I think so, yeah," she replied.

"You saw him, did you?"

"I did."

"And you spoke to him?"

"Only to ask where his mate had gone," she replied. "He was a bit...I don't know. Out of it, if you know what I mean?"

"Not really, no."

She rolled her eyes.

"He was drunk or something," she said. "Like Lee. The two of them could barely string a sentence together."

"I thought you said you and Lee were chatting," Gillespie said.

"We were. Well, not really chatting. He was rambling on about something. God knows what it was. I couldn't make out a word."

"Because he was drunk?" Ben asked. "Or something?"

"The music was loud," she said. "He was slurring."

"But still, you carried on talking to him?"

"Of course," she replied. "He was nice. He wasn't aggressive or anything. He was one of those happy drunks. I was looking after him."

"What was he drinking, Margot?" Gillespie asked. "Was he on the beer?"

"I don't know," she replied, then stared at the ceiling in thought.

"So, you sat with him while he mumbled and slurred, and with the music too loud to hear anything, and you don't know what he was drinking?"

"No. I suppose I thought he must have had a warmup some-where, you know? England were playing, so I suppose he'd been in the pub."

"Tell me what happened next," Ben said. "You sat with him for how long?"

She shrugged. "Half an hour or so," she said. "I went to the bathroom, and when I came back, he was gone. I mean, I looked around but couldn't find him. That's when I saw Paul. He was in the kitchen chatting up some girl."

"And what did Paul have to say?" Ben asked.

"He was quite rude, if I'm honest," she said. "Said he wasn't Lee's mum and that he's probably taken himself off home."

"And did you go looking for him?"

"Well, no. Why would I? I don't know him. He was just some bloke at a party who made me laugh."

Ben perched on the window ledge and plunged his hands into his trouser pockets.

"The thing is, Margot," he said. "The bloke who made you laugh at a party on Saturday night, the same bloke you spoke to and must have at some point exchanged numbers, was found in the quarry not far from here."

"I told you. I don't know anything about it."

"No, I don't suppose you do," he said. "But what's troubling me is that he reached the quarry through the fields."

"Right, so? Is that supposed to mean something?"

"Whose house backs onto that field?" Ben asked, and he watched as his line of questioning began to make sense.

"No. No, you don't think my brothers had anything to do with it, do you?"

"Right now, I don't know what to think," Ben said. "When did you see them last?"

She cast her gaze downwards and bit down on her lower lip.

"Margot," Gillespie cut in. "It's worth mentioning that, right now, all we're trying to do is piece together what happened when Lee left the party. We just want to speak to people. When did you last see them?"

"I saw them at the weekend," she said quietly, then looked up at them both in turn. "They were at the party."

CHAPTER TWENTY-EIGHT

Ben waited for the team to settle before speaking. It was a trick he'd seen Freya do a hundred times or more. She would sit patiently, making no eye contact with any of them, until the hum of chatter had ceased and the clatter of typing had faded.

"Margot Major," Ben said, and he tapped her name on the board with the end of the marker. "Younger sister of Colin and Andrew Major, whose names you might all recognise as being the owners of the house in which Cruz discovered the weed farm, not five hundred yards from where Lee Constantine entered the field."

"Actually, Ben," Cruz said, raising his hand like a timid school-boy. "It was Jewson who discovered the farm. I can't claim credit for it."

Ben smiled politely, nodded once, and then continued.

"As I understand it, the brothers are missing, but DI Wilt-shire upstairs has every officer in the county on the lookout for them."

"Sorry, Ben," Chapman cut in. "They're in custody now. I saw Sergeant Priest this morning as he was processing them."

"Well, that's not going to help us right now," Gillespie said.

"Wiltshire has warned us off them. Said he doesn't want us interfering with his drugs investigation."

"No, he said we couldn't speak to them until they've been charged," Ben said, turning to Chapman. "Get Sergeant Priest on the phone, will you? Ask him to let you know when they've been charged and to have them ready and waiting in separate interview rooms." He turned to Gillespie. "We'll be interviewing them this morning, so get your game face on."

"Do you have an angle for them? Other than their house being in close proximity to where Lee Constantine entered the field? We're going to need something more than that," Nillson asked.

"As it happens, we do have something," Ben told her. "This is where it starts to get interesting. Chapman looked into Constantine's last calls and text messages and found three messages from a number registered to Margot Major."

"Not much of a link, Ben," Nillson said.

"Who we paid a visit to this morning, while you were all eating your cornflakes," Ben added, which raised a few intrigued eyebrows. "Margot claims that she was talking to Lee at the party and that he was rambling and slurring his words. The music was loud, so she couldn't quite understand him, but given how drunk he appeared, felt compelled to look after him."

"Drunk?" Gold said. "I thought he'd taken LSD?"

"There's no mention of alcohol in the toxicology report," Chapman said, then glanced up at Ben. "It came through last night."

"Was Pip close to the truth?" Ben asked.

"Spot on," she replied. "Right down to the estimated time he died."

"Good," Ben said. "Anyway, Margot used the bathroom, and when she came back, Lee was gone. She looked for him and spoke to the only person she knew who knew him. A Paul Stoneman."

He watched as each of them made a note of the name, and then he turned and wrote it on the board.

"What we do know about Stoneman?" Nillson asked.

"Only that he knew Lee Constantine and that he works at the quarry."

"At the quarry? Jesus," Cruz said.

"Let's not jump to conclusions," Ben said. "Chapman, do some digging on him, will you? Find out what you can while we deal with the Major brothers."

"Will do," she replied, making a neat note in her pad.

"And to answer your question, Nillson," Ben continued. "According to their sister, both Colin and Andrew Major were at the party on Saturday."

"Bloody hell," Cruz said, voicing his thoughts. "Sounds like we were the only ones who weren't invited."

"Not just us," Gillespie said, turning to Gold. "Vicky Fraser wasn't there."

"She has a newborn baby, you idiot," Gold said. "She's hardly likely to go out partying, is she?"

"And alibis don't get much stronger than that," he replied.

He had a glint in his eye and Ben recalled the conversation they had had moments before they had knocked on Margot Major's door.

"Care to expand on that, Jim?" he said. "You mentioned something about having a direction for us." He sat back on the desk behind him and waited.

"Aye, well," Gillespie began, which was his standard method of buying himself time to gather his thoughts. "The way I see it, we need to look at this from Lee Constantine's perspective."

"Isn't that what we've been trying to do?" Nillson asked.

"Not really," he replied. "See, what do we know about him?"

The team shared thoughtful glances, but it was Gold who spoke up first.

"He had a baby," she said.

"Right," Gillespie said. "He's a new dad. Anything else?"

"He worked at Dicks Appliances," Anderson suggested and Gillespie pointed at her, clicking his fingers.

"Good. Keep them coming. What do we know about Lee Constantine? What we know. Not think. What do we know?"

"He was out of his head on LSD," Cruz said.

"Bingo," Gillespie said. "And the winner is the little short arse with coffee on his shirt."

"Eh?" Cruz said, and he glanced down at his front. "Oh, for God's sake."

"What do we know about LSD?" Gillespie said, then peered around the room at the blank expressions. "How many times have any of us nicked somebody for taking, possessing, or even dealing LSD?"

"Not many," Ben said. "It's not exactly a drug of habit, is it? As far as I know, it's not even addictive. Not like coke or heroin, or weed for that matter."

"No, it's a pleasure drug, is it not?" Gillespie said. "It's something you would only take if you knew you had nothing to do for the next day or so, right?"

"Right," Ben said, seeing where he was leading the team.

"And it's something you would only take with good friends," Gillespie continued. "Let's face it, you take an acid tab and you're accepting that you're going to have absolutely no control over your actions for the next twelve hours. It's not like doing a line of coke or popping a pill. It's nothing like smoking a joint, is it? When you take LSD, you're in for one hell of a ride."

"Are you speaking from experience, Jim?" Nillson asked.

"No," he said. "No, I'm not. But when you've been a copper all your adult life, like I have, Anna, you hear things. You pick things up." He turned to Ben and jabbed an index finger at his desk. "What else do we know? Or what else have we surmised?"

Ben shook his head. "Enlighten me," he said.

"Something his girlfriend said," Gillespie continued. "Or should I say, something she nearly said?"

"He was in trouble?" Ben said.

"Right," Gillespie said. "So, if he was in trouble, or if something had happened, why the bloody hell would he go to a party where he didn't know anybody and pop an acid? The man had a wee bairn and girlfriend at home. Why would he do that?"

"He could have been reckless," Gold suggested. "Christ, you hear it all the time, don't you? Blokes going out on a Friday night and not coming home until Sunday with no idea of where they've been."

"Going out and getting drunk is one thing," Gillespie said. "But popping an acid?" He shook his head. "That doesn't sit right with me. I think we need to establish if the party was linked to his death, or if it was part of the plan."

"The plan?" Gold said.

"Aye, the plan," Gillespie replied. "You see, I don't think Lee knowingly took the drugs. I think he was spiked."

"Oh, come on," Cruz said. "That's just conjecture."

"It's a theory," Ben said, holding his hands up to keep them all calm. "And right now, it's the best we've got."

"How do we know he didn't pop acid every week?" Cruz said. "It might not be addictive, but it's obviously a good buzz or people wouldn't do it, would they?"

"Actually, I can answer that," Nillson said. "As much as it pains me to say it, I agree with Jim. I think he was spiked."

"Oh, not you as well," Cruz said.

"What makes you say that, Anna?" Ben asked.

"Well, Anderson and I paid a visit to Lee's parents last night," she began. "We had to tell them their remaining son had been found dead."

"Remaining?" Cruz said. "What do you mean?"

"It means they've already lost one son," Ben said, studying Nillson's expression. She nodded gently. "And my guess is the other son died through drugs as well." Nillson's expression said it all and Ben's heart tightened at the idea of parents losing both of their children to drugs. "Right, who do we know is involved with drugs and was at the party?"

"The Majors?" Cruz said.

"Right," Ben agreed. "Chapman, call Priest. Get them set up in interview rooms with duty solicitors if need be."

"What about DI Wiltshire?" she asked.

"Leave him to me," Ben said. He opened his notebook to the page he had used inside Margot Major's house and placed it in front of Nillson. "This is the address of the party. I want you and Anderson to pop around there and see what you can find out. I want the names of the hosts and who they invited. We're looking for a connection to Lee Constantine or the brothers."

"Okay," Nillson said, exchanging glances with Anderson, who seemed indifferent to the task. "Are we bringing them in?"

"Not yet," Ben replied. "But I want them to know we're closing in. I want everyone to know we're closing in. Especially the Major brothers. Am I clear?"

"Aye," Gillespie said, voicing the team's sentiment.

"Good, we'll meet back here this afternoon. If Lee was in trouble, then who with? We find that out and we have our motive. Any questions?"

"Just one," Chapman said politely, and Ben turned to her, eyebrows raised.

"You asked me to check a phone number last night," she said, discreetly asking if the knowledge should be shared among the team.

"From the burner phone, you mean?"

She nodded and winced.

"I did a little digging," she said. "And I know who the number belongs to."

"Hold up, what's this?" Gillespie asked. "A burner phone?"

"It was among the items taken from the weed farm," Ben said without looking at him. "It was an old Nokia, fully charged with one number in the call history."

"You know we can't use that, don't you?"

"I'm well aware of the risks to the investigation," Ben said, waiting for Chapman to finish.

She slid a piece of paper across the desk and watched as he reached for it, read the name, and then folded it in half.

"Nillson, Anderson," Ben said, "when you're done with the party house, I have a job for you."

He turned to the whiteboard and stared at one of the names.

"The suspense is killing me, Ben," Gillespie said. "Whose number was it?"

Ben took five steps forward and handed him the folded slip of paper, before retreating to the whiteboard to connect the Major brothers' names to the name he had been staring at.

"Barry Coleman?" Gillespie called out, handing the paper to Nillson. "What the bloody hell has a man who repairs and sells fridge bloody freezers have to do with two kids growing weed?"

"Barry Coleman connects Lee Constantine to the Major brothers," Ben said, collecting his file from his desk. "That's our link. I don't expect either Colin or Andrew Major to talk." He looked across at Nillson. "What's your thoughts on Coleman?"

"Oh, he'll do more than talk," she said with a smile. "I'll make the bastard sing."

CHAPTER TWENTY-NINE

The party house was as ordinary as ordinary came. As far as new builds were concerned, the houses were well-finished, and judging by the cars on the drives, it had fast become a respectable community. There were no unique features that set the party house apart from the rest of the new builds around it, save for an overflowing wheelie bin.

"Jesus, they threw these up quick," Nillson said as she pulled into the new estate. "They're nice, too. I was expecting to find an old, run-down council house with a rotting caravan on the drive and a manky sofa on the lawn."

"A little judgmental, don't you think?" Anderson replied.

"Well, come on. Someone throws a party and invites drug dealers. One guy has his drink spiked and winds up dead. It's easy to think we'd be visiting a hovel."

"Well, this isn't a hovel," Anderson replied. "I wouldn't mind living here myself. Where I grew up in London, new builds are renowned for being poorly built and small. Perfect starter homes, but not exactly ideal for a family of four. But these? These are nice."

Nillson switched the engine off and climbed from the car, then waited for Anderson to join her on the pavement.

"I don't suppose you've had second thoughts, have you?" Nillson asked.

"Look," Anderson replied, "can we agree not to discuss it? I shouldn't have said anything, and I've been dreading you bringing it up."

"Well, what do you expect? I'm not just going to let you go without a fight."

"I came here to work with Freya," Anderson replied. "If she isn't coming back, then why am I here? I'm not a local. I don't know anyone–"

"You know me."

"Friends, I mean. I don't have any friends here."

"Oh, cheers. And here's me thinking we'd grown to be pretty close."

"You know what I mean–"

"No, I don't," Nillson said. "I took you under my wing. I showed you around. I even stopped Gillespie from hitting on you, if you remember?"

"I do," Anderson said with a smile. "I just... It doesn't feel right. I feel like an outsider. When Freya was around, I had a connection. I had someone I looked up to–"

"You're really stroking my ego now, Jenny."

"I meant before," she replied. "Before I came, I knew I would be working with Freya." Her shoulders seemed to deflate, and she turned her gaze towards the large pond in the middle of the new houses. "I need to find my own way. Can't you just support me in that?"

"Find your own way?" Nillson said, shaking her head.

"What? What's wrong with that?"

"Nothing," Nillson said. "Nothing at all. You find your own way, Jenny. And best of luck with it."

"You're disappointed," Anderson said, as Nillson started up the footpath.

"Of course I'm disappointed," she replied, as she reached up and rang the doorbell. She turned to face Anderson. "I'm going to lose a friend. And a bloody good one at that."

Anderson's expression altered, and for a moment, Nillson thought she saw a tear form in the corner of her eye. But there was no time to watch it roll. The door opened in a rush and a man stood on the doorstep, staring down at them.

"Yes?" he said.

He was tall, dark, and clean-cut. Nillson estimated him to be in his early thirties. He wore smart trousers, polished shoes, and a tie hung around his neck waiting for a knot.

"Justin Greaves?" Nillson said, waiting until the last minute to produce her warrant card. "Sergeant Nillson. This is DC Anderson." She pocketed the little leather wallet, hoping his expression would give her some kind of indication of his thought process.

"So?" he said. "How can I help? Be quick, because I'm leaving in two minutes."

"We were hoping to talk to you about a party you held here last Saturday," Nillson said, and again he held his hands out in frustration.

"So what? I had a party. Nobody complained. We kept the music down after eleven."

"Well, to be precise, we wanted to speak to you about some of your guests," Nillson replied.

He sighed and peered back into the house, which from the doorstep appeared to be immaculate.

"Look, can we talk while I finish getting ready? I've got a meeting in twenty minutes, which means I'm..." He checked his watch, an expensive-looking smartwatch with a tan leather strap. "Fifteen minutes late."

"Do what you need to do," Nillson told him. "As long as we can come inside."

"Whatever," he replied, then darted off into the kitchen. Nillson found him in the open-plan kitchen working on a double Windsor, which he finished with a flourish and slipped the tail into the little loop, before tugging on his suit jacket. "Lee Constantine," Nillson said. "Recognise the name?"

He strode over to the kitchen counter where some kind of green smoothie was waiting for him.

"Should I?" he asked before he took a large mouthful and then yanked off a piece of kitchen paper from the roll to wipe his mouth.

"He was one of your guests," Nillson replied.

He downed the rest of the drink, giving him a good ten seconds to consider his answer, then wiped his mouth, rinsed the cup, and put it into the dishwasher.

"There must have been seventy-odd people here on Saturday," he said. "You can't expect me to know them all."

"I don't expect you to know them all," Nillson agreed. "But you would know most of them. Only a fool invites seventy strangers to their house."

"Alright," he said. "So, I know most of them. So what? Who is this Lee Constantine, anyway?"

"A friend of Paul Stoneman. Does that name ring a bell, or don't you know him either?"

"I know Paul. He's a mate. We play squash on Thursdays," he said, then looked up at the ceiling in thought. "You must be talking about the bloke he brought along. Bit shorter than me, stocky, with a bit of a beard going on?"

"That's him. That's Lee Constantine," Nillson said. "Well, it was."

The final part of her response caught his ear. He cocked his head to one side.

"Was?"

"We found his body on Monday night. His last known location was here in this house."

"Jesus," Greaves said then held his hands up. "Look, I didn't even speak to the bloke."

"I didn't say you did," Nillson replied.

"Look, if you need me to come to the station, I can come tonight after work."

"Right," Nillson said. "You have a meeting."

"It's important," he replied, suddenly appearing uneasy.

"Another name. Colin Major."

"Eh?"

"What about Andrew Major?" she asked. "Do you know either of them?"

He reached for his car keys from a hook beside a wall calendar.

"What station is it?" he said. "I can be there for six-thirty."

"Do you know either of them?" Nillson said.

He presented the hallway door with a sweep of his arm.

"I really need to get going," he said. "I understand the gravity of the situation, and honestly, who Lee was, I feel for his wife and... Did he have kids?"

"A son," Anderson said. "Six weeks old."

"Jesus Christ," he said. "Look, alright. I get it. I can give you a list of names tonight. I know who was there and who brought guests."

"I just want to know about the Major brothers," Nillson said. "Were they there?"

He looked away, clearly battling with the truth and betrayal.

"I'll take that as a yes," Nillson said.

"I didn't say that—"

"You didn't have to," she replied. "What time did they get here?"

He shook his head, clearly frightened of speaking out, so Nillson gave him prompts.

"Just nod your head when I say the right time," she said. "Five, six." She watched his face and fingers for a muscle twinge. "Seven, eight—"

He gave a slight nod, and Anderson made a note in her pad.

"And when did they leave?" Nillson asked. "Same rules apply. Nine, ten—"

"They weren't here that long," he said. "Fifteen minutes or so."

"Fifteen minutes? Wow, must have been a terrible party," Nillson said, with a smile which she let fade as fast as it had formed. "Unless they weren't here to party."

"Look, I really need to get going."

"What you need to do, Justin, is answer my questions or I'll drag you down to the station and you can answer the questions under caution."

"What? You can't do that—"

"Did they come here to sell drugs?" Nillson asked.

"I'm not answering that."

"Look, just so we're clear," Anderson said, stepping into his line of sight. "We're not here to make an arrest about some petty class B drug. Somebody died, Justin. Imagine if that was your friend. Imagine if it was your brother or your son."

"I don't have a son or a brother."

"Right," Nillson said. "Justin Greaves, I'm arresting you on suspicion of conspiracy to murder—"

"Alright, alright," he said, tugging his tie loose. He stared at them both, his face white with fear. "They brought some weed. That's all. It was a party. People wanted to kick back."

"Just weed?" Nillson asked. "Or did they bring something else? Something with a bit more kick in it?"

"Eh? No. I don't know."

"Did you buy some?" Anderson asked.

"Me? Well, yeah. I had a bag of weed. So what? It's gone now."

"But you don't know if they supplied anything else?"

"How would I know what they gave to anybody else? And what has this got to do with this Lee bloke?"

"What's it got to do with Lee Constantine?" Nillson asked. "He left this party out of his head on LSD. From here, he somehow got to the fields behind the quarry, which he ran through as naked as the day he was born."

"Yeah, acid will do that to you."

"And then he was either pushed or fell into the quarry wildlife pond."

Greaves was silent for a moment.

"Drowned?" he asked.

"No," Nillson said. "No, he broke his neck on the rocks. The thing is, forensics tells us that he wasn't alone."

"Eh?"

"Somebody was with him. Most likely somebody from this party."

"And that's where I come in, is it?" He took a moment to rub his face, then pulled his phone from his pocket, tapped a message out, presumably to his workplace to tell them he was not going to make the meeting, and set it down on the kitchen counter. "Alright. Alright, there is something you should know."

CHAPTER THIRTY

It was reaching ten o'clock in the morning when Cruz pulled his little hatchback to the side of Dunston Heath Lane, and already the sun was beating down. He leaned across to the passenger seat and pulled open the glove box.

"What the hell?" Jewson said, pulling her legs to one side.

"What?" Cruz said.

"You touched my legs."

"Eh?" He snatched his hand away.

"You touched my legs."

"I did not. I opened the glove box."

"Your hand grazed my knee. What is it you want? I'll pass it to you."

"For God's sake," he said. "Alright, alright. Can you pass me the sun cream, please?"

"Sun cream?"

"It's under the tissues and the foot powder somewhere," he said. They had been in the car for less than twenty minutes and already he was gaining an insight into what the day would be like for him.

"Foot powder?"

"Yes, foot powder. I have athlete's foot."

"You have what?"

"Athlete's foot. It's a condition, you know?"

"I know what it is. It means you have manky feet."

"It means I walk a lot," he told her. "Spend half my life knocking on bloody doors. It's a wonder my feet haven't worn away."

With her nose scrunched in disgust, she picked up the shaker bottle of anti-fungal powder with a finger and thumb and deposited it into the rear footwell.

"Hey?" Cruz said, but she ignored him entirely and fished the sun cream from the glove box. He snatched it from her, shook the can, and with one hand covering his fringe, he sprayed his face and neck in one long burst. "What the bloody hell are you doing?" she said, fumbling for the door handle. She stumbled out, making a show of sucking in the fresh air. "You could have warned me."

He tossed the can back into the glove box, slammed it closed, and then climbed out of the car, rubbing the cream into his skin to cover the areas behind his ears and nape.

"Don't want to burn, do I?" he said. "You can use some if you want. We'll be out here all day, so you should really protect your skin."

"It's not my skin I'm worried about. It's my bloody lungs," she said.

"It's your mouth that worries me," he mumbled to himself, as he scanned the field before him. They had parked in a layby where a break in the hedge that surrounded the field provided access to farm vehicles. The tarmac road merged with the field, where the mud was hard and cracked, resembling elephant hide.

"What did you say?" Jewson said, moving around the car with purpose.

"Me?" he replied. "Oh, I was just saying that we should start over by that tree." He gauged her expression to see if she believed the lie, then continued. "Maybe we should split the field up into segments? Might be easier to deal with."

She stared at him; she had not believed his little lie. But with no evidence to go on, she reluctantly engaged with the new topic.

"It's not a big field. I say we walk the trail while it's still fresh, and then work backwards," she said. "The search team has covered a lot of it already. We should focus on the trail and the surrounding area."

"Yeah," he replied, conceding that, of the two, hers was the better idea. Yet he couldn't let her dictate terms. He was, after all, supposed to be in charge. "Yeah, if we work back towards the car, we'll stay motivated." He clapped his hands, pulled his rucksack from his car, and looped it over both shoulders. He hit the fob to lock the doors, and then, as if they were about to start a long hike, clapped once. "Let's get to it, shall we?"

She shook her head and rolled her eyes but joined him.

"I'll take the left of the trail, you take the right," she said. "We don't want to disturb any prints."

"I was thinking the same," he replied. Then he muttered to himself, "The further away from you I can be, the better."

They walked slowly, stopping on occasion to refind the trail of flattened crops, which after a few days, had already started to recover.

"Careful where you tread," she told him when he stepped too close to the trail.

"I'm minding every step," he replied, with as much positivity as he could muster.

"The last thing we want is for one of your size fives to smudge one of the Reebok prints."

"I'm a seven," he replied, unable to hide his indignation. "A seven and a half in trainers."

"Wow," she said. "Move over Arnold Schwarzenegger."

"Can I remind you that you threatened to report me for commenting on your size the other day?"

"It wasn't the comment on my size that bothered me," she replied, with a wry grin forming on her face. "It was the sexist comment."

"It was not a sexist comment."

"You alluded to me being weaker and scared of an intruder due to me being a female."

"I did not," he said, then stopped. They were halfway along the trail and had a long day ahead of them. "Look, ask anyone who knows me. I'm not like that. Any officer in the station will tell you I'm a nice guy."

"I did ask, as it happens," she replied. "And do you know what I was told, by more than one individual, I might add?"

"Go on."

"That you are a pathetic loser. You're a people pleaser, which means you try too hard."

"Who said that?"

"It doesn't matter who I spoke to," she said. "The fact is that you're stagnating. You're heading for the record as the longest-serving constable—"

"Detective constable," he corrected her.

"A constable is a constable," she said. "The detective part is not an elevation of rank."

"Coming from a PCSO, that's rich."

"Ah," she said, grinning. "How long have you been a constable? Five years?"

"Seven," he said proudly.

"Seven years?" she said, sounding shocked. "I might be a PCSO now, but in seven years, I'll be telling you what to do."

"Yeah right," he said, and started off again. "I shouldn't have to remind you that I'm leading this search. Not you, alright? I don't mind a bit of banter, but you won't dictate to me. You're with me to learn. You'll do well to remember that."

"I thought I was here because we work so well together," she replied, as she too started off on the far side of the flattened crops. "That's what MacAllister told me anyway. He said you spoke so highly of me that he was happy for me to spend more time in Major Crimes. He said it would do me good to gain some experience in other teams, so when the time comes for me to move up, which won't be long, I have an idea of what path to take."

"You in Major Crimes?" he scoffed. "Do me a favour. You haven't got what it takes."

"Oh really. And what does it take, then? I mean, you should know considering you've spent so long in the same team at the same rank."

He bit his tongue and picked up the pace.

"Come on then, Constable Cruz. What is it that you've got that I haven't?"

He stopped, spun around to face her, and saw the smug expression on her face. If he chose to voice the thoughts in his head, she would no doubt use it against him. He turned away, staring past her into the field.

"Ah, see. Nothing. I reckon I'd be a good fit. I can see myself with a cushy little number like yours."

He said nothing. He tried to block her irritating voice from his mind.

"There might even be a space opening up," he heard her say, the words barely registering as his eyes fell on a small patch of field where the crops weren't quite upright but weren't quite flattened either. It was as if, like those on the trail Lee Constantine had made, the affected crops were in the process of recovering. "Especially when I tell them about you touching my leg in the car."

He heard her but her words were insignificant. He strode forward across the trail and stopped before the area he had seen.

"Did you hear what I said?" she asked. "Have you any idea what MacAllister will say when I tell him—"

"Oh, shut up," he told her, then jabbed an index finger at the small patch of land. "This is why you wouldn't make it in Major Crimes."

"What?" she said, her smug tone replaced by one of concern. "What is it?"

"This is what we call a game changer," he told her, shaking his head in disgust. "And you walked right past it."

CHAPTER THIRTY-ONE

In the centre of the quarry, the huge, spider-like machine spewed various-sized aggregates into separate piles ready for lorries to load up and deliver to construction sites or roadworks.

To the left of the car park, where Ben and Gillespie sat on the rear bumper of Ben's car donning their boots, a yellow digger fitted with a hydraulic rock breaker was hard at work, kicking up clouds of dust that seemed to hang in the hot, still air.

"Christ, would you look at it?" Gillespie said. "Can you imagine it? Out in all weathers for a living? If it rains, you get wet. If it snows, you get cold."

"And if the sun shines, you get a tan?" Ben added.

"You get bloody sunstroke is what you get," Gillespie replied.

"Reminds me of harvest time," Ben added. "Without the crops."

"And the clouds of dust?"

"Have you ever seen a harvest?" Ben asked. "When it comes to dust, mate, this is nothing. Two or three combines working a field, the same again in tractors and trailers." He shook his head. "It's stunning."

"Stunning?" Gillespie said, stamping his boot on. "Sounds like the outer circle of hell."

Ben laughed and closed the boot lid as Mr Willis, the quarry manager, descended the steps from the upstairs office.

"What's in the inner circle?" Ben asked under his breath.

Gillespie gave it a moment to consider as Willis strode towards them with two visitor hard hats and hi-visibility vests.

"Celibacy," he said, which took Ben by surprise. "Celibacy and Cruz. I wouldn't want to spend a moment with either of them." He winked at Ben, then called out to their host. "Mr Willis, thanks for seeing us," he said, as he took one of the hats and vests. He extended an arm to Ben. "You'll remember Detective Inspector Savage."

"I do," Willis said. "Though I'm not quite sure what more you expect to find. You had the place closed down long enough. We've only just reopened. Damn crusher will be working day and night to catch up."

"Day and night?" Gillespie said. "I thought you only operated the noisy machinery during off-peak hours. That's what you said, wasn't it?"

"Well, we might have to break our own rules to catch up is all I'm saying."

"Actually, it's not what we'll find," Ben said. "Rather who."

"Sorry?"

"Paul Stoneman. One of your employees, I believe."

"Paul?" he said.

"That's right. We were led to believe he works here."

"He does," Willis replied and gestured with his chin at the heavy digger breaking rocks on the east face of the quarry. "S'him over there."

"Mind if we…" Ben said.

"More delays," Willis said.

"I'll be as brief as I can be," Ben told him.

"What do you want with him, anyways? He's a good lad is

Paul. Hard worker, and you'll know as well I do, they're not easy to find. Not these days. Kids rock up here and want the moon on a stick, they do. Never been told the word no, that's their problem."

"I just want to ask him a few questions," Ben said.

Willis eyed them both then reluctantly nodded, before starting off towards the machine.

"It'll be a set-up nonetheless," he said. "Place don't run on hot air, you know?"

"I imagine it doesn't," Ben said. "But then, a few questions with an employee is far better than being shut down, isn't it?"

"Sorry?"

"Malpractice," Gillespie said. "Or negligence. One of the two."

"Excuse me?"

"Well, how else would you explain how somebody gained access to the top of the quarry, fell in, and broke his neck?"

"What on earth? That's not the fault of the quarry—"

"Well, I'd pray it doesn't get picked up during the inquiry."

"What inquiry?"

"The inquiry into the death," Ben said. "Believe me, they will go into great detail to understand how it happened, and I didn't see a fence up there."

"Of course there's no fence. There's a hedge."

"Your hedge?" Ben asked.

"No, it's the farmers. He maintains it. Always has done, to my knowledge. If somebody fell into the pond, then it'll be him you want to talk to, not me."

"It's not me who wants to talk to you, Mr Willis," Ben said with as charming smile as he could find in his arsenal of defences. "But when the day comes, you should be ready for somebody to ask some questions. That's my advice, Mr Willis. You don't have to take it."

They closed in on the breaker and Willis held a hand up to keep them at a safe distance then waved his arms to gain the attention of the digger operator. Once the driver was looking his way, he ran a finger across his throat, a sign for him to cut the engine.

A few moments later, the great machine's engine chugged a slow death, then silenced.

"Ah," Ben said. "That's better. Can barely hear myself think."

Willis waved the operator over to them then turned and stared at Ben.

"If the day ever comes when I'm to be questioned, Inspector Savage, you can be sure I'll give a full account of your officers' actions while they were here."

"And what actions were they, Mr Willis?" Ben asked. But Willis simply eyed them both, then turned to address Stoneman.

"Everything alright, boss?" Stoneman called as he approached.

"These fellas want to ask you a few questions, Paul," he said, then grumbled beneath his breath. "I'll be in my office should you need me."

"Thank you, Mr Willis," Ben said, then produced his warrant card to present to Stoneman. "DI Savage. This is Sergeant Gillespie. Mind if we ask you a few questions?"

Stoneman was a stocky man in his late twenties. With a few days' growth on his face and eyes wrinkled from the sun, he was the type of man Ben was used to dealing with. A grafter. The type of man his father would have hired in a heartbeat. There was a look about grafters that his father had always favoured. He could tell from one look at a man if he was a grafter or not. And Paul Stoneman had the look.

But it wasn't just his look that Ben recognised or the way he carried himself. He recognised the man from somewhere.

"About?" he said.

Ben watched him for a sign of deceit in his eyes but found none. It was only when he turned and spat on the ground, that Ben placed him.

"I'm sure you can tell me," Ben said, and Stoneman nodded.

"Lee?"

"Unless there's something else you'd like to talk about."

Stoneman shook his head sadly.

"Hit us hard," he said. "Is there any news?"

"News of what?" Ben asked to which Stoneman shrugged.

"How he died, or... I don't know."

"We can come to that," Ben said softly. "I'd like to talk about Saturday night. You were with him at a party in Metheringham, weren't you?"

Stoneman nodded.

"Justin's place. Yeah, I was there. For a while anyway."

"What's for a while? An hour? Two?"

"I don't recall," Stoneman replied. "But I was home by eleven and sober enough to get myself a kebab from Nick the Greek's."

"In Metheringham?" Ben asked. "If we asked them, they'd confirm that, would they?"

"Should do. I'm there often enough."

"What about Lee? When did he leave, Paul?"

"I don't know. He was pretty hammered."

"Drunk?"

"More than drunk," Stoneman replied. "Couldn't understand a word he was saying."

"Was that a common occurrence?" Gillespie asked. "Like a drink, did he?"

"He didn't have it easy," Stoneman said. "His brother and that. You know about his brother, right?"

"We do," Ben said. "We've spoken to his parents."

"Are they alright? Must be bloody awful for them."

"Do you know them?" Ben asked.

"Yeah, I know them. Known Lee for years. His brother, too. You know how friends' parents become like second parents when you're a kid? That was them with me."

"Oh, so you grew up with Lee?"

"Well, not much grew up with, but our parents were close. We went to the same scout group, and I suppose we just stayed mates."

"I imagine you're feeling it right now, then," Ben said to which Stoneman nodded and wiped his eye, leaving a wet smear on his dusty skin. "So, I'll cut to the point. We need to establish what time Lee left the party on Saturday night."

"I told you, I don't know."

"But you knew he was inebriated?" Gillespie said. "And you just let him go? Is that what mates do?"

"I'm not his mother," Stoneman said then softened. "I wasn't his mother. He could get like that sometimes. We all can, can't we? I wouldn't expect my mates to hold my hand when I'd had too much."

"What was he drinking?" Ben asked. "To get in such a state, I mean."

"I have no idea. All I know is he was sitting on the floor in the hallway talking to Margot. They were getting pretty close–"

"Close?"

Stoneman eyed him.

"It was a party. People hook up at parties."

"But what about Vicky? What about their son?"

Stoneman held his hands up and opened his mouth to speak.

"I remember, you weren't his mother," Ben said, which seemed to silence him. "So, you didn't see him leave?"

"Nope," Stoneman replied, shaking his head and meeting Ben eye to eye. "And you didn't speak to him afterwards?"

"No, I didn't get a chance. I just wanted to get home, you know?"

"And the next day? The Sunday? You didn't call him?"

"I wasn't really in the mood for a chat," Stoneman said. "You know, late night and all that."

"Eleven o'clock is hardly a late night. I would have had you down as a man who can handle his drink."

"Listen, I work hard and I like my Sundays to kick back," he said. "My mate's just died. I'm trying to focus on my job. So if there's nothing else?" He pointed back to the digger.

"There is one more thing," Ben said. "What were you doing on Tuesday morning?"

"Sorry?"

"Tuesday morning," Ben said. "I saw you visit Vicky's house. What for?"

He stared at them both, his mouth ajar. Eventually, his head snapped too.

"Got a call from Mr Willis. He said the place was closed for a day or so," he said. "Went to see Lee, didn't I?"

"And that's when you found out, is it? That Lee had died?"

"S'right," he said, nodding.

"And how did you leave it? I notice you didn't go inside the house."

"No. No, one of you lot was there, asking questions and whatnot."

"So, what did you do?"

"Me? What could I do?" he said. "How would you feel if your best mate had just died?"

"Paul, I'm sorry, I know this must be painful, but I need to know," Ben said. "Did Lee know Andrew or Colin Major?"

"The Majors?" he said, his eyes widening. "Don't know. Not that I know of."

"And you have no reason to believe that anybody would want to harm Lee?"

Stoneman adjusted his feet and put his hands into his jean's pockets. "Why on earth would anyone want to hurt Lee?" he said, shaking his head. "He was the salt of the earth, that man. The salt of the earth, you hear me?"

"Loud and clear," Ben replied. "If we need to ask more questions–"

"I'll be here," Stoneman said. "Though I don't know what else to say other than..."

"Other than what?" Gillespie asked, and Stoneman gave the question some thought.

"Other than that you need to get to the bottom of this. If somebody did this to him," he said eventually, then paused on that thought.

"Go on," Ben said. "If somebody did this to him?"

"Then he'd be better off inside," Stoneman replied, his tone filled with bitter hatred. "Because if I get my hands on them, it'll be me who winds up in the nick."

He nodded a farewell then turned and made towards the digger.

"What do you make of him?" Gillespie asked.

"I think he has more to tell us," Ben said. "Trouble is, so does everyone in this bloody investigation."

CHAPTER THIRTY-TWO

"Get what you need?" a voice called out as Ben and Gillespie sat on the rear of his car to remove their boots.

"I got what I expected to get if that counts," Ben replied. "As for what I need, well, that's an entirely different story."

Willis came to a stop a few feet from them, his fingers tucked into his pockets so that his elbows swung freely. He was what Ben's father would call a man with idle hands, and idle hands belonged to the rich or the lazy.

"Listen, I spoke out of turn–"

"I'm used to it," Ben said, as he tied a shoelace. In contrast to Willis' boots, which were relatively new, Ben's shoes were so old and worn that they felt like part of him. They looked awful and he knew it. Freya had even bought him a new pair, but they didn't feel the same and they didn't suit him. He'd tried them a few times and despite the exuberant cost, he felt like a fraud wearing them.

"Do you foresee any more action here?" Willis asked.

"Action?" Gillespie said.

"You know what I mean. Am I going to have to shut the gates again? Can I line up the lorries?"

"You can line them up all you like," Ben told him. "I have absolutely no intention of coming back here if I can help it."

He stood, waited for Gillespie to move, and then slammed the boot lid closed.

"And Paul? Was he helpful?"

"You know, there's such a thing as asking too many questions," Ben said.

"I was just—"

"I know what you were doing. You were fishing for clues. How far have we got? Do we have anybody in mind? It's a guilty move. Did you know that? Do you know how many murderers have managed to worm their way into an investigation under the guise of being a helpful neighbour? Ever heard of Ian Huntley?"

"Whoa, I'm not a—"

"Or maybe you were worried that we're planning on arresting your employee."

"Are you?"

"We're not *planning* it," Ben said. "But I haven't ruled it out." He stepped over to Willis, noting the two-inch difference in height. He stuffed the high-viz vests inside the borrowed hard hats, then pressed them into Willis' chest. "I haven't ruled anybody out."

Willis held his stare, accepted the hard hats, and then stepped back to put some distance between them.

"Noted," he said. "Well, if you need anything—"

"I'll call," Ben said, and he turned back to his car, tugged open the door, and fell into the driver's seat.

A few moments later, Gillespie climbed in, and the entire car rocked on its suspension. He pulled his door closed, cleared his throat, and waited. But the wait proved to be longer than his intrigue could bear.

"Something on your mind, Ben?" he asked to which Ben said nothing. "Bit harsh on the fella, don't you think?"

"A bit harsh?"

"Aye. He was helping us out, Ben. He could have told us to go away and come back with a warrant."

"Are you standing up for him now, Jim? The last time you spoke to him, if I remember rightly, you didn't exactly send him home with a pat on the back for being a good citizen."

"Aye, but I didn't treat him like suspect number one."

"He is suspect number bloody one, Jim. He's in first place and he shares it with Paul Stoneman, Andrew Major, Colin Major, Barry Coleman, Margot Major, and even Vicky Fraser. That's the bloody issue. All we're doing is building a list of people who don't know what happened."

"One of them knows."

"It doesn't matter what they know, it's what we can prove they know," he said, then turned away to stare out of the window at the digger. For a moment, he thought he saw Stoneman staring back at him. "And right now, we can't prove a bloody thing. Message Chapman, will you? Ask her to set up one of those group calls. I need to speak to the team."

Gillespie pulled his phone from his pocket and Ben felt his chest loosen.

"Sorry, mate," he said.

"Eh?" Gillespie replied in a tone Ben had heard a hundred times or more from him. It was his way of saying *nay bother* without actually saying the words. Somehow the silent rendition had more punch.

Gillespie tucked his phone into his pocket and sat back.

"You forgot one," he said.

"Sorry?"

"You forgot one," Gillespie repeated. "Another first placer." Ben shook his head. "The host of the party itself. Greaves."

"Right, so all three Majors, Vicky Fraser, Paul Stoneman, Barry Coleman–"

"Willis?" Gillespie added.

"Yep, him too. This Greaves bloke," Ben said. "Bloody hell.

One of them must give something up soon. All we need to know is how Lee Constantine got from the party to the field. How hard can that be?"

"Have we checked doorbell footage?" Gillespie asked. "It was in that new estate. Bound to be one somewhere."

"I asked Nillson to check when she went."

"Yeah, well, that podium needs to be a big one, Ben," Gillespie replied. "Because if those people you just mentioned are telling the truth, we're going to have to start with the rest of the party guests."

"Jesus, do we know how many that is?"

"Nope, but we're about to find out," Gillespie replied, and he nodded at Ben's buzzing phone on the dashboard.

He reached forward, took a breath, and hit the green button to answer the call.

"Chapman?" he said.

"Oh, hi, Ben. I've got the team on the call."

"Everyone?"

"All but Cruz and Jewson. He's not picking up, but I sent him a message to call when he gets it."

"Alright," Ben said. "We're getting nowhere fast. Let's have an update from you all. With any luck, we might just have a fragment of something shiny to go after. Nillson, you might as well tell the team what you told me about Justin Greaves."

"Well, you should put whatever picture you have of debaucherous shenanigans in a rundown council estate to the back of your mind," she began. "Justin Greaves is not some low-life drug addict living in squalor. He's, on the surface at least, successful, clean-cut, and well-spoken.

"That doesn't mean he's not a low-life," Gold said.

"No, you're right. It doesn't," said Nillson. "But it does give him a certain amount of credibility."

"How so?" Gillespie asked. "Just because he washes behind his ears, doesn't mean he's not a lying toe rag."

"I think what Anna is trying to say, Jim, is that there's a difference between somebody whose life is embroiled in crime and a man who might dabble in the odd bit of class-A drugs here and there," Ben said. "Drug addicts and low-lifes rely on crime to survive. They go from crime to crime to feed their habits, and if they get caught, so what? What have they got to lose? At best they'll get a stint inside, be fed three times a day, and have a roof over their head. Someone like Justin Greaves, however, has significantly more to lose. He might try to squirm out of our hands, but when we corner him, as it sounds like Nillson and Anderson have, he'll have his priorities straight."

"Right, so we take what he says as gospel then, do we?" Gillespie said.

"Right now, we're not in a position to ascertain fact from fiction. I'll take whatever leads we get and run with them until we hit a dead end."

"Well, if you ask me," Nillson said, "Justin Greaves is a dead end."

"That's not what you told me when you left his house."

"I said we shouldn't cross him off," Nillson said. "But he's not our primary suspect, that's for sure. He confirmed that the Major brothers were at the party, but not for long. Probably long enough to deliver whatever had been ordered, and most likely to a number of people. However, we don't know that they supplied anything other than weed. We have no evidence of them being involved in LSD. "

"Agreed," Ben said. "As much as it pains me to say it. There was nothing on the inventory to suggest any links to LSD whatsoever."

"But he did say this," Nillson said. "Greaves thought Lee Constantine was drunk, but we know otherwise. According to Greaves, Lee was upset about something. He sat on the floor most of the time he was there. Margot Major went to speak with him. Shortly after that, he was gone. Greaves presumed he'd had enough to drink and had taken himself home."

"So, Margot Major was telling the truth?" Gold asked.

"She may have been telling the truth about speaking to him," Ben said. "But somebody must have seen him leave."

"Have we checked for doorbell cameras?" Gold asked. "Surely somebody has one in a new estate."

"It's a dead end," Nillson replied. "Greaves' is the first house you come to in the new estate. Anybody could have come and gone unnoticed."

"We seem to have an abundance of dead ends," Ben said. "We need to keep going. One of these leads will take us somewhere."

"I'm starting to think the party had nothing to do with it," Gillespie said. "Think about what I said earlier. We need to understand if the party was a key part of Lee Constantine's death. What if he was in trouble somehow, but it had nothing to do with the party? He goes to the party, leaves, and is picked up on his way home."

"If that's the case, then it could have been anybody who wasn't at the party," Ben said. "Somebody who held a grudge against him."

"Unless, of course, whoever those Reeboks belong to was at the party, but only for a short time," Anderson suggested. "Long enough to see him and know where he was."

"That's not a bad shout," Ben said. "But we need a link. We need a motive."

"We've got the link," Nillson said. "Coleman was in touch with the Major brothers. Lee was sitting with their sister. What if she spiked his drink? What if they were waiting down the road for him?"

"That's not a motive," Ben said. "But it is a theory we can work with—"

"Ben, sorry, but I've got Cruz on the other line," Chapman said. "Said he needs to speak to you."

"Can you patch him into this call somehow?" Ben asked.

"Hold tight," she replied. There was a brief silence, and then the line grew noisier as a breeze washed across Cruz's phone.

"Cruz, how's it going out there?" Ben asked. "Enjoying the sunshine?"

"I wouldn't say I'm enjoying it," Cruz replied. "But I've got a feeling we're going to be out here a lot longer than we anticipated."

CHAPTER THIRTY-THREE

"For crying out loud," Gillespie muttered to himself, but loud enough that Ben heard it.

They stared down at Cruz's morbid find, and the warm breeze tickled the tips of the crops. It was a stain on an otherwise beautiful scene.

"Alright, let's head back to the car. We need to preserve the scene," Ben said. "Cruz, have a uniformed officer positioned out on the lane, will you? Gillespie, find out who owns this field and give them the bad news."

"What bad news is that?" Gillespie asked. "That a woman's body has been found amongst their crops? I'm not sure they'll be too bothered."

"The bad news is that their field is now off-limits and will be for the foreseeable," Ben replied. "Cruz, what's the ETA on the medical examiner?"

"An hour from when I called him," he replied, then checked his watch. "So anytime now."

"And CSI?"

"They're here already," Gillespie said, then nodded with his chin at the two white vans parked at the entrance to the field not far from the Major brothers' house. The rear doors were open and Ben could see three people pulling on their white suits and boots. But before them, halfway across the field, were two other women. "Oh, Christ. And so is Nillson."

"You didn't think to call me sooner?" Ben asked, to which Cruz shuffled his feet a little.

"Well, you were busy. And I mean, it's not like I don't know who to call. Sorry, was that wrong?"

"No, not at all," Ben told him. "I'm just surprised, that's all. In a good way." He checked his watch, then clapped once. "Right, it's midday. And we have a lot to do."

"Think it's linked, Ben?" Gillespie asked.

He stared down at the hand protruding from the mud.

"That's not my major concern right now," he said quietly.

"Go on," Gillespie said, and Ben turned away from the find.

"Well, put it this way, we've found a hand in the soil. I'm just hoping the rest of her is still attached."

Gillespie's eye widened and he puffed his cheeks. "Hadn't thought of that."

"Yeah, well. Call me cynical, but the way things are going, nothing would surprise me right now."

"How's it going?" Nillson called out as she and Anderson approached. She jabbed a thumb over her shoulder. "I see you've called your girlfriend in, Jim. What's the matter, losing your stomach for dead bodies? Has she come to hold your hand?"

"For your information, it was Cruz who made the calls," Gillespie replied. "And anyway, why don't you take a look for yourself?"

With a sweep of his arm, he invited her to take a peek at the gruesome discovery.

"Oh, Jesus," she said, turning away.

"He won't help you," Gillespie replied.

"I wasn't expecting that," she said.

"So, what were you expecting?" Ben asked.

"I don't know. A body?" she said.

"Well, there's a bit of one," Gillespie replied.

"Yeah, I can see that. Makes you wonder what the rest of her is like, doesn't it?"

"If the rest of her is even here," Gillespie suggested.

"Well, it's been here a while," Nillson replied, dropping to a crouch to get a better view without disturbing the area. "Looks like a female."

"Nice one, Sherlock," Gillespie said. "Aside from Cruz, what other bloke do you know with fingers that slender?"

"Hey," Cruz said, while his new PCSO friend, Jewson, made no attempt to hide her amusement.

"Right, let's get to it," Ben said, clapping his hands. "Cruz, Jewson, out on the road. Gillespie—"

"Aye, aye," he said. "Get onto the farmer. I know."

"What about us?" Nillson asked. "Where do you want us?"

"Here," Ben told her. "This one's yours."

"Sorry?"

"I want you to manage the crime scene and the investigation."

"But you're the SIO—"

"I'm leading the investigation into Lee Constantine's death," he said. "We're two days in and we still can't be sure if he committed suicide or if there was any foul play. As for whatever this is, we have no evidence to suggest they are linked, and given that Lee Constantine is taking up so much of my time, I find myself in need of a pair of capable hands to manage it."

"Right," she said, clearly surprised.

"Liaise with Katy. Keep me informed. You know the drill. Check missing persons and call hospitals. See if you can get a head start on an ID, otherwise, it'll be a day or so until either Pip or Kate can check her DNA."

"Right," she said. "Leave it with me."

"Good. Use Chapman where you need to. She can span both investigations from the office. Cruz and Jewson are out on the road, but it would be good to replace them with more uniforms. All this activity is going to attract the media or worse."

"Worse?" Gillespie said.

"The public with their smartphones," Ben replied. "Once we have an ID, we'll know if the investigations are linked. Until then, we need to be pragmatic."

"Ah, come on, Ben. Lee Constantine was found a hundred metres away. There's pragmatism and then there's pragmatism."

"Alright," Ben said. "Imagine this is your daughter, or your wife, or your mum. Imagine if we assume her death was linked to another murder and, by doing so, wasted a week or two. Judging by the colour of her skin, we're already a week behind. We don't have a week or two to waste." He held an index finger up to accentuate his point. "We treat these as separate crimes until we know more. Understood?"

"Aye," Gillespie replied.

"Nillson?"

"Understood," she said, then peered into the distance where Katy Southwell and her colleagues were picking a path towards them.

"Keep me informed, Anna," Ben said, then nodded at Gillespie for them to leave. He had gone only two steps when a thought struck him, and he turned, walking backwards for a few paces. "How did you get on with Coleman? Did you break him?"

"Haven't had a chance, Ben," she replied. "Want me to get there after this?"

"No," he said. "No, we'll deal with it. You just focus on our mystery hand."

He turned again and ran the few steps to catch up with Gillespie, who said nothing. "She asked for it," Ben said, answering a question that had not been voiced. Gillespie looked his way. "You had the quarry, she's got this. I've got to be fair."

"Aye," he grumbled in reply. "Aye, I know. And she's welcome to it. I bloody hate digging up bodies. Like that last one in Haverholme." He shook his head at the memory. "Bloody awful business, you know? Can't help but wonder what their last moments were like."

"How's that different to finding a body above ground?" Ben asked.

"Ah, I don't know. It just is. For once, I agree with Anna on it. Bloody awful."

"Well, it's not like we have to wield the spades and shovels, is it?" Ben said, as he looked up and saw Katy and her team approaching. She carried a heavy bag on one shoulder and one end of a large crate in her other hand. At the other end of the crate was one of her colleagues, who also carried a large tuff box. The last of the threesome had their hands full with a large, cardboard box containing the stainless-steel steps they used to get close to the body whilst preserving the evidence. "Hope you've got shovels in one of those boxes," Ben called out.

"Shovels?" Kate said, and the threesome of investigators came to an abrupt stop as Ben and Gillespie reached them. But Ben didn't stop walking and Gillespie kept pace. He called over his shoulder to Katy, "Unless of course, you fancy digging with your hands. But knowing what goes into the soil, I wouldn't recommend it."

They left Southwell and her colleagues to make their own plans and pressed on. The sun was high in the sky and there was barely a cloud in sight to promise a few moments of shade.

"So, we're off to see Coleman then, are we?" Gillespie asked. "Do you think a man who sells appliances and white goods has air conditioning?"

Ben laughed and felt the vibration of his phone in his pocket. He pulled it out, shielded the screen from the light and saw Chapman's name flash up, so he directed the call to loudspeaker.

"Chapman," he said. "How cool is it in the office?"

She laughed. "A balmy twenty-one degrees," she replied

happily. "Listen, I didn't get the chance to talk to you before. Cruz's news kind of took precedence."

"Alright, well to give you an update, we're looking at a female. She's been there a few days. Doctor Saint will be able to tell us more, but be warned, I've left Nillson in charge and she'll need you to do a ring around for her."

"Noted," Chapman replied, and Ben imagined her neat handwriting as she recorded the task. No doubt by the time Nillson got around to calling her, Chapman would have all the answers she needed. "Listen, I've been looking into Barry Coleman. You know, Lee Constantine's boss?"

"Right, and what have you come up with?"

"Well, I don't know if it's linked or not, but something doesn't sit right with me."

Ben felt Gillespie's stare and they stopped to huddle around the phone.

"Go on," he said. "What have you found?"

"Well, it's his son. He's currently serving a five-year sentence in Maidstone."

"He's inside? What for?"

"Well, that's just it," she said. "Supplying class A drugs. He's a convicted drug dealer."

CHAPTER THIRTY-FOUR

"Wow," Southwell said. "He wasn't kidding when he said we'd need shovels, was he?"

They were an easy six metres from the find, from where they could see the offending hand jutting from the soil like a scene from a horror movie. Nillson studied Katy's face as she observed the scene.

"You do have them, don't you?" Anderson asked, to which Southwell simply grinned.

"They don't use shovels, Jenny," Nillson said. "They use hand trowels, and if memory serves, it's a long and laborious process."

"She's right," Southwell added. Then she turned to her team member who was holding the box of stainless-steel platforms. "Let's make a path from the far side up to where the crops have been flattened. That's the least likely area the killer would have taken." She turned to her other colleague and gestured at the large box. "Cordon the area off, Pat, will you? I want ten metres all the way around. We're going to need casts, trowels, sieves, and bags. Lots of bags."

Pat nodded, then immediately set to work, leaving Southwell free to assess the situation some more.

"What do you need from us?" Nillson asked.

"Water," she replied, without looking up. "And lots of it. How many of you lot were here?"

Nillson thought back to who had attended. "Cruz and Jewson, Ben and Jim, Jenny and me. Six."

"Quite the party," Southwell said. "I'm going to need your boot prints. Has anybody touched it?"

"Why the hell would we touch it?"

"I'll take that as a no, shall I?" Southwell said, and she watched as Pat took a few tentative steps across the platforms and crouched beside the hand. A few deft strokes with the trowel and more of the wrist was exposed. "Not too deep, Pat. Let's not get carried away."

Pat peered up at them but said nothing. In fact, in all the crime scenes at which Nillson had encountered the quiet investigator, never once had she heard Pat speak. There was speculation among the team that Pat was a rather feminine man. Although, Gillespie swore blind that Pat was a butch female. The argument had soon been quenched by Freya, who cited common decency as a reason not to make assumptions about other people's gender, stating that type of discussion could land them all in trouble with the woke police. It had been her way of saying, 'I agree with you, but we can't go there'.

But even though only Pat's eyes were visible beneath the hood, the mask, and the goggles, there was something in the way he or she moved that had captured Southwell's attention. Pat was fumbling with something and, after a few moments, held up a wristwatch in a gloved hand. Southwell strode across the platforms with purpose, taking the watch from her colleague.

"It's expensive," she called out to Nillson.

"Well, we can probably rule out a mugging gone wrong," Anderson said.

"Agreed," Nillson replied, but Southwell wasn't finished.

"There's an engraving," she said, then read aloud. "JW. Yours for all of time. JW."

"Is there a wedding ring?" Anderson asked, to which Pat simply shrugged.

"We'll let you know when we uncover the other hand," Southwell said.

But Pat had already begun tracing the arm beneath the top few inches of soil. Instead of the adjoining arm delving deep into the soil, it bent at the wrist, running almost horizontally a few inches beneath the dirt. Nillson watched as Pat, who held the wrist, glanced up at Southwell for approval. Southwell nodded and carefully brushed the soil away as Pat exposed the limb.

"Shallow grave," Southwell called out. "What does that tell you?"

"The dirt was too compact to dig?" Anderson suggested, to which Southwell shook her head.

"This field has been farmed for two thousand years or more," she said.

"Two thousand years? Maybe not that long," Anderson said, but Southwell maintained her stance.

"There's a reason the metal detectors are over here every summer," she said. "Roman coins, brooches, and God knows what else. This place is ploughed at least once a year, sometimes twice. No, this is loose. Whoever did this used their hands to dig."

"They didn't have a shovel or a spade," Nillson said, cottoning on to Southwell's idea. "It wasn't planned."

"It's likely she was killed here, too. Or somewhere close, at least," Southwell continued. "I've seen this before. If she had been killed elsewhere and brought here to get rid of the body, the killer would have brought something to dig with. This? This was unplanned."

With the arm exposed, Pat laid it on the ground and carefully felt beneath the soil for the torso, stopping after just a few seconds to give Southwell a discreet nod.

"Alright, let's expose what we can," Southwell said. "I want this soil sieved, so let's go easy on her."

Pat set to work, and Southwell stood then deftly made her way back across the platforms. She crouched beside their equipment and began rummaging through the boxes.

"Whatever happened here," she said, "she didn't go down without a fight."

"What makes you say that?" Nillson asked, and Southwell stopped rummaging to look up at her.

"Her fingernails," she said. "Whoever she was, she took care of herself. Nails like Freya, if you know what I mean? A woman who takes that amount of pride in her appearance doesn't leave the house with a broken fingernail, and if they do, it's filed and tidied." She shook her head. "No, my guess is that she put up a fight." She produced a box of evidence bags from the crate, followed shortly after by a reel of labels and a Sharpie pen. "There's no sign of much disturbance, other than the area you and your colleagues have trampled—"

"Hey come on."

"It's okay, we're used to it," Southwell said. "At least you had the sense not to disrupt the immediate area too badly. But my guess is that the missing fingernail will be in the dirt around here somewhere. When I find that, and when Pat has fully exposed the cadaver, we'll be in a position to start developing a narrative as to what happened here."

Nillson took a deep breath and then exhaled long and slow.

"An hour or more is the answer you're looking for," Southwell added.

"Sorry?"

"An hour or more. Before we expose the body."

"And the fingernail?"

"Much less," a voice called out from behind them, and they all turned to find the junior investigator, who had been busy cordoning off the area, driving a little, white plastic flag into the soil not five feet from where Pat was meticulously exposing more of the body.

"Well done, Sam," Southwell said, then grinned unabashedly at Nillson. "Sorry, I just enjoy being right."

"That explains your choice of man," Nillson replied.

It was strange to think of the great, hulk of a man she had come to both love and loathe being with somebody so intelligent, articulate, and coordinated. Gillespie was a man who, in Nillson's mind, lived on takeaways and beer, burped during meals, and most likely picked his nose. Yet his girlfriend was the opposite. As far as refinement was concerned, she was somewhere between Nillson, who cared little for her fingernails and kept grooming to a minimum, and Freya, who was meticulous about such things and rarely had a hair out of place.

"He's a project," Southwell said with a wry grin. "And I'm making progress with him. He just needs somebody to love him, that's all."

"Is that all?" Nillson said, appalled at the idea of being close to the man, let alone sleeping with him.

"He speaks highly of you, you know?"

"Who, Jim?"

Southwell nodded. "He likes strong people. He admires them."

"And weak people? I suppose he loathes them, does he?"

"I presume you're referring to Gabby Cruz?" Southwell replied. "No, actually. Jim has a deep affection for him. Unfortunately, Jim uses Gabby's weakness to distract from his own weaknesses."

"Which are?" Southwell opened her mouth to speak, but then tapped her nose with her index finger. "Let's just say his weaknesses are what I'm working on," she said, as Pat gave a slight cough to gain their attention, before holding something up for them to see.

Immediately, Southwell retraced her steps across the platform to retrieve the item.

"It's a receipt for fuel. It was in her jacket pocket," she called out. "Looks like she was at Metheringham petrol station last Friday."

"Cash or card?" Nillson asked.

"Card," Southwell replied, then dropped the receipt into a clear, plastic evidence bag. "You're looking at a Mrs J Willis."

"Willis?" Anderson said. "Why do I know that name?"

Nillson stepped over to the hedgerow a few metres from where the body had been buried. She peered through the gap that Lee Constantine had forced himself through.

"Because we've met her husband," she said. "He's owns the bloody quarry."

CHAPTER THIRTY-FIVE

The last time Ben had walked along Lincoln High Street, Freya had been by his side, and despite his requests, she had refused to shop at the lower end of the street, stating that the best shops were further up the hill. What she had really meant was she preferred to shop in the expensive shops alongside like-minded people. She was a snob, and nothing could change that. Ben far preferred the bottom end of the street, favouring the little shops that sold the same things as the top end, only for a far lower price.

Walking with Gillespie, however, was a far different experience. He stopped to peer into a charity shop window, leaving Ben talking to himself until he realised he was alone.

"Jim, we're not shopping, mate."

"Aye, I know, I know. But have you seen this? A bloody saxophone for thirty quid. Thirty quid?"

"I didn't know you could play the saxophone."

"Eh? I can't. But for thirty quid, I'd give it a damn good go." He admired the faded brass instrument for a few moments longer. "I always wanted to learn an instrument. Might give me something to do when Katy works late."

"Come on," Ben said, tugging him away from the shop. "I think you left it a bit late to become the next John Coltrane."

"You what? He was the fellow that played the big guy in Harry Potter, wasn't he? Is he a saxophone player as well? Jesus, some people are just talented, eh? I loved him in that old detective show."

"Yep, he's not short of talent," Ben replied. The urge to ridicule Gillespie's knowledge of all things art and culture was overshadowed by the fact that, had Freya not provided a subtle education over the past year, he too would have made the same mistake. "Here we go. Dick's Appliances."

He looked the shop up and down, noting the ageing signboard and the bright yellow cardboard stars on which somebody had scrawled in black marker *50% off*.

"Jesus, would you look at this?" Gillespie said, opening the door of one of the dishwashers on the pavement. "An entire dishwasher for eighty quid. Eighty quid?"

"Free delivery, too," a voice said, and they both looked up to find a man in the shop doorway. He was what Ben's father would have called thick-set, with shoulders like a rugby prop forward and a waist like that of a twenty-year-old boy. He removed his glasses and slid them into his breast pocket. "It's a good model, that one," he said. "Only had it in a few days."

"A few days?" Ben said, and he peered both ways along the pedestrian street. "Somebody just came and dropped it off, did they? Perhaps they were on the way to get some milk and thought they'd kill two birds with one stone."

"Ha," Coleman said, and as a true salesman, he elected not to rise to Ben's sarcasm. "We offer a collection service. Quite busy, as it happens."

"You must have a good team working for you," Ben said. "Good people are hard to find. I mean, anyone can drive a van, can't they? But trusting someone in your customers' homes. That's a different story altogether."

"Right," Coleman said, his head cocking to one side. "They are hard to find, as it happens."

"And this was collected a few days ago, was it?"

"S'right," he said, still clearly unsure of the men before him. "Only needed a new bearing. But you know what people are like these days. They don't want the hassle. People don't like to be pestered. They just want to be left alone, don't they? Absolutely nothing wrong with this now, and I'll put my name to that."

"Your name?" Ben said, and he glanced up at the fading sign written in an old-world gothic-style font. "You're Dick, are you?"

"Me? No. That was my old man. Took over from him, didn't I? Course, he's dead now, but people still remember him, you know? They still ask after him."

"Which makes you Barry Coleman, then," Ben said. "Is that right?"

The mention of his name added weight to his suspicion, and his eyes narrowed a little until Ben produced his warrant card, and he shook his head in dismay.

"Detective Inspector Savage," Ben said. "This is Sergeant Gillespie."

"There should be a law against that," Coleman said. "Thought you were here to buy something, didn't I? If you're not interested in anything, perhaps next time you'll get straight to the point. Save me going through my pitch."

"Oh, I'm interested," Gillespie said, checking with Ben, who shook his head. "Ah, maybe next time."

"I believe you spoke to two of our colleagues," Ben said. "Sergeant Nillson?"

Coleman studied them both for a moment, then gestured at the shop door.

"You'd better come inside. Don't want my customers to see me talking to you lot, do I? Hard enough to get them through the door as it is."

He held the door for them, peered along the street, then closed the door, and turned the sign to closed.

"Better be quick," he muttered. "Said all I had to say to the lass."

"In that case, I will get straight to the point," Ben said, gazing around at the dozens of white and silver machines on display, each with their price marked on a yellow, cardboard star. "Do the names Andrew Major and Colin Major mean anything to you?"

"Sorry?" he said, which Ben took to be an attempt at buying time to construct a more suitable reply. Ben said nothing and Coleman shrugged. "I don't think so, no."

"You've never met an Andrew Major?" Ben asked.

"Not to my recollection."

"And Colin Major?" Ben asked. "Name ring a bell, does it?"

It was clear by the look on his face that Coleman did indeed recognise the names but looks on faces provided scant argument for the Crown Prosecution Service.

He shook his head. "No. No bells ringing here. Should I know them?"

"Yes, actually," Ben replied. "Seeing as your number was in the call history of a mobile phone found in their house."

Again, Coleman shrugged those huge shoulders and shook his head.

"I get dozens of calls every day. Probably just a customer, or something. Happens all the time. People call up and make enquiries to see what their machine is worth, then–"

"And that same phone number was called from your phone," Ben replied, offering a smile of condolence. "We checked your statement."

"What? I don't know them. Maybe I called them back with a price or something–"

"Nine times?" Ben said.

"Maybe. It's not unheard of, you know?" he said, and he

flipped open an old ledger. "What're their names again? I'll see if I made a note."

Ben reached forward and closed the ledger, then let the weight of the front cover slam down.

"You also called them last month."

"I did?"

"And the month before," Ben said. "Regular as clockwork. I mean, it's possible they had several items to get rid of, isn't it? A fridge one month, a dishwasher the next. I suppose people often fancy an upgrade, don't they? Sergeant Gillespie is a prime example," Ben said, nodding at the big Scotsman who was perusing the wares. "He only bought a new dishwasher last year."

"Does this one come with a warranty?" Gillespie asked, peering inside yet another dishwasher near the door to the back office.

Coleman ignored the question and turned back to Ben.

"I don't know what to tell you," he said. "I don't know the names, and if their number has been dialled by my phone—"

"Every month," Ben added.

"Right. Every month. Then it has to be some mistake. Either that or they're suppliers of mine. What is it they do?"

"They grow cannabis," Ben said, and Coleman's face paled. "Which is an interesting line of work, isn't it? Do you have much call for cannabis, Barry?"

"Never touched drugs in my life," he spat.

"Good for you," Ben said. "But your son has, hasn't he?"

"Sorry?"

"Your son," Ben said. "The one in prison for supplying a class A drug. Bit of a coincidence, isn't it?"

"I don't...I don't know what you're talking about. I've nothing to do with them. What my boy does is his business. It's none of mine."

"Yeah well, you see, that's not really an alibi, is it?"

"An alibi? What do I need an alibi for? I ain't done owt," he said, glancing between Ben and Gillespie with fear in his eyes. Then his head snatched back to Gillespie, who was peering inside the back office. "Hey, that's private. You can't go in there."

Gillespie pulled his head out, his eyes wide. He nodded sideways at the office.

"Business going well, is it, Barry?" he said, and Ben gave Gillespie a questioning look. But Gillespie was too good at playing games with suspects to divulge a find immediately. Coleman took a step back, his chest rising and falling fast. "There must be twenty grand there," Gillespie continued. He reached into the office and then held up a large zip-up cooler bag, which he held open for Ben to see. "What is that, a month's takings? We're in the wrong game, Ben."

The meaning of the cash was not clear, and by rights, it could very well have been a month's takings for Coleman. But no businessman with twenty thousand pounds in cash or more ever wore a fearful look the way Coleman did.

"Barry Coleman," Ben said, catching Gillespie's attention to drag him away from appliance shopping. "I'm arresting you on suspicion of conspiracy to murder. You do not have to say anything. But it may harm your defence if you do not mention when questioned something that you later rely on in Court. Do you understand what I just said, Barry?"

Coleman shook his head in disbelief.

"I don't understand," he said, as Gillespie pulled his arms behind his back and fished a pair of handcuffs from his pocket. "Honestly, I haven't done anything. I don't know who they are. I don't understand."

"That makes three of us," Ben told him, as Gillespie led him towards the door. "Maybe we can work it out together, eh? At the station."

CHAPTER THIRTY-SIX

By the time a unit had arrived to cart Coleman off, he was a snivelling mess. It was late in the day, and Ben and Gillespie rode in silence, each of them lost in their own thoughts, developing their own theories, internalising. The air conditioning in Ben's car wasn't the best, but it was better than nothing. The cool breeze on Ben's feet was welcome, but his shirt still clung to his back, adding weight to his already darkened mood.

"You thinking what I'm thinking?" Gillespie asked.

"About buying a new car?" Ben said.

"Ah, tosh," Gillespie spat. "A new car is the last thing on your mind. I know that much."

"Right, well. Thanks for clearing that up, Jim. The next time I need somebody to interpret my thoughts, I'll know where to come."

"You're thinking of one of two things," Gillespie said. "Either the investigation, specifically Coleman, or..."

"Go on, you can say her name," Ben said.

"Ah, what's the point," Gillespie grumbled. "So, it's her, is it? She's the reason you're quiet?"

Ben rubbed the growth on his chin, then ruffled his hair, hoping to invigorate some desire for conversation.

"I don't know, mate. If I'm honest, my head is a mess. Lee Constantine probably wasn't even murdered. From what I can see, he fell into the pond, broke his neck, and died. If it wasn't for the bloody footprints, we'd have closed this off and handed it over for an enquiry to establish if it was suicide or an accident."

"But we do have the prints, Ben, aye? And if we hadn't had the prints, then we wouldn't have found the hand. So, what then? Another murder goes unrecorded? A killer walks free? A family has to go on not knowing if their loved one is missing or worse?"

"It's just a mess, Jim, that's all."

"Aye, I mean, yeah, we're lacking direction for sure. But we've made progress."

"Progress? Jim, all we know is that Lee Constantine was upset about something. He was hiding something. Something he'd done or somebody else was doing to him. We have no idea. What we can assume is that his state of mind was off-kilter. He went to a party. Why would you go to a party if you had something on your mind? Would you be in the mood for a party? I know I wouldn't. At around nine p.m., he took the drug. Now, we don't know if he did this willingly or if he was spiked. We know he sat on the floor talking to Margot Major. We know he was upset about something, so I can only assume it was related to whatever it was that Vicky Fraser wanted to tell us. Margot uses the bathroom and Lee vanishes. Nobody sees him. There's no doorbell footage, no cameras anywhere, and nobody saw a thing."

"Well, nobody is keen to admit they saw anything," Gillespie added. "They could be too frightened to speak up."

"Well, if that's the case, then we'll need to widen our questioning to all those who attended the party." He glanced across at Gillespie. "And we all know what a complete waste of time that'll be. The Major brothers did some kind of delivery service, so you can imagine how tight-lipped the guests would be."

"I think they're linked somehow," Gillespie said. "I mean, they sell drugs, for God's sake. Just because they have a little weed farm going, which by the way is small fry. They're not exactly competing with the big boys with that set-up." He shook his head. "No, these boys deal locally. They know their target audience and their target audience knows them. The question is, would the locals have reason to be afraid of a couple of local dealers?"

"It doesn't matter how big or small they are, Jim, they're obviously a force to be reckoned with. They have something to hide. Lee was found in a quarry near their house and their farm. They're in cahoots with Lee's boss about something. They're connected, I'll give you that. But how, I don't know."

"Maybe Lee knew something? Maybe he found something out or told somebody and they were after him?"

"You still think they waited up the road for him?"

"I think we need to speak to the brothers, Ben. What did they do when they left the party? Where did they go?"

"Right, and you think they're just going to tell us they waited for him?" Ben said. "Or maybe they went on to do more deliveries? Do you think that's their alibi?"

"I presume, given that Chapman hasn't called, that DI Wiltshire hasn't finished with them yet?"

"No," Ben said. "No, we'll have to wait our turn, I'm afraid."

"Okay, so we've established some kind of direction," Gillespie said. "They were after Lee. They delivered something to somebody at the party to give to him, and then waited for him to leave, spaced out of his brain with no idea where he was or who he was, probably."

"That's a theory, Jim. That's not a direction."

"Ah, that's where you're wrong," Gillespie said, and Ben took his eyes off the road to give him a hard stare. "With respect," he added. "What we've established is that Lee took the drug at the party. We've established that, despite whatever he had going on, somebody convinced him to go."

"So?"

"So, the party is a factor. A major factor," Gillespie said. "That's a direction. That's premeditated."

"You asked what I'm thinking," Ben said. "I'm thinking all of that. Everything we just said is on my mind, with the unwelcome addition of Freya."

"Ah, for God's sake. Get a grip man."

"Sorry?"

"Get a grip, Ben. Look at you," Gillespie said. "Every single officer in the station admires you. Did you know that? Every one of them. Not one person has a bad thing to say about you, and do you know why?"

"Because I've been at the station longer than most of them?"

"Tosh," Gillespie said. "It's because you're solid, man. You're a rock. You're infallible. Nothing vexes you. And then along comes Freya. She captures your heart and your mind, and now you're like a week-old balloon languishing on the floor. You're filled with the ideas and the knowledge, but you're letting the weight of the world keep you down."

"That's a terrible analogy."

"Aye, I know. I'm winging it. Just hear me out, will you?" he said. "Just let her go. Let her do what she needs to do, Ben. If she wants to go back to this Greg knobhead, then let her. There's nothing you're going to say that'll stop that happening. If she doesn't come back to work, then send her off with a bang. Pat her on the back and be a bloody mate to her."

"And if she does want to come back?" Ben said.

"You're not listening to me. Whatever she decides to do, just go with it. Think of it this way. She could probably retire right now. The force will give her a payout, early retirement. She's set for life. She could go off with Greg the Smeg if she likes. And if she does, then great. Private healthcare, a ready-made family, big house in the city. Wish her well and move on," Gillespie said. "But if she comes back to you, mate. If she comes back to you..."

"Then what?" Ben asked as they approached the station. He slowed and indicated, ready for a break in the traffic to turn in.

"Then you know she's mental," he replied with one of those Gillespie grins. "I'd stay well away if I were you. If she chooses you over her other options, she's obviously a nutjob."

Ben laughed as an oncoming car flashed to let them go, but two men were crossing the road, forcing Ben to wait a few moments. He pulled into the station yard, parked, and climbed out.

"Thanks, mate," he said to Gillespie. "I needed that."

"Ah, Ben. Listen, all I'm trying to say is that you can do this. You're Ben bloody Savage," Gillespie replied. "And anyway, you've got me by your side. If that doesn't fill you with confidence, I don't know what will."

He'd clearly designed the last statement to raise another smile, but something sat uneasily on Ben's mind. He glanced at the gates and the road beyond, then up at the door to the custody suite.

"Ben?" Gillespie said. "What's up? I mean, I know it wasn't funny, but—"

Ben strode across the yard, shoved open the door, and found DI Wiltshire speaking to Sergeant Priest.

"You bastard," he said, and Wiltshire turned to face him.

"I'm sorry?"

"What's wrong with you? I asked you to hold them here. I just saw them walking across the road."

"You must be referring to the Major brothers." Wiltshire shook his head sadly. "Had to bail them, Ben. Claiming the weed is all for personal use, and unless I can prove otherwise, I've got nothing to go on."

"I don't give a monkey about the weed, Chris. I'm running a murder investigation here, and they're mixed up in it."

"Oh, come on, Ben. Those two aren't murderers. I'd be

surprised if they had the balls to kill the greenfly on their bloody weed plants."

Ben turned away and took a few paces, rubbing his hair in frustration. He looked to Sergeant Priest but kept Wiltshire in his peripheral.

"Has my suspect arrived yet?"

"Barry Coleman," Priest said, then looked down at his computer. "Cell three. Processed and ready for questioning."

Wiltshire made no indication that he recognised the name, which meant that whatever resources he had working on the seized goods had yet to establish the owner of the phone number.

"Want him brought through?" Priest asked. "There's a duty solicitor knocking around somewhere if he needs one."

"No," Ben said. "Not yet. Not until I've got the Major brothers back in here. I want to speak to them first."

"I wouldn't do that if I were you," Wiltshire said. "I've got an entire team going through the seized goods and a few leads we're following up on. All being well, I'll have them back in custody on a possession with intent to supply charge."

"They're key players in my investigation, Chris."

"And key players in mine, too," Wiltshire replied. "Elections are coming up. The DCC wants a few positive outcomes to demonstrate his position on drugs in the county. What do I tell him if the two suspects I had lined for bust with a street value of more than two hundred grand are embroiled in a murder enquiry, for which they obviously played no part? Should I send him your way, Ben? Because I certainly won't be taking the flack for it."

Ben closed the gap between them, stopping just two feet from Wilshire and staring him in the eye.

"What do you have on them? So, what? They grow weed. That could be a year's supply for all you know. You know as well as I do that times are hard. People can't afford to feed their habits. What do you have on them to prove they have intent?"

"Nothing yet. But we will. They've made a mistake somewhere, and we'll find it."

"Interesting," Ben said. "How about this for a deal? Tomorrow morning, my team are going to their house to question them. We let them have a night at home. Right now, they have no idea that I want to speak to them, and you've bailed them, so they won't run."

"And what's in it for me?" Wiltshire asked. "Why would I risk my investigation?"

"Oh, it's not a risk," Ben said, confidently. "Because I know where they're washing their money."

"Of course you do," Wiltshire said mockingly. "You haven't got a clue about my investigation."

"Barry Coleman," Ben said, and he nodded to the door to the cells.

"You can prove that, can you?"

"I'm closer to proving that than you are to proving their intent to supply the drugs they grew," Ben said. He turned back to Gillespie near the door, who then unzipped the cooler bag from Dick's Appliances. Wiltshire's eyes widened and the confidence in his eyes faded. Ben jabbed his chest with an index finger. "If you want to speak to my suspect, then I want to speak to yours." He waited a few seconds for Wiltshire to process the information and come to a decision. "That settles it," Ben said. "I'm hitting the Major brothers first thing tomorrow morning." He nodded once to Wiltshire to cement his victory.

"When do I get to speak to Coleman?" Wiltshire asked.

"When I'm done with the Majors," Ben said. He turned to Gillespie. "Make the arrangements, Jim, will you? I want to hit them early, preferably before they've had a chance to roll their first joint of the day."

CHAPTER THIRTY-SEVEN

Gillespie concluded that NHS shifts worked differently from the police force. Arriving at nearly the same time as he had the previous day, he had expected to meet the same nurses. In fact, there was one he was particularly keen on meeting again. But there were different faces, different smiles, and varying degrees of welcome when he walked onto Freya's ward, and even that bemused look of nonrecognition from the nurse at the nurse's station, forcing him to explain who he was for her to grant him access to Freya's room. He knocked and opened the door, and she pushed herself into a seated position before fumbling for her glass of water to wet her lips.

"And which one are you?" she said. "Don't speak. Just sit."

He slid the visitor's chair across the room, then sat and folded one leg over the other. Freya cocked her head, moving her good ear forward. The room was silent for a while as she listened.

"So, he's still sulking, is he?" she said. "I must admit, I thought he'd give in by now."

"He's a bit distracted by the investigation," Gillespie told her. "There's been a few developments."

"Oh, goody. I could do with something to keep me going."

"Freya, listen, I'm not sure if I should be—"

"Divulging sensitive information to your DCI?" she said. "I am still your DCI, am I not? I haven't received a letter to tell me otherwise. Detective Superintendent Granger hasn't been for a few days, but I'm sure he would have said something if he wanted me to step aside."

"Well, aye. I mean—"

"The party," Freya said. "I believe you were tasked with finding out if the party was merely coincidental, or if it was a key factor in Lee Constantine's death. What did you find out?"

He sighed and found himself grinning. After all, the reason he had decided to visit her was to progress the investigation, but he hadn't imagined having to do so on her terms. It was no longer an experienced officer offering advice. The way she spoke, he was now beholden to her. She expected news. She was part of the investigation.

He arranged the facts in his mind, then puffed his cheeks, seeking a place to begin.

"We believe the party was a part of it," he began.

"Ah, thought so."

"The more I think about it, the more I believe you were right. If he was worried about something or had something on his mind significant enough for Vicky to be worried about it, then I don't see why he would attend a party, and I definitely can't see him taking acid willingly."

"So now you're looking at suspects," she said. "The weed farmers. They're your most likely."

"Aye, but growing weed is very different from making acid tabs. Besides, there was bugger all in the house that suggest they were up to that sort of thing."

She smiled with confidence.

"Gillespie, how many times have you arrested somebody for crimes relating to LSD? Before you were in Major Crimes, you had a stint in CID, am I right?"

"Aye."

"And I imagine that cannabis formed the majority of the drugs-related offences, followed closely by cocaine. You may have had some involvement in anything heavier, but not often."

"Aye, true."

"Let me ask you something. If you left this room and asked ten people to get you a bag of weed, how many bags of weed do you think you'd get?"

Gillespie gave it some thought, then shrugged.

"If I asked the right people, maybe five or six."

"Right. Five or six people would know somebody who knew someone, etc. Ask those same people to get you some LSD. How many do you think could?"

He shook his head.

"I'd be lucky to get one, I would think."

"Exactly. The only people who really know how to get the stuff are people heavily involved in drugs. Usually cannabis, too. Anyone involved in the heavier side of things has neither the time nor inclination for such a small market. The LSD came from the brothers. What were their names again?"

"Major," Gillespie said. "Andrew and Colin."

"Right. There you go. And were they at the party?"

"That's the thing," Gillespie said. "They were there for fifteen minutes."

"Enough time to see what they needed to sell and then get out," Freya said. "Somebody there requested it. Either that or they had someone on the inside to spike Lee Constantine. What's the theory?"

"That somebody spiked him, and the brothers were waiting up the road for him to stagger home."

"Cameras?"

Gillespie shook his head, though she wouldn't have known.

"Not a thing."

"Right, so you need two things. You need to know who was on

the inside to spike his drink, and what it was that Lee Constantine knew that made two, let's face it, minor weed farmers go to such lengths. Had he upset them? Did he know something?"

"Well, there's the small matter of a second body," Gillespie said, and the unbandaged parts of her face shifted into a new, surprised expression.

"A second body? Do we have an ID?"

"Ben left Nillson in charge," he said. "She seems to think it's Jenny Willis. She was about twenty yards from where Lee Constantine broke through the hedge and fell into the pond."

"Jenny Willis. Jenny Willis," she said to herself. "Willis? The name is familiar."

"Jacob Willis," he said. "He owns the quarry."

She fumbled for her glass again, then held up her hand, irritated when Gillespie tried to help. She sipped, thought, then sipped again.

"So, the obvious conclusion would be that the brothers had something to do with her death. Could Lee have known about it? It's a big jump to accuse two weed farmers of being murderers, but if they'd done it once, then they'd have enough to lose. They'd want to keep Lee quiet, whatever the cost."

"And as for somebody on the inside, as you put it, Lee spent the night talking to Margot Major. The sister of—"

"Andrew and Colin, yes," Freya said. "Yes, I think you're getting somewhere. It's time to put Lee Constantine's murder to one side and focus on this new body, Jenny Willis. You need a motive. Why would the brothers want to murder her? Could Lee have seen them do it? Was he in the area at all? Did he have reason to be near their house and witness something?"

"He was a delivery driver," Gillespie said. "He could have been anywhere."

"There will be records. His boss will have routes for him," Freya said, and Gillespie heard that same passionate enthusiasm she demonstrated in the incident room. Whatever damage the fire had done to her ear and face, it hadn't made a mark on her ability.

"That's the other thing," he said. "Among the goods seized from the Major brothers' house was a mobile phone. A burner with one number in the call history."

"Go on," she said, intrigued.

"Barry Coleman. Lee's boss," she said, and she shook her head as if she was agitated that the piece of information did not fit the theory she was developing. "Ben and I paid him a visit earlier today."

"Did you arrest him?"

"We did, aye. We only went to speak to him, but..."

"But you found proof of his guilt. Ben wouldn't commit without being sure. He might have the emotional intelligence of a pubescent boy, but he's not stupid."

"I found a large amount of cash in his back office," Gillespie said. "It's not been counted, but it's twenty grand or more. Has to be."

"And the business?'

"He buys and repairs white goods. Washing machines, dishwashers, that sort of thing."

"And he had twenty grand in his back office? Even businesses with a large cash turnover don't keep that kind of money on the premises. Not unless they're happy to be robbed of it." She turned her head away as if she had the power of sight and could stare at a blank area on the wall. "He's washing the money for the Major brothers," she said.

"Aye, we thought the same."

"The question is, why?" she told him. "Why would a man who owns a crummy old appliance repair shop wash money for two young weed farmers?"

"Ben doesn't want him interviewed until we've brought the brothers in for questioning."

"And when is that?"

"In the morning," Gillespie said. "I've got the team all lined up to hit them while they're still in bed."

"Good. I'd have done the same. You want the brothers to give you a lead. You want them to tell you how they know this Coleman fellow. Otherwise, you're no better off than you were, and you might as well have interviewed him in his shop. No, he needs to be scared. Ben did the right thing. But mark my words, Gillespie. You need to understand why the brothers would have killed Jenny Willis, and why Bary Coleman would help them. Do that, then report back."

"Eh?"

"Don't give me that," she said. "I'm in this now. You said Ben is struggling, did you not?"

"Well, aye, but—"

"So, help him," she said. "He knows the answers. He knows what he has to do. Help him realise it." She reached out and groped for his hand, then squeezed hard. "Make him realise he doesn't need me, Gillespie."

CHAPTER THIRTY-EIGHT

If Ben had stayed in the family farming business, he might have felt pleased to see such a glorious morning sky. The low humidity meant that the crops would be sold at their maximum value. Harvest was a joyous occasion, and often he would help his father and his brothers. It was a time when the surrounding farms all came together, helping where help was needed. The days were long, but it wasn't work. Not really. In police terms, it was akin to spending a year investigating, questioning, and developing solid accounts that the CPS could not question and then purging society of the criminals in one fell swoop.

But policing wasn't like that, especially in Major Crimes. It was an endless cycle of death and lies, until either somebody broke, or the decision-makers withdrew resources. A farmer could adapt to challenges. A farmer could call upon his neighbours to complete a harvest before the onset of rain. He could build additional grain stores should the logistic chain break, or he could wait if the moisture levels were too high, in the hope that a few more days might bring in an extra ten or twenty per cent.

But Ben had no such avenues in which to manoeuvre. He had processes that had to be followed. He had the risk of charges being dropped should a rule be broken. But most of all, his challenges lay within people. People for whom there was no greater good, and all actions served only one purpose – self-preservation. People would do anything to help themselves or to avoid prison.

The fields around the Major brothers' house were similar to his father's. To the untrained eye, the fenland farms were much of a muchness. Even those who could see the differences could see the similarities – the pride a farmer took in his crop lines, the maintenance of the surrounding and often unfarmable lands in which landowners accepted government grants for the planting of wildflowers, or the development of wildlife ponds.

From where Ben parked, a couple of hundred metres from the house, he could almost read the history of the Major house. It was in a central location with fields to the east and west. A hundred years ago, it would have been considered a large farm. But the land had clearly been sold to one of the giant nearby operators and the house had retained a few acres, perhaps to lift the sale price.

Either way, the house no longer enjoyed the pride a farmer would take. It was a stain on the otherwise idyllic landscape – decrepit, stained with moss and damp, and fit for tearing down. Somewhere, very likely close by, a farmer would be turning in his grave at the state of his old house.

In his rear-view mirror, Ben saw movement and found Gillespie's old Volvo trundling along the track, followed closely by two transporters – vans with secure cells for the removal and transportation of prisoners, often referred to as meat wagons. He had requested two, one for each of the brothers. When the door was kicked in and the brothers were taken into custody, he planned to keep them from conferring for as long as possible within the confines of the law.

Ben had parked a hundred meters from the house, and as Gillespie and the transporters approached, he raised a hand through his open window to wave them forward, then followed on foot. By the time he had caught up with them, half a dozen uniformed officers had climbed from the van, one of whom carried the ram, and Gillespie was stretching as if he had climbed from his pit only minutes before.

"Ah, I love waking people up," he said, stretching his neck in search of a gratifying click.

"Really?" Ben asked.

"No, I was kidding. It's going to take all I can not to find a spare bed and get in it."

"Late night, was it?"

"Ah, Kate came round after work. I did us a wee dinner."

"Oh? What did you cook?"

"Meatballs," he said proudly. "She's not exactly a girl who craves all that fancy muck. I could probably do her a Pot Noodle and she'd still want to jump my bones."

"Well," Ben said, "didn't take long for you to lower the tone, did it?" Sergeant Macallister caught his eye, and Ben was grateful for the distraction.

"Ready when you are," he said, reassuringly efficient.

"Right," Ben said, and he clapped his hands once to gain the team's attention. It was only after he had clapped that he recognised the technique as one of Freya's, which then forced him to recollect himself before briefing the officers. "A few days ago, Colin and Andrew Major were arrested on suspicion of possession and intent to supply a class B drug. The house was searched, items were seized, and they were subsequently taken away. Now, we have reason to believe they are involved in a murder inquiry. This is entirely separate. When the suspects are in custody and locked in the transporters, Sergeant Gillespie will be leading the search. I want this done with fresh eyes. If you were involved in the search earlier this week, then I want you to forget what you did and what you saw. This is new. Do not forego searching a cupboard because you did it a few days ago. Do not leave a single item unturned."

"What is it we're looking for?" Macallister asked.

"Weapons," Ben replied. "Drugs, specifically LSD."

"LSD? Does anyone even do that anymore?" one officer murmured.

"Apparently so," Ben said. "In case you do not know, LSD tabs are sold to the consumer in tiny squares of paper soaked in the drug. We're talking pieces of paper an eighth of an inch square. These tiny tabs, as they are known, are torn from larger sheets, perhaps A6 or A7 size pieces of paper. They usually have some kind of design on them, a yellow smiley face, or a purple star, which means the sheets that will have a repetitive pattern of some kind. But let's not let our ignorance stand in the way. I want every piece of paper in that house collected. If they're making the stuff themselves, then there's no guarantee they've gone to such lengths. We could be looking for a plain piece of paper for all we know."

"You mentioned weapons," MacAlister said. "Can we narrow that down?"

"No," Ben said. "Not yet anyway. When we've got them in custody, and the search is underway, I'll be attending the autopsy. I'll call Sergeant Gillespie if the pathologist is able to give us a clue. Are we ready?"

The team nodded as one and the officer with the ram held it up. Ben gave him the nod.

Ben pointed to three of the officers. "You three take the rear. The rest of us will enter through the front," Ben said. "And one last thing." The team were keen to get going, but there was something very important to convey. "No brutality."

"I can assure you—" Macallister started.

"I know," Ben said, cutting him off. "Your officers are highly professional. But we've all been there. We've all felt the pump of adrenalin, and we've all been on the receiving end of somebody who not only has just been woken up but could be facing a significant prison sentence. If we give these two an excuse, they'll walk.

Not just from two murders, I might add. But from the drug offences, too. I'm not having that on my conscience."

"Right you are," Macallister said, then addressed his team. "You heard the man."

They walked in single file, then the three officers split off to cover the rear. Radios were turned down low, and on Ben's approval, MacAllister gave the signal for the ram to be used. So rotten was the old wood that it took a single hit to burst open, and in moments, the morning was alive with shouts and cries of officers, following protocol by warning the homeowners of their presence. Ben waited at the front of the house. There was often so much commotion during a raid that he felt in the way. Besides, as Freya had taught him, there was much more enjoyment in being the first to greet a handcuffed suspect as he was led through his own front door.

"Good morning," he said, with a smile, when the first of them was shoved into the front garden in his boxer shorts. He stumbled and fell at Ben's feet, rolled, and stared up at him. "And which one are you, then?"

"No comment," he replied, his bare chest rising and falling with fear and adrenalin.

Ben dropped to a crouch beside him to read the tattoos on his chest. A line of writing ran from one shoulder to the next, and what Ben could only describe as a scene from hell sat beneath it on his right pectoral.

Moments later, the next brother was dragged through the door. He tried to cling to the doorframe with his bare feet, but a hard tug broke his resolve, and he dropped down beside his brother.

Ben needed no way of identifying one from the other. Not yet anyway. So, he addressed them collectively.

"Colin Major and Andrew Major. You are under arrest on suspicion of murder. You do not have to say anything. But it may harm your defence if you do not mention when questioned something that you later rely on in court. Do you understand?"

Neither said a word, so Ben looked up at MacAllister.

"Take them away, Sergeant," he said. It was only when the pair were on their feet that Ben addressed them again. "You do know that no comment only works in the movies, don't you?" The officer leading them allowed them to stop and turned them to face Ben. He strode over and stood before them. "I suggest you say goodbye to each other now. It'll be a long time before you speak again."

"Guv?" an officer said from the front door. But Ben remained focused on the brothers, searching for something in one of their eyes to tell him he was right.

"What is it?" he replied, the brothers leering at him.

"It's Sergeant Gillespie," the officer replied. "He's found something. He thinks you'll want to see it."

"What is it?" Ben said again, hoping the answer would invoke some kind of reaction from the brothers.

The officer leaned into the house and called up the stairs. "Sarge. Guv's busy. He wants to know what it is?"

Suddenly, an upstairs window opened, and Gillespie leaned out waving a piece of paper in the air.

"Got it," he said and grinned at the brothers.

"LSD?" Ben asked, to which Gillespie shook his head.

"No, it's even better than that, Ben," he said. "This here...is a motive."

CHAPTER THIRTY-NINE

As arranged, Nillson met Ben at the hospital entrance. As usual, she was punctual, and as usual, she walked with purpose. She was one of those people who wore a permanent scowl. To strangers, she must have been quite intimidating, but to those who knew her, she was just no-nonsense Nillson. Her face rarely brightened unless she was witnessing Freya tear Gillespie to shreds in the incident room. Those moments, she savoured.

But the one thing that was different about her that morning, that Ben took a few moments to recognise, was her attire. She was never scruffy or improperly dressed, but today, she had taken smart to a new level. It was as if she had raided Freya's wardrobe, stolen a loose, white blouse, and trouser suit, and picked up a pair of her heeled boots on her way out.

"Morning," Ben said, leaning against the building with a take-away coffee in his hand.

"I'm going to be honest with you, Ben. I'm not looking forward to this."

He shoved off the wall as she drew near and held the door for her.

"Thought dead bodies would be right up your street," he said. "You've never had a problem before."

"Dead bodies I can deal with. What I can't deal with is a certain Welsh pathologist who irritates the bloody hell out of me."

She marched on until Ben stopped her.

"Wait a minute," he said. "Look, let's get a coffee and make a plan. She can be difficult to deal with, but honestly, she knows her stuff. What we can't do is get her back up. That's not going to help us at all." He nodded at the little coffee shop near the entrance. Nillson considered it.

"No," she said, then continued walking. "The more I think about it, the worse it'll be. Let's get it over with."

"Over to you," he said. "It's your murder."

Two women drinking coffee both stopped and stared at him, mouths open. It was enough to bring a wry smile to Nillson's face and ease the mood.

"How did you get on at the Major house?" she asked, clearly a little more at ease.

"Not bad. They're in custody. We'll be interviewing them when we're done here."

"The clock is ticking, Ben. Shouldn't we start the preliminary questioning to get the ball rolling?"

"No," he said. "No, I think we've got enough to get an extension, and by proxy, Coleman too."

"Sounds big," she said, hungry for something to work with.

"Well, let's just say that Gillespie found something that potentially connects them to Jacob Willis."

They turned into the pathology corridor and felt the heat from the glazed walls almost immediately.

"Come on, Ben. Stop teasing," she said.

"Alright," he replied. "I'll tell you what we've got. But you have to promise me that you're not going to fall into any of Pip's traps. She'll try to corner you. She'll pick up on everything you say, believe me. She slaughters me every time I come here. You just have to rise above it, alright?" They came to a stop and Ben waited with his finger poised over the button. "Alright?"

"Okay, okay. I won't let her get to me," Nillson replied. "What did you get?"

"A piece of paper," Ben said, enjoying the tease.

"Paper? LSD? You got a full sheet of acid? Ben, that's great—"

"Not LSD I'm afraid. It's just regular A4 paper."

Nillson's eyes narrowed.

"I tell you what, if you don't tell me, I'm going to make a scene. That little lunatic behind these doors will not know what hit her."

"It's a letter to the brothers," he said. "A letter from Jacob Willis. He wants to build a road from the quarry, around the edge of the field, and out onto the road beside the house."

"The Major house? Why would he want to do that?"

"They can't expand the quarry and transport the material out of the main gate. Too many lorries or something. The council have denied them permission. But they'll grant it if they provide access via another route."

"So? How is that a connection?"

"They denied him," Ben said. "They said no and now we understand why. Their entire operation would be at risk."

"I still don't see the connection. How does that link the brothers to Jenny Willis' death?"

"It wasn't the only letter. Looks like things turned nasty."

"So, they went after the man's wife? That doesn't make sense?"

"Doesn't it? What if the wife went round to have a word and, just as Cruz and Jewson did, got an eyeful of what they shouldn't ought to?"

"That's a huge leap. We need more than that."

"I agree," he said. "You do need more than that."

They heard the sound of shuffling feet from behind the doors. And they readied themselves to greet Pip.

"Now then," she said when she opened the door. "My best customers." Immediately, Nillson entered, forcing Pip to stand to one side. Ben remained where he was, savouring the look of horror on her face. "Come in, why don't you?"

"Morning, Pip," Ben said. "And for the record, it's not like we're responsible for anybody's death. We just find them. But it's nice to know we're your favourite customers."

"I said best," she said. "Not favourite."

She nodded to Ben to enter and scowled at Nillson who was already preparing the necessary PPE from the cupboards.

"So, who's your favourite?" Ben asked, hoping to break the obvious tension between the two women. "And what do we have to do to earn that accolade?"

"George Larson," she replied.

"Larson?" Ben said, as he caught a cellophane-wrapped gown Nillson had tossed him. "Why do I know that name?" He racked his brain to put a face to the name. "Doesn't he work out of Mablethorpe?"

"Used to," she replied. "They closed the station down. Incorporated it with Skegness and Boston. Some sort of cost-saving exercise, I suppose. He's covering the Wolds now. Works out of a station near Horncastle."

"A change of scenery is as good as a rest," Ben said. "And what is it about George that I lack?"

"I don't know," she replied thoughtfully. "He's a gentle old soul. Reminds me of my old grandpa. Maybe that's it."

"Are we going to waste the morning reminiscing?" Nillson asked. "Or are we going to deal with a murder investigation?"

They both turned to Nillson, who was dressed in full PPE, and stood with her hands on her hips impatiently.

"Someone's keen," Pip muttered, then shoved open the heavy, insulated door that led into the chilled room. "Come through when you're ready, Ben."

Nillson followed her through, leaving Ben to dress in peace.

He struggled with the gown cord, remembering that Freya often had to help him. By the time he pushed through into the morgue, Nillson and Pip were studying the cadaver.

"Here he is," Pip said. "The boss man, come to make sure no corners are cut."

"Come on then, Pip. What are we looking at here?" he replied, pulling the mask down to inhibit the smell. Pip carefully removed the blue sheet to reveal the Y-shaped incision she had already made, with the two arms of the Y stretching down from beneath each ear, meeting on the victim's breastplate, where a single cut reached down to her navel.

"We'll start with the ID, shall we?" Pip replied. "The lab has already got back to me with confirmation. You're looking at Jennifer Jane Willis. Forty-nine years old. Ex-smoker, judging by her lungs, but was still a heavy drinker. There's no sign of anything else right now, but of course, we'll know more once the toxicology report comes in."

Of all the bodies Ben had seen lying on Pip's bench, he concluded that those in the early stages of decomposition, of which Jenny Willis was included, were by far the hardest to deal with. He was always surprised at the condition of the cavities Pip had made. They were still vivid and pink, compared to the flesh that had already begun putrification and had taken on a greenish tinge.

"No broken bones that I can find," Pip continued. "However, she didn't die without putting up a fight."

"Katy Southwell said the same thing," Nillson added and crouched to study the hand which, from the difference in colour, was clearly the limb that had been exposed.

"She was right," Pip said. "Broken nails, grazes on her elbows and knees, and..." She raised the victim's right arm. "Some slight bruising here, which suggests she held her arms up to protect herself."

"Somebody really went at her, then?" Ben asked.

"If you ask me," Pip continued, "she was on her knees with her arms held above her head, while the attacker rained blows down on her."

"Weapon?" Ben said, and Pip moved the victim's hair from her face to reveal a large gash in her temple. "Jesus. They didn't hold back, did they?"

"They most certainly did not," Pip replied, her strong Welsh accent turning the statement into song. "From the debris in the wound and the grazed skin, I'm leaning towards a large rock. I suppose you want to know when, do you?"

"It would be helpful," he replied, to which she, bravely, took a deep breath.

"I've examined the contents of the stomach. She ate, I'll give her that much. Spinach, salmon, and what I think is quinoa. Either that or bulgar wheat. Whatever it is, it's a healthy meal, and given the condition of her bowel and colon, she took care of herself."

"You said she was a drinker," Ben said. "Heavy?"

"More than many, but I'd put her as a woman who enjoyed a glass or two of wine with her dinner. Maybe the occasional gin and tonic."

"So, not the sort to neck a bottle of cheap white wine to blur reality, then?" Nillson asked.

"No," Pip replied. "No, this woman had taste. She had class. You can see by her nails."

"Like Freya's?" Nillson said to which Pip agreed.

"She took care of herself," she said. "Anyway, given the early stage of putrification, the contents of her stomach, and the condition of her head wound, I would say she's been dead for a week. Not much more."

"A week?" Ben said. "She looks like she's been in the ground for months."

"If she's been in the ground for months," Pip replied. "She

would have been much harder to remove from the ground in one piece."

The image turned Bens's stomach and he looked up at Nillson, who remained totally unfazed.

"Putrification," Pip continued, announcing the word as if she were at the head of a classroom about to give a talk on decomposition, "ordinarily begins after around seven to ten days." She leaned on the bench, her face not twelve inches from the rotting corpse, and she lowered her voice to a grave tenor. "However. It's hot, is it not? Hotter than usual. Hot enough to speed up that process significantly. Six to seven days is my estimation. No more, and certainly no less."

"Six to seven days? So, sometime last week. Last Tuesday or Wednesday?"

Pip nodded gravely. "Now," she said, shoving off the bench, "what baffles me is where she was found. Katy tells me she found a fingernail close to the body. That right, is it?"

"It is," Nillson said. "We're quite sure the struggle occurred close to where she was buried."

"Hence the shallow grave," Pip added, then turned and led them over to the bench that ran along the side wall, on which was a clear, plastic crate, not unlike those which had been used to seize the Major brother's possessions. "Now, you might be asking, what was a woman who clearly took care of herself and her appearance doing out in a field?"

"We might have the answer to that," Ben said.

"Oh?" Pip replied and paused with her hand on the crate lid.

"Her husband owns the quarry. It's a family business," Ben said. "There's some correspondence between them and a couple of brothers who own one of the only nearby houses. As far as we can make out, to expand the quarry, they need another access road."

"And the brothers denied the request, did they?"

"They did," Ben replied. "I can't go into details, but let's just say that both the quarry owners and the brother's businesses were affected. Stop the road being built, and the quarry hits a limit to what can be extracted. Build the road and the brothers' business goes down the pan."

"So, you think she was out there talking to these brothers, do you?"

"Something like that," Ben said, as Pip opened the crate and pulled out a clear plastic bag containing a pair of high-heeled shoes. Louboutin stilettos?"

Both Nillson and Pip stared at him with expressions of surprise and disbelief.

"What?" he said, then pointed at the shoes. "It's the red soles. Louboutin, aren't they?"

"You seem to be adequately informed on women's high heels, Ben", Nillson said.

"When your ex..." he began, then corrected himself. "When you spend enough time with Freya, you soon get to learn these things."

"The question is," Pip said, shaking her head to continue with her train of thought. "What was she doing in a field wearing a pair of Louboutin heels?"

CHAPTER FORTY

"What are you doing here?" Gillespie said when he looked up to find Anderson in the doorway of the bedroom he was searching. The contents of the wardrobe had been piled in a corner of the room, as were the contents of an old chest of drawers, behind which he had found a pile of letters, both opened and unopened.

He was sitting on the carpet, leaning against the radiator. To his right was the pile of papers he had found, and to his left were those he had examined.

"Anna said I should come to give you a hand while she's at the hospital with Ben," Anderson replied. "Looks like you're busy."

"Aye," Gillespie said. "Pull up a seat, why don't you?"

She peered around the room in disgust, and to be fair, she had a point. The bed sheets were dirty even by his own poor standards. The carpet hadn't been vacuumed for some time, and there were more used cups and glasses on the furniture than he had in his entire house.

"I'll just crouch," she said, dropping down beside him. "What are we looking for, anyway?"

"Well, put it this way," he replied. "I wouldn't lick any of the sheets of paper, if I were you."

"Sorry?"

"LSD," he replied. "We're trying to link the brothers to Lee Constantine's murder. So far, we're failing. We can link them to the quarry, and therefore Jenny Willis, but not to Lee."

"What if they're not connected? What if it's a–"

"Don't say it," he said, holding his hand up. "Whatever you do, don't say the C-word." He set the letter down to his side. "Look, if we're going to have these wee bastards, then we need more. We know they were at the party. We know they're mixed up in drugs, so it makes sense that they supplied the LSD that Pip found in Lee Constantine's system."

"Right. But just because they may have supplied it, it doesn't mean there's more here. It also doesn't mean they meant for Lee to take it," she said. "They went to a party to supply drugs. We used to get this in London all the time. The host would know somebody who knew somebody else. He or she would make a list of what people wanted. The dealer would turn up, make the deal, then leave."

"Aye, I know how a drug deal works, thanks," he said. "You spoke to the host, didn't you?"

"Justin Greaves," she said, nodding. "Yeah, he pretty much said the same thing. Everything but the list, anyway. Maybe they turned up and sold what they could."

"Was anybody else on LSD?" Gillespie asked. "I mean, you don't buy a single acid tab, do you? It comes on a sheet. The dealer would buy a sheet, split it into tabs, and then sell them individually. So, we're looking for the sheet."

"Right, and you expect to find a sheet with one tab missing, do you?"

"I don't know what I expect to find," he said. "But in lieu of any camera footage, any Reebok trainers, and any witnesses, it's our best chance of proving they had something to do with it." He rested his head against the radiator. "Of course, it would help if we knew why they wanted to hurt him."

"Jenny Willis?" she said. "What if he saw them do it?"

"Ah," he replied. "Now that's where things get a little interesting." He held up the paperwork to his left. "Letters from the firm that owns the quarry, addressed to the owners of this house."

"The brothers?"

"Right. The quarry needs to build a road. The only way out is either through this property or across the farmer's field."

"The farmer won't give up his field. Not for a road to be built. No chance."

"Exactly. Which is why there are more than a dozen letters from the quarry, offering increasing amounts of money, all of which were turned down by the brothers."

"And then Jenny Willis is found in the field by the quarry," Anderson said. "Well, there's a link there, but it's not exactly robust, is it?"

"Aye, I know. But we're getting somewhere. We've got motives," he said. "She's been in that ground for days. Weeks, maybe? Lee Constantine died last weekend. What if he saw the Major brothers kill her, or bury her, or something, and they went after him?"

"By spiking him with acid? Wouldn't it be easier to just run him over, or hit him over the head or something?"

"Could be," he agreed. "But Lee Constantine called in sick last Wednesday and that was the last time he was there. If he was scared, or hiding, he wouldn't have left his house."

"But he went to the party? That doesn't make sense."

"No," he said. "No, it doesn't. Hence why I'm sitting here reading through all this garbage trying to make a connection. Somebody convinced him to go to that party. Somebody needed him to go to that party, so they could put that tab in his drink, so they could be there when he left the party. Waiting. And they did that for a reason. They had a reason for doing that. They had a reason to hurt him. A reason to stop him talking or to take revenge. I don't know."

"You sound like Freya," Anderson said.

"Eh? Behave."

"You do," she said. "You're passionate."

"You think she's passionate?"

"About this kind of stuff, yeah. As it happens, I do."

"Well, I suppose there are worse people to sound like. Cruz, for one. Whining wee bastard, he is."

"Ah, he's alright," Anderson said. "He means well. And he's actually pretty switched on. Just a little naive. Freya has a lot of time for him, so she must see something in him. She's not exactly one to waste her time, is she?"

"Sounds to me like you've a wee crush, eh?" he told her. "If you and the boss were blokes, I'd call that a bromance. I'm not actually sure what the female equivalent is."

"Just admiration," she replied, her voice carrying more than a hint of sadness. She smiled, then picked up a handful of the papers.

"Something you want to tell me, Jenny?" Gillespie asked.

She tossed the first sheet of paper onto the pile to Gillespie's left and stared at the second for a moment.

"No," she said. "No, I just—"

She paused, sniffed, cleared her throat, then blinked a few times.

"Just what, Jenny?" he said. "You okay, mate?"

"I just think you're a good team, that's all. It seems like you all have your place here."

"Well, aye. And I hope you included yourself in that."

She hesitated, bunched her lips like a teenager stifling tears, and then took a deep breath. But before she could speak, a voice sang out from the hallway downstairs.

"What the bloody hell is this?"

The voice was female and agitated.

Anderson looked at Gillespie, a puzzled expression forming on her brow.

Immediately, they both rose to their feet and rushed to the top of the stairs, as the woman began yelling at the uniformed officers who had stayed to conduct the search.

"Get out. You've no right to be here," she screamed. "You've been through all this." Gillespie took the first few steps down and bent to peer into the living room. Then she stared back at him. "Where are my brothers?"

"Margot," he said, and slowly descended the stairs, nodding to the uniformed officers for them to leave him to it. "What brings you here? You're going to have to leave, I'm afraid."

"It's my brothers' house. I'm not going anywhere. Bloody hell, they've only been out a day. What's the matter, couldn't leave them alone?"

"Margot, I'm not going to ask you again. What are you doing here?"

"What do you think I'm doing?" she said, and she pointed to a plastic tray filled with cleaning products and rags. "I've come to fix the mess you lot made last time."

"I'm afraid that's not going to happen," Gillespie said. "Not today, at any rate."

"Where are they?" she spat.

"In custody, Margot. Where else do you think they would be?"

"You can't do that. They were bailed. You can't nick them again. Not for the same thing."

"Well, it's a good job we've something else to talk to them about, eh?"

"Oh, yeah? Like what?"

"Murder, Margot," he said. "Murder."

"What? No. Not that Lee fella? I told you about that. I told you they had nothing to do with it."

"Well, actually you didn't," Gillespie said, as Anderson moved slowly down the stairs to cover the front door. "In fact, Inspector Savage and I spent an entire hour with you. An hour, Margot. And in all that time, you never once mentioned that your brothers were at the party. Not once. Doesn't that strike you as odd, Anderson?"

"It does, Sarge, yeah," Anderson replied.

Gillespie nodded and he watched as Margot's confidence waned.

"I think we need a wee chat, Margot."

"We chatted. I told you everything I know."

"We need a wee chat, and what you tell me, Margot, will determine whether or not you leave this house under your own steam, or if we carry you out, handcuffed, and bang you up with your brothers."

"Bang me up? What for? I've not done owt, have I?"

"Well, that's just it. I don't know," he said. "You see, what we do when we have an investigation like this, and by that, I mean, an investigation in which nobody is willing to point the finger, for one reason or another, what we do, Margot, is build theories. Do you want to know what my theory is?"

"Theory? What's that, another word for conjecture?"

"Not really. Think of it more as a hypothesis based on the little amount of evidence that we do have, which we then work with to either eliminate the theory or add substance to it," Gillespie said. "Your brothers were at the party. They went there, sold their weed, and then buggered off. But it wasn't just weed they were supplying, was it? Oh no. No, there was something else in there, wasn't there?"

"I have no idea, what you're talking about."

"Margot, we know your brothers were there selling drugs. We know how long they were there, what time they arrived, and we've got it all in a written statement. I'm not looking to put any more drug charges on them. I couldn't care less what drugs they do or sell. They clearly haven't a brain cell left between them if they think they're going to get away with it, alright? So, you don't have to plead ignorance. It's pointless, and if I'm honest, it's not going to help your cause."

"My cause?"

"Aye, your cause. See, who did they know at the party? Who were they close to, who could have slipped a wee acid tab into Lee's drink? Eh? Think of anyone, Margot? Somebody who spent the night talking to him?"

"What? He was drunk. He was upset."

"Aye, he was upset, but as for being drunk, I think we both know that's not entirely true, eh?"

"Well, whatever. He was upset," she said. "So, this is your theory, is it? You think my brothers gave me acid to spike his drink? Why would they do that?"

"Well, you can't say I haven't given you ample opportunity to tell me, Margot. So how about we have this chat down at the station, eh?" He gave Anderson the nod. "Nick her and call some transport for her."

"You can't do that," Margot said. "I just helped the bloke. He was upset. He could barely speak a word."

Gillespie held up his hand to halt Anderson, who was reaching for a pair of handcuffs from the pouch on her belt.

"Well, he can't speak at all now, can he?" Gillespie said, shaking his head. "He's dead. Your scumbag brothers are looking at prison, regardless, Margot. But you? You've got a chance here. You've got an opportunity to do the right thing here." Her quivering lip belied her confidence. "What's it going to be, Margot? Are you going to help me quash this theory of mine?" he said. "Or are you going to prove me right?"

CHAPTER FORTY-ONE

Ben burst through the incident room doors with purpose. Even the squealing hinges failed to rise above his dogged determination. Chapman glanced up, her fingers frozen over her keyboard, and her eyes darted from Ben to Nillson, who followed far more casually and took her seat.

"Chapman, group call. Get them all on the phone in ten minutes, please," Ben said, snatching up the whiteboard marker. He started by adding Jenny Willis to the board, then sought a way to link her to the other names. But the investigation was all over the place. The space he found for her lacked prominence, so he snatched up the rag and wiped the entire board clean.

"You alright, Ben?" Nillson asked. "Not giving up, are you?"

"Not giving up," he said, as he removed all traces of the previous notes. "Just starting over. We're looking at this all wrong."

"Is there a right way?"

"There is," he replied. "And I'm going to find it."

He began by drawing a horizontal line across the top of the board, marking an X in the centre, which he noted with *21:00 LC takes LSD.* He then went on to make a series of other key times. *20:00 LC and PS arrive at party. 22:00 - 03:00 LC dies.*

He then added a second timeline beneath the first, dividing the line into segments, which he annotated with days of the week running from ten days prior, ten days being the maximum date that Jenny Willis could have died. He circled the Wednesday, noting that LC called in to work sick. He circled the Saturday, noting the party.

"You might want to put a ring around the Sunday before the party," Nillson called out, and he turned to face her, dragging his mind from the whirlwind of thoughts and ideas. "We found a receipt for petrol in Jenny Willis' pocket, so I requested the footage." She turned her laptop for him to see. "This is her."

"What petrol station?"

"Meg," she replied.

"Metheringham?" he said. "So she was in the area, filling up with fuel. What did she do after that? Did she go to the quarry?"

"Hard to say," Nillson replied. "It's not exactly a metropolis with cameras everywhere."

"Which way did she turn when she left the petrol station? Did she go out onto the main road, or did she turn left into the village?"

"Give me a minute," she replied, and Ben returned to his board. He circled the previous Sunday, noting Jenny Willis at the petrol station, then, on the left-hand side of the large space beneath the timelines, he wrote Lee Constantine's name along with the known information:

Fell/Pushed. Broken Neck.

Twenty-five years old.

Partner – Vicky Fraser.

Six-week-old baby.

Driver for Dick's Appliances.

He stepped back to gain a broader view, then leaned in again, adding one more line to Lee Constantine's column. He hesitated, deeming the addition subjective, or unevidenced, but wrote it anyway.

Troubled.

On the right-hand side of the board, he wrote Jenny Willis' name and added the information gleaned on her beneath:

Blunt Force Trauma. Rock?

Fifty-one years old.

Husband – Jacob Willis.

No children.

Director at husband's quarry.

Stilettos.

"We need more on Jenny Willis," Ben said.

"We also need to speak to her husband," Nillson replied, and Ben winced at the prospect of not only talking to the man again but having to relay the bad news.

"I'm well aware, cheers," he replied.

"Plus, we have Barry Coleman in custody," she added. "He'll need to be charged or bailed today."

"I know," he said, as politely as he could.

"And then there's our green-fingered friends," she continued.

"I know," he said, a little sharper than he perhaps should have. "I know what we have," he said, softly this time. "I'm doing what I can, alright? I just need to get my head around this."

In the centre of the board, beneath the timelines and between the victims' names, he wrote Party, beneath which he added the known attendees.

Justin Greaves.

Colin Major.

Andrew Major.

Margot Major.

Paul Stoneman.

"How are we doing on that call, Chapman?" he asked.

"Ready when you are," she replied. "I just need to dial them in."

"Where are they all, anyway?"

"Cruz is with his new girlfriend in the field," Chapman said, and Ben looked quizzically at her.

"That's my doing," Nillson added. "I asked them to broaden the search."

"Why?"

"Well, we've two bodies within fifty metres of each other. Who's to say there isn't more?"

"I hope there isn't," he said. "I'm running out of space on my whiteboard."

She smiled back at him, and Chapman continued.

"Gold has gone to Vicky Fraser's house to see if she's calmed down."

"Right, if she's playing at being the grieving girlfriend, I want some support sent. It's been days now and we're getting nowhere."

"Gillespie and Anderson are at the Major house," Chapman continued. She knew better than to comment on an instruction, whether she agreed with upsetting a grieving girlfriend or not.

"Right, well they should be done soon," Ben said, then nodded. "Get them on the line."

While he waited, he made the known connections on the board with dotted lines. Paul Stoneman to the quarry. The Major brothers to Dick's Appliances.

"We're ready," Chapman announced, and then set the call onto loudspeaker before opening her notepad and clicking her pen open.

"Everyone here?" Ben asked.

"Aye," Gillespie said, the only discernable confirmation among a handful of "Yep," as well as Gold's, "I am."

"Good," Ben said, collecting his thoughts. "So, here's the working hypothesis. There's an ongoing battle between the Major brothers and the quarry. I believe that last Sunday, Jenny Willis paid the brothers a visit. It's likely that if she went to the property, then she could have discovered their little illegal enterprise. She was wearing heels. Expensive heels, at that. If they found her snooping around their polytunnels, then she could have run. They could have given chase and caught up with her. It's possible that she ran towards the quarry, knowing that somebody would be there. Her husband, maybe? But they got to her before she crossed the field and things took an unexpected turn. Cause of death, according to Pip, was blunt force trauma, and she thinks the weapon was a rock. So, I need somebody to contact Katy Southwell. I don't suppose they analysed every rock they found, but you never know."

"We can have a look," Cruz said. "We're here now, and the crime scene has been closed down. We can have a look round, if you like."

"Good. Yes, do it," Ben said, then remembered his manners. "Thank you. So that's our first challenge. We need to link the brothers to Jenny Willis' murder. When we're done here, Nillson and I will be questioning the brothers, and subsequently Barry Coleman. What I need is some leverage. Gillespie, Anderson, what have you got?"

"Nothing that links them to Jenny Willis' murder," Gillespie replied. "Except for the letters regarding the access road. There are dozens of them, Ben. It's been going on for months."

"Anything else?"

"Well, I've Margot Major in a pair of handcuffs. Would that do?"

"In handcuffs?"

"We don't want to know about your sex life, Gillespie," Nillson called out, grinning from ear to ear.

"Very funny," Gillespie replied. "She turned up to clean her brothers' house. Though, I will say this. She's not exactly dressed for housework."

"Oh, yeah. Trust you to notice that," Nillson added. "What's she wearing?"

"Hey, come on. I'm a happy man," he replied. "Besides, it's not what she's wearing. It's more what she's not wearing, if you know what I mean."

"No, I don't know what you mean," Nillson said. "Describe her outfit."

"Alright, alright," Ben said. "I'm not interested in what she is or isn't wearing. I want to know what she had to say."

"Ah well," Gillepsie said. "Started mouthing off. You know? The usual abuse. She didn't exactly tread new ground."

"But she was on the defensive, was she?"

"Without a doubt," Gillespie said.

"Right, hold that thought," Ben said before the new line of rhetoric strayed off the path in his mind. "So, we have reason to believe that Jenny was killed last Sunday. We've got her on CCTV in Meg petrol station–"

"From there, she heads into the village," Nillson said, nodding at the footage on her laptop. "She turns left out of the station. If she was going to the quarry, she would have turned right and used the main road."

"Okay," Ben said, nodding more out of politeness than understanding. "Let's get somebody on the ground out there. Somebody on Metheringham High Street must have a doorbell camera. I want to build a picture of where she went and who she saw."

"She could have been going to see Margot Major," Gold said. "She lives in the village, and if her brothers aren't playing ball, then perhaps she had an idea to enlist Margot's help."

"Not a bad thought," Ben mused. "Gillespie and Anderson, can you ask her if Jenny Willis paid her a visit?"

"Shouldn't we wait until we've got her in custody and we've read her rights?"

"Ordinarily, yes," Ben replied. "But we've got three in custody right now, and I haven't spoken to one of them. I don't want any more. Not just yet. Ask the question, will you?"

"Aye," Gillespie replied. "She's in the back of a car out front. Anderson's just popped out for a wee word."

"Good," Ben said. "Chapman, talk to Sergeant Priest, will you? See if he can free up a couple of PCSOs to walk the streets. I want every house with a doorbell camera and every business with CCTV listed."

"Righto," Chapman replied.

"Which leads me to Lee Constantine," Ben said. "And this is where it gets interesting."

"Interesting or just plain baffling?" Gillespie asked, and Ben felt a pang of surrender forming. Had Freya been there, she could see a way through the facts. It was a skill that Ben had once but in recent days seems to have mislaid.

"I'm sticking with interesting," Ben said. "I'll save *baffling* for when my theory is proved wrong."

CHAPTER FORTY-TWO

Pressing on before the clouds descended and fogged the bigger picture, Ben took a deep breath.

"Lee Constantine called into work on Wednesday morning to say he wouldn't be in and he never showed up again. What does that tell us?"

He stared at Nillson and hoped that she, or at least somebody, would make a suggestion. But nobody did.

"It means," Ben continued, "that if the reason Lee called in sick had anything to do with whatever it was that worried him, then it clearly didn't worry him on Monday or Tuesday." He waited for somebody to add some thoughts, but his mind was bursting with ideas he just had to lay on the table. "I think whatever happened to Lee that caused him to be upset or worried happened on Tuesday evening or Wednesday morning. Given that he called in early on Wednesday, I would imagine it was Tuesday night." He let that theory settle for a moment. If any of the team had an argument against it, they would voice their opinions soon. But nobody did. "Gold, if Vicky Fraser doesn't let you in, I want you to let Chapman know. She's had time to come to terms with Lee's death. It's about time she answered some questions."

Gold's inhale rasped over the speaker.

"Alright," she said. "I'm just outside the house now, ready to go in."

"Well, just remember. What was Lee doing on Tuesday evening? Why was he upset? And lastly, who invited him to the party? How did that conversation go? Was he reluctant to go? Was whoever it was persuasive? This is the level of information we need to fill in these gaps, Jackie."

"I think I can answer that last one," Chapman said, and she rifled through some papers to find what she was looking for. "This is Lee's phone statement. The network provider sent it through. There's not much activity at all. Seems he wasn't much of a talker," she began. "But there are quite a few text messages. All of them to Vicky."

"Did they send the transcripts?" he asked, to which she nodded.

"Photos."

"Of the baby, I'll bet," Gold added. "If he was at work, then she would be sending him pictures whenever the baby did something like smile or something. It's natural, isn't it?"

"That does make sense," Chapman said. "His responses were short and sweet. A few Xs here and there. Some love heart emojis. But nothing of substance. In fact, that's how most of their chats went."

"What about Saturday?" Ben asked.

"Well, he didn't work on Saturdays," Chapman said. "He was probably at home, so there was no need for her to text him."

"I know, but did anybody else?"

She scanned through the statement and then made a show of cross-checking the phone numbers.

"There's a few from Paul Stoneman," she said while she read. "I'll see you there, then? Eightish?"

"That's them arranging to meet at the party," Ben said. "Anything else?"

"Nothing that looks like Paul was pressuring him to go," she replied. "But there is one from Barry Coleman earlier in the day." She looked up from the statement. "Well?"

"Well?"

"That's all it says," Chapman replied. "One word."

"I suppose that's him asking if Lee will be at work the following Monday?" Nillson suggested.

"Could be," Ben replied. "Either way, it's a nice segue. So, let's say that Lee witnessed, saw, heard, found, whatever it was on Tuesday evening. We know, as much as we can, that Jenny Willis was murdered on the Sunday before. So, he couldn't have seen the murder take place, which means that it's something else." He stared at the whiteboard. The answer was in there somewhere and verbalising his thoughts had done little to bring the truth to light. "What else do we know about Lee Constantine?" he asked the team loudly, so they all heard him in their various locations. "He broke his neck, he was twenty-five, he had a small child with Vicky Fraser, he worked for Barry Coleman, who in turn is in cahoots somehow with the Major brothers."

"What about his brother?" Nillson suggested.

"His brother?"

"Yeah, he died a few years back," Nillson added, checking her notes. "Five years ago. Overdosed on ecstasy."

"Overdosed on ecstasy," Ben said aloud, but to himself. "Alright. Alright, how about this? How about if the Major brothers were responsible for his brother's death? How about if Lee had found this out somehow? How about if he found this out and..." He stopped, the train of thought running dry even as he uttered the words.

"I get you," Gillespie said to Ben's relief. "What if he wasn't upset about something? What if he was planning something? Paul Stoneman is his best mate. He could have heard about the access road argument and mentioned it to Lee in passing. I mean, that could have been harmless, right? It's just chit-chat. But if

Lee knew, or thought, that the Major brothers were involved in his brother's death, he'd be pretty bloody annoyed, would he not?"

"Annoyed?" Nillson said. "He'd be out for blood."

"Okay, okay," Ben said before the two most senior of his officers began ridiculing each other. "That doesn't explain why he called in sick on the Wednesday morning."

"Not directly," Gillespie said. "But let's say Lee knew about the whole access road affair and wanted to stitch the brothers up."

"What, so he killed Jenny Willis to frame the Majors?" Nillson scoffed. "Behave, Jim. All he would have had to do was grass them up for growing weed. It takes a lot for the average person to commit murder. It takes huge emotions, huge frustration, desperation."

"Nillson's right," Ben said. "That's just bordering insanity. We might only have theories to work with, but let's not enter the realms of absurdity. Not yet, at any rate." He sighed and sat back on the desk, where Freya often sat. "So, there we are. That's what we need to prove. We need evidence to support that the brothers had the means, motive, and opportunity to murder Jenny Willis. We have a motive, of sorts. She went to the house and discovered the weed farm. It's down to Gillespie and me to understand their movements on Sunday, which, with any luck, will give us the means and opportunity. When we can prove that the Majors killed Jenny Willis, then we need to be in a position to link Lee Constantine's murder to Jenny's. Gold, you know what to do. Gillespie, what news from Anderson?"

"I'm here, Ben," Anderson said, her voice slightly distant for a moment until she moved closer to Gillespie's phone. "According to Margot, she's never heard of a Jenny Willis."

"Do we believe her?" Ben asked.

"Right now, I wouldn't even ask her for the time and expect the right answer."

"Thanks anyway," Ben replied.

"Are we bringing her in?" Gillespie asked. "She's been in the back of the car for an hour now."

"Can you question her there?" Ben asked. "We've got nothing on her to make an arrest except suspicion, and even that is based on conjecture."

"She's ready to talk," Anderson said. "I think Sergeant Gillespie made quite the impression on her."

"You mean he terrified her into submission?"

"I wouldn't say that" she replied, and Ben could hear the smile in her voice. "I think he just articulated the potential outcomes in a way that made her see sense."

"Aye and being locked up in a car in the sweltering heat helped," Gillespie added.

"For God's sake, get her out," Ben said. "I want to know what time exactly she attended the party. What time her brothers were there, and what time exactly Lee Constantine decided to up and leave."

"If you're trying to connect her to the spiking of Lee's drink, Ben, I think I can put that one to bed."

"Oh, great. Is this the first line of my theory about to crumble?"

"She arrived at the party around eight-thirty," Gillespie said. "Lee was already there, but her brothers must have already been, as she didn't see them all night."

"Right, so basically she's saying that her brothers couldn't have passed her something to spike Lee's drink with?"

"That's about the size of it."

"Well, as lovely as Margot is, I'm not about to take her word for it," Ben said. "Can she evidence this, somehow?"

"She can," Gillespie said.

"She can?"

"Aye," he replied. "She claims to have stopped in the Co-op on the way to the party to buy some wine. She was wearing a red and orange summer dress, and she had a wee chat with the fellow behind the counter."

"Brilliant," Ben said. "Well, let's get this claim proved. Gold, can you stop into the Co-op when you're done? If it wasn't Margot who spiked his drink, then we'll need to speak to somebody else, and if we have to expand our investigation into the list of other guests, then this will be a very long process."

CHAPTER FORTY-THREE

"The Major brothers?" Ben said, leaning into the custody suite.

Sergeant Priest, a stout and diligent Yorkshireman with rosy cheeks and a warm heart that concealed the iron rod he produced during moments of escalation, looked up from his computer.

"Andrew Major in interview room one. Colin Major in room two," he replied.

"Duty solicitors?"

"All present and correct," Priest replied.

"Thanks, Sarge," Ben said, then headed back into the corridor where Nillson was waiting. "Room one. Andrew Major."

"Is he the older one or the younger one?"

He stopped at the door and stared back at her, shaking his head.

"I haven't a clue," he said and shoved through into the interview room.

Andrew Major was a rough-looking young man. Not hard. But rough. Rough like he hadn't washed his clothes for a month. Rough like he could have planted his weed plants in the grime behind his ears. He was just one of those people that his father often commented on. 'Looks like he could do with a good bath,' he would say. On appearances, he looked like the type of young man who couldn't fight his way out of a paper bag, but if one of his dirty fingernails drew blood in a scrap, you'd be straight down the hospital asking for a tetanus jab.

Nillson hit the button to initiate the recording while Ben was preparing his notes, and once the long buzz that announced the beginning of the recording and avoided the loss of data by speaking too early had ceased, Ben cleared his throat and announced the time and date, then introduced himself and Nillson. He waited for the duty solicitor to follow suit.

"Pierce Garrott," he said. "Duty solicitor."

There was little need to educate Major with the process, seeing as he had likely sat in the same chair the previous day while talking to DI Wiltshire.

"Andrew Major," he mumbled.

"Andrew Major," Ben began, glad to have the formalities out of the way. "You have been arrested on suspicion of conspiracy to murder. Before we begin, is there anything you would like to say?"

"Actually, yeah," Major said, looking a little bemused. "What's the conspiracy bit mean?"

"It means they suspect you had some involvement in the murder, but do not have sufficient evidence to place the blame on you in its entirety," Garrott said. He was young for a duty solicitor, no doubt gaining experience before delving into visions of grandeur in a much more lucrative role within a private law firm. He wore a smart suit, he was well-groomed, and his eyes were keen and confident.

"It means we believe you to have played some part in a murder," Ben said. "Or murders."

"Murders? As in two?"

"Or more," Ben said cryptically.

Major shook his head and for the first time appeared frightened.

"But I ain't done owt. I ain't."

"Well, if that's the case, then you have nothing to worry about, and perhaps I can expect full participation?"

"At this stage, my client will be refraining from answering in full," the brief cut in.

"On your advice?" Ben asked, to which the solicitor nodded. "Well, Mr Major, let me add a few words of advice of my own. You and your brother, who is sitting in the next room by the way, are in a lot of trouble. I hope I don't need to press the matter. Enough cannabis was discovered on your property to secure the maximum sentence allowed for the supply of a class B drug."

"I would prefer it if, during this interview at least, we keep to the charges, Inspector Savage," Garrott said.

"Oh, I'll be keeping to the charges," Ben told him. "But before we begin, I just want to ensure that your client is aware of the procedures and the weight an honest account can have."

"Eh?" Major said.

"He means that, if you speak candidly, it will be taken into account when dealing with any other charges against you," Garrott said.

"Candidly?"

"It means honestly," Ben said before Garrott could interrupt. "Look, you're going to be sentenced for the cannabis. You're not going to get away with a fine and slap on the wrist." Major stifled a tear and licked his lips. "And this charge isn't going to help your cause. If you play hard to get, you could easily wind up with the maximum sentence for both charges."

"But I never done nothing," he said.

"Then convince me," Ben replied. "Convince me of your innocence. Were you responsible for the death of Lee Constantine?"

"Eh? No. Course, I weren't."

Garrott winced at his client's response, but Ben continued before he could offer advice.

"Were you responsible for the death of Jennifer Willis?" Ben asked.

"Willis? Eh?" he said, becoming quite obviously irritated and scared. "No. No, I weren't."

"And your brother?" Ben asked to which Major silenced and stilled. "To your knowledge, was he responsible for either of those deaths?"

"Colin? No, course he weren't. Neither of us were. We're not like that. We're just—"

Garrott placed his hand on Major's arm before he could finish his sentence.

"You're just what, Andrew?" Ben asked, but Garrott had warned him with a shake of his head. "Andrew, this is the part where being honest counts," Ben said. "Give us something to work with here."

"I am being honest. Neither of us did anything. I don't even know...what was his name?"

"Lee Constantine?" Ben said.

"Right, yeah. Never even met him."

"You've never met him? Oh, that's interesting."

"If you have evidence of my client and your victim being acquainted, Inspector, then please do let us know," Garrott said, and he rifled through his files. "As of yet, I have seen no evidence which suggests otherwise."

The smile Ben found was short-lived. More of a camera flash than a prolonged display of amusement.

"Andrew, perhaps you could describe your ongoing correspondence with representatives of Willis Aggregates?" Ben asked. "In particular, Jacob and Jennifer Willis, owners of the quarry near your house."

"Eh? Who?" he replied. "You mean the bloke who owns the quarry? The rich twat?"

"I'm referring to Jacob Willis," Ben said. "And yes, he owns the quarry which is situated less than a kilometre from your house."

"Never met the bloke," Major said.

"But you have been corresponding with him?"

"Eh?"

"Letters, Andrew. You've been exchanging letters. Can you tell me what the subject was?"

"The letters?" he replied, shaking his head as if they meant nothing. "They wanted to put a road through our property. We said no."

"And they offered a reasonable sum for the inconvenience, did they?"

"Don't matter how much they want to give us. We'll not sell. Our grandad built that house. We're not selling it to some dick-head who wants to build a road."

"Even though they offered more than the market value."

"Market value don't really mean much, does it? Not when your grandad built the house with his bare hands."

"So, it's an honour thing, is it? You refused to sell your land to retain your grandfather's honour?"

Major contemplated the question, then nodded.

"It's always been Major land," he said. "Start putting roads through, and then what? You get another, then another."

"I have to concede I agree with you," Ben said. "These things do have a way of building momentum, but I do question your sense of honour when you've given over some of that land for the purpose of growing an illegal drug."

"I think we've crossed the line, Inspector," Garrott said. "I'm failing to understand how this is linked to the murder charge—"

"Andrew, did Jacob or Jennifer Willis ever pay you a visit in person?"

Major stared hard at Ben. Not into his eyes, but close. It was as if he was studying the tiniest detail of Ben's face.

"No," he said. "Couldn't even tell you what he looked like."

"Except that he was posh?" Ben said, and Garrott leaned in to whisper in his client's ear. "Funny detail to have gleaned from correspondence alone. Perhaps it was his use of the English language? Some of those legal letters can be quite stuffy, can't they?"

"No comment," Major said, realising his mistake.

"You've never met him, then?"

"No comment."

"And his wife? Can you describe her?"

"No comment."

"We found more than a dozen letters from the quarry addressed to you, Andrew. Were they all delivered via post?"

"No comment?"

"Have you ever seen either Jennifer or Jacob Willis at your property, either delivering one of these letters or otherwise?"

"No comment," he said, although, by his tone, Ben guessed his resolve to remain silent was waning.

"Okay," he said. "Why don't you tell me what you did the Saturday before last? That's twelve days ago now, but I'm sure you can recall your movements."

"No comment."

"Did you tend your plants at all?"

"No comment."

"Perhaps you went for a nice walk in the field behind your house?"

"No, I didn't," he said. "I was at home."

"Ah," Ben said, and Garrott closed his eyes in dismay. "All day?"

"All day," he replied, then looked across at Garrott. "What?"

"Nothing," Garrott said. "Nothing at all. Inspector, my client clearly has nothing to contribute regarding this matter—"

"Clearly?" Ben said. "There's nothing clear about any of this. Not a single thing. I don't know if he met Jenny or Jacob Willis, if they ever had an argument, or if they got on like a house on fire. Your client, Mr Garrott, is proclaiming innocence. He agreed to a level of candour in respect of other charges against him. But so far, I can see no reason why any officer would see fit to cut your client some slack. He's not helping me and he's not helping himself. The only person gaining anything from this interview is you."

"I can assure you–" Garrott began, but Ben knew a brick wall when he saw one. He knew a wasted cause.

"What if I asked your client about his movements last Saturday evening? What would he have to say about that?" Ben asked, then turned to Major. "Where were you last Saturday, Andrew? At home all day, were you?"

Major said nothing, and Garrott was not one to be silenced easily.

"May I suggest–"

"No, Mr Garrott, you may not," Ben snapped, then berated himself internally for allowing his composure to slip. He turned back to Major. "I can put you and your brother at a party in Metheringham, where Lee Constantine was given drugs that later led to his death. Do you know how serious that is, Andrew?"

Major shrugged like a teenager caught playing truant.

"That's hardly enough for the CPS to rub their hands together, Inspector, and you know it," Garrott said.

"Okay then. Not only can I place you there, but I also have statements from other guests confirming that you and your bother attended the party for the sole purpose of supplying drugs."

"Eh?" Major said.

"I have witnesses," Ben said. "And if need be, I'll get more. I don't need them, believe me, what I have is enough, which when coupled with your little enterprise will see you locked up for a long time." Ben took a moment to breathe and caught Nillson's encouraging nod. "Andrew, look," he said. "You're not cut out for prison. You might think you are, but you're not, mate. They'll eat you alive in there. You might think you're hard, but really, you would be going in on the lower end of the food chain. Now, that's not a big deal if you're looking at a three-month sentence for possession of a little bag of weed. But the sentence you're looking at is much larger. I know you were at the party. All I need to know is who you gave the LSD to."

"Eh? Acid? I ain't never done no acid."

"I'm not asking if you took it, Andrew. I'm asking who you gave it to. A friend? You knew some people there, didn't you? Who did you hand it to? Justin Greaves?"

Major's head flicked up at the mention of Greaves' name.

"Now we're getting somewhere," Ben continued. "What about your sister, Margot?"

"Now listen," Major said, his index finger jabbing at the table. "You leave her out of this."

"I'm afraid I can't do that," Ben said. "You see, she was the last person to talk to Lee. As far as we know anyway. Everyone is telling us the same story. You and your brother turned up to sell your wares, your sister spent the evening talking to Lee, and then he vanished." Ben sat back in his seat. "But if you insist on lying about being at the party, I can only assume that whatever response you give me regarding the LSD and Lee Constantine, is also a lie. You're losing credibility, Andrew. I've got nothing to work with here."

Ben waited for Garrott to offer his advice, and then made some notes in his file.

Major's trembling hands linked before him and he picked at a fingernail, then wiped the offending debris onto the floor.

"If I were to say I was at the party–"

"Both of you," Ben said. "Your brother and you."

"Right," he agreed. "If I were to say we were there, and we sold bags of weed there, then you'd have me for intent to supply."

"Correct," Ben said. "But if I'm honest, the fact that you had five polytunnels filled with the stuff tells us you had some kind of intent anyway."

"But that does buy me credibility. Is that right?"

Ben cocked his head, intrigued at the young man's sudden display of acumen.

"To a degree," he said. "The more truth you tell us, the more credibility you earn. That goes for anybody in all walks of life."

"But if I say we weren't there, that neither of us were at the party, then you would deem everything I say a lie."

"Potentially a lie, yes. We'd have no reason to believe a word you said, would we?"

"But if I said nothing?" Major asked, his eyes narrowing at the idea that somewhere between those two poles.

"Then I'd have no choice but to charge based on the evidence we have, and you would be handing your liberty over to twelve strangers sitting in a courtroom. But I'll be honest, you haven't painted a pretty picture, so far. Certainly not one they would buy."

He nodded, then conferred with his brief, and Nillson slid her notebook over to him. He turned to the page she had marked by folding the corner and read her writing.

This is going nowhere, it read.

He closed the pad and slid it back to her.

"The way I see it," Major said, "you ain't got much on me or my brother. Not for this, anyway. I didn't even know the bloke, and as for acid, I ain't seen one for years, let alone sold any. And all that weed was for personal use. We smoke a lot, don't we?"

"So, you'll take your chances then, will you? Actually, before you answer that," Ben said, and he turned to Nillson. "Can you please fetch the statement from Barry Coleman?"

Nillson immediately saw the direction Ben was taking and nodded, then stood, preparing to leave.

"Eh?" Major said. "Who?"

"Barry Coleman," Ben said. "You know Barry Coleman, I'm sure. His number was found on a mobile phone seized from your property. And anyway, he certainly knows you."

"He told you that, did he?"

"He's in custody now," Ben said coolly. "And given that Lee Constantine was one of his employees, we not only have you using Mr Coleman to clean the money you make, thus proving your intent to supply, but we have a direct link to Lee Constantine."

Major's face said it all. Without revealing whatever secrets he had, he confirmed the fact that there was a secret.

"The truth is, Andrew," Ben said, "Mr Coleman's part in this is only really a bit part. He has a business, a bona fide registered business, and a home. He's got much more to lose than you, and as a result, he's earned himself quite a bit of credibility."

"What's he said?"

"Ah," Ben replied, striking the hook into Major's spotty lips. "Why don't you tell me what you think he said? This is your last chance to earn yourself some of that credibility. Give me a reason to believe you, Andrew. Come on. Give me something."

Major stared at his hands and then up at his brief, who offered only a shake of his head following his client's disregard for his advice. So, Major turned to Ben. He jutted his chin out briefly, steeling himself.

"You reckon they'll take my honesty into account then, do you?" he said.

"I know they will," Ben replied. "Judges favour honest and remorseful individuals."

"This isn't me owning up to anything, though. I still say I'm innocent."

"You say what you need to say," Ben replied, as casually as he could through his thumping heart and calm exterior.

"Alright," he said, laying his hands flat on the table. "Alright then." He stared up at Ben and his entire gullet rose and fell as he swallowed his fear. "Alright, I'll tell you."

CHAPTER FORTY-FOUR

Had there been an event titled Office Olympics or The Officeathlon, Ben would have been a clear runner-up, having let the rage that had been building inside him for the past week or so erupt in a single moment of madness. His phone left his hand at something like fifty miles per hour, a decent speed for the event, and his aim was spot on. It hit the desk's surface with arrow precision. But he hadn't factored in velocity. The phone slid across the surface in a blur, reentered the air, and then bounced into his chair before careering off in an altogether new direction, where it landed at Chapman's feet.

She said nothing, and Ben, seething, strode over to the board while she reached down, grabbed it, and set it down on her own desk within reach of him.

"Sorry, Chapman," he said, as Nillson entered the room. He felt, rather than saw, some kind of silent dialogue between them. Perhaps Nillson was shaking her head to warn Chapman from saying anything.

And then it dawned on him. It dawned on him like the day he'd woken up and stared at his cigarettes in disgust. Granted, that had been years ago, but the sensation was the same. The realisation that smoking made him feel awful. It was exactly as he felt now, realising that his behaviour mirrored Freya's temper.

And that wasn't a pretty sight. It wasn't the message he wanted to send to the team.

"Well, that went well," Nillson said.

Ben considered her comment. The interview hadn't gone well, and she knew it. But when he saw the expression on her face, he couldn't help but smile.

"What are we going to do?" he said. "What the bloody hell are we going to do? We've spent a week on the Major brothers and all we've done is help out DI Wiltshire. He's got himself a nice little case to put forward. And what do we have?"

"A smaller suspect list," Gillespie said, and Ben spun to find him sitting beside Anderson.

"How long have you been here?"

"A wee while," he replied.

"And Margot Major?"

"Ah, she's useless, Ben. Let her go," he said. "I mean, it's not like she's a flight risk, is it?"

"Agreed," Ben sighed. "I doubt Sergeant Priest has any cells left, anyway. We've got three people in custody and we've interviewed one of them. If I don't start working this investigation instead of skirting around the edge, he's going to start charging me rent."

"Well, let's start doing it, then," Gillespie said. "Let's process them. What did the Major brothers have to say?"

"I've only interviewed Andrew," Ben said. "That was enough. And where the bloody hell do they get these duty solicitors from these days? They used to sit there, make notes, and observe. These days they all think they're Kings bloody Council."

"Tell us about Andrew, then," Gillespie said. "What's got you all hot and bothered?"

"What's got me hot and bothered, Jim, is that we've spent the entire week trying to get something on them and all we've managed to secure is a confession for intent to supply a class C drug. He admitted to being at the party but was there for less than ten minutes. He admitted to going somewhere else to deliver weed. He wouldn't tell us where, but he assures us that his number plates would have been picked up on the other side of Lincoln. He was there all night."

"What about last Sunday?" Gillespie asked.

"Have a guess?"

"I was never one for guessing games, Ben."

"With Coleman. Again, we can check the local CCTV."

"And have we? Checked, I mean."

"Not yet. But I'm also loathe to waste another bloody second of valuable resources looking into what has been a dead end from the start. He even told us they used to sell the harder stuff. Didn't say what, of course, he's not a complete idiot, but these days they just do the weed. It's virtually legal anyway."

"No, it's not."

"I know, but the sentence is so low you might as well be given a week at Butlins," Ben told him. "The amount they had in those polytunnels was nothing compared to some of the busts they make down south. Any decent lawyer could get them a reduced sentence."

"Oh, so it wasn't all personal then. Surprise Surprise," Gillespie said. "He's basically said that, yes, they're selling weed, but are too scared to do serious time for it."

"Which is brilliant for DI Wiltshire. He and his team are probably upstairs right now cracking the champagne. He'll be ironing his tunic ready for the deputy chief constable to pin a bloody medal on his chest. Me? Us? We're still looking at two murders with two MOs, and absolutely bugger all in the way of submissible evidence."

"I might have something," Chapman said. To Ben, it was as if they were lost in a cave deep underground and her voice had led them to a pinprick of light. "I've been looking into the CCTV footage Nillson found. You know, the petrol station footage."

"I already looked at that," Nillson said. "She goes through the village. Gold is checking for doorbell cameras."

"I know," Chapman replied. "I wasn't questioning anybody's work. I just wanted to see if she paid by card or cash, and if it was card, then maybe that could give us a clue."

"Right?" Ben said, noting the pinprick of light growing ever so slightly larger.

"Well, look," she said, turning her laptop for them to see. Chapman had paused the footage of Jenny Willis at the counter. Her arm was extended and her hand held onto a credit card. "Credit card."

"So? Haven't you checked them already?"

"Well, I did, Ben," she replied. "But she doesn't have any."

"Eh?"

"She doesn't have a credit card."

"Of course she has a credit card. Look, she's driving a Range Rover. She's a director of a bloody quarry and a road-building firm. She was a wealthy woman. Wealthy people have credit cards."

"Not this one," Chapman replied.

"So, what's that she's using?" Ben said, pointing to the image. "That's a credit card or a bank card, or something."

"I've checked all her accounts," Chapman said. "I've even got the account numbers from the petrol garage to see who they belong to."

"And?"

"It's being dealt with," she said. "Maybe an hour or two from now."

"Right, well, that's a start," Ben said. "A wealthy woman without a bank or a credit card. Whoever owns that card she's using in the footage I want to speak to them."

"Thought you'd say that," Chapman said proudly.

Ben moved back to the whiteboard. He struck a line through the Major brothers, hoping that the smaller pool of suspects might invoke some kind of motivation.

But nothing happened.

"What's this?" Nillson said. She was bent over Chapman's laptop and moved the cursor to Jenny Willis' neck. "A necklace."

"So what?" Ben said.

"Well, she wasn't wearing a necklace in the morgue."

"Of course not. Pip would have removed her clothing—"

"No, I mean. She wasn't wearing one when she went in."

"How would you know?"

"Well, because I was there when she pulled it from the ground, Ben," Nillson said. "You ask Jenny. We were talking about her clothes, saying how she looked like a taller version of..."

She lingered on that last word.

"Of who?" Ben asked. "Freya?"

Nillson hesitated. "I just meant that she dresses well, that's all," she said. "The point I'm making is that the necklace you see there in the footage was not on the body when we dug it up."

"Are you suggesting this could have been a robbery?" Ben said.

"I'm suggesting that there could be another avenue for us here. If it was a robbery, then it's probably been pawned."

"Chapman," Ben said, but before he could give her an instruction, she relayed exactly what he was going to say.

"Call round to all the local pawn shops and jewellers?"

"Thank you," he said. "When you're done there, run through the inventory of seized goods, will you? You never know, it could be downstairs as we speak."

"You really want to get them on something, Ben, eh?" Gillespie said.

"I just don't like wasting time," Ben told him. "How can they be linked to Coleman, who in turn is linked to Lee Constantine, who via Paul Stoneman, is linked to Jenny Willis? How can that be possible? There's a narrative here that explains it, but I'm buggered if I can see it." He folded his arms and took a few deep breaths. "Chapman, if you find something, have Cruz and Jewson check it out, will you? They've spent three days sunbathing in the field. It's about time they did some real police work."

She nodded with the phone's handset held between her shoulder and ear.

"What next?" Gillespie asked, but there was an underlying question in there. The real question had nothing to do with what they were going to do. It was who Ben was going to work with. Was he going to continue working with Nillson, or go back to working with Gillespie?

"I think it's time we paid a visit to Jacob Willis," Ben replied, then turned to Nillson. "Anna, I need somebody to keep things moving here. Chapman's run off her feet, Gold is out there on her own, and with any luck, Cruz and Jewson haven't been rolling around in the field. Keep things moving, will you? It'll be good practice for you. Oh, and do some digging into Jacob Willis, will you? If you find anything out, give me a call."

"Will do," she replied after a moment to think about it, and she stared at Gillespie. Clearly, the two of them were now engaged in a war of promotion. Who could make the biggest difference to the investigation?

"You could also contact Pip," Ben said. "You've got a way with her. See if the necklace was missing and ask if she had a credit card in her effects. I'm pretty sure she didn't, but it's worth checking."

"I have a way with her, do I?" Nillson said, grinning.

"Let's just say, you have a way with most people, Anna," Ben said.

"We off to deliver the bad news, then, are we?" Gillespie asked. "I'll restock on tissues, shall I, eh?"

"We are," Ben replied. "With any luck, the next news we deliver after this will be good news. Something like, we've found the person who killed your wife, Mr Willis, and your boyfriend, Miss Fraser, and they're going to prison for a very long time." Gillespie looked up from his chair, eyebrows raised in amusement. "But the way my life is going right now, Jim, I very much doubt it will be."

CHAPTER FORTY-FIVE

"What's on your mind?" Gillespie asked as he and Ben descended the fire escape stairwell. "Aside from the obvious, of course."

"The obvious lack of progress, evidence, and motivation, you mean?" Ben replied. "Actually, if you must know, it's this credit card thing. She didn't have any effects. If they'd found anything, we'd know. There's no phone, no purse, no credit cards"

"You know what else we haven't found?" Gillespie asked as Ben held the door for him. "Lee's clothing."

"I hope you don't think I'm that incompetent, Jim," Ben said. "That's the main reason Cruz and Jewson are still out there. The dive team would have found something if his clothes had been thrown in after him. And that field? It might be small, but believe me, when you have a field of crops, searching for something is almost impossible. I remember this time my brother dropped the keys to a tractor. Four of us, it took. Four of us. All bloody day. My dad was apocalyptic."

"Inspector Savage," somebody called out from behind them, Ben turned to find DI Wiltshire walking the corridor, his face beaming with joy. "I hear there's a few people in the county you haven't arrested for your murder charge. Are you off to get them now?"

"Very droll, Chris," Ben said. "You should consider a career on stage."

Wiltshire grinned back at him. Their relationship was old enough that such remarks had little effect. If push came to shove, Wiltshire would have his back.

"The deputy chief constable is delighted, I hear," he said.

"Wow," Ben replied, doing his best to sound enthusiastic. He checked his watch. "So, in under an hour, you've charged the brothers, built a case for the CPS, and had time to send the message to the top brass. I suppose you had plenty of time, given that I did all the hard work." Ben eyed him, hoping to see a sign of guilt, but found not a single shift in Wiltshire's expression. "But then, I doubt my name was even mentioned, was it?"

"That Coleman lead was a good one," he replied, changing the subject. "That was what I would call the clincher. I mean, a confession is good. But we both know how confessions can change. They'll be held on remand for six months while the CPS get their facts straight. By the time they go up in front of a judge, that confession could easily be turned on its head. Police pressure, confused state of mind. You know how these things go."

"I do," Ben agreed.

"But that Coleman lead," Wiltshire continued, shaking his head. "Washing the money for them. You know what that means, don't you? It means that HMRC will step in. They'll want to know when they'll receive their share of the tax owed, which means that not only will I have the CPS backing me, but His Majesty's bleeding Revenue and Customs. They'll tear this Coleman bloke apart. Honestly, Ben. I don't know how you did it—"

Ben opened his mouth to speak, but Wiltshire held up his hand to stop him.

"But rest assured, your diligence has not gone unappreciated."

"You do realise Barry Coleman is still a live suspect in our murder investigation," Gillespie said, and Ben gave him a warning look. Wiltshire was alright peer to peer. But he wouldn't take kindly to banter from a lesser rank.

"Did you just hear what I said?" Wiltshire said. "I've got the DCC, the HMRC, and the CPS backing me on this. What have you got? What have you got apart from some muddy old corpse, some footprints, and a floater?"

Ben stared hard at him, quite unable to believe that at one time they had been friends, both navigating the ways of the police force together.

"There's more to Coleman than simply a means to wash money," Ben told him.

"There's nothing more to Coleman," Wiltshire replied. "He's just a poor, old fool with a failing business who relies on a few grand here and there from two spotty youths trying to find a way to live off their earnings. It's simple. The Major brothers take Coleman twenty grand, he invents a few transactions, probably one or two per day, and by the end of the month, he's cleaned up the money. He takes a few grand and they have the balance."

"That doesn't make sense," Gillespie said. "How does he then extract the cash? How do they claim to have earned the money? That's not cleaning cash."

"They take a dividend," Wiltshire said.

"A what?" Ben replied. "A dividend. But that means—"

"They're shareholders," Ben replied, to which Wiltshire nodded slowly. "Brilliant, eh? Find yourself a failing business that runs on cash. Buy into it, keep it going, and you've got yourself a means to wash your money. Those five polytunnels were on a cycle. Every month, one of them is ready to harvest. That means their stock is replenished every month. By the time the fifth polytunnel is harvested, the first one is nearly ready. And on the cycle goes."

"And all the cash is put through Dick's Appliances?" Gillespie asked.

"Every single penny," Wiltshire replied. "Not a bad little number if you can find the right failing business to exploit."

"Doesn't it make you feel like Coleman is a bit of a victim, in all this?" Ben asked. "I mean, they've just exploited him. Makes you wonder if the jury will see through their dirty tactics."

"No, families like the Colemans only go one way," Wiltshire said. "I got the son and now I've got the old man. The only thing I'm wondering is if the wife is up to something."

"Sorry?" Ben said.

"The wife," he replied. "Makes you wonder if she's up to something, doesn't it? You know? Sons in the nick for drug dealing. The husband's about to go down for tax evasion, conspiracy, and who knows what else."

"No," Ben said. "Before that. You said you got the son. Coleman's son?"

"S'right," Wiltshire said. "Gary Coleman. Must be what, six years ago now, give or take? Took a year or so for the trial to come around."

"So, let me get this straight," Gillespie said. "It was you who arrested Gary Coleman?"

"Yeah," Wiltshire said. "Course, it wasn't just drug-related. The original charge was manslaughter, believe it or not."

"Manslaughter?"

"Yeah, he sold some poor kid a few dodgy pills at Hollywood's over in Nottingham. Took us a while to trace it back, and even then, it wasn't enough for a conviction."

"What was the boy's name?" Ben asked.

"Oh, I don't know. Don't matter now, does it?"

"I'm just curious," Ben replied.

Wiltshire peered up at the ceiling in thought.

"Michael," he said, finally. "That was it. Michael–"

"Constantine," Ben replied. "Michael Constantine."

"That's it," Wiltshire said, and he clicked his finger and thumb to accentuate his remark. "Terrible, it was. How did you know? Not on your growing list of cold cases, is it?" He grinned, hoping the jibe had struck a chord. But it had done far more than that.

"No," Ben said. "No, I just seem to remember it, that's all. You know? Dead boy, failed CID investigation. It's always nice to see a fellow colleague struggle as much as you do, isn't it?"

"Right," Wiltshire said.

"Anyway," Ben said, glancing up at Gillespie. "Shall we go and tell a man his wife has been found battered to death? That should be the icing on the disastrous cake my week has been so far."

CHAPTER FORTY-SIX

"Bloody hell," Gillespie said, the moment he'd slammed the passenger door closed. "Coleman's lad was responsible for Michael Constantine's death?" He made himself comfortable and noticed a slight irritation in Ben's expression as the car rocked from side to side. He shoved the seat back as far as it would go and sighed when he extended his legs. "Have you had Cruz in here? Bloody seat's set up for a child."

"I think there's more to the whole Coleman thing. I think he played a bigger part," Ben said, checking his mirror to make sure Wiltshire hadn't followed them out. "Who do you think sold Coleman the drugs in the first place?"

"Eh?"

"Who told us today that they used to sell more than just weed but the risk got too much for them?" Ben said. "It wasn't the risk, Gillespie. They were part of it. They knew Gary Coleman sold the lad the dodgy pills because they *supplied* him with the dodgy pills in the first place. Make's total sense."

"To you, maybe."

"All this time, we've been trying to work out why Coleman

would let two spotty kids exploit him," Ben said. "Isn't it obvious? His son is inside for serving up pills. What they know could add a manslaughter sentence to his term. What's he going to do? Watch his business go down the pan and let his son get another ten years? Or give in, keep his business going, and get his son out as soon as possible?"

"Jesus," Gillespie said. "I sometimes have trouble deciding if I should have porridge or Crunchy Nut Cornflakes in the morning."

"Hardly a life-changing decision, Jim," Ben said, although mildly amused.

"Aye, not life-changing for me," he agreed. "But the porridge does have an adverse effect." Ben pulled out onto the main road and glanced across at him, hoping for an explanation. "Poor air quality," Gillespie added.

"Ah," Ben said, his finger poised over the button to lower the window. "What did you have this morning?"

"Kate made me one of her smoothies, as it happens," he replied. "Kale, cucumber, pineapple, and God knows what else."

"Right, so how are you feeling?"

"Hungry," Gillespie replied. "Bloody hungry."

It was a natural place to end the discussion on Gillespie's digestive system and allowed Gillespie time to contemplate his world. The differences Kate had made since coming into his life were astronomical. His habits had changed, his house had been, with the help of Cruz, completely redecorated, and even his eating had improved. In fact, he wouldn't be surprised if he came home one day to find the local Chinese takeaway up for sale.

Then he reflected on the changes happening in Ben's life. His girlfriend had been involved in a nasty accident and was moments from disappearing from his life altogether, taking with her his confidence. He felt sorry for Ben, although pity was the last thing he needed. But he couldn't help it. Ben was the type of bloke who would help anyone. He had been a rock in a river, parting the current with his stubbornness and tenacity. Now he was more like a pebble on the riverbed being tossed this way and that.

There was no furrowed and determined brow, no focus in his eyes. But there was hope. Hope that maybe a piece of the information they had gleaned would become evidence, a direction for them to follow.

It was mid-afternoon, and they had known for sure that the body belonged to Jenny Willis for nearly a full day, and yet only now were they paying a visit to her husband. It wasn't the way things should have been done, and Ben must have known it. Yet he seemed so absorbed in the investigation. His attention appeared, on the surface, at least, to be solely focused on the Major brothers, or Coleman, or any of the other individuals embroiled in the mix. Yet it had been at least two days since Freya's name had even been brought up. To some, this might have been a sign he was moving on. But for Gillespie, who knew Ben better than anyone, this was a sign that she weighed heavy on his mind.

By the time they pulled into the quarry, Ben had to visibly shake himself from his thoughts and get his game face on.

His demeanour was even evident in his parking. As a rule, Ben would reverse into a spot. It was a habit that many people who drove the unreliable cars of the eighties and nineties adopted. It was always best to park in such a way that the bonnet could be opened and jump leads could be attached. Young drivers of today would never know the anxiety the older generations experienced whenever they walked out to their car.

"Right, let's do this," Ben said, and he shoved open the car door, allowing a cloud of hot quarry dust inside.

"Christ, it's like the bloody desert," Gillespie said. "Any more of this and I'll need one of those scarfs the Arabs wear." He shoved open his door and climbed into the oppressive heat. "Or a camel. Now that would be interesting, eh, Ben? Imagine riding back to the station on a pair of camels, dragging the Major brothers behind on a length of old rope."

"If I were you, I'd keep those ideas to yourself, Jim," Ben said. "There are some that might find that offensive."

"Christ almighty. I can hardly fart without offending someone."

"No, Jim. Your farts are offensive. No question about it, mate. But talk about other cultures and what they wear," Ben said, "that's going to get you in bother."

"Aye, the world's gone mad. Why is it that people feel like they have a right not to be offended? I get offended every day and you don't hear me complaining."

"Who offends you?"

"Everyone," Gillespie said. "I can see it when I speak. They kind of screw their faces up like I'm talking nonsense. It's not my fault I've got an accent, eh? What am I supposed to do, shove a silver spoon in my gob and a plum up my–"

"Back then, are you?" a voice called and they looked up to find Jacob Willis peering down at them from the top of the steel stairs. "Thought we'd agreed we were done."

He started down the stairs until Ben held up a hand.

"Actually, Mr Willis, it's probably best if you stay up there. We need to have a chat with you."

"I can chat down there."

Ben started up the steps.

"Why don't you have a wee sit down, eh?" Gillespie said.

"What's happened?" Willis asked, a bemused expression forming on his face. "Don't tell me you need to close the gates again. This is ridiculous. We've only just opened. We've got projects all over Lincolnshire on hold because of this. Do you know how much it costs to close a road, let alone resurface it?"

Ben stepped past him and into the uppermost portacabin, leaving Gillespie to usher Willis inside.

"How about a cup of tea, eh?"

"I'll report this, you know?" Willis continued. "Whatever it is you need to do, you've had ample opportunity to—"

"Mr Willis, I have some bad news for you," Ben said, cutting him off. He took a seat at the large meeting table and proffered the seat opposite with a wave of his hand. There was something in this movement and the tone of Ben's voice that seemed to knock Willis off kilter. Gillespie sat down in the seat beside Ben and together they waited for Willis to lower himself onto the chair wearily.

"Go on," Willis said, his eyes darting from one to the other.

"Yesterday afternoon, we discovered another body."

Willis shook his head dismissively.

"Yesterday afternoon? You couldn't have. Not here, anyway. We were open. You came and spoke to Paul—"

"Not here," Ben said. "Actually, it was in the field at the top of the quarry." Ben gestured in the general direction but held Willis's gaze. "Mr Willis, I'm sorry to tell you, but it's your wife, Jennifer."

"Eh?"

Ben said nothing. To speak now would only delay the inevitable. He would either enter into a state of denial or fall into dismay. Anger usually followed both of those initial reactions. Only once those phases had passed could any real insight be gleaned.

"My wife?" he said, his voice soft. He shook his head as if they had gone mad. "You're wrong. Can't be her."

"I'm afraid we were able to identify her through her DNA, Mr Willis. We're quite sure."

"But it can't be her. She's in Spain."

"She's what?" Ben said.

He stared at them like they had completely lost the plot.

"She's in Spain."

"Spain?"

"Yeah. Went Sunday before last, she did. Bloody good

riddance, if you ask me." He gave a little laugh at them both, his hopes clinging to the reality he had laid out. "At least with her out of the picture and you lot gone, I can get some bloody work done."

"Mr Willis, does your wife drive a Range Rover?"

"Yeah, my Range Rover," he said. "Well, the business' anyway."

"And apologies for the questions, Mr Willis, does she wear a necklace?"

"Yeah? Course she does. It's the one thing I bought her that she still wears. She might hate the hours I work and she might berate me for breathing, but she won't take that off. No. It's antique. Some lady this or that wore it more than a century ago while she bossed her servants around. Seems quite apt that Jenny should wear it everywhere she goes."

"When exactly did she go to Spain?" Ben asked.

"Sunday. Like I said. We've got a little place out there. She goes there when we argue. She'll be back in a month or so with her tail between her legs." He sat back. "I'm sorry, gentlemen, but whoever it is you found up there is not my wife. I can assure you."

Ben suddenly pulled his phone from his pocket, glanced at Gillespie to take over, and then slipped out of the room to take the call.

"Blimey," Willis continued. "I knew you lot were bad, but this? This is beyond bad. You're lucky I'm a busy man, let me tell you. Anybody else would sue you for emotional damage."

"Mr Willis, I hope you don't think me brash or irresponsible, but I think you should seriously consider the prospect that the woman we found up there is actually your wife."

"How can it be?" he said. He leaned forward across the desk and spoke slowly as if Gillespie had difficulty hearing. "She's in Spain."

"She's not in Spain, Mr Willis," Ben said from the doorway. He let the door close behind him but didn't bother retaking his seat.

"She's lying in the morgue in Lincoln County Hospital. The sooner you come to terms with that the better."

The shift in tone was clear. Ben's expression portrayed severity. And Willis shifted in his seat.

"Eh?"

Ben opened the photos application on his phone and held it up for Willis to see.

"Do you recognise this woman, Mr Willis?"

"Course, I do. It's her, ain't it?"

"This is your wife paying for petrol at Metheringham petrol station, just down the road here, two Sundays ago."

"Must have been on her way to the airport," he said with a shrug.

"And she would leave the Range Rover there, would she? Must be quite expensive."

"The very idea of her taking a taxi to Heathrow would kill her, Inspector," Willis said to which Ben gave a half smile, merely acknowledging the sentiment.

"What if I was to tell you that, about an hour ago, your Range Rover was found parked up just outside Metheringham."

"Eh?"

"In fact, where she parked is just a short walk from the field in which her body was discovered."

"I don't understand. It can't be—"

"Do you see this credit card in the photo, Mr Willis? The one she's using to pay for the fuel."

"Yeah, so what?"

"I've just learned that this credit card was cancelled the Monday after she paid for the fuel," Ben said. "Cancelled by you."

He rolled his eyes.

"So what? It's not like she bloody earns anything, is it? The only reason she's on the bloody payroll is for tax efficiency, and before you say it, it's not a crime."

"Oh, I'm not interested in tax dodging," Ben said, again with a half-smile. "But I am interested in your mobile phone statement."

"What?"

"Your mobile phone statement," Ben replied. "We've been doing some digging of our own. Our researcher has discovered a rather strange connection to Victoria Fraser. Does that name ring a bell?"

"Eh? Victoria who?"

"Fraser," Ben repeated. "Or perhaps it would be easier to describe her position." Ben pocketed his phone and gave Gillespie a sly nod to be ready. "Lee Constantine's girlfriend."

"I don't get it," he said, growing more flustered by the second. "What are you saying?"

"Me? What am I saying?" Ben replied. "I'm saying that you're under arrest, Mr Willis. On suspicion of murder."

Willis's face was a picture of horror and fear. He looked between Ben and Gillespie, perhaps seeking a way out between them. But before he could say anything, the door burst open, and Paul Stoneman walked in, abruptly stopping when he saw Ben and Gillespie.

"Sorry," he replied, then saw the expression on his boss's face. "Everything alright, Jake?"

"Do you have keys to the quarry?" Ben asked him.

"Eh?"

"Do you have keys to lock the place up?"

"Well, yeah, but..." He started as Gillespie moved around to pull Willis' hands behind his back. "You can't nick him. He's not done owt."

"Then see to it the quarry is closed, will you?" Ben said. "Your boss is going to be unreachable."

"Eh? But we've got lorries due. We're barely making ends meet as it is after all that's happened. How long's he going to be gone for?"

"For the foreseeable future, Mr Stoneman," Ben said. "And

when you understand why, perhaps your loyalty would be better served elsewhere." He turned to Gillespie. "Get him some transport back to the station, will you?"

"You're going to regret this, Inspector," Willis said, as Gillespie encouraged him to his feet.

"Take a good look around, Mr Willis," Ben replied. "It might be the last time you see all this."

CHAPTER FORTY-SEVEN

Ben's entry into the incident room was met with trepidation which eased when Chapman, Nillson, and Anderson noted the new expression on Ben's face. He walked as though buoyant on the stuffy air. He even felt light on his feet.

"I take it he's in custody," Nillson asked, the only one brave enough to prod the lion.

"Hold on," Ben told her, as he stared at the board. "I need to make sense of all this. We need a theory."

"We need a miracle," Nillson replied, and Ben turned on her, then relaxed. "Sorry. Couldn't help myself."

"No, you're right," he told her. "We do need a miracle. But in lieu of having one to hand, we'll have to make do with brute force."

"I didn't mean anything by it, Ben–"

"I know," he said. "DI Wiltshire said something about me nicking everyone in Lincolnshire. And do you know what? He's right. Lee Constantine died out of his mind on drugs. Jenny Willis died in agony, probably scared out of her wits. If I have to nick everyone in this county, then I bloody well will." He tapped the board with the end of the pen. "Jenny Willis. Last seen at Meg petrol station two Sundays ago. According to her husband, he thought she was heading to the airport to go to their holiday home. However, why then did she drive through the village and not out onto the main road? It doesn't make sense."

"You clearly have a reason in mind," Gillespie said.

"I do," Ben replied, without letting his eyes leave the board. "She paid somebody a visit."

"Well, that much is obvious."

"Is it?" Ben said, finally turning to see him. "Tell me what's obvious. You can't, can you? None of this is obvious, Jim. The two bodies were found less than fifty meters from each other, which obviously makes them linked, right? There's nothing tying them together apart from misfortune. The Major brothers' house backs onto the field which makes them obvious suspects, right? Wrong? The Major brothers have a direct link to Coleman, Lee's boss. Again, obvious, or not? Jacob Willis has a direct link to Vicky Fraser. Now tell me what part of all that is obvious." He waited a few seconds. "You can't, can you? Because none of this is obvious. Maybe she took the route through the village to avoid being seen by somebody?"

"Aye, well, there's that—"

"Maybe she was never going to Spain," Ben said. "Maybe she just told her husband that." He waited a few more seconds for the sentiment to well and truly bed in before turning back to the board. "What we do know is that, whether she drove straight through the village and out the other side, or whether she paid somebody a visit, she wound up on the main road less than a hundred metres from the field. We know she was dressed in expensive heels, so the only obvious thing surrounding her death is that she wasn't planning a gentle walk in the fields. She died later that day. An hour, two hours, eight hours? We don't know. We can't know. Not yet."

"I'll tell you what we don't know," Nillson said, to which Ben turned and waited with bated breath. "We don't know if she was alone in the car. CCTV doesn't really show the occupants. All we know is that she filled the car up and paid, and then the car left the forecourt. For all we know, her husband could have been in the car with her."

"That's another thing we don't know," Ben said. "I think it's worth keeping that in mind, but I'd like to focus on what we do know."

"Fair enough," Nillson said. "We know she was wearing an expensive necklace, which wasn't on her body when she was unearthed. Chapman, any news on that?"

"We might have a hit," she replied. "There's a little boutique jewellers in town that bought one off a customer. The manager isn't in today to give us a description, so Cruz and Jewson are on their way there to see it."

"Right, let's get our heads into this," Ben said, circling Jacob Willis' name on the board. "Jacob Willis has already told us he and his wife had an argument and that she was off to the house in Spain. He cancelled her credit cards and her bank cards the day after she died. Why would he do that?"

"To piss her off?" Gillespie suggested.

"Or to protect himself," Ben said. "If you killed somebody—"

"Easy tiger," Gillespie said.

"If you killed somebody," Ben said again, "what would you do with his or her effects?"

Gillespie shrugged. "Bin them?"

"Oh, come on. How many times have we seen it? The killer dumps the belongings elsewhere to stop the victim from being identified. The more time passes between the death and the identification, the harder it is for us to pin the murder on the killer. He dumped her possessions somewhere. We'll need to widen the search. There's miles and miles of dykes and ditches, not to mention the surrounding fields."

"So, you think he ditched her belongings but saved her necklace," Nillson said, pulling a face to suggest she wasn't quite in agreement.

"What if somebody found her belongings?" Ben asked. "They'd have access to his bank account. Imagine that? And he'd have no recourse, would he? What's the first thing you do when you lose your wallet? You cancel your cards. He cancelled every single one of them."

"Right, so this happened within a stone's throw to the quarry, which gives him the opportunity and the means, but what's the motive?"

"That's where we need to get to," Ben said. "My guess is that it has something to do with Lee Constantine. He's been talking to Vicky. Why?"

"What if they were having an affair?" Chapman suggested, to which Gillespie laughed aloud.

"It's a good job Cruz isn't here, eh? You know his thoughts on affairs. If he had his way, affairs and dog walking would be punishable by death. Both of them inevitably wind up either creating a dead body or finding one."

"Regardless of Cruz's opinions on the trends we have to deal with, Chapman could be right," Ben said. "What if Willis and Vicky Fraser were seeing each other?"

"Well, if that's the case, then he's obviously got some weird fetish," Anderson added, then realised the whole team was looking at her. "What? He's been calling her for what, five or six months? She's just had a baby. She would have been the size of a house."

"I'm not sure the CPS would go for a theory that involved him having a fetish for pregnant women," Ben said.

"No, it's the Major lass," Gillespie said. "If anybody's putting it about, it's her. Did you see what she was wearing at the house? Vicky Fraser is not really the sort a man like Willis goes for."

"Are you speaking from experience?" Nillson asked, a smirk spreading across her face.

"As it happens, aye, I am. I'm a red-blooded male, Anna. You ask me to choose between the two of them and I'd go for—"

"Let's not have this chat, please," Ben said. "They very likely both have their good points and bad points, like the rest of us."

"Aye, sorry," Gillespie said, his face reddening.

"Look, the point is that if Jacob Willis was responsible for Lee Constantine's death, then he would have needed help. Where did he get the drugs, for a start?"

"Local dealers?" Gillespie said.

"Right. And who are the only two people we know with access to the drug community?"

"The Major brothers," Nillson said, clearly disagreeing with him. "Why on earth would they sell drugs to Jacob Willis?"

"For the same reason Coleman was helping them. Blackmail."

"Oh right. So, you think that during the whole access road debacle, he discovered their weed farm and blackmailed them? What do you think he said? Can you get me some acid? I want to spike this fella's drink so he can drown in the pond on my property? We searched their house and there was no sign of LSD. There was no sign of anything, apart from a lorry load of weed."

Ben dropped down onto the desk behind him, the wind gone from his sails.

"We can't force this, Ben," Nillson said. "We can't bend the truth to make it fit our hypothesis."

"I know," Ben said, his voice tired and cracked.

"I've got Cruz on the line," Chapman said hesitantly. "He said he's got the CCTV from the jewellers."

Ben eyed Nillson and Gillespie and then sighed.

"If it's the Major brothers," he said, "then I want them back in here this evening."

"What if it's Willis?" Gillespie asked, to which Ben gave another sigh and dropped the marker pen onto the little shelf beneath the whiteboard.

"Then we have to accept that the two murders are not linked," he replied. "And do you know what? A part of me thinks it will be easier if they weren't."

"What do you want me to do?" Chapman asked, holding the phone's handset away from her ear.

Again, Ben checked Gillespie and Nillson's expression for some kind of guidance and then gave Chapman the nod.

"Let's hear what he has to say," he said.

It took a few moments for Chapman to engage the loudspeaker, and then she sat back, her pen poised.

"You're on loudspeaker, Cruz," Ben said. "Everyone's here apart from you and Gold."

"Oh, is there a briefing?" he asked as if he felt he was missing out.

"Yeah, we thought you'd prefer a few more hours with your new girlfriend," Gillespie announced. "Besides, we've concluded that the entire murder investigation revolves around dog walkers and affairs."

"Eh?"

"Ignore him," Ben said. "He's teasing you. What do you have for us? Is it the necklace?"

"Looks like it," Cruz replied. "It's on sale for eleven grand. It's over a hundred years old."

"Eleven grand?" Ben said.

"Yeah," he said. "Who the bloody hell walks around with an eleven-grand necklace?"

"Somebody who drives a Range Rover and has a house in Spain," Ben replied. "So, who was it then? Who sold it to the shop? Willis or the brothers?"

"Neither," Cruz said, clearly not understanding the magnitude of his news.

"Neither?" Ben said.

"Don't tell me it was Coleman," Gillespie added. "If it's him, I'll go down to the cells and bloody extract a confession myself–"

"It wasn't him, either," Cruz said, cutting him off. He took a long breath and cleared his throat. "It was Lee Constantine."

CHAPTER FORTY-EIGHT

For the second time that day, Jackie Gold walked up the footpath to Vicky Fraser's house. But unlike the first visit, when nobody had answered the door, this time she heard movement from inside. It was late in the day and she had considered leaving it until tomorrow, but after walking the village, noting any doorbell cameras in use, she had found herself just one street from Alfred Avenue.

The movement stopped and she imagined Vicky frozen to the spot, too scared to open the door. It was either that, or she was still mad at Jackie for staring at her baby.

But Ben was right. It was time Vicky spoke to them.

She recalled the last conversation she'd had with Ben. He hadn't seemed himself. He was lost somehow. Even the whiteboard was a mess of ideas. There was no single thread that ran through the evidence like there often was. That's what Freya would have done. She would have noted down everything they knew and weaved a thread of a theory throughout, giving them a direction to follow. Lighting a path through the chaos.

But Ben had no such path. There was no light. Only chaos.

She knocked on the door again, harder this time, then bent to peer through the letterbox.

"Vicky, it's Jackie Gold," she said. "I know you're there. Can you open the door, love? We need to speak."

She waited, watching for movement in the hallway. But it wasn't the hallway as she remembered it. There were boxes and bags at the foot of the stairs.

"Vicky, it's Jackie Gold. Can you open the door, please? Come on. I only want to talk to you."

"Go away," a voice called, and Jackie processed the voice. The tone. It wasn't the voice of a grieving woman clutching her child, pondering a bleak future. It was the voice of a teenager, mad at her parents, in a cloud of hormones, facing the transition from childhood to adulthood.

"Vicky, I just want to talk. There are things we need to discuss," Jackie said, then peered around her to make sure she wasn't being overheard. "Things about Lee, Vicky. We need your help."

"I don't want to talk about it," Vicky replied. "Just go away. I'm not ready to talk about him."

"I can't do that, I'm afraid. Listen, Vicky, do you remember Inspector Savage? He needs to know a few things. He's been very understanding so far. He's given you time. But now he needs answers. If you can't do it for me, Vicky, then do it for Lee. Help us, will you?"

"I don't want to talk about it," Vicky yelled, and she walked from the living room into the hallway and saw Jackie peering through the letterbox. "Just go away."

"Vicky, this is your last warning. If you don't let me in, then I'll be forced to come back with a warrant. Let's not go down that path. There's really no need."

Jackie straightened and waited, her eyes closed, picturing Vicky inside. The seconds passed, and then a full minute.

"Have it your way, Vicky," Jackie said, loud enough for her to hear, but not too loud that curtains in the neighbouring houses would twitch. She started back towards the road and unlocked her phone. Among her recently dialled numbers was Ben's name and she hit the button. But it was only when she put her phone to her ear that she heard a gentle click from behind her. Slowly, she turned and found Vicky Fraser in the doorway, her head bowed and her face a picture of darkness. Dark rings surrounded her eyes and her skin had an unhealthy sheen, as if she hadn't washed.

Jackie ended the call and pocketed the phone.

"Vicky," she said.

But instead of replying, the girl simply held the door open and wandered back inside. In the hallway, Jackie closed the door behind her and peered down at the bags and boxes.

"His stuff," Vicky said quietly, as footsteps came from inside the living room, and Paul Stoneman stepped into view. Vicky glanced back at him, and then at Jackie. "I asked Paul to help me. I couldn't face it alone," she said. "I couldn't bear to look at it all. I couldn't bear to..." She dropped onto the stairs and sobbed into her hands. "I can't do this alone."

"Then don't," Jackie said, and she looked up at Paul. "It's kind of you. I know it can't be easy. For either of you."

"I wanted to help," he replied. "Besides, it's not like we've any work. Your boss put pay to any of that."

Gold felt the sting. Resentment under the circumstances was a bitter pill to swallow and one that Jackie found herself forcing down her gullet far too often. The entire team were hell-bent on bringing justice to Lee's name, yet their help was met with little more than ungracious hostility.

"Why don't we have some tea?" Jackie suggested.

"I don't want tea," Vicky said. "Whatever you've to say, you can say it here."

"Should I leave you to it?" Paul asked, but Vicky startled.

"No. No stay, would you? It shan't take long." She looked up at Jackie. "Shall it?"

"If I could just explain," Jackie began. "You see, when we investigate matters such as this, we need to understand the victim's movements."

"And Lee is the victim, is he?"

"He is," Jackie said softly. "But if I'm honest, we're having a hard time understanding what his movements were over the past week. Ben said...that is, Inspector Savage mentioned that you thought he might have been troubled by something."

"I said no such thing."

"He's under the impression that you thought he was...I don't know, frightened of something, or someone. Either that or he was in some kind of trouble."

"Trouble?"

"I don't know," Jackie said. "We can't seem to get to the bottom of it."

"Well, that's because it's not true. He was fine."

Jackie winced. Extracting information from a grieving girl-friend without it becoming an interrogation was a challenge she had yet to master.

"He called in sick," Jackie said. "What was he doing on the three days before his death?"

"Helping me," she replied, and she nodded up the stairs. "I've been struggling, see? With the baby. Doctor's given me something for it. Said, it's common for women to fall into depression. I just had a bad week, is all. He took a few days off to help me."

"I see," Jackie said.

"If he was troubled, then it was probably my fault. He was worried about me. Said I shouldn't be left alone, if you know what I mean."

She stared at Jackie, daring her to challenge her candid response.

"Postnatal depression, you mean?" Jackie said and felt for the girl. "I had that, you know. In fact, I can name a dozen mums who had it too. What did he give you?"

"Who?"

"The doctor. You said he gave you something. What was it?"

"I don't know," she replied. "I need to get it from the pharmacy."

Jackie frowned and dropped into a crouch before her. "Vicky, if he's prescribed you something, then you need to get it. Now more than ever."

"I've been getting on with it," she said. "I'm okay." She looked up at Lee's best friend, who stood awkwardly with his hands in his pockets. "Paul's helped me. And Lee's parents have been in touch. They're making the arrangements. You know?"

"I do," Jackie said. "It must be hard for them, too. What with Lee's brother—"

"They're just worming their way in," Vicky said. "They never liked me, and had we not had littlun, they probably wouldn't even have called. They would have buried him without me even knowing about it."

"Well, stand your ground," Jackie said. "Lee loved you. He must have seen a future with you, or else he wouldn't have..." She glanced up the stairs. "He wouldn't have committed as he did."

"S'what I told her," Paul said. "And you're right. He did love her. His parents have always been like that. They look down on people. Even me. And I've known him for years."

Jackie beamed up at him. He was a good friend to have.

"Tell me about the night of the party," she said. "You see, the thing we can't get our heads around is why he even went. If he was worried about you, Vicky, then surely, he wouldn't have left you alone."

"He needed the time away," Vicky said flatly. "He'd been stuck in here all bloody week. I told him to go. I told him to let his hair down. He was so...so tense."

Jackie straightened and smoothed her blouse.

"So, to your knowledge, he wasn't worried about anything?"

"Not as far as I know."

"Nor me," Paul said. "Except Vicky, of course."

Jackie took a deep breath. The next question could go one of two ways.

"I'm sorry to ask," she began, "but did Lee take drugs? Of any kind?"

"I'm sorry?" Vicky said, the first line of defence being drawn.

"I know, it's a horrible thing to have to say, and nobody would be in any trouble, it's just that...well, our lab technicians found traces of LSD in his system. Is that something he would have done?"

"Lee never even smoked a joint," Paul said before Vicky could speak. "You know how his brother died, don't you?"

"Yes, we know. It's just that –"

"So, you'll understand if I told you that Lee was against drugs of any kind."

"Right," Jackie said. "Right, of course. I'm sorry to have brought it up."

"Is that all?" Vicky asked, her tone sharp and uninviting. "We need to get all this out to Paul's car before the next feed."

"Oh, I can help," Jackie replied, hoping to repair some of the damage the final question had caused. She bent to pick up two of the bags.

"No," Vicky said, and she reached out to stop her.

"It's no bother," Jackie said as she straightened, feeling the weight of the bags cut into her hands. "Tell you what, why don't you pop upstairs and see to littlun? While Paul and I deal with this lot? Won't take a minute with two of us."

"No, honestly," Vicky said, and she grabbed onto the bags. But as she pulled the bags, Jackie's grasp on the handles gave, and the content of one spilled to the floor. "Now look what you've done." Vicky dropped to the floor, hurriedly stuffing the contents back into the bag. It was clothing, mostly – t-shirts and boxer shorts, and something else. Something that caught Jackie's eye the way a kestrel homes in on a tiny mouse in the field below.

She dropped to a crouch again and placed a gentle hand on Vicky's, who stopped her frantic repacking and lingered there, her head bowed.

A tear fell from her eye onto Jackie's wrist.

"Vicky," Jackie said. "Vicky, I'm going to ask you something, and I need an honest answer."

Vicky was still. Her head remained bowed, and still, the tears fell.

"He wasn't worried about you, was he?" Jackie said. "All that about the doctor. You made that up, didn't you? You made it up to protect him, didn't you?"

"He was a good man," Vicky sobbed. "He didn't deserve this. If only you could have known him. If you'd met him, you'd know."

"I'm sure I would," Jackie replied, and she glanced at Paul, who had turned away shaking his head. "Vicky, what was it that Lee was worried about? It wasn't you, was it? Why did he call in sick, Vicky? Come on. It's time to be honest with me."

Vicky stared up at Paul, who closed his eyes, took a breath, and then muttered those fateful words.

"Alright," he said and then held Vicky's stare. "Tell her, Vic. Tell her what really happened."

CHAPTER FORTY-NINE

"Sorry?" Ben said, after the silence in the room had grown stale. "Lee Constantine sold the necklace to the shop?"

"Yeah," he said. "It's definitely him. You should see the CCTV here. It's like watching it in high definition." He waited for a response, but none followed. "What is it? Is that good news, or..."

"Cruz, I need you back here, please," Ben said. "Thank the staff, get the CCTV, and see what we need to do to have the necklace taken away. We might need some kind of warrant if it's worth that much."

"Yeah, will do," he said, sounding a little unsure if his news was indeed newsworthy. The right thing to have done would have been for Ben to tell him he'd done a good job and end the call. But any energy he had had waned. He let his head fall into his hands and felt his fingers scrunching his hair.

"Cruz?" Gillespie said. "Ah, well done, mate. Listen, it's getting late. Why don't you and Jewson get off, eh? There's no point coming back here now. You'd only have to turn round and go home."

"Well, I don't mind—"

"I'll see you tomorrow, eh," Gillespie said, then gave Chapman the nod to end the call. She did as requested, then waited. Ben, meanwhile, closed his eyes and tried to find a way through the maze of information. "Actually," Gillespie said, the words muffled and barely registering in Ben's fogged mind. "Why don't you all get off, eh? We can't do much more here tonight."

"We've got Willis in custody," Nillson said.

"Yeah, and he'll still be there in the morning," Gillespie replied. "Just let me and Ben deal with Willis. Let's have a briefing first thing, eh?"

Ben heard the words but was unable to respond. He'd messed the entire investigation up. He'd followed the wrong paths, not listened to advice, and had, as Wiltshire had said, arrested nearly everyone involved in the hope that a shred of evidence might come to light.

"Just let him go," Ben said.

"Eh? Willis?" Gillespie said. "You want to let him go?"

"And Coleman. If Wiltshire wants him, he'll have to rearrest him. Let them all go."

"Ben, let's not be too hasty."

"Just let them go, Jim," Ben said, snatching his hands from his face and feeling the burn of the blood under his skin. "I've got nothing on any of them. Nothing the CPS would back us with." He shook his head. "Just let them go. I need to rethink it all."

Slowly, the team filed out in silence, and as discreet as Gillespie was, Ben still noticed the encouraging nods and winks he gave them. It was his silent way of saying, 'He'll be alright,' or 'Leave it with me, eh?'.

When the last of them had left and the double doors had closed, even the reassuring squeal that had returned offered little in the way of motivation.

Ben shoved himself off the desk and stood before the whiteboard that held more names than facts. Every name had been circled yet they had all come to a grinding halt. Not one name before him could be aligned with a means, motive, or opportunity.

"Right then," Gillespie said, dragging his chair over to the board. "Let's have a wee look at this, shall we?"

Ben laughed to himself. It was just the sort of thing he had come to expect from Gillespie. But Ben reached out with his bare hand and ran it straight through the centre of the scrawled names, places, and circles.

"Hey, mind out," Gillespie said. "We could have used that."

But Ben was in full flow now. His hand was covered in ink, but he cared little for a stained palm. He dragged it back across the board, his vigour growing in intensity, until the last remnant of information was little more than a smudge. Then he sat back on the desk and looked up at Gillespie.

"Go home, Jim," he said.

"And what'll you do, eh?" Gillespie replied. "We could always go for a pint."

"Thanks," Ben said. "But no. I think I'll stay here a while."

"Well, I could stay—"

"Please don't force me to be rude, Jim," he said, then smiled up at his old friend. "I need to be on my own. I need to sort my life out."

Gillespie remained where he was, and when Ben stared up at him, he saw an expression of absolute disgust. His top lip was pulled back in a sneer, eyes narrowed as if they couldn't bear to witness the sight before them.

"You're pathetic," he said.

"Sorry?" Ben replied before he could digest the statement thoroughly.

"You're pathetic," Gillespie said again. "Look at you. You're a snivelling mess, Ben. You're giving up at the first sign of a battle."

"I am not giving up," Ben said. "I just need to get my head—"

"Your head, my head, all our heads," Gillespie continued. "It's not about our heads, Ben. Can't you see that? It's not about you, it's not about me, and it's certainly not about Freya."

"I didn't mention Freya—"

"You didn't have to," Gillespie said, cutting him off. "It's written all over your face, Ben. Ah, you've been knocked down. That's fair. You know, there's a million people out there who get knocked down every day. The one time, the one time, Ben, that you come up against a challenge, and what do you do? You crumble. You make me sick."

"Now listen here—"

"Ah stick it up your backside, Ben. If you're going to give me some spiel about how difficult this one is, then I don't want to hear it. If you're going to spout on and on about how nothing seems to make sense, keep it to yourself. Because you know what? I don't want to hear it. What I want to hear, and what the team needs to hear from you, is how we address the challenges. You were so close. You were so close to holding it together. When we first went to the quarry, you were just about keeping your head screwed on. And do you know? I've been doing my damndest to help you through the fog, Ben. We all have. We've been trying to make you see that you've got this. You've relied on Freya for so long that you no longer see how bloody talented you are. You can't see it, Ben. What did you do before she came along?"

"I had David Foster," Ben retorted.

"Right, and when he died?" Gillespie said. "What then? You didn't fall to pieces. You remembered him, and bloody right, too. David was a good bloke. But you didn't fall to pieces. You seized the opportunity, Ben. You grabbed it with both hands. Not because you were driven, oh no. You're not in this to see how far you can get up the ladder. No. No, you seized it with both hands because you didn't want what David had created to fade away. You wanted to keep it alive. And now look at it. Look at us. Look at the team. Do you think any of us would be here if it wasn't for you?"

"Surely Freya had something to do—"

"Ah, did she hell, you halfwit. We put up with Freya and her ways because of you. You're the bridge between us and her. If I piss her off, yeah, she might give me an earful, but I don't get the full whack, do I? No, it's you who takes that. Right? It's you who has to listen to her rant on about how slovenly I am, or how me and Anna drive her nuts with our bickering, or how Cruz is a feeble moron, or Gold is more of a wet nurse than a police officer. It's you who has to take that on. Not us." He stood, plunged his hands into his pockets, and stepped over to Ben, where he bent so their faces were just inches apart. "People work for people, Ben. This team. Anna, Anderson, Chapman, Gold, and even that little, short-arse Cruz. They all work for you, mate."

"Is that what you think?" Ben said, after a pause.

"It's what I know, Ben," Gillespie said, straightening. "And if you can't see that...well, then you're an idiot. You don't deserve to crack this investigation, Ben. You don't deserve to be a DI." He shook his head and turned away. He stopped halfway to the door and glanced back over his shoulder. "And you don't deserve our loyalty," he said. "Go home, Ben. Go home and think about that. Go home and think about your future. Because if this is the future..." He waved his hands, gesturing at the room in its entirety. "Then you'd better start looking for a new team."

CHAPTER FIFTY

Gillespie marvelled at the range of individuals who entered and exited the hospital's main entrance. The place was, as he had come to learn in his middle age, a leveller. There were individuals from across the spectrum of classes, if the class system was still a thing, that is. Some clearly found life a struggle. He tried not to judge, but sometimes the pains of life were all too evident. And in much the same way, others seem to have spent time dressing for a hospital appointment as if they were popping out after to see the opera. The place was undoubtedly a leveller. When you walked or were carried through the doors and needed help from the nurses and doctors, life on the outside didn't matter. It didn't matter who you were.

It was that thought that carried him through the maze of corridors and allowed the mental freedom to reflect. It wasn't that long ago that a chat like the one he'd had with Ben would have played on his mind for hours afterwards. But he felt calm. Perhaps it was Kate's positive influence on him, but he felt more rounded somehow. More reasonable.

He was mid-maze when he felt the rumble in his pocket, and

he imagined Ben, still sitting in the same position with his head in his hands, calling to apologise.

But it wasn't Ben's number that flashed up on the phone's screen.

"Jackie?" he said. "Bit late for you, eh? Everything alright?"

"No," she said, sounding flustered, and he heard her slam her car door. "I've just got out of Vicky Fraser's house."

"Ah, right. She didn't have you doing the ironing, did she?"

"It's Lee," she said, spurting the name like it was poison.

"What's Lee?"

"Jenny Willis," she said.

"Lee is Jenny Willis? Jackie, are you okay, love?"

"He killed her," she said. "It was Lee. Think about it. It makes total sense. The Reebok footprints were found near her body. We can't find a single connecting factor among all the suspects, and it's not like we haven't had enough of them."

"Have you had some kind of revelation, Jackie? This isn't something you read in the tea leaves, is it?"

"The trainers fell out of the bag, Jim," she said, sounding more and more flustered as the conversation developed.

"His trainers? The Reeboks?" he said. "What bag?"

"The bag with all his gear in. They were getting rid of it all. Clearing it out."

"They?"

"Vicky and Paul," she said, then took a breath. "Look, Paul was helping her clear Lee's stuff out. The hallway was full of bags and whatnot, so I offered to help while she took care of the baby. She tried to stop me and I dropped the bag. The trainers were inside, Jim."

"That doesn't mean it was him—"

"She said it was him. She tried to hide it at first. She lied about Lee taking the time off work to look after her. She said she was suffering from post-natal depression, and he was concerned she would do something stupid, but all along he'd bloody killed her and was terrified of leaving the house."

"And she just came out and told you this, did she?"

"No, I had to...coerce it from her. But Paul was there. He heard it."

"So why not just tell us that in the first place?"

"Because she loves him, Jim. She loved him. She doesn't want the last memories of the man she loved to be him being labelled as a killer. Think about it. He took the time off, he was edgy, he sold the necklace, which presumably he took from her."

"Have you mentioned this to Ben?"

"I tried," she said. "I've called him three times and he's not answering his phone."

Gillespie found a quiet spot in a side corridor and leaned against the wall.

"Okay, let's not bother him right now. He's quite a bit going on, right now. Let's put the pieces together," Jim said. "Why?"

He left that single word hanging there like it was the last apple on the tree, and with every passing moment, the rot was setting in.

"I don't know," she said eventually. "I've racked my brains, and I can't think of anything."

"You know, Ben mentioned this. It was one of the theories we discussed. We've got an idea that Jenny's husband and Vicky were...you know?"

"An affair?"

"He's been contacting her for the last six months. Chapman found her number on his phone statement."

"Six months?" she said. "Jim, she would have been pregnant."

"Aye, she would have been what, four months pregnant? The baby's barely showing at that point, is it?"

"Jim, this isn't a question of aesthetics. It's about her mental state. She's pregnant. The last thing she's going to be thinking about is...well...that."

"Do you know that for sure?" Gillespie said. "I mean, I know you had a wee bairn, but that doesn't mean every woman out there has the same sex drive as you."

"Excuse me?"

"Ah, you know what I mean. We're all different. For all we know, she could be a nymphomaniac. She could have been shagging half the village for all we know."

"I'm not sure we're in a position to make that assumption—"

"All I'm saying is that..." He faltered. "Ah Christ, I don't know what I'm saying." He cleared his throat and gathered his thoughts. "Are you sure about this?"

"I'm certain," she said.

"Okay. Okay, how about if Willis and Vicky Fraser were...up to no good?" Gillespie started. "Ben's theory was that Lee could have caught wind of it and approached Jenny."

"What? He killed her because her husband was sleeping with his girlfriend?"

"Aye, I know. Sounds a bit farfetched, right? But it doesn't have to be. Think about it. This wasn't planned. Jenny's body was just a few inches beneath the surface. Katy reckons whoever buried her dug with his hands. If it had been planned, they would have a spade or a shovel or something, right?"

"Right?"

"How about if he tried to tell Willis' wife about the affair? Maybe he was hoping she would put a stop to it. Maybe she took offence and lashed out. Maybe he fought back, and before you know it, he'd caved her head in. How many times do we have to deal with this type of thing? The average person isn't a murderer. The majority of murders are unplanned. Things just...escalate."

"And so, Jacob Willis took revenge."

"It's plausible," Gillespie said. "Right now, Ben's working on the theory that Willis killed his wife. But I can't see it. There are too many unknowns. But this, Jackie. This is the first time something actually makes sense."

"Well, it's not set in stone."

"Don't play it down, Jackie. This is good work. This could be what we need," Gillespie said. "How are their finances?"

"Vicky's and Lee's?"

"Aye. Are they struggling or..."

"They're on the breadline," Jackie said. "They don't have much at all."

"Right, so the prospect of a few grand for the necklace would be an appealing one, eh?" Gillespie said, leaving her with that thought. "I'm going to call a briefing tomorrow morning. Try and get in early, eh? We need to draw this out and get Ben's buy-in."

"Shouldn't you call him?"

"No. No, let's leave him. What that man needs right now is a team behind him. He's carrying a burden and we need to carry our share."

"Alright," Jackie said softly. "I suppose I'll see you in the morning then?"

"Good night, Jackie," he said. "And hey, well done. Really well done."

He pocketed his phone, puffed his cheeks, and exhaled long and slowly. There were still gaping holes in the theory, but Jackie had been right. It was the first time there had been an idea that could come to something.

He marched into the ward filled with hope yet weighed by doubt. He thought of Ben, and how Freya usually shared the burden with him. And now he was alone, the weight of it all was pulling him down.

"Evening, ladies," he called out to the nurses on the ward reception. It was the same nurses as the previous day, and when he had left, he had done so in a manner that left it almost impossible for them not to remember him. A bit of a flirt and wink went a long way. But even his flirts and winks these days were dumbed down compared to 'life before Kate'. He carried the confidence, not of a single man with nothing to lose, but of a taken man, to whom nobody could offer more. The difference, on the outside at least, was nominal. But on the inside, he felt good. He wondered what life would be like without her now. Now that he'd had a taste of what a real relationship could be like. A loving relationship.

And it was with that thought that he paused at Freya's door.

A loving relationship.

He couldn't be. Surely not. Did he? Did he actually feel that way about her? Did she feel that way about him? Is that why Ben was behaving like a lovesick teenager who'd lost the girl to the school bully?

"I can see you, you know?" a voice called out from inside. The tone was sharp and left no room for nonsense, each syllable pronounced as if a headteacher was standing close by with a wooden ruler, ready to slap the owner's knuckles should she dare to drop a vowel or mispronounce a single word.

He pushed open the door, and to his surprise, found Freya resting on the bed. Not in the bed, as she had been during his previous visits, but *on* her bed. She was dressed in loungewear, not unlike the type of thing Kate would wear around the house when it was too early for pyjamas and too warm for a dressing gown.

"I was hoping you'd come," Freya said. She was perched on the bed, with one leg hanging free and her head turned away from him, busying herself by folding a few items of clothing and placing them into a holdall. "I was beginning to wonder if you'd cracked it without me."

"And what if I had?" he asked, closing the door behind him and making his way over to the guest chair.

"Then I would have been disappointed," she replied. "Severely disappointed."

He dropped into the seat, as he usually did, and folded one leg over the other.

"I can't help but notice, boss, but..."

"I'm dressed?" she replied, as she zipped the holdall and gently placed it on the floor beside the bed. It was only then that she heaved herself onto the bed wincing at the discomfort, and then sat cross-legged. It took a few moments, perhaps, for her to ready herself, and then she turned to face him, finally turning the injured side of her face into the light.

He had to hold his tongue. He had to mask his surprise. Yet, every muscle in his body wanted to cry out, '*Bloody hell, boss*'.

Only the previous day, her injuries had been swathed in bandages. And now, for the first time, he saw the full extent of the damage that terrible fire had done to her.

Her hair had been styled in such a manner that it fell over her injuries whilst retaining a certain classical look. He glimpsed the shiny and smooth skin beneath her hair and the jet-black fabric that was an eye patch.

"Am I a monster?" she said, her voice far less confident than it had been only moments before.

"Eh?" he said, realising he'd been staring. "No, boss. No. Just..."

"Just what?" she asked, pressing him for some negativity.

"Brave," he said finally. "Just bloody brave."

"That wasn't the word I thought you'd say," she said, and for the first time, he saw a shyness to her. As if beneath her shell-like exterior, she was actually human.

"Oh aye? What did you expect me to say?"

"Oh, I don't know," she replied, turning her head away again. "Probably something like, 'Bloody hell, boss,' or, "What the bloody hell have you done, eh?'"

Her Glaswegian accent wasn't bad, he had to admit, and she'd been closer to the truth than he'd ever let on.

"You know what?" he said, sitting back in his chair and making himself comfortable. "You carry it well. And the eye patch? It's like you've always worn it. Like that singer. What's her name?"

"Gabrielle?"

"Aye, that's her. What a cracker she was, eh? And a belter of a voice."

"Sadly, singing isn't really my forte," Freya said, and they shared an awkward smile.

"Am I the...you know? The first to, erm..."

"What?"

"See it," he said. "Is this your way of testing the look?"

She sighed and shifted her position so that her elbows rested on her knees.

"No," she said flatly. "Anyway, how are things progressing?"

It was as if she had discussed her new look enough and was keen to move on to a new topic. One of her choosing.

"Ah, bad. Pretty bloody dark, if I'm honest," he replied. "There's been a few developments, none of which make complete sense, but there's a glimmer of hope."

"Well, let's focus on that glimmer, shall we?" Freya replied. "Let's see if we can give it a little polish to make it shine."

"Aye," he said. "Aye...it's just..."

"Gillespie, if there's something you want to say, then say it. Or are you put off by my injuries?"

"No, it's not that—"

"My eye patch, then?" she said. "Pretty, isn't it?" She turned so that he could see it in full. "I bought this one from the internet. You should see the ones the NHS provide. Long John Silver wouldn't have worn it, I can tell you. You know, I didn't even know there was such a demand for these things. But apparently, there is."

"Freya it's not your...eye thing."

"Oh, I see," she replied. "It's my hair then." She stretched her legs before her and let her hair hang in front of her face. "It's real hair, you know? My own hair will grow back in a few months. The doctor says that the scar tissue doesn't extend to my scalp." She grinned. "He said I'm lucky."

"Lucky?"

"You don't agree," she said. "One side of my face has severe burns and even with plastic surgery will never be the same. My eye will regenerate tissue over time. But I'll need to wear this thing for a few months, and my hair will grow back." She turned again so that the shadows fell across that side of her face. "It could have been worse, you know. It could have been far worse. They want to transfer me to Nottingham to see a specialist."

He stared at her, wondering if she realised what she had said, and if she did, then if she credited him with enough of an inquisitive mind to question her words.

"I didn't know you could buy things off the internet," he said, "and have them shipped to a hospital."

She stilled, then did that thing that resembled a smile but wasn't. Not really.

"You'd be amazed at what you can do when you put your mind to it," she replied.

"Somebody bring it in for you, did they?" he said. "It didn't come to the station. You must have had it sent to your home."

"Gillespie, I hope you don't think that our little meetings have extended beyond the investigation and into the realms of my private life."

"No, they haven't," he told her. "But my loyalty to Ben hasn't altered. Not a single bit."

"Well," she said, "and I thought I was lucky. But how fortunate he is to have a friend like you."

"Listen, Freya. Ben might not be able to give you the private healthcare and a readymade family–"

"But he can give me so much more, can he?" she said. "And what is that exactly? Where is he? What is it he can give me, Gillespie?"

The two locked stares for what seemed like an eternity until he nodded at her bag.

"You're leaving?"

"I can't stay here forever. And even if I could, I'm not sure my palette would ever recover."

"Are you coming back, Freya?" he asked, and her expression shifted. She cast her eyes down and then dabbed at her good eye.

"Damn you," she said with a laugh. "Look what you've done."

"Freya, I need to know. I need to know if you're coming back. Ben needs to know. He's hanging by a thread right now. We all are. We're all in limbo here. It's hard enough to know if the injuries would keep you away, but with..."

"Greg?" she said. "You can say his name, you know?"

"We just want to know," he said. "It's not just your future. We're a bloody team."

She ran her tongue around her front teeth.

"Well, seeing as we're now suddenly on first-name terms, I'm sorry to disappoint you, Jim," she said. "I have a meeting with Superintendent Granger later today." This time she really did smile, although he felt it was more to mask her shame than through joy of any description. "I'm afraid you're going to be rather disappointed. In fact, you all are."

CHAPTER FIFTY-ONE

If he had entered the hospital buoyant and Gold had halted his ascent, then Freya had done little more than to send him plummeting to the ground.

"Bye then," the nurse on the ward desk said, her eyes wide with anticipation of a witty remark from him.

"Eh?" she said, the voice registering moments later and the meaning of the words a few moments after that.

"I suppose this will be the last time we see you," she said.

He stopped and once more cleared his throat.

"She's really going then?" he asked, keeping his voice low in case Freya heard him from her room.

"Miss Bloom?" she asked. "She discharged herself. Against the doctor's advice, I might add. I was hoping you could convince her to stay."

Gillespie laughed, a single stab of laughter to accentuate his point. "I don't think you, me, or the bigman upstairs could convince her to stay, love."

The nurse checked that nobody was listening.

"That's a shame," she said. "I'm finishing soon. Perhaps we could go for a coffee or something."

"A coffee?"

"Yeah. You know? Between us, I'm sure we could devise a way to convince her to follow the doctor's advice."

"I'm sure, between us, there are lots of things we could do," he said. "But she's quite strong-minded."

"And you? Are you strong-minded? I suppose you have to be in your line of work."

He grinned and couldn't believe the words he was about to say were actually his own.

"Let's just say I'm better than I once was."

"What does that mean?"

"It means that however nice going for a coffee with you might be, however innocent that might be, somebody will get hurt." He smiled at her, a genuine smile of appreciation. "You take care of her, eh? And yourself, now that I think of it. You lot do a grand job." She said nothing in response and maintained a neutral expression, which he acknowledged with a wink. "Enjoy your evening."

He walked from the ward into the corridor feeling torn. Lost in a blend of emotions. The high the nurse's affection had produced was dulled by the prospect of seeing Ben fall to pieces when he learned of Freya's intentions. The pride he carried from staying true to Kate was sullied by the idea of being the one person who had the opportunity to stop Freya and hadn't. But like he had said to the nurse, he doubted he could stop her from doing what she wanted to, even if he tried.

The question was, did he really want to stop her? Was some part of him longing for her to leave so that Ben could find his way again? For as long as she held him at arm's length, keeping him in limbo, he wouldn't find his way through whatever fog he was lost in.

He was halfway across the car park when he heard a voice call out. But just like the nurse's, it took a moment to register.

"So, this is goodbye, then," the voice said. "It's Gillespie, isn't it? Or can I call you Jim?"

Gillespie looked up and found a man in tight jeans, a pressed, black shirt, and shiny, brown, leather shoes at the rear of a nice-looking Volvo estate, similar to his own Volvo, only the number plate suggested this one was less than a year old. Had his own Volvo been a person, it would have passed through school, puberty, college, and university, and would be looking to settle down with a partner by now.

"It's Gillespie," he said, unable to hide the snarl that curled his top lip.

"Is she ready for me?" he asked, gesturing at the building behind them. "I presume you've been to see her."

Gillespie stared at him, and regardless of his ever-increasing expression of disgust, Greg seemed oblivious to his position.

"You bastard," he spat.

Greg closed the tailgate, locked the car with the fob, and then swirled his keys on his finger. It was all Gillespie could do to walk away.

"I thought you'd be pleased for her," Greg called out. "Private healthcare. That's what she needs. People who actually care for her wellbeing. Unlike this lot."

"This lot?" Gillespie said, stopping and turning on his heels. "This lot saved her bloody life, man. This lot is the reason she's alive."

"And your lot is the reason she was here in the first place," Greg said. "All the nurses here care about is getting somebody well enough to give their bed to somebody else. No, mark my words. She'll be looked after where she's going. No expense spared, proper food, proper beds..." He paused to ensure he had Gillespie's attention. "And a loving husband by her side."

That was all Gillespie needed to cast off the weighty burden and march over to the lanky prick. Gillespie's height and size were usually more than enough to put an assailant on their back foot, but Greg seemed to stand his ground. Being a copper's husband for God knows how many years had probably ingrained in him a certain amount of self-restraint. He knew that most police officers would stop short of physical violence, reaching their limits of verbal profanities and staying on the right side of the law.

But Greg Bloom was clearly unaccustomed to Lincolnshire folk and he was certainly unaware of the loyalty the team enjoyed. So far removed was Greg's understanding of local reality that he still wore that smug expression when Gillespie grabbed hold of his expensive shirt and dragged him onto the bonnet of the Audi in the next parking spot. That was when his eyes widened, that was when he knew he'd crossed the line, and that was his first lesson in local dos and don'ts. The next lesson came when Gillespie's hand closed around his throat. The third was when he pulled the smug bastard's head from the car. And the fourth and final lesson was when he shoved him back down, hard enough to crack the windscreen.

Greg cried out in pain and tried to fight him off, but Gillespie, merely tightening his grip, both silenced and stilled him long enough to hear a few extracurricular lessons.

"You lost her more than a year ago, sunshine," Gillespie said, the anger in him calling on every Glaswegian grumble he could summon. "You've no right to her. You've no right to come here and do this."

"I'm calling the police," Greg said, but his attempts to reach his phone soon faltered when Gillespie slammed him down once more, and with one look, warned him of what was to follow.

"Oy, get off him," a voice called. "You can't do that."

The voice belonged to a man, mid to late middle age, and carrying more weight in his chins than Greg was carrying in his expensive underpants.

"You can bugger off, as well," Gillespie told the man. "Go on, now. Off wi' you."

"Leave him alone," the man cried. "What's he done to you?"

"What's he done to me?" Gillespie said, still pinning Greg to the Audi. "Never you mind what he's done to me, you old bastard. You want to mind what I'll do to you when I'm done wi' him."

The man backed away, shaking his head as he went.

"Well, I…I'll call the police."

"I am the police," Gillespie yelled at him. "So go on. You call them, and while you're at it, why don't get them to send an ambulance to the hospital car park?" He turned back to Greg and lowered his voice. "Tell them there's a man in critical condition. Both his legs are broken, hands broken, and a fractured skull."

"You wouldn't," Greg said.

"No? I wouldn't, eh?" Gillespie heard his own laugh and it was the laugh of a madman. "You've no idea what I'd do to you."

"Lose your job?" Greg said, and the beginnings of that smug expression began to form.

With a final pang of absolute hatred, Gillespie wrenched him from the car and dumped him onto the concrete, where he stood over him.

"You want her?" he said. "You take her. If that's what she wants, then you take her." He bent into a crouch and Greg flinched, holding his face at a distance. "But if you come back, Greg," he said. "Not here. Not to the hospital. Oh no. If you ever come back to Lincolnshire, I'll have a dozen men and women hunt you down, and a dozen more ready to kick you back to London. You'll need more than private healthcare then, Greg. You'll need a bloody care home, a lifetime supply of straws, and a full-time nurse to wipe your backside, you smarmy, wee bastard. Do you understand me?"

Greg's face was a picture of fear. But he said nothing.

"I said, do you understand me, Greg? Or do I have to make myself clearer? Because I will. Aye, I will."

"You'll lose your job over this."

"Don't you get it? Are you really that thick or ignorant, or whatever it is you are? I couldn't give a toss about my job right now. What matters to me are the people I love. The people I work with. They mean more to me than my job ever will," Gillespie said. "So, take her. You take her and you see what good she'll do you." He raised his index finger and held it two inches from Greg's nose. "Don't tell me I never warned you and don't ever come back here. You hear me? You won't get a second chance."

CHAPTER FIFTY-TWO

It had taken an entire six-pack of Stella Artois, one portion of beef in black bean sauce, chicken fried rice, sweet and sour chicken balls, and when she got home, a shoulder massage from Kate, for Gillespie to finally relax enough to sleep.

By the time morning had come around, and he had found her in his kitchen preparing one of her special green juices, the previous day was little more than one of those memories you can never forget but held no real significance. Even when the driver of a dark blue BMW had taken a chance and overtaken on a bend, Gillespie had eased off the accelerator, insulted the other driver under his breath, and moved on with his life.

The behaviour change had little to do with being comfortable with himself, being happy with Kate, or even enjoying the idea of not having to see Greg the knob again. In fact, the behaviour was just a show. A mask. The real Gillespie was a wild beast that he had pinned against the wall of his mind. He held it there to let the traffic flow. His thoughts.

And there it would stay until they could put the investigation to bed and restore normality. He deserved that. Ben deserved normality.

To his surprise, he wasn't even the first in the incident room. Gold was there, and it was nothing short of sheer pleasure to see her come alive. Her belongings were strewn across her desk, her jacket had been dumped on Nillson's chair, and she stood at the whiteboard as if she was... Gillespie smiled to himself.

"Thought you were the boss for a wee moment," he said, and he let the door squeal closed.

"Sorry," she said, startled slightly. "I just had to get it all out of my head. I've been thinking about it all night."

"Ah, you're not the only one," he told her, and he dropped into his own chair and tossed his keys onto his desk. "I've been going over it and over it, and I can't see a way through." He rubbed his face with both hands and sighed heavily. Then he caught a faint aroma. "Is that coffee?"

"Oh," she said, and from Freya's desk, she collected the mug of coffee and placed it on his desk. She saw his confused look, then gestured at the window. "I heard your car pull up, and well...I was making one for myself, so..."

"Where are we then?" he said, nodding his appreciation and taking a sip of the coffee.

"I think I've got it," she said excitedly. She turned back to the board and then took a moment to collect her thoughts.

"It's as we said," she began. "Willis was sleeping with Fraser. Lee finds out, but what's he going to do? Willis is a local business owner. A grown man. It's not like he could even pay someone to help him. He was skint. He had a young baby and a girlfriend to support."

"Aye, well, I mean, if a lass cheated on me, I wouldn't be too concerned about supporting her—"

"With a child?" she said. "Your child."

Gillespie saw her point and nodded.

"Go on," he said, and she turned back to the board, tapping the various names with the pen, just as Freya used to do, and how Ben still did.

"So, he arranges to meet his wife. But he doesn't want to kill her. He just wants to ruin their marriage. He wants to tell her what's been going on."

"Aye, right," he said, agreeing that so far, the story was plausible, if a little difficult to prove.

"But he can't meet her at home. Vicky would be there with the baby. And he can't meet her at the quarry, so he arranges to meet her elsewhere. Maybe they go for a walk, or something."

"A walk?"

"I don't know," she said. "It's a gap, but it's plausible."

"His timing would have to be good. She was on her way to the airport, wasn't she?"

"Maybe he knew she was on her way to the airport and had to talk to her before she left."

"How would he know that? She'd had a row with her husband." Gillespie held his hands up in defence. "Don't shoot me. I'm only questioning the theory. It's what Ben would be doing."

"Right. I know, sorry. Look, I don't know the mechanics of how this works," Gold said. "But please. Hear me out." He took a few moments to enjoy his coffee and then let her continue. "Paul Stoneman works at the quarry. What if the row was there?"

Gillespie pondered the solution.

"Feasible," he said. "If they'd had the row in the top office. I mean, when Ben and I were there yesterday, Stoneman just walked right in."

"And he was close to Lee. They were friends. What's to say he didn't pop round and just mention it in passing?"

"Gossip, you mean?"

"Right," she said. "Gossip."

"Like two old dears with bugger all better to do with their time," he replied, then immediately held his hands up again. "Sorry, my bad."

"So, Lee has an idea that Vicky is sleeping with Willis, hears

Paul mention the row, and then what? How does he get her to meet him? His phone statement," she said, and immediately started towards Chapman's desk.

"Nope," Gillespie said. "Nothing on there. She's been over that phone bill."

He let his head fall back, while he searched among the chaos for a means for Lee Constantine to arrange a meeting with Jenny Willis.

"He didn't," Gold said, her eyes sparkling with hope. "He didn't contact her. He saw her. That's all. He saw her."

"Saw her where, Jackie?"

"We found her car parked up on the main road near Metheringham. Paul didn't tell him anything. He didn't need to. He waited for her outside the quarry and followed her. Probably flashed his lights or something and got her to pull over."

"She went to the petrol station," Gillespie said. "We would have seen his Dick's Appliances van on the CCTV."

"Well, I don't know, Jim," Gold said. "I'm trying here, and all you're doing is finding holes in my theory."

"Because that's what the CPS will do," Gillespie said. "They'll find the holes, then they'll decide if the holes are, first of all, significant enough to affect the outcome, and secondly, they'll decide if they need to be filled prior to or during a trial. I'm not trying to be an arse, love. I'm on your side." He leaned forward and set his mug down. "Let's forget about how he found her for the time being, alright? We'll need a statement from Vicky and Paul today. They can fill in the gaps."

"Right," Gold said.

"Right, so we move on," Gillespie said, prompting her. "Jenny died on the Sunday. Lee called in sick on the Wednesday morning. What was happening before all that?"

Gold shrugged. "I suppose he was just trying to be normal. Isn't that what people do, act normal?"

"Actually, no," Gillespie told her. "Most people turn themselves in. The guilt is too much to bear. Only a small percentage actually try to get away with it. Hence, why we're a team of nine and not fifty-bloody-nine."

"So, he was one of the few, then?"

"Maybe," he said. "He was desperate. Desperate enough to take the necklace to the jewellers on Tuesday after work."

"Why Tuesday? Why not Monday? If he was that hard up, then surely he would have—"

"Because Willis was on to him," Gillespie said. "Would Willis have had to pass the car on his way to work?"

"No, he would have turned off unless he was going to Sleaford for some reason."

"Okay then, what if he found the body?"

"What?"

"What if he found the body? He was looking at expanding the site. He could have been up there for any number of reasons."

"The fingernails," Gold said. "Nillson mentioned her nails were done like Freya's. He would have recognised them."

"Right, so why wouldn't he have called the police? Why would his first thoughts upon, let's face it, finding his wife's dead hand sticking out of the mud be to go after Lee?"

"Because he'd had a row with her. He'd even cancelled her credit cards. He would have been the prime suspect. There had to have been some kind of dialogue between Lee and Willis. They had to have crossed paths and argued or something."

Again, Gold was growing excited as the possibilities unveiled themselves.

"Unless, of course..." Gillespie started.

"Unless what?"

"Well, I was going to say that if Willis and Vicky were doing the nasty, as they say, then it's possible she told him that Lee knew."

"So, when he discovers his wife's body, it can only be one person," Gold said.

"Or it could have been a few people and he started with Lee. Struck it lucky the first time, if you like. He could have arranged for Lee to be drugged and waited down the road for him. Same theory as we had for the Major Brothers but replace them with Willis. He would have been upset. He would have taken Lee to the place. To the field. To show him what he'd done."

"Where did he get the drugs?" Gillespie asked. "He's a man of social standing, not some spotty scrote who wakes up with a spliff in one hand and can of Super Tennent's in the other."

"You back on the weed, Jim?" Nillson said as she barged through the door. "Didn't have you down as a Super Tennent's man, though. I would have said Stella Artois."

"We've got a theory," Gillespie said. "And for your information, my past might not be black and white, but there's certainly no green in it."

"Right," she said, disbelievingly, as Anderson followed her in, and then Chapman shortly afterwards.

"I thought the boss was back for a moment," Cruz said, coming in last. He dumped his bag on his desk and slumped into his chair. "So, what's happening? Where's Ben? He's usually in before any of us."

"Gold and I have been working on a theory," Gillespie said. "And given that we've nicked everyone in a half-mile radius of Metheringham and let them go without charging them, I think we should crack on and interview Willis." He sank the rest of his coffee and caught Gold staring. "And by we, I mean you and me, Jackie."

"Without Ben?"

"Without Ben," he replied. "The man has a million things on his mind right now. Let's take care of one of them, shall we?"

CHAPTER FIFTY-THREE

There was a time when suspects could be divided into two categories – those who could afford private legal representation, and those who couldn't and therefore relied on a duty solicitor, of which there was always one on call or to hand.

A decade or more ago, the private legal representative was typically deemed to be experienced and effective. Whereas the duty solicitor merely protected the suspect's rights and did very little to act on their behalf in terms of proving their innocence.

But things had changed in recent years. There was always the chance, albeit slim, that a private solicitor could turn out to be useless and disengaged. Their salary depended on a positive outcome. But the duty solicitors of late seemed to have far more fire in their bellies, far more desire for the charges to be dropped, and a far greater hunger to make a name for themselves.

Perhaps it was the economy or the state of the country. Perhaps it was the lack of opportunity, Gillespie thought. Or perhaps it was the rise in crime, which led to the decrease in apathy.

Either way, when Thomas Shaw introduced himself, fetching an expensive-looking business card from his leather portfolio,

Gillespie was left with no doubt at all as to which category the man fell into.

Gold set to work on the recording, while Gillespie gathered his notes and thoughts. They waited for the long buzz to initiate the interview, and then Gillespie began by introducing himself and Gold, followed by Shaw and his client, Jacob Willis.

"Mr Willis," Gillespie started, "do you understand why you are here?"

The man who Gillespie had first met at the quarry was gone. Where his confidence had grown into arrogance, his shoulders now sagged under the weight of death. Where his sharp rhetoric had been clear and crisp, he mumbled his name, and the hard stare that had dared to be challenged now sought refuge on the empty table before him.

"I'm a suspect," he said. "You think I killed my wife."

"That was part of the initial charge, I agree," Gillespie said. "But there was more to it, than that. Jacob Willis, you are under arrest on suspicion of the murders of Lee Constantine and Jennifer Willis. You do not have to say anything. But it may harm your defence if you do not mention when questioned something which you later rely on in court. Anything you do say may be given in evidence. Now do you understand?"

"Lee Constantine? Are you kidding me? I bloody found him."

"And grateful we are, too," Gillespie said, silencing him before he entered into a rant. "You see, while you're under arrest on suspicion of both counts of murder, I don't truly believe that you did it. Not both of them, anyway."

"Eh?"

"He's dropping the charges for your wife's murder, Mr Willis," Shaw said, searching Gillespie's face for a clue. "Am I right, Sergeant?"

"Not quite. I'm not dropping the charges entirely. Not yet anyway. We've a way to go before we get there. You see, one of the things we do when we're investigating a murder is to establish a means, a motive, and the opportunity," Gillespie said. "We do this by developing the victim's back story. Who were they? Who might have held a grudge against them? Where were they when they died? That type of thing. By understanding their last few days or weeks, we get an idea of who might have been responsible for their death. Once we have a name, we then apply the MMO thinking to the name."

"And that's what you've done to me, is it?"

"Naturally," Gillespie replied. "Although, in this particular case, the answer is not necessarily straightforward. We have your wife's murder..." Willis winced at the mention of his wife. He closed his eyes and swallowed hard. All natural behaviours for a grieving man. "Followed nearly a week later by Lee Constantine's murder," Gillespie said. "The second murder, although discovered first, adds a certain amount of complexity, as you can imagine."

"I can't imagine," Willis said. "All I can think about is my wife. You..." He stifled the tears in his eyes and emotion in his throat. "You came to inform me yesterday afternoon then immediately arrested me. I've been sitting in that cell since last night wondering how, why, and who bloody did it."

"I think it's only fair that my client knows the extent of his wife's injuries," Shaw said. "He's clearly not of sound mind, right now."

"Not of sound mind my left foot," Gillespie said. "He knows how she died, when she died, and he knows why."

"I'm afraid unsubstantiated claims are little more than accusations without grounds–"

"Oh, I'm not accusing him of murdering his wife," Gillespie said. "I'm merely stating that he knows who did it and why." He turned to Willis. "Isn't that right, Mr Willis?"

Shaw leaned over and whispered into his client's ear, although, for the life of him, Gillespie could never understand why they whispered. The advice would be to follow a path of 'no comment' with a view to pushing past the allotted time period for which a suspect was legally allowed to be held in custody without being charged.

"No comment," Willis said, as if reading Gillespie's thoughts.

"We will be filing for an extension on this," Gillespie said. "I believe we have grounds to hold you for thirty-six hours." He sat back in his seat to ease the tension and to find some of that zen that Kate had instilled in him. "But I doubt we'll need it."

"Has the request been submitted to the judge?" Shaw asked.

"As we speak," Gillespie replied, then turned back to Willis. "Mr Willis, I'm going to run through what I think happened. The sequence of events that led to your wife's death, and subsequently, Lee Constantine's death. There are pieces of information that are missing. Perhaps you'd be kind enough to fill them in for us? But rest assured, I believe we have enough of an evidence-backed hypothesis to pursue a case with the CPS. So, it is my advice that you offer any information you can during this interview. Remember, if you do not mention something you later rely on in court…" He let the sentence hang there for a moment. "This whole sordid affair begins with you and Paul Stoneman, one of your employees. I believe that, through him, you either met Lee Constantine and Vicky Fraser, or you met her without Lee. Maybe it was the Christmas party. Maybe it was some other event. This is a key piece of information that we'll be seeking."

"An introduction to Lee Constantine's girlfriend?" Willis said. "That doesn't mean anything."

"No," Gillespie agreed. "But up until now, I certainly haven't mentioned her relationship with Lee." He grinned. "Which tells me you do know her."

Willis shook his head and sighed heavily.

"What we can't establish is the date of that first meeting, but we can deduce that you entered into some kind of relationship with her."

"What?"

"We've been through your phone records, as we explained yesterday."

"That doesn't mean I was in a relationship with her."

"True, but you were in contact with her. Frequently, I might add. I wonder if Lee got the wrong idea. I wonder if he approached you. Maybe he warned you to back off. Maybe you used your wealth and position to put him back in his box. I mean, after all, who was Lee Constantine to you? What could he possibly do to you, even if you had slept with his girlfriend?"

"There is no evidence of Vicky and me..." He glanced up at Gold, and then back at the table. "You can't prove we had sex."

"This is just a theory, Mr Willis. We can refine it as we go, and if you're innocent, then it would be in your best interests to set us straight. I mean, if you've nothing to hide, then set us on the right path. We might not even need that extension, with your help. That would be something, wouldn't it?" His smile was lost on Willis but had the required effect on Shaw, who lowered his head to make notes on his plush-headed paper. "So, what could Lee Constantine have done to you? He couldn't hit you financially, and I doubt he could have tried anything physical. I'm sure you would have overpowered him. So how could he get to you? How could he hit you where you hit him?"

"You think he killed my wife?"

"Not purposefully, but yes," Gillespie said. "I think it's a plausible solution that we will be looking into."

"But you arrested me for her murder?"

"Aye, well. First of all, you were arrested before certain information came to light."

"Has this new evidence been submitted?" Shaw asked. "I've nothing to suggest that."

"It will in due course," Gillespie assured him. Such enquiries indicated that Shaw was a man who would use every possible legal loophole to bring the charge to a halt. "But you have to admit, it makes sense," Gillespie continued. "I mean, had I been in Lee's position, with the girl I loved entangled in some kind of love affair–"

"It was not a love affair–"

"And without means to affect the offending third party effectively," Gillespie said, overriding Willis' interruption. "I would have gone to the man's wife. I would think she deserved to know the truth. Perhaps she would help me bring it to a stop." Gillespie left a pause for Willis' imagination to run wild. "Perhaps she denied it. Perhaps she defended you, Mr Willis? Was Jenny somebody who would have defended you? Was she the type to have fought your corner? Pushed the wrong buttons, as it were? Perhaps she stirred something inside Lee? Perhaps he'd put so much hope into having Jenny on his side that when she entered into a state of denial, he lost control."

"That's your theory, is it?"

"It's a work in progress," Gillespie replied.

"But you think he, did it? You think Lee killed my wife?"

"Which would halve the sentence you receive, Mr Willis," Gillespie said. "So, before we move on to Lee's murder, do you have anything to add to our hypothesis? Anything at all?"

CHAPTER FIFTY-FOUR

There had been few times in Ben's life when he simply could not foresee the future and even fewer times when the possible outcomes weren't even clear. With Freya, anything was possible, and the way his heart and emotions had been behaving of late instilled little in the way of confidence. He likened his situation to a soldier exiting the battle to go home for tea with his wife. Around the next corner, she could be sitting there, teapot at the ready. Or he could face a barrage of gunfire, grenades, and airstrikes. Knowing Freya, however, there would be fewer airstrikes and gunfire. She preferred a tactical approach, sneaking up on her prey and squeezing their heart until life and hope simply faded away.

Ben rounded the corner and was met with neither gunfire nor a pretty China tea service. Instead, the nurse at the ward reception lowered her glasses, smiled, and then watched as he made his way to Freya's room. The lights were off inside, and after a few moments of hesitation, he decided against knocking, preferring instead to move out of the nurse's inquisitive line of sight as fast as humanly possible.

He closed the door behind him and searched the darkness for

her. He listened to the shadows for her breathing. There was plenty he had to say to her but waking her up to tell her would not be the most effective approach.

Less than ten seconds had passed when he knew. He didn't know how. It didn't matter how he knew. What mattered was that she wasn't there. The little en-suite door was open and the light was off, which meant that she was likely off somewhere having tests or being examined by some kind of specialist.

That was good news. It meant that he could prepare. He could acclimatise and enter into what was to be the worst chat with her he'd ever had with the upper hand.

He didn't drag the guest chair to the bed. Instead, he simply dropped into it where it was, beneath the window in a slice of light the blind couldn't quite prevent.

Where to begin? He'd been over and over what he wanted to say, yet without knowing how she felt, he was entirely at her mercy. Did she want to stay in Lincolnshire, and if so, would she still work? Or was there more to her existing marriage than she had let on? And now that it was in the open, was it prudent for her to return to London with Greg? There was little to be gained from him pouring out his heart, or by laying his cards on the table if her heart was elsewhere.

The question was how to establish her truest wishes and part on good terms. That was the key, he thought. To part on good terms. Not to simply up and leave and move on. This wasn't a teenage foray into the world of relationships; it was, or it had been, an adult relationship. Something real. It had been the foundation of dreams, excitement, shared interests, and, of course, it had been the foundation of love.

To walk away without saying goodbye would be to slice open his chest and leave the wound to heal. No, he would need sutures. He would need closure. He hoped that she would too, although knowing her, as he did, she would choose the path of suffering over a torturous goodbye, knowing that the decision had been her own. The price of a tortured ending would pale in significance to wielding control in her manicured fingernails.

And so, he would wait. The one thing he could control was to force the conversation. It was his only chance of taking back that control, to give him an ending. His sutures.

The door opened and the light from the ward spilled into the room. His heart seemed to hit the floor of his stomach. In an instant his hands became clammy, and he found himself holding his breath as a feminine form stood in the doorway.

She stopped, as if unsure of the space. Perhaps she saw him sitting there in that slice of sunlight.

He saw her reach up for the light switch and he positioned himself accordingly. A strong posture and a confident expression to mask his deepest fears.

But it wasn't her. It wasn't Freya. It was the nurse from the ward reception.

"I wondered where you'd got to," she said.

"It's okay, I'll just wait for her to come back. Would you mind turning out the light?"

"Eh? She's not coming back."

"She's what?"

"She's not coming back. She discharged herself last night."

"Last night?" he said. "But how? Why?"

"Well," she said and checked behind her to make sure nobody could hear, "the doctors tried to keep her in here, but she was having none of it."

"That sounds like Freya," he said, his heart still lying on the floor of his stomach, wounded.

"To be fair, she didn't really have much of a decision, did she?"

"What do you mean?"

"Well, she's lucky. She has options. The doctors were going to send her to Nottingham to see the burns specialist. In a year or two, her injuries would barely be noticeable."

"And the alternative?" Ben asked, knowing the answer already.

He didn't know why he asked because when she spoke, her words seemed only to stab at his dying heart.

"Her husband," she said. "Sorry, I thought you would have known. He's taking her to a private clinic down south. We don't all have that luxury, do we?"

Ben closed his eyes and held his head in his hands.

"Are you okay?" she asked. "Sorry, I thought you would have known. You seemed quite close to her."

"I was," he said. "And it's fine. I did know. I was just hoping to say goodbye, that's all."

"She's lucky to have friends like you," the nurse said, reaching past him to tug on the blind's string. The light was blinding and for the first time, he saw the room in full daylight. Void of life but his own and the nurse's. Even the flowers had gone and the picture he'd brought in. The bed had been stripped and made ready for a new patient. "Well, you and the other fellow, that is."

"Her husband, you mean?"

"No, not him. The big chap. Scottish guy. It's a shame. He was alright, he was. Nice smile, if you know what I mean."

"Scottish?"

"Yeah. I think so, anyway. He works with you, doesn't he? He said he did, anyway."

"I know who you mean," Ben said. "It's okay. And yes, he's alright. Did he come often?"

"The Scottish guy? Yeah, every night. Well, for the past week or so, anyway. I thought you were taking turns. You know? You stopped coming and he started. Thought it might have something to do with your shifts. You're police, right?"

"Right," he said. "Yeah, shifts. That's it. I've been on lates. Very intuitive of you."

She smiled at him. "Not really. We're on shift, too. Plays havoc with your digestive system, doesn't it? That and your social life."

"Right," Ben said. "Yeah, it takes some getting used to, that's for sure."

"Well, I'm glad you're here, anyway," the nurse said, and from the bedside table, she collected a small bag that Ben recognised immediately. It was a heavy, linen tote that Freya had bought to carry some shopping back to their hotel in Paris. She despised bags or clothing with unsightly logos and so thought the bag would come in useful one day. Ben had carried the macarons he had bought in a paper bag, which he had thrown away the moment he had finished the little carton of six. "She left this here. Maybe you could get it to her, somehow?"

She handed him the bag, and his first reaction was to tell the nurse he wouldn't see her again. But something inside him clung to the linen handles. It was a connection he savoured.

"Okay," he said, and she gave him a questioning look before letting go. "I've got her London address somewhere. I'll get it to her."

"She must have been keen to get away," the nurse said. "She even came back in to get something she'd forgotten, and she still left that behind." She gestured at the bag.

"Yes, I expect she was keen to get home."

"Well, if that's all," the nurse said. "I need to finish the room. We've got someone coming in, you see?"

"Right," Ben said again but remained where he was. "Actually, would it be okay if I just had a minute?"

"A minute?"

"I just want to sit for a minute, that's all. Freya nearly died in here. I just want to remember her recovering. It's been quite a journey, you see."

"Erm...well, I suppose—"

"Just a minute," he said. "That's all I need. I'll turn the light out when I leave."

"One minute," she said, offering him a playful smile as she left the room, closing the door behind her.

Ben took it all in. The closure he had sought would never

happen. He had, in his own mind, opened his chest and only time would heal the wound.

He opened the bag and peered inside. He didn't know what he expected to be in there. Her make-up and clothing would be in the holdall he and Gold had brought in for her. Her work things would be in her satchel and any personal effects would be in her handbag.

He reached inside and pulled out the only item, the leather-bound diary she used to manage her appointments. He browsed to the current date where the little satin marker lay across the page and found solace in her impeccable handwriting.

But it wasn't her flamboyant serifs or her exquisite looping tails that caught his eye. It was the words, the ideas, and the hope they brought.

CHAPTER FIFTY-FIVE

"We're in," Gillespie said, as he burst into the incident room. He slapped the weighty file down on Cruz's desk and took his place at the head of the room, perching where so many others had perched before him.

"No way," Nillson said, and for once, her disbelief in his abilities was not filled with spite.

"Way," he replied. "We've got a good case to put before the CPS. Lee Constantine killed Jenny and Willis returned the favour."

"He confessed?" Anderson said. "Christ, that theory was full of holes. He could have held on a bit longer."

"Well, aye, I mean, he didn't confess in so many words."

The pressure in the room dropped a little, taking with it the expressions of joy and excitement.

"He didn't confess?" Nillson said.

"Not exactly," Gillespie said. "But there's enough there for the CPS to sit up and listen."

"Like what?"

"Like the lies he told about being at golf last Sunday."

"So where was he?"

"Well, he wouldn't say. But when he realised we'd be checking with the golf club, he soon changed his statement."

"Right, so that's it, is it?"

"No, Anna, that is not it."

"So, did he at least admit to sleeping with Vicky Fraser?"

"Well, no. He denied being in a relationship with her, formally or informally."

"Okay then," Nillson said, closing her laptop and turning in her seat to face him. "What part of all of this makes you so sure you can get a conviction? All we've got is an idea that Lee somehow thought Willis might have been sleeping with his girl-friend, and that the only way to get at him was through his wife."

"We've got a statement from Vicky Fraser saying exactly that," Gillespie said. "It's less pie in the sky than you think."

"You've got a statement, have you?"

"Well, Gold's on her way there now. She needs to get Fraser to say what she told her yesterday and sign it off."

Nillson said nothing. She studied Anderson's expression while she considered her next attack on Gillespie's success.

"So, you've got word that Lee murdered Jenny Willis. You still need the mechanics of how that happened."

"I'm well aware of the shortfalls, Anna. Jesus, why can't you be happy for once? If Freya was here saying the same thing, you'd have been gushing all over it."

"You're not Freya," Nillson spat. "And I don't gush, thank you. Besides, Freya wouldn't have pressed charges without getting the facts in place first."

"The facts are in place," he said. "His bloody girlfriend confessed on his behalf. She'd hardly do that without having reason to, would she?"

"Well, on your head be it," Nillson said. "And Lee? How exactly did he convince somebody to spike Lee's drink?"

"Spike his drink?" Gillespie replied. "Spike his drink? Nobody spiked his drink. That was a theory. That was a theory that we worked with from the outset but had no evidence of."

"Oh right, so evidence is actually a factor in all of this, is it?"

"We were basing our entire investigation on Lee being scared of something or somebody. We thought he was in trouble, in which case, taking an LSD tab would be the last thing he would have done. But we were looking at it all wrong. We didn't know then that he'd just killed Jenny Willis—"

"Well, we don't really know it now, do we?" Nillson said. "Not for sure, anyway."

"How would you be if you'd just accidentally killed someone, Anna? How would you be if you'd just buried them with your bare hands?"

"Depends on who it was," she replied thoughtfully.

"You'd be a mess and you know it. The man was terrified of his own shadow." He turned to the board and tapped on the timeline they had created. "Lee killed Jenny Willis on the Sunday. That gives Willis Monday and Tuesday to make the discovery. We know he was up there in the field because of the access road, and we know he and Paul Stoneman got along pretty well. Who's to say Stoneman didn't mention the party?"

"Did he?"

"I don't know until we ask him. Now we've got Willis in custody indefinitely, we can iron these details out."

"Oh, so you admit it's not a closed case?"

"It's far from a closed case, Anna, but it's a damn sight closer than it was an hour ago."

"Closer?'

"Ah you know what I mean," he spat. "The fact is that it is not implausible for Willis to have learned about the party, known Lee would be there, and waited for him up the road. Tell me. Tell me what you would do to the man that killed your wife or husband, Anna? You'd make them suffer, eh? You'd want to do to them exactly what they did to the person you loved." He beat his chest with his fist. "That's where we've been going wrong. We've been looking at this objectively—"

"Because investigations are usually built on facts, Jim."

"But not this one," he said. "Not this one. This one's built on emotions. It's not until you put yourself into the mind of Lee Constantine or Jacob Willis that you really see how things could have played out. You have to feel it."

She silenced, and to his surprise, she nodded.

"I get you," she said, nodding again. "And for what it's worth, you're probably right. I'm just making your life hard."

"Is that an apology?"

"Not quite," she said. "But I agree. If we have Willis on remand, then we've got time to iron out those details. We still need to work out where the acid came from."

"I don't think it came from anywhere," Anderson cut in. "He could have had that for ages."

"Sorry?" Nillson said.

"Well, we've been saying it all along. The streets aren't exactly rife with LSD, are they? I'll bet none of us could go out and pick some up if we wanted to. It's probably been in his drawer for years. Five years, to be precise."

"Before his brother died, you mean?"

"Exactly," Anderson said. "Lee probably enjoyed the odd dabble in drugs as much as his brother did, until he died. Then he gave all that up. You heard what his parents said. He never touched the stuff. But before his brother died, who's to say he wasn't on something every weekend, like any bloody college boy?"

"Feasible," Gillespie said.

"And to be honest, details like that won't get in the way of a conviction," Nillson said, and she sat back in her chair. "I hate to say it, Gillespie. But I think you might be on to something here. I think we can get the CPS to back us on this one."

"Aye, really?"

"Aye," she said, mimicking his accent, but sounding more like a pirate than a Glaswegian. "Nice one. So, what do we do? What do you need us to do to get this over the line?"

"I need you to drop the charges on Jacob Willis," Ben said, and the team turned to find him in the doorway.

"Jesus, Ben," Gillespie said. "You alright, mate?"

The room was silent. He moved slowly, studying each of them in turn. "Where's Gold?"

Gillespie looked nervously at Nillson, who shrugged.

"It's *your* conviction," she said to which Gillespie sighed.

"She's gone to see Vicky Fraser."

"To tell her we've charged Willis?" Ben said.

"Aye," Gillespie said. "And to get a formal statement. She owned up to why Lee was acting odd. She said that Lee had met with Jenny. He found out about Willis and Vicky and went to have a wee chat with her."

"And then things escalated, did they?"

"Aye looks that way," Gillespie said, and he pointed at the whiteboard. "I can bring you up to speed if you like?"

Ben turned to Chapman.

"Get Gold on the phone, will you? See if you can stop her before it's too late."

"Ben, I think we've passed that point, mate. We've charged Willis—"

"Sooner rather than later," Ben said, cutting Gillespie off, but keeping his eyes firmly on Chapman's desk phone.

Gillespie looked at Nillson, who in turn looked at Anderson. The cycle of bemused expression stopped with Cruz, who simply shrugged and pulled a blank expression.

"Cruz, where's the officer you had working with you?"

"Erm, she called in sick."

"Do you need somebody with you?"

"I suppose not. Where am I going?"

"You're going to Coleman's shop. Dick's Appliances. Call me

when you get there," Ben said, then turned to Nillson. "I need you and Anderson at the quarry."

Nillson opened her mouth to question the task but thought better of it, and Ben waited for the pair to grab their belongings and, along with Cruz, head out of the door.

"No answer from Gold, Ben," Chapman said. "I've tried twice now."

"Thanks, Chapman," he said. "Get your stuff, Gillespie. You're with me."

"Okay, where are we off to?" he asked, snatching up his phone and his bag. "I'm guessing it's not the coffee shop?"

"Nope. Not the coffee shop," Ben replied.

"Well, do we need backup or a warrant?"

"We're following a hunch," he said. "That's all you need to know."

"What about me?" Chapman asked. "I was going to write up the reports for the CPS."

"Hold fire on that," Ben said and placed what looked like a journal on her desk. He turned to face Gillespie, and using the little ribbon page marker, blindly opened the book to the right page.

"What's this?" Chapman asked, and she looked up at Ben, who remained focused on Gillespie. "This is Freya's handwriting."

"Do you see the questions on the page?" Ben asked.

"I do," she replied, working her way through what looked like a bullet-pointed list.

"Good," Ben told her. "Call me as soon as you have answers to them." He started towards the door and stopped to wink at Gillespie. "I didn't say whose hunch it was, did I?"

CHAPTER FIFTY-SIX

"Good to have you back, mate," Gillespie said, as Ben pulled out of the station car park, found second gear, and pushed the old Ford as hard as it could handle.

"Did I go somewhere?" he said, then before waiting for an answer, he tossed Gillespie his phone. "Get some support lined up, will you?"

"Eh? What are you expecting here?"

"I'm not," he replied. "Dreading is what I'm doing, Jim. Dreading every bloody minute of it."

It was times like this that Ben wished he had let himself be swayed by Freya's advice and upgraded his car. She had said the old Ford had had its day, and it was time to get something with a bit more poke.

But like his father, who among the fleet of less than three-year-old Claas and John Deere tractors had retained his old Massey Ferguson, he felt it still did the job, albeit somewhat slower.

"So, what's this new direction we're taking?" Gillespie asked. "I feel like I'm being taken to a surprise birthday party."

"You went to see Freya, Jim," Ben replied, to which Gillespie squirmed a little.

"Aye, well. I mean, who else was going to see her? She was there all alone."

"She had her husband, Jim. I told you she had her husband, so why go?"

"Look, mate—"

"No, it's not *look, mate*. You told me to move on. You told me to move on and forget about her and then you went to see her yourself."

"You were lost, Ben, for God's sake. You were so deep into the investigation, that you couldn't see the wood for the trees."

"And you could?"

"No. No, that's my point. None of us could. We needed some... perspective. Some outside perspective."

"So you went through the investigation with her? You went behind my back and discussed the confidential details of a live investigation with her."

"She was still the guv, Ben. Unless I've missed something here, which I don't think I have."

"Was?"

"Eh?"

"Was. You said *was*," Ben said. "She *was* still the guv. As in, she no longer is."

"Aye, well. She was, wasn't she?"

"And now?" Ben asked. "Is she still the guv, Jim?" Gillespie turned to stare out of the passenger window. "I went to see her this morning, Jim. She's discharged herself. But I suspect you already know that." He glanced across at his old friend, who sighed and refused to meet him eye to eye.

"I was going to tell you, mate," he said. "You know? I had this grand plan of nailing the investigation, giving you one less thing to think about, and then...I don't know, taking you out for a drink or something. Break it to you gently." Suddenly, he spoke with a far greater enthusiasm. "I needed you to see that you don't need her. You don't need anyone. You're an incredible detective."

Ben heard the words but believed few of them.

"And I suppose all those great ideas you had, the theories, they were Freya's, were they?"

"Well, they weren't all hers. It was more of a...collaboration, of sorts. You know? We talked through the details—"

"I know how it works, cheers," Ben said. "And if I'm honest, it's one of the reasons I could see through the information." He took his eyes off the road to look at him. "I didn't have her to bounce ideas off."

"That's not the reason you couldn't see through it, Ben."

"Sorry?"

"You couldn't see through the information, because you thought you needed her. But obviously, you don't."

"What are you on about? The reason I asked for Willis to be released is based on Freya's bloody theory. The reason we're in this car right now and not stuffing him into the back of a meat wagon is because of Freya's bloody theory."

Gillespie grinned at him.

"Ah, you're still stuck in the bloody trees, Ben."

"Excuse me?"

"You're stuck in the trees. You can't see it, can you?" Gillespie said, as Ben took the car over the railway crossing outside Metheringham and then increased the speed again. "Every one of Freya's theories was based on the information that you brought to the table. Her ideas were all guided by you."

"What are you saying?"

"I'm saying that all you need to do, is listen to yourself, you bloody idiot." The insult earned him a glare from Ben but made no impact. "It was you who did all this. Freya had the luxury of being removed from it all. Freya had the luxury of having you, me, and the others all running around like headless chickens, while she remained composed. Logical, of sorts." He watched as Ben disgested that twist of fact, and as he turned into Alfred Avenue, Gillespie worked out what they were doing and removed his seat belt. Ben pulled the car to one side to let a silver Transit van pass then idled forward when the road was clear. "Anyway," Gillespie said, "that's enough praise for one day. The sooner you realise you've got this, the better."

Ben brought the car to a stop behind Gold's hatchback, and Gillespie was out of the door in a flash. Jackie emerged from the side of the house, and when she saw Gillespie she ran to meet them.

"I've been knocking and knocking," she said. "The back door is open, so she must be in there. I don't know what could be the problem. When she finally told me about Lee, she seemed fine. Like a weight was off her chest or something. I don't know what could have changed." She looked up at the top windows. "Oh God, I hope she's okay."

"Jackie, when you last saw her, what did she say?"

"I told you what she said. Lee had found out about her and Jacob Willis and had gone to speak with her. She said that when he came back, he was acting odd. He had a bath. She said he never has baths. It's always a shower."

Ben nodded and met Gillespie's concerned stare.

"And Paul Stoneman was there, was he?"

"Yeah. He was helping her get rid of Lee's stuff. God knows it must be hard enough to do, but with a six-week-old baby to look after. Christ, the poor girl."

Ben was about to offer some reassurance when his phone rang inside his car. He leaned into the door Gillespie had left open and hit the button on the screen to answer the call.

"DI Savage," he said, eyeing Gillespie and Gold, who stared at him in anticipation.

"Ben, it's me, Chapman," the voice said. "You said to call you regarding Freya's list."

"Freya's list?" Gold said, looking to Gillespie for an answer.

But he simply held his finger to his lips and listened to what Chapman had to say.

"Paul Stoneman was arrested six years ago for possession of a class A drug," Chapman said. "He was never charged on the basis of it being such a small amount."

"Any more details?"

"It's brief," Chapman replied. "But according to the report, local police found an LSD tab tucked inside his wallet when they arrested him."

"So they didn't arrest him for possession in the first place?" Ben said as Gillespie and Gold stepped closer, intrigued by the fresh direction.

"No, he was arrested in conjunction with an investigation into an overdose."

"Michael Constantine?" Ben said.

"Apparently, he was there when it happened," Chapman continued.

Despite the incessant sun and the bright blue sky, the clouds descended on Ben's mind.

"Anything else?" Ben asked.

"I've made enquiries with the archive team," Chapman said. "I wondered if the LSD tab could be matched to the one Pip found in Lee's stomach."

"Good work," Ben replied. "Keep me posted, will you?"

He leaned inside the car to end the call and met both Gillespie's and Gold's stares.

"What does this mean?" Gold said, the only one to voice what they were all thinking. But immediately, the silence was broken by Ben's phone once more.

Again, he reached inside and answered the call.

"DI Savage," he said, reading Gillespie's expression and seeing a mirror of his own thoughts.

"Boss, it's me," Cruz said, his light, boyish voice almost sing-song, melodic in the quiet street. "I'm at Dick's Appliances."

"How's Coleman?" Ben asked.

"Closing down," Cruz replied. "I think he knows he's looking at a prison sentence. You said you wanted me to call you when I got here."

"I want you to look inside the van," Ben said. "It's parked out the back, or at least it was when I was there."

A few moments of silence followed, and they heard Cruz's muffled voice talking to a grumbling Coleman. Then they heard the jangling of keys and Cruz's casual manner. "One sec, boss. Just popping out the back."

"Yeah, take your time, Cruz," Gillespie said. Then he muttered, "Grab a coffee or something on your way, eh?"

Ben grinned at the big Scot's persistent bias against Cruz.

"Nothing in the cab," Cruz announced. "A KitKat wrapper, a box of tissues–"

"What's in the back?" Ben asked.

"Oh, right. Hold on," Cruz said.

"One of Freya's hunches?" Gillespie asked.

"Actually, it's one of mine," Ben replied. "Do you remember what was framed on the wall in Vicky Fraser's living room?"

Gillespie puffed out his cheeks and looked to Gold, who stood wide-eyed and guilty of not paying attention.

"What's this?" Cruz said, followed by the sound of the phone being set down and a plastic bag being ruffled. Ben waited for Cruz to make his discovery and eyed Gillespie. "Roman coins," he said.

"Eh?"

"Roman coins. They're everywhere around here. Coins that have lain dormant for two thousand years, dragged to the surface by ploughs and cultivators."

"Coins?" Gillespie said as Cruz picked up his phone.

"Erm, boss?" he said. "I'm not sure if it's relevant, but–"

"You've found something?" Ben said, grinning at the still bemused Gillespie. "A metal detector."

"How did you know?"

"Never mind that," Ben told him. "Just bring it back to the station, will you? And well done, mate."

For the last time, he reached inside his car and ended the call.

"I don't get it," Gold said. "Sorry, I just don't get the relevance."

"What it means," Ben said, gesturing for Gillespie to get in the car, "is that Lee Constantine didn't kill Jenny Willis."

He ran around to the driver's side and climbed in. He immediately found Chapman's number in his recently dialled numbers and hit the button to initiate a call. Gold was still by Gillespie's seat, bending to see exactly what was going on.

"So who did then?" she said, as Chapman answered the phone.

"Chapman, it's Ben," he said, meeting Gold's stare to answer her question. "I need you to do something for me. I need to know what Paul Stoneman drives." He put the car in gear but kept the clutch held firmly down. "And I need all units on the lookout for it."

"I'm in the DVLA database now," Chapman said and then tapped away on the keyboard. "It's a silver Ford Transit van."

CHAPTER FIFTY-SEVEN

Jackie was in the rear pulling on her seatbelt as Ben's old Ford sped to the end of Alfred Avenue, where he indicated to turn left and came to a stop as a line of traffic ambled past with no end in sight.

Gillespie's silence was enough of a sign that he was processing the new information, and the more Ben nosed the car out, the more indignant the other drivers seemed to be.

"Jackie, when you finally got in to see Vicky Fraser, what exactly did you say?"

"I don't remember," she said. "Not exactly, anyway."

"Give me an idea. You didn't just walk in there and she confessed. You must have prompted her."

"Well, yeah, of course. But—"

"You asked what it was Lee was worried about, right?"

"Yeah. That's what you wanted me to find out."

"And what did she tell you?" Ben asked, finally able to pull out of Alfred Avenue. "What did she say?"

"She just said that he was worried about her. That she was suffering from post-natal depression and he was worried about her."

"But she changed her story?"

"Well, yeah, eventually. But only because I found Lee's Reeboks. They fell out of a bag, and..." She paused as if recalling the moment.

"Jackie?"

"Sorry, I had it then. It was right there."

"When the trainers fell out of the bag, Paul Stoneman was there, right?"

"Yeah, he was there all along. I suppose he was looking after her."

"Jackie, was it Vicky or Paul that changed the story? I need you to think."

She was silent for a moment, then spoke softly.

"He did," she said. "Now I think about it, it was him. He saw the game was up and dropped down beside Vicky. He said it's time they told the truth about Lee."

"Right, I need you to think hard now," Ben said. "How long did it take to get into Vicky's house?"

"Well, I tried in the morning but nobody answered, so I walked the village looking for doorbell cameras to check out. That's when I found Jenny's car parked up."

"Right, and in the meantime, Jim and I were at the quarry putting the cuffs on Jacob Willis."

"I suppose so, yeah," she said.

"And Paul Stoneman was there. He knew we were looking into Jenny's murder. He heard it all. He heard us talking about an affair between her and Willis."

"I'm not following," Jackie said.

"It means he saw a way out. Lee wasn't there to defend himself. We bloody gave him everything he needed to come up with a story about Lee murdering Jenny."

"I don't understand. Why would he do that? Why would he blame Lee?"

"Because we can't charge Lee, can we? He's dead," Ben said, and he looked over his shoulder. "Paul bloody killed her."

"But why? This is crazy," Jackie said. "Why would Paul Stoneman kill his boss's wife?"

They rounded a corner and the entrance to the quarry came up on their left-hand side, so Ben indicated, changed down a gear, and pulled off the main road, where they were greeted with the sight of Nillson and Anderson standing at the quarry gates and Nillson's car parked to one side.

He turned in his seat and held Gold's eye.

"Would it be too much to suggest that he did it for love?" Ben asked, and left her with that thought, lowering his window to speak to Nillson who was running towards them.

"It's locked," she called out. "No sign of anyone." She stopped at the side of the car and leaned on the door.

"Anyone inside?" he asked.

"Hard to tell. Can't see much from the gates."

Ben stared ahead at the steel fabricated gates, the wire mesh fencing and the chain holding them closed.

"Is the padlock on the inside or the outside?" he asked.

"Eh?" Nillson said.

"The padlock," Ben said. "Is it locked from the inside or the outside?"

"Oh, Christ," Nillson said, realising her mistake. "It's on the inside."

Ben engaged first gear and disengaged the handbrake.

"Get Anderson out of the way," he said, raising his window to suggest his instruction would meet no argument.

"Ben, what are you doing?" Gillespie said, and slowly he began to fumble for his seatbelt. Ben glanced over his shoulder to check Gold was strapped in. "Ben, think about this, mate."

But where Gillespie saw only mess, paperwork, and perhaps danger, Ben saw a glimmer of hope.

"It's time I bought a new car anyway," he said and revved the engine once before letting go of the clutch.

"Jesus Christ, Ben," Gillespie said, scrambling for the handle above the door. "You're a bloody madman, Savage."

The end of that fear-filled statement was lost to the sound of a snapping chain, twisting steel, and the rattle of the metal chain link fencing as it scattered across the car roof. Ben slammed on the brakes and the car slewed to a halt, sending the unfettered gate sliding to the dusty ground.

"There," Gillespie said, and he was out for the car like a shot. Nillson and Anderson came running towards them, but Gillespie was off, running at full pelt in the pit to their left, where besides the great spider-like machine that sorted aggregates into sizes, a silver Transit was parked.

But as Ben climbed from his car, the van in his mind wasn't silver. It was white.

He walked slowly at first, but with every step, his pace increased and the image in his mind grew evermore vivid, contrasting with the details before him. It was his mind altering reality to devastating effect. The van doors were closed, but in his mind, the side door was open.

He was no longer running through a hot and dusty quarry, but a field, with mud and tufts of grass impeding his progress.

And as Gillespie came to the side of the van and peered in through the driver's window, it wasn't him. It was Freya.

"No," he called out, and Gillespie stared back at him. "Get away."

"The engine's running," Gillespie called back, clearly oblivious to what Ben was seeing. He made his way around the back, and still Ben stumbled through the imaginary field, tripping over rocks that in his mind were great clumps of rich and fertile earth.

And there he stopped, peering down at the exhaust pipe. Frantically, he tugged on something. A hosepipe ran from the exhaust into the van's cargo area.

"Get away," Ben said, growing close enough now to see the expression on Gillespie's face as he reached for the side door handle. "Jim, no," he said and he ran at him, planted his shoulder into his midriff, and drove the big Scotsman to the ground.

"What the bloody hell are you doing, you madman?" Gillespie said, shoving Ben off him. "You trying to bloody kill me?"

And like it had all been a little more than a dream, the white van, the mud, the grass, and Freya had gone, replaced by the silver van and the dusty ground.

"You're losing the bloody plot," Gillespie said, as Nillson, Anderson, and Gold finally reached them and came to a stop at the side of the van.

Ben reached up to stop them, but his effort lacked conviction, so strong was the doubt in his own mind.

It was when they dragged a coughing and spluttering Paul Stoneman out of the van onto the ground that the remnants of that vivid dream finally dissipated and reality came into focus as if he'd opened his eyes from a deep slumber.

"Paul Stoneman," Gillespie said. "I'm arresting you on suspicion of murder—"

"Wait," Anderson said, dropping to the suspect's side. His head rolled from side to side, and despite his close call, he seemed amused at the world and his surroundings. She pulled his eyelids back, then let him go, and looked up at the team, her face grave. "He's as high as a bloody kite."

Ben dragged himself to his feet, not bothering to dust himself off. He walked over to where Stoneman lay on the ground, apparently lost in the great, blue sky above.

"Get an ambulance here," Ben said, to nobody in particular, and Gold turned away with her phone in her hand. He dropped to one knee and held Stoneman's head still. "Paul, I'm Inspector Savage. Do you remember me?"

"Savage?" he replied, his voice almost a laugh. "Savage. Savage. Savage."

"Jesus Christ," Ben said, standing again and taking a few steps to calm down.

"A few moments later and he'd have been a goner," Gillespie said.

"That would have saved a lot of paperwork," Nillson added, never one to restrain her truest thoughts.

"Not necessarily," Ben said, as Gold returned, pocketing her phone and giving Ben the nod.

"Nillson, Anderson, stay here and wait for the ambulance. Gold, Gillespie, I need you with me."

"Now where are we going?" he replied. "We've got the bastard."

"Do you really think he did this to himself?" Ben asked. "Do you honestly believe that this man took what I can only presume is LSD and then drove his van here, put a hose pipe in the exhaust, and climbed inside?" They each lowered their heads to stare at the grinning mess in the dust. "He can barely bloody stand, let alone drive."

"Vicky Fraser?" Gillespie said.

"No..." Gold added.

Ben stared towards the quarry's sheer face. To the spot with the path where, only a few days before, he and Gillespie had climbed up to see what Cruz and Jewson had found.

"You think she's up there?" Gillespie called out, seeing where Ben was heading.

"Well, she's on foot, and she has a six-week-old baby with her," Ben replied. "Besides, this is where it all began. It makes sense that this is where it ends."

There's nothing up there but a field," he said. "Ben, come on, man. This is no time to work on a hunch."

"She's played us," Ben replied, then caught Gillespie's questioning expression. "And by us, I mean *all* of us." He continued for a while then he stopped to make an addition to his conclusion. "And that includes Freya."

But Gillespie was no longer staring at him. His expression was no longer one of frustration, but horror, and Ben followed his gaze to where, at the top of the quarry face, directly where Lee Constantine had fallen to his death, Vicky Fraser appeared, the baby in her arms.

CHAPTER FIFTY-EIGHT

Gillespie was on his toes, sprinting off to the path that led to the top of the quarry. Gold was on her phone calling in every form of support available – the dive team, the air ambulance, and uniformed support to close off the roads. With the large wildlife pond between Ben and the quarry's sheer face, Ben couldn't get close enough to break her fall should she decide to jump...or worse. It was all he could do to keep eyes on her, to maintain contact, and to somehow delay her until Gillespie could get near.

"Vicky?" he yelled. "Vicky, stay where you are. Don't move. The ground is loose."

"Go away," she said. "Why can't you people just leave me alone?"

"I'm not going anywhere," Ben said. "But I won't come any closer. Is that good enough for you?"

It was vital to let her think she controlled the situation, which in light of Ben's predicament, wasn't too far from the truth. "It's over," he called. "It's all over now."

"Nothing is over," she said. "It'll never be over. Don't you see?"

"Paul's alive," he replied. "He's going to be okay." He watched her find the van a hundred metres away, and how her face seemed to sag at the sight. "What's he going to tell us, Vicky? What's he going to say when he's able to?"

She said nothing, instead choosing to stare down at the rocks below her and the water's edge, which lapped and lapped against the rocks.

"Can I tell you what I think, Vicky?" Ben said.

"No," she screamed, almost losing her footing. She scrambled back a foot or two, clutching the child to her chest. "I don't want to hear it."

"Well, I'm going to tell you anyway," Ben said, his patience as thin as a single strand of hair. "You've watched us struggle, Vicky. For days now, we've been working for you. Working tirelessly to understand who killed Lee. And do you know why? Do you know why we did it? To bring you peace. Justice, Vicky. Justice. To let you move on." He shook his head and found her staring at him. Gillespie was only halfway up the footpath and still had more than a hundred meters of ground to cover when he was up there. "That's not Lee's baby, is it?" Ben said. "He wasn't the father, was he?"

She stilled, and even from afar, he could see her hand stroking the baby's soft hair.

"I think you killed Jenny," Ben said, then waited for her to react. But she didn't. She was lost in some far-off memory that even after hours of interviews, Ben would never be able to understand. "I think Jenny Willis found out about you and Jacob," he said. "I think she wanted to speak to you. But you couldn't do it at the house, could you? You couldn't risk her being there, in case Lee found out, or came home. You'd lose everything, wouldn't you? Lee would have left, you'd have lost your home, your everything. So you agreed to meet her up there. Up there in the fields where nobody could see. There's a house not far from where you're standing. It's a weed farm, Vicky. The owners grow weed there for the very same reason. It's private."

"I didn't mean to do it," she snapped back. "I didn't plan for this to happen. For any of this."

"I know," he told her, their voices echoing off the quarry walls. "I know. Things escalated."

"And I didn't lead her here. It was her. I met her on the road, and she went for me. I was trying to get away."

"So you ran into the fields?" Ben said. "The same fields Lee would have told you about. You must have known them like the back of your hand. All those times he came over here with a metal detector. Am I right, Vicky?"

"There was nowhere else to go. I was trying to get to the house," Vicky said, her shrill voice carried by the warm breeze. Then she was lost to her thoughts again, the words becoming fainter the more she drifted into history. "She pulled me down and hit me, but I got away," she said, then ran her hand along the back of her leg. "I felt her nails in my skin. I felt one break and she cried out. I knew it was my chance. I knew I had to get to the house, but she grabbed onto me. She was strong and I was scared, and..."

"Take your time, Vicky," Ben said, spying Gillespie on his hands and knees edging along the hedge as far from the edge as he could.

"I don't know what came over me," she said. "I was scrambling away from her. My hand found a rock and I didn't even think. I just..."

"You lashed out?" Ben suggested. "You hit her?"

She nodded, then almost immediately shook her head.

"I didn't mean to kill her. I never would. I've never hurt anybody. It just happened. And then I had this rock in my hand, and it was too late. I tried to help her. Honestly, I didn't just leave her. I tried, but it was too late. She was gone."

"It's okay, Vicky. Everything is going to be just fine."

"It's not though, is it? Not now."

"There are degrees of fine," he told her. "The best thing you can do now is tell the truth."

"The truth?"

"What else have you got?" he asked. "Nobody can hurt you for telling the truth, can they? The truth is all that counts."

"The truth? The truth is that my life is over," she said, and once more, she peered down at the drop. "My life, Lee's life, Paul's life. It's over."

"Did Paul help you?" Ben asked. "He's a good friend. Did you ask him to help you? Is that it?"

She nodded and seemed to settle in the new direction.

"I called him. I didn't know what else to do. He's a friend. He's always been a friend, and..."

"And he likes you?" Ben suggested. "Nothing wrong with that. You're a good-looking girl. When you like someone enough, there's nothing you wouldn't do, right?"

"Right," she said. "Right, yeah. He climbed up and I showed him what I'd done. He went ballistic at first. I was frozen still with fright. I didn't know what to do. I didn't want to go to prison." She wiped a tear from her eye and rocked the baby back and forth. "So he helped me bury her. We had to dig with our hands, but I had the baby back home."

"You left the baby alone to meet Jenny?"

"I didn't know what else to do," she said. "I wasn't going to be long. It was just going to take ten minutes or so."

"So Paul buried her and together you came up with a story. Is that right? Is that the truth?"

"The truth is what killed Lee," she said. "If only he hadn't bloody well..." She held the baby in one arm and tore at her own hair with her free hand, then growled up at the sky like an injured beast.

"Did he find her, Vicky? Is that it?" Ben asked, then watched for some kind of reaction. The dialogue seemed to keep her calm. It was only when she was allowed time to think and reflect that her emotions got the better of her. "I'm right, aren't I? He came over here with his detector, didn't he? Is that when he found the necklace lying in the dirt? He must have thought he'd struck gold. I know I would have." She stared with her mouth wide open. "We know about the necklace, Vicky."

"He bloody ruined it," she said. "Nobody would have found her for weeks if he'd bloody stayed away like I said. I told him not to come out here. I said it was too hot, but he said he had a hat. I told him dinner wouldn't be long, but he said he weren't hungry. He said he just wanted to cover some ground while the days are long." Gillespie was just twenty metres from her now and signalled to Ben that he'd stay put until needed. "Then he came home with it. The necklace, I mean. He came home. You should have seen his face. It was like he'd bloody killed her himself. He was white. Like pure white. His face... And I knew it. I knew even before he said owt what he'd found."

"But he didn't know it was you," Ben said, to which she shook her head. "The only people who knew were you and Paul."

"He said we had to get rid of it and fast. And we told him he shouldn't. We said he should wait—"

"We? You and Paul, you mean?"

Again, she nodded.

"Paul reckoned they'd be harvesting in a few weeks, and that they were bound to find her. But a few weeks would be alright. In a few weeks, any traces of us being there would be gone. All we had to do was wait. But Lee had to, didn't he? He just had to bloody go and sell it. He wouldn't listen to us. Paul told him that if somebody found out he'd found the body, then they'd come after him. It was meant to keep him quiet, but it only made him worse. He sold the necklace the next day, then called in sick. He wouldn't leave the house after that. It was all Paul could do to get him to go to the party. Said it would do him good to get out. And it was only up the road. Everything would be fine. He could go out, let his hair down, and everything would be fine."

"But that's not how it happened, is it, Vicky?" Ben said and eyed Gillespie, hoping he would pick up on the cue. "Everything wasn't fine, was it?"

She shook her head and rocked the baby in her arms.

"He wanted to tell the police," she said. "I don't know what he was thinking, but the longer he stayed cooped up in the house, the more it began to get to him. He had this wild idea that the body would be found, somebody would be arrested, and he'd get some kind of reward. And if they ever found out he'd sold the necklace, he'd just tell them he didn't know it belonged to the dead woman. He was mad on the idea. Anyways, as the week went on, we couldn't talk him out of it. We said he should go to the party, have a good time, and then we could discuss it after."

"Who's idea was it to spike his drink, Vicky?" Ben asked. "Paul's? Or was it your idea?"

Gillespie was inching closer now, moving slowly so as not to make a noise. If she stood up, he would have just seconds to reach her, and Ben was running out of story. Soon they would discuss what happened to Lee, and that could literally send her over the edge.

"It was mine," she said, finally. "Paul had nothing to do with it. He didn't even know I'd done it."

"He didn't know?"

"Of course not. If he knew I'd spiked his drink then..." She stopped.

"Then what?" Ben asked. "Vicky, what would he know?"

But before he could press her further, she had shoved herself to her feet. Gillespie readied himself. If he broke cover now, she would see him, and only God knew what she would do.

"Vicky, talk to me. What would he know? Have you done it before? Is that it?" Ben asked, and then it hit him. "Vicky, did you know Lee when his brother died?"

Her shoulders sagged under the weight of the baby in her arms and of the story that Ben knew was about to unfold.

"Vicky?"

She took a step closer to the edge, lost now in a different memory. A memory that since aired could change the lives of so many people. Innocent people.

"Vicky, did you know Michael Constantine?"

"Yes," she screamed. "Yes, of course I bloody knew him. Who do you think sold him the pills?"

Ben stared at her. There were so many things he wanted to say. So many things he should have said or done. But with the pond and rocks between them, all he could do was buy time and extract the story before it was too late.

"Vicky, was it you who brought Lee here?" Ben asked gently. "Was it you or Paul, Vicky? Come on. Stay with me now. Talk to me. You're doing great, okay?"

"I did," she said. "Paul said he couldn't be a part of it. He said he wouldn't be a part of it. You can't put this on him."

"I'm not putting anything on anyone right now," Ben said. "I just want to understand what happened. Alright? Things aren't as bad as they look. You've had a rough time. Anyone can see that."

"I took his van," Vicky said. "I knew he would be too drunk to drive, so when he came to get Lee, I said he should leave the van at my house and walk. It's not far. It's not worth the risk. They had a few beers at my house before they left. That's when I did it. That's when I spiked Lee's drink."

"Vicky, we're nearly there now, okay? I'm going to come up and get you. Everything is going to be fine."

"It's not though, is it? It's going to be fine for you. You get to go home. I don't have a home. Not now."

"You have a son, Vicky. He needs you. They can't take him away from you. Not yet. Not for a long while."

"You don't get it do you?" she sobbed. "You don't bloody get it. I don't want him. I don't want a baby. I don't want his baby. I want Lee." She held the baby out over the ledge, and his tiny feet danced in the air.

Gillespie jumped to his feet and Vicky saw him. She turned to face him and backed away, stepping too close to the edge, where the soft ground beneath her feet gave way. A cascade of rocks and dirt fell into the water below with a huge splash, and a cloud of quarry dust rose high into the still air. Ben ran to the water's edge, peering out at the rocks where Lee had fallen, squinting for a view through the thick dust.

Slowly, the dust cleared, teasing him with a view, inch by terrible inch. The ripples in the water reached his feet, and then slowly, they too stilled.

"Vicky?" he said. "Jim?"

Nobody said a word.

"Jim? Vicky?"

Nothing. Gold ran to Ben's side, her face white with horror.

Then a hand rose from atop the quarry wall.

"I've got them," a voice said, gruff, exhausted, and a very dusty and bedraggled Glaswegian raised his head above the lip of the newly formed edge. "It's okay. I've got them."

CHAPTER FIFTY-NINE

The last time Ben had walked into the second-floor incident room, where CID operated from, nobody had looked up, and if they did, then they soon got their heads back down. Too much work, not enough time, and no real desire to take on any more.

But this time, it was as if he had stepped into a saloon in the wild west, and the old honky tonk piano came to a tinkling halt. There was one group of officers in the far corner who were so engrossed in their work that they hadn't noticed the dimming of the din or the hushed murmurs that had been hissed around the room.

It was only when Ben slapped a file down onto Wiltshire's desk that he looked up. His eyes widened at the sight of Ben, with a layer of dirt across his shirt, trousers, and tarnished shoes. Even the skin on his face resembled a hippopotamus wallowing in the sun.

"S'that?" Wiltshire said, his eyes flicking to the folder and then back to Ben's.

"That's me returning a favour," Ben replied.

Wiltshire appeared wary of Ben and his dishevelled appearance, a sentiment shared by his team members, who daren't say a word.

"In the desert, was it?" Wiltshire remarked, but his team were too stunned to join in the laugh that followed. And so it fell flat, leaving a silence for Ben to speak quietly.

"This makes us square, alright?" he said, to which Wiltshire cocked his head and dragged the file towards him. He flicked open the first page, where Chapman had provided a summary.

"Michael Constantine?" he said, shoving the file back towards Ben. "Been there, done that. Wasted too many man-hours on it, Ben. Five or six years ago now. The chances of proving anything are slim to none. You know that better than anybody."

Ben shoved the file back towards Wiltshire.

"It's a confession," he said, which seemed to catch Wiltshire's attention. "But you'll have to wait until we're done with the suspect to question her."

"Her?"

"That won't be a problem, will it?" Ben asked drily.

Wiltshire shook his head.

"No," he said. "No, I'm sure we can work with that. But what about the Coleman boy? This isn't going to bring me a retrial, is it? We're busy enough, Ben. The last thing I need is to reopen old wounds. His sentence is nearly up now."

Slowly, he pushed the file towards Ben and sat back in his seat, daring Ben to push more.

"You nicked Coleman for supplying class-A drugs, Chris," Ben said quietly. "You couldn't get him on the manslaughter charge, and do you know why? Because he didn't do it." He shoved the file towards Wiltshire. "If I had a nice little bow and a little more energy, maybe I could pretty it up for you." He turned and started back towards the door, and called back over his shoulder. "But frankly, mate, I have neither."

He let the doors swing closed behind him and made his way towards the fire escape stairwell. His feet were heavy, his filthy clothes clung to his skin, and even his ears seemed to be full of the quarry grime. On the first floor, he shoved the door open and stepped into the corridor.

And then he sniffed.

That smell.

He strode over to the incident room, burst through the doors and found the room in total darkness. He half expected to find her there, sitting in her chair, a wry smile on her face. He reached for the lights, hesitated, and then with a deep breath, he turned them on.

The lighting circuit was older than Ben and the fluorescent tubes were as old as the car he'd left at the quarry. They pinged on, flicked off, and then eventually settled into a hum.

But sadly, their efforts went unrewarded. The room was empty.

He scanned the room. The desks had all been tidied, computers were shut down, and the bins had been emptied. All ready for a new week next week.

All that remained to do was to wipe the board clean, which was a task Freya used to enjoy. She used to say that it marked the end of an investigation. The end of one story and a blank page for another.

She used to clean the board with care, being sure to remove every last sign of the turmoil they had been through. But it was as much as Ben could do to run his hand through the names, dates, and places, so they became illegible. It was nearly the same.

He gave the room one last look, then flicked off the lights and headed back into the corridor.

And there it was again.

That smell.

It was rose with oud. As distinct as the nose on his face. He had been there in Paris when she bought it. He had waited impatiently while the shopkeeper had devised it to her own design.

And he had laughed to himself when she told him that no other woman in the world had that exact same bouquet.

He followed the aroma to what was supposed to have been her office, had she not been a control freak and insisted on being out in the field. The room was empty, and he moved through the corridor, the scent growing stronger until he burst into Superintendent Granger's office.

Only he hadn't expected him to be sitting behind his desk.

The big man with the oversized hands looked Ben up and down, his brow furrowing with every inch of him he studied.

And then Ben saw it. The file in his hands. It was red. An internal file. Not blue, as an investigation would have been. And he saw the name on the front, among the force's logo and various stamps.

Freya Bloom.

"She's been here," he said, as Granger placed the file beneath two more.

"Ben, listen," Granger began.

"She's been here. I know she has."

"Ben, there's going to be some changes," Granger said, then presented the visitor chair with his broad palm. "Sit down, will you?"

"When?" Ben said. "When was she here?"

Granger pulled the top two files from the pile and dropped them close enough to Ben for him to read. The first was dog-eared and labelled *DC Jenny Anderson.* The second was a much newer file and labelled *Jewson.*

Ben nodded slowly, enough to let Granger know he understood what each of them meant. Anderson was leaving and Jewson was joining. It wasn't what Ben wanted to learn, but now wasn't the time to discuss transfers.

"She's been here," Ben said, his eyebrows raised expectantly.

Granger bit his lip. He had known Ben long enough for the

two of them to enjoy some sort of informality. It was those flexible relationships that made the rigidity of the force bearable.

He sighed.

"You've just missed her," he said. "If you run, you might catch her."

Ben's heart fell from the perch he had managed to wedge it onto from the morning's dismay. He rushed from the room, back into the incident room and over to the wall that was lined with windows overlooking the station yard. He fumbled for the string to raise the blind and hauled it up in time to see a dark Volvo estate parked in the centre of the car park. A beam of light from the custody suite door spread across the concrete, illuminating a familiar figure. Ben pressed his face against the glass, hoping to glimpse her face. But to his dismay, Greg emerged from the driver's side of the Volvo. He made his way around to the passenger side, opened the door, and held his arm out to greet her.

Ben banged on the glass, but it was useless. He was too high up and the glass was too thick to be heard through.

He ran across the room, sending Gillespie's desk clattering. The doors squealed open and he was in the fire escape before they could even squeal closed.

He took the steps three at a time, shoved his way through the doors and out into the yard, as the Volvo's rear lights switched on. Without stopping for breath, he erupted into the car park and sprinted at the car as it began to pull away. But the harder he ran, the faster Greg pushed the car as if he knew that if Ben had the tiniest opportunity to see Freya, she might change her mind.

The Volvo roared towards the gates with Ben just ten metres behind. He was closing in as Greg checked for oncoming traffic, the boot lid just out of reach.

"Freya!" he yelled, but if Greg had heard him, it only served to push the car harder. "Freya, stop."

The car slowed and his heart raised its weary head.

But then the Volvo indicated and turned into a sidestreet.

And then it was gone.

She was out of reach. He was out of time and out of hope. Ben stood in the centre of the exit, drained. His legs gave and he dropped to his knees, as the woman he loved disappeared from sight.

He sat back on his haunches, not caring if a car came, not caring if somebody in the security team was watching him.

Nothing mattered. Not anymore. None of it mattered.

It was as if the universe had been following him. It was as if the powers that be had waited for him to fall to his knees. With nothing left to give and only a heart filled with despair, he felt the first kisses of rain touch his filthy skin. They were light at first, and he almost laughed at the sight of himself. The heavens opened, and he let his head fall back, feeling the warm rain cleanse his skin.

And then he heard them. Like two clicking fingers marking the beat of some unheard melody.

Heels.

Expensive heels.

And they stopped just metres behind him.

He daren't look for fear of another letdown. He couldn't face another heartbreak. He couldn't let himself build hope only to have it whisked from his grasp.

Not again.

He closed his eyes. Perhaps he'd imagined it. Perhaps, his mind was playing tricks. It wouldn't be the first time that day.

"Congratulations," she said, and it was her. There was no doubt. It had to be her.

"I'm not sure I can take the credit," he replied, hearing the weakness in his voice, but not caring in the slightest.

"Oh, I don't know," she said. "I never had a problem with

taking the credit. As long as you share the spoils, I don't think anybody minds."

It had to be her. Nobody else carried the calm, the confidence, or the arrogance. That delightful arrogance.

"I mind," he said. "I can't exactly claim this as my own, can I? Not when you had Gillespie working as one of your puppets."

"I suppose it depends on your perspective, Ben. Was he my puppet?" she said. "Or was he yours? I wasn't the one on the ground developing the investigation, was I?"

"Is that your way of telling me you couldn't have done it without me?" he asked, and he heard her smile, or felt it, somehow.

"Something like that."

"Well, if you want your share of credit, you'll be pleased to know that Vicky Fraser will spend the foreseeable in a secure mental hospital, the baby will disappear into the system, unless, of course, Jacob Willis steps forward, and Paul Stoneman will wake up to find himself looking at an accomplice to murder charge. Everybody loses."

"Isn't that always the way?" Freya asked, but Ben had tired of the small talk.

"What about the private healthcare?" Ben said. "You missed your ride. Your ticket to marital bliss just drove off."

He heard her smile again. That little click of saliva that she would deny if ever he mentioned it. He could smell her now. She was closer. Maybe if he reached out behind him, he could touch her.

Maybe if he reached out, though, she would be a dream.

"It's not all it's cracked up to be," she said.

"And Nottingham? I thought you'd be undergoing surgery. I thought that was the plan."

"Oh, you know?" she replied. "I've had plenty of time to think. Do I really need it? Do I really need a year's worth of surgery? Or should I let people take me for who I really am?"

"That all depends on your perspective," Ben told her.

"And that's my point," she said. "My perspective. It's...altered, somewhat. I have new priorities."

"New priorities?" he said, and let a laugh slip out with those words.

"Like I said..." she replied, and those heels clicked twice more. He couldn't believe what he was doing. He reached forward, pushed himself to his feet, and turned to face her. She was real. As real as she had ever been. Even when he reached out and pushed the hair from her face to reveal the angry scar that had claimed her entire cheek and eye, she was real. It was her. Freya. He choked, but held onto his emotions, not willing to let them be trampled any more. Never again. But then she smiled softly and everything changed. "I've had time to think. I've made some decisions."

She reached for his hand and she held it to her chest.

Ben opened his mouth to speak, but she silenced him with a manicured finger.

And then she kissed him. It was the kiss to end all kisses. No other kiss would ever rival it. He pulled her close and felt his body mould into hers. How long it lasted, he couldn't know. But when it ended, he stayed there, his lips parted and poised for more.

"There's something you should know," she whispered, and for a moment, his heart froze. Not now. She couldn't do this to him. Not now. But, as if she could read his thoughts, she beamed up at him. "You asked me a question once, and I'm afraid to say, I wasn't entirely honest with you."

"We don't have to go through that—"

"Just..." she said, silencing him once more. She peered into his eyes, the hardness gone from her, and that single eye wet with emotion. "Ask me again," she said, and Ben felt his knee give for a second time that night. And down he stayed, on a single knee, until he heard the words he had been waiting to hear. "Yes," she said, crying unabashedly at the sight of him and the meaning of those words. "Nothing would make me happier."

The End.

Click here to get your copy of Run From Evil

RUN FROM EVIL - PROLOGUE

The air brakes hissed, and regardless how hard he pulled on the steering wheel, the lorry just seemed to slide forward in slow motion, the front wheels screeching against the tarmac like nails on a blackboard.

And then he felt it. The slight knock as the man on the bike, the man he had taken great pains to avoid, collided with the twelve ton lorry then disappeared from sight.

Eamon's heart stopped.

Another car swerved in front of him, knocking an oncoming vehicle from the road and spinning into the nearby shops. Finally, as if on a delay timer, one more set of car tyres screeched, and he jolted forward as one more car ploughed into the back of the lorry.

A terrible, deafening silence followed, where the only sound he could hear was the thumping of blood in his ears. A stampede.

That was when somebody screamed. It was shrill and alarming, and conveyed everything he needed to know in a fraction of a second. Far more effective than words might have been.

There was a protocol for these incidents. He was sure of it. Stay calm. Turn the engine off and remove the keys from the ignition, and then climb from the cab. He did all this, and dropped down to the road. But his knees buckled at the sight.

The tiny Lincolnshire village had become a scene from a movie. A woman fell from her open car door and crawled to the side of the road. A man, whose face was a smattered in dark red, wrenched open the rear door of his car, presumably to check on his child.

The last screech he had heard had come from a red Vauxhall, which had buried itself into the rear of his lorry.

And then there was the bike. It was laying on it side with the front wheel slowing to a stop. And beside it, a smear of red had stained the road, disappearing beneath the truck.

His stomach muscles clenched suddenly, and he leaned forward, spewing the bacon rolls he'd had for breakfast onto the road. Again and again, his body rejected the meal, and the kebab he'd bought the previous night, and God knows what other meals he had consumed.

He stayed there, bent over with his hands on his knees and a string of bile and saliva hanging from his mouth.

"He's dead," somebody called. A passer-by, or maybe somebody from one of the other cars. "Call an ambulance," she screamed. "Help me."

But Eamon couldn't move. He wanted to. He wanted to do the right thing. But if he moved an inch, he would heave again.

The man he had seen earlier was carrying a child in his arms. He fell to his knees on the side of road and screamed for somebody to help.

The driver of the red Vauxhall stared through the windscreen. His gaze seemed to cut straight through Eamon. And then he saw the gash on the man's head. The trickle of blood that seeped from his nose.

There were sirens somewhere. Far off, maybe? He couldn't tell. Nothing seemed real. None of it.

"You okay there, mate?" a voice said, and Eamon looked up to find a thick set, middle-aged man approaching. He spat the remains of the bile from his mouth.

In his head, he had responded. He had told the man to help the others. That he would be okay. That others needed seeing to. The man in the red Vauxhall, for instance.

But the reality was that he hadn't uttered a word.

The thick set man placed a hand on his shoulder.

"Let's get you out of the road, eh?" he said. He had a Scottish accent, and a way about him that Eamon felt comfortable with. "Ambulance's are on their way."

He let himself be guided, and sat in the shop doorway. The Scotsman gave him his coat, wrapping it around his shoulders.

"Now listen, fella. Shock will be setting in right about now. So I need you to keep talking, okay? I'm a police officer. You've been in a collision, but you're alright."

"You're a..." Eamon started. "You're police?"

"Aye, for my sins," the man said, as he scanned the scene of devastation.

"Is he...?" Eamon said, nodding at the lump still beneath the lorry.

"Let's not worry about that right now, eh?"

"He's dead, isn't he?" Eamon said. "I know he is."

The officer looked down at him, appraising him perhaps, to see if he could handle the truth.

"Aye. Aye, he's dead."

Eamon's heart stopped for the second time in the space of a few seconds, or minutes, or however long it had been. Every muscle in his body seemed to tense, and every ounce of heat dissipated, leaving his skin icy cold.

"It was me," he said, feeling his lower jaw tremble. "It was all my fault."

"I'm sure we'll get the bottom of it, Mister...?"

"Price," Eamon said. "Eamon Price."

"Right, well Mister Price. Do you want to tell me what happened? Are you up to it?"

"I was in a hurry," Eamon started. "I should have held back, but the man on the bike..." He took a breath. "He was in the way. We're supposed to give them a metre, but there wasn't room."

"You were overtaking him, were you?" the officer said.

"Yeah. I was behind him for ages. He was taking up the road. You know how it is. What they do? They don't seem to care, do they?" The officer said nothing, but he had begun making notes in his little notepad. "Anyway, I was on the wrong side of the road. I was paranoid about hitting him. Probably paying too much attention to the mirror and not enough on the road ahead. That's when he pulled out of that side turning. I didn't stand a chance. You have to understand. I had nowhere to go, except..."

"Who?" the officer said. "Which car pulled out?"

"The blue one," Eamon said, and he looked about him, unable to see much from where he was sitting. "I thought he'd wait until I'd passed. I thought it was obvious what I was doing."

"And he still pulled out, did he?"

A glimmer of hope shone briefly, then faded. It might not be his fault. But it was. It had to be his fault.

"I ran into the back of the car. Just caught the rear left hand side. I heard the lights break, but..."

"But what, Mister Price?"

"But I suppose I was more worried about the bloke on the bike," he replied. "Lot of good that did, eh?

"You're sure it was a blue car?" the officer said.

"Positive. It was bright blue. Like the sky."

The officer pulled his phone from his pocket, then took a few steps away to make a call.

Eamon stretched his legs out before him, doing everything he could to avoid looking under his lorry. The child was now awake, and limping to the pavement with the help of her father. Local residents and shopkeepers had emerged from their houses and shops. A few tended the wounded, but mostly they stood huddled in groups, shaking their heads.

The officer returned, pocketing his phone.

"Can I get my things before you take me away?" Eamon asked.

"Take you away?" he said. "You're not going anywhere until you've been seen by a medic, Mister Price. You just stay there, eh?"

"I thought you'd want to take a formal statement. At the station, you know?"

"Oh aye, I'll be taking a statement in due course. I'm more interested in talking with the driver of this blue car you mentioned."

"Is he okay?" Eamon asked. "Is he hurt?"

"Hurt?" The officer said. "I let you know when we find him."

"Sorry?"

"There's no blue car here, Mister Price," he said. "So either you're misremembering the events, or he's done a runner."

Click here to get your copy of Run From Evil

VIP READER CLUB

Your FREE ebook is waiting for you now.

Get your FREE copy of the prequel story to the Wild Fens Murder Mystery series, and learn how Freya came to give up everything she had to start a new life in Lincolnshire.

Visit www.jackcartwrightbooks.com to join the VIP Reader Club.

I'll see you there.

Jack Cartwright

ALSO BY JACK CARTWRIGHT

The DCI Cook Murder Mysteries

A Winter of Blood

A Secret to Die For

The Wild Fens Murder Mysteries

Secrets In Blood

One For Sorrow

In Cold Blood

Suffer In Silence

Dying To Tell

Never To Return

Lie Beside Me

Dance With Death

In Dead Water

One Deadly Night

Her Dying Mind

Into Death's Arms

No More Blood

Burden of Truth

Join my VIP reader group to be among the first to hear about new release dates, discounts, and get a free Wild Fens novella.

Visit www.jackcartwrightbooks.com for details.

A NOTE FROM THE AUTHOR

Locations are as important to the story as the characters are; sometimes even more so.

I have heard it said on many occasions that Lincolnshire is as much of a character in The Wild Fens series, as Freya is, or Ben. That is mainly due to the fact that I visit the places used within my stories to see with my own eyes, breathe in the air, and to listen to the sounds.

However, there are times when I am compelled to create a fictional place within a real environment.

For example, in the story you have just read, the quarry is very real, and *Burden of Truth* has been written with the approval of the management. The towns and villages mentioned are all real places, too. However, the houses that are described are fictitious, as is Dicks Appliances. The reason I create fictional places is so that I can be sure not to cast any real location, setting, business, street, or feature in a negative light; nobody wants to see their beloved home town described as a scene for a murder, or any business portrayed as anything but excellent.

If any names of bonafide locations appear in my books, I

ensure they bask in a positive light because I truly believe that Lincolnshire has so much to offer and that these locations should be celebrated with vehemence.

I hope you agree.

Jack Cartwright

AUTHOR

AFTERWORD

Because reviews are critical to an author's career, if you have enjoyed this novel, you could do me a huge favour by leaving a review on Amazon.

Reviews allow other readers to find my books. Your help in leaving one would make a big difference to this author.

Thank you for taking the time to read *Burden of Truth*.

Best wishes,

Jack Cartwright

AUTHOR

COPYRIGHT

www.ingramcontent.com/pod-product-compliance
Ingram Content Group UK Ltd.
Pitfield, Milton Keynes, MK11 3LW, UK
UKHW010955300625
6643UKWH00019B/81